Praise for *The Saboteur*:

'This'll keep readers up all night. It's a hugely entertaining read, featuring the nastiest, most charismatic villain of recent years, and barely pauses for breath throughout'
Mick Herron, author of *Slough House*

'There's a healthy crop of younger spy writers just now, and Simon Conway is among the pick of the bunch. His military background renders the action scenes bloodily and the novel's apocalyptic scenario all too plausibly . . . Fire in the hole'
*The Times*

'Conway has created, with Jude Lyon, a very modern hero, and one who will run for many more stories, I hope. Basically, if you are going to read any thriller this year, make it this one'
*Shots Magazine*

'Violent, authentic and alarmingly believable story about modern spying'
*Sun*

'The most brilliant spy thriller'
Charlotte Philby, author of *A Double Life*

'Brilliantly written, this sequel manages to be even more exciting and nail-bitingly intense than the original'
*Irish Independent*

'A superb writer, with great imagination, inventiveness and the ability to portray events with simplicity and urgency'
Michael Jecks, author of *Act of Vengeance*

*About the Author*

Simon Conway is a former British Army officer and international aid worker. He has cleared landmines and the other debris of war across the world. As Co-Chair of the Cluster Munition Coalition he successfully campaigned to achieve an international ban on cluster bombs. He currently works for the charity The HALO Trust opening up access to hazardous areas.

He lives in Glasgow with his wife, the journalist and broadcaster Sarah Smith. He has two daughters.

A LOYAL SPY, his third novel, won the 2010 CWA Steel Dagger Award for Best Thriller of the Year.

Visit Simon Conway's website at www.simonconwaybooks.com and follow Simon on Twitter @simongconway and Instagram @simongconway

*Also by Simon Conway*

Damaged
Rage
A Loyal Spy
Rock Creek Park
The Stranger

# THE SABOTEUR
# SIMON CONWAY

HODDER

First published in Great Britain in 2021 by Hodder & Stoughton
An Hachette UK company

This paperback edition published in 2022

1

A CIP catalogue record for this title is
available from the British Library

Paperback ISBN 978 1 529 33433 3
eBook ISBN 978 1 529 33431 9

Typeset in Plantin Light by Hewer Text UK Ltd, Edinburgh
Printed and bound by in Great Britain by Clays Ltd, Elcograf S.p.A.

Hodder & Stoughton policy is to use papers that are natural, renewable
and recyclable products and made from wood grown in sustainable
forests. The logging and manufacturing processes are expected to
conform to the environmental regulations of the country of origin.

Hodder & Stoughton Ltd
Carmelite House
50 Victoria Embankment
London EC4Y 0DZ

www.hodder.co.uk

For Sarah Smith

Thanks to: Nick Sayers, Mark Stanton, Paddy Nicoll, Elizabeth Smith, John Robb, Callum Glenny, Thomas Nash, Allan Little, Kate Keehan, James Cowan, Nick Boreham, Louise Vaughan, Misha Glenny, Helen Parham, Andy Greenberg, Karen Geary, Zoe Conway, Ric Paterson, Nicholas Torbet, Diana Roberts, Phil Robertson, Peter Macfarlane and Kirsty Lang.

'The defeat of the enemy's objectives is conducted throughout the entire depth of his territory'

General Valery Gerasimov, *The Value of Science in Prediction*

'If we continue to expect the next major terrorist attack to look like the last one, we will always be one step behind'

John Robb, *Brave New War*

# Follow the money

The Piper Malibu glides out of a cobalt sky and the control tower flicks on the runway lights just a few moments before it lands.

As they taxi towards the darkened hangars, Jude Lyon, an officer in the UK's Secret Intelligence Service (MI6), pulls the Velcro straps tight on his body armour, secures the chinstrap on his helmet and pulls a waxed-canvas messenger bag over his shoulders. He checks the magazine is secure in the pistol in the pancake holster at his waist. As soon as the jet has come to a halt and the cabin is depressurised, the pilot opens the door and extends the steel frame steps.

'Welcome to Syria.'

Jude exits and she pulls the steps up behind him.

He jogs across the concrete apron past a row of Humvees towards the waiting Black Hawks from US Joint Special Operations Command. Ducking under the spinning rotors of the nearest heli-copter, he climbs aboard.

Within seconds he is airborne again, in the row behind the flight deck. He buckles himself into the side-gunner's chair beside two members of the SEAL team wearing balaclavas and night vision goggles with their assault rifles between their knees. The Black Hawks fly low across the desert with two Apache helicopter gunships as escort and somewhere far above a couple of F-22 Raptor fighter jets as top cover. They swoop over the dark ribbon of the River Euphrates, crossing the de-confliction line.

The Black Hawk's pilot's voice over the intercom crackles in Jude's ears. 'Welcome to enemy territory.'

'Which enemy?' someone asks.

'Does it matter?' another replies.

Their route may be straightforward but the journey taken is complicated. It passes over an extraordinary patchwork of competing militias that fight, form alliances and fall out again at the whim of God or their proxy masters in Damascus, Tehran, Ankara and Moscow.

'We have two Sukhois inbound.'

The Raptors release chaff and flares. Burning magnesium rains down either side of the helicopters, lighting up the ruins of an abandoned town. They listen to the pilots on the emergency channel warning the Russians, in their forty-year-old jets, to leave the area.

Outgunned, the Sukhois peel off and fly away.

Ahead of them the desert gives way to a rocky landscape that appears to have been shaken by an ancient earthquake. Hiding amongst the piles of boulders and steep gullies are the last remnants of the Caliphate, the Islamic State group that once controlled huge swathes of territory across Syria and Iraq.

Tonight's target is a Kuwaiti national, Wahab Mutairi, former finance controller of Islamic State. It is just over two weeks since one of the worst terrorist acts in the United Kingdom's history. A former British Army officer named Guy Fowle killed two hundred and sixty-five people in London, in coordinated attacks on Westminster underground station and the Houses of Parliament. Mutairi is believed to have funded the attacks from the Caliphate's extensive cryptocurrency holdings derived from oil sales, extortion, kidnap and ransom, drug smuggling and antiquities trading. A Jordanian agent who has infiltrated the group has revealed Mutairi's location. He is on the move, overnighting in an isolated safe house close to the edge of their territory, prior to an attempt to cross the border into Turkey.

They touch down a kilometre short of the target and the team huddle together in the downdraught as the helicopters lift off into a holding pattern. The SEAL team leader issues his orders and the assault team make ready their weapons. They advance across a fractured landscape lit up in fluorescent green by night vision goggles.

The building is on a promontory at the edge of a ravine, a single cinder-block structure with a flat roof. The snipers take out the sentries using supressed rifles and the team crouch against the walls either side of the door. Jude draws his pistol and holds it against his thigh.

'Go!'

The team kick in the door and move from room to room, shooting Mutairi's guards as they tumble out of their beds.

They find Mutairi cowering under a bed in one of the back rooms. The team leader drags him out on his stomach and cuffs him before holding up his head for Jude to identify him.

'That's him,' Jude confirms, squatting down beside him and slipping the messenger bag off his shoulder. He removes a laptop from its padded sleeve and wakes it up. He logs on via a satellite uplink. 'I am authorised to make you a one-time offer, Wahab, immunity from prosecution and lifelong witness protection. In return for which, you give us everyone in your contacts book: the extortionists, the kidnappers, the drug smugglers and the antiquities traders. Then I want the tribal leaders and politicians who laundered the money for you, and finally, all your cryptocurrency. What do you say?'

Mutairi stares up at him.

'I know you can speak English, Wahab. You have a Master's degree from the London School of Economics.'

Jude taps the screen and opens up an aerial view from a drone flying overhead. He shows the screen to Mutairi.

'Just after we leave, two Hellfire missiles will destroy this building and everything in it. There'll be no evidence that we were ever here. You can stay behind and die here or you can come with us. It's up to you.'

'I'll come with you,' Mutairi says.

'I'll require a gesture of good faith.'

'What?'

Jude opens a Sapling-compatible wallet on the screen.

'To prove you're actually worth saving. Show us how much money you transferred to Guy Fowle.' He looks up and nods. The team leader runs a blade up through the cable ties and the Kuwaiti's hands are free. He shakes his wrists and Jude hands him the laptop.

'Show me the transfer.'

Mutairi looks up at him.

'Now.'

Mutairi's fingers dance across the keyboard. He sits back and Jude takes the laptop back. On the X-cash page there is a shielded X-to-X transfer, with an anonymous recipient, but the amount visible:

*$480,000,000*

'Fuck!'

'What?' the team leader asks.

It's the largest terrorist war chest in history. The 9/11 attacks cost al-Qaeda less than half a million dollars to pull off and inflicted $100 billion in property damage alone, with estimates of the economic damage ranging up to $2 trillion. There is enough money in Guy Fowle's account to finance almost a thousand similar attacks.

'Guy Fowle is a very rich man,' Jude tells him. 'Come on, let's go.'

They cuff him again and drag Mutairi out of the building while the team leader summons the circling helicopters to the site for extraction. Within minutes the Black Hawks have touched down long enough for the team and their prisoner to board.

They race north while behind them the building is lit up by two almost simultaneous detonations.

They are about a mile short of the Euphrates, passing over the ruins of the town, when they hit a wall of flak. Tracer like crimson flecks lights up the sky. Cannon rounds punch through the floor and the soldier beside Jude spasms in his harness and sprays arterial blood across the flight deck. The Black Hawk takes a hit on the tail rotor and goes into an immediate spin, spiralling out of the sky in a cloud of smoke.

The Apaches return fire. Rockets streak across the sky.

'Seven One going down,' the pilot says. 'Seven One going down.'

The helicopter clips the top of a building and slams belly-first down onto a dirt road intersection. Because the heavy machinery is on top, the rotors and engine, the helicopter rolls over. The rotors gouge scars in the ground before snapping and spinning away, or digging to a halt.

When he comes to, Jude is on his side. His face is wet and his clothes are sodden. The cabin is murky with floating dust and pissing hydraulic fluid. From what he can remember of his crash course at Yeovil, closing your eyes is important.

'Obstacles, darkness, and disorientation is what's out there,' an instructor known as Crash-Test Bob had barked at the class with unnerving zeal. 'It's best if you close your eyes. If they're open, you just get bad data.' Then something urgent about finding your exit: 'When the violent motion stops, identify your exit path and get fucking moving.'

Jude reaches out with one hand to locate the frame of the gunner's exit window and pushes. It's jammed shut. Which means that he is at the bottom of the pile and up is at the opposite side of the cabin.

The buckle of the seat harness is slippery and he fumbles with it for a few seconds before he manages to release it and pull himself free. He reaches up and to his right, patting the body of the man above him, but finds no response. Jude then climbs, hand over hand, up the corpse into the empty seat beyond, and then crabs sidewise to the open window. He drops out into the shallow crater formed by the crash.

When he opens his eyes, Jude sees the remainder of the team spread out in fire positions at the edge of the crater, forming a perimeter around the helicopter. He scans the surrounding buildings. They vary between two and four storeys, and are in a ruinous state. Several have partially collapsed floors. One of them is pancaked flat. Others are little more than skeletons of steel-reinforced concrete columns.

He looks back at the helicopter, which is riddled with bullet holes and fragmentation from the high explosive canon rounds. The windscreen looks like a spider's web and the cabin door like a colander and he can see moonlight through the punctures where the rounds have exited. The pilots are both slumped in their seats, presumably dead.

Jude hears gunfire and sees sand kicked up by tracer fire at the edge of the crater. They need to move. The SEAL team leader yells a command and points to the nearest defendable building, which is fifty metres or so away across a moonlit expanse. They fire and manoeuvre their way there, with the wounded slung between them, rubble pile to rubble pile, taking it in turns to move or provide covering fire. Jude prods a cuffed Mutairi into a sprint and empties a magazine in the direction that he judges to be the source of the incoming fire.

They reach the building without incurring further casualties and the team leader places the chalk members by windows and other points of ingress while a medic attends to the wounded. Jude logs on to his laptop and accesses mission control on an encrypted link. He learns that they are about seven hundred metres south of the river that marks the de-confliction line and the other helicopters have made it across into safety, albeit shot up and with casualties. He opens the aerial view of the drone and watches tracer flailing like tentacles towards it.

The SEAL team leader joins him. It's hard not to wince as bullets strike the building. Most of the incoming fire seems to be coming from positions to their north and west, between them and the river.

'We're about half a mile short of the bridge,' Jude tells him. 'Can we fight our way there?'

'Too many wounded,' the team leader says, 'and we're not leaving them behind.'

'You better talk to control,' Jude tells him. 'We're going to need fire support.'

It's not long before artillery fire so thick it froths the air starts bracketing them, flattening remnants of the surrounding buildings to create a perimeter and deter any attack, but at the same time preventing them from moving.

They are trapped in a box.

## 2

# Night owl

From the window of her study at the top of the house, Yulia Ermolaeva, an officer in the Russian Foreign Intelligence Service (SVR), can see the unmarked car parked beside the iron railings across the street. While she is watching, the furthest door opens and one of her four FSB minders gets out. He moves a short distance into the shadows between streetlights with the dark slope of London's Primrose Hill behind him. Moments later the flame of a lighter illuminates the severe planes of his face and then the red tip of the cigarette end glows.

They are there to protect her – her husband calls them her guard dogs – but she knows that they are there to watch her too. And they do with a kind of hunger that makes her skin glow.

It is not long before dawn and Yulia is still at her desk, in stockinged feet, working her way through the night's briefing papers for Moscow. In the urgent file there are a number of one-page summaries compiled by her executive team. They include an evaluation of ongoing MI5 counter-surveillance activities against her own officers; a demand for financial assistance by an increasingly greedy asset inside the Barrow-in-Furness shipyard that is building the new *Dreadnought*-class submarines; a file deletion instruction for a long-redundant asset; and a draft of the Ambassador's latest warning, due to be delivered in two days' time at Chatham House, that continuing Western interference in Syria is neither welcome nor prudent. The reports on other agencies include a hacking operation against the UK Treasury that bears the extravagant hallmarks of a GRU operation and is, in all likelihood, her lumpen husband's brainchild. There is also an FSB surveillance operation against a Chechen dissident who was granted asylum in the UK. She fears that it may result in an assassination attempt that will further restrict her room for manoeuvre.

Hers has become an increasingly complex task: she is reporting an unprecedented level of animosity and hostility towards Russians at the same time as her intelligence-gathering efforts are hampered by the lack of resources resulting from the expulsions that followed the GRU's ham-fisted and grandiose nerve agent attack in Salisbury. She has assets carefully cultivated over years that she is struggling to service. She needs more support. But hers is not the only voice given credence in Moscow these days. Military intelligence, the GRU, and the state security service, the FSB, are both briefing the Kremlin on foreign policy, flattering their way into positions of power and encroaching on the traditional turf of the foreign intelligence service, the SVR, and the foreign ministry. As one embittered fellow SVR officer recently put it to her, 'our mistake is to keep talking about the world as it is, not as the president would like it to be.'

She fears that the one man who decides Russian strategy has become cocooned in an ever-thickening web of half-truths, dubious interpretations, and ludicrous optimism, which may make him prone to increasingly dangerous adventures: deeper engagement in the Syria quagmire, a wider invasion of Ukraine, or tangling directly with Western nations. In the long run, the GRU and the FSB may well be as dangerous to the president as to the West.

She leans back in her chair and parts her legs, running her hands across the insides of her thighs, from her stocking tops to her knees. Since she has been taking testosterone to combat the menopause, she has found herself with increased energy and greater concentration but she's also horny as hell. She can practically make herself come with the swish of her own legs and she can't look at a well-presented man in a suit without wondering if there isn't a nearby hotel room. Right now, she wants Jude Lyon, the young British intelligence officer whose caressing hands and urgent desire evoke such delicious memories, but who has been assiduously avoiding her messages since the Westminster attack.

She will have to ambush him. He likes her to be brazen.

It is her strength. She knows how to value the simple things in life and is able to adapt to any situation. She does not regret that she was born and grew up in a socialist country. She has seen how difficult life can be and she appreciates what a luxurious life brings. She will never forget who she is or where she came from but she will grab pleasure wherever she can and by whatever means.

Across from her desk and beneath an Armenian carpet on the wall, there is a sofa that is all that remains of her parents' carefully hoarded belongings. When they died not long after each other, she burned everything that they had been unable or unwilling to throw away. The things they could not say goodbye to because of that particular Soviet anxiety that you might need them in the future. Everything went on the bonfire except one piece of furniture. A product of Moscow Furniture Factory #3, it is a beech wood and textile sofa influenced by constructivist designs from the 1920s.

She remembers the day that her father added theirs to a list of more than a hundred names at the furniture shop. Every day after that it was necessary to go to the shop to meet the person responsible for maintaining the list and sign that you still wanted the sofa. If you missed one day, you were crossed out and had to start over again. Eventually, they got the sofa. Yulia has had it reupholstered several times, variously covered it in throws and scatter cushions but it defies her every effort to make it comfortable.

It is her most vivid memory of childhood in the Soviet Union: the lines of hundreds of people standing one after another in queues. It wasn't easy. There were only a few basic food items available – bread, sugar, salt and oil – and they were carefully rationed. Forget vegetables. If you wanted fresh meat, you had to get up early morning and stand in a very long line for several hours. Both her parents were working and didn't have enough time to queue so she had to do it.

A lot of people criticise those times and there's no doubt that it was a hard upbringing. But it made her what she is. A tough survivor who knows how difficult life can be. In the queues, she learned to live by her wits and to value people for their usefulness and not for their social status. It was in the queues that she had her first cigarette and, despite the ham-fisted efforts of a similarly inexperienced young man, her first sexual fulfilment.

It didn't seem to matter how much school she missed, she still excelled. She secured a place for herself at Moscow State University, graduating with an A-5 grade, in Russian *'otlicho'*, literally great. From there, she was hand-picked for the KGB's Moscow Academy, graduating just as Mikhail Gorbachev became the General Secretary of the Communist Party of the Soviet Union. At the Academy she learned the fundamentals of acquiring sources and working with them; methods of conducting surveillance and evading it. And in doing so she overcame the longstanding and ill-founded prejudice against the employment of women as agents.

She was noticed by the General in charge of a secretive wing of the KGB known as Directorate S and became one of his protégés. She still remembers standing to attention on her first day at the Directorate while he delivered his opening speech.

'In the West they have their Dr Spock method but here at the Directorate we have our own ways of making people.'

Their job was building legends for sleeper agents – 'illegals' – working across the West, creating detailed back stories and putting people in positions in public service and industry, who were expected to rise in their professions and become assets that would in time yield rewards. It was rewarding and creative work and she had a flair for it. She came to know and understand the West in all its unruly glory, its cut-throat economy and its myriad tolerances.

And then, all of a sudden, her world fell apart. As devastating as a tsunami, the collapse of the Soviet Union swept away the certainties and destroyed her hard-won status. The 1990s was a particularly nasty time, when survival demanded ruthlessness and self-sacrifice. When unsavoury alliances were required. Nonetheless she survived and ultimately thrived.

She gets up and walks across the study to the walk-in safe that contains her asset files. She presses her thumbs and then fingers on the biometric scanner and the vault door opens with a hydraulic hiss. Inside there are racks of steel filing cabinets. She opens a drawer and shuffles the hanging file dividers until she finds the right name and retrieves the file. She flicks through it as she walks towards the shredder. Pilar Allan. A retired widow in her sixties living on the Suffolk coastline, who was married to a metallurgist in the Department of Trade and Industry. No record of financial or other inducements and so, by inference, a believer. But no contact for five years. Perhaps she no longer believes. Yulia feeds the sheets of paper one after the other into the shredder, watching them spool out like ticker tape.

Her phone rings. She is momentarily startled.

She crosses to the desk and answers. The caller is Russian, well known to her, and currently inside Syria. She listens to the brief in silence. When the caller is finished, she finds herself staring out across the park. Jude Lyon is, once again, on the wrong side of a bridge, and again it is up to her to decide whether he lives or dies.

'Ma'am?'

'Forgive me,' she says, composing herself. Briskly, she issues her orders and the caller confirms his understanding of them.

'If anything happens contrary to what I have just told you,' she says, 'I will ensure that something significantly worse happens to you and your family. Is that clear?'

The caller pauses to digest the information.

'Yes, ma'am.'

She ends the call.

# 3

# A bridge too far

It's been quiet for a couple of hours with no incoming or outgoing fire but no one expects it to last.

Inevitably, Jude's been asking himself *what am I doing here?* What is it about this work that draws him? Why does he find himself so often in dangerous and life-threatening situations? The answer is not an easy one. There is something that he believes and simultaneously doubts. He believes that he was lucky to be born in one of a cluster of countries on either side of the North Atlantic, where citizens, for the most part, enjoy the benefits of legitimate government and the rule of law. And he believes that with rights go responsibilities. That means that he feels he has a duty to be engaged in the world, to know what is going on.

With that goes recognising that there are people and ideas that threaten this way of life. And from there, the biggest leap, the belief that it is necessary to do something about it, to *'take arms against a sea of troubles'*, and accept the risk of dying in the process.

Of course, he is ready for death.

His will is written and the executors named. He doesn't have much to speak of, he has no property and he's never been a hoarder, but the beneficiaries of what savings he has are his two beloved nieces. An envelope contains instructions for what is to be done to dispose of his ashes and the lock of hair that his employers keep on file as a record of his DNA. There are letters for his sisters thanking them for their forbearance. And one for his stepfather, who played more of a role in shaping who he is than anyone else.

Of course, there are regrets, principal among them that he has not found someone to share his life with and he has no children of his own. But it's hard to see how this work is compatible with that. And besides, there is a part of him that is wary of perpetuating his genes: both his parents died young: his father, a victim of depression, by his own hand, and his mother of cancer of the blood and bone marrow.

He admires his sister Hannah's determination to have a normal, happy English family and her apparent success at it. But like his other sister, Tamar, he will always consider himself an outsider. Someone who has tried but never quite succeeded to belong. Which leads him back to the same question, *What am I doing here?*

The previous months have sorely tested his faith in the legitimacy of his own government and its adherence to the rule of law. He has seen innocent people suffer and die to protect the reputations of politicians and so-called public servants working for the intelligence services. He has started to doubt that his actions are necessary or even moral.

Even so, he cannot imagine doing anything else. There is a stubborn part of him that believes in things as they should be and not as they are.

By the grey light of dawn, a man wearing *Flecktarn* camouflage and carrying a white flag navigates the rubble of demolished buildings that creates a no man's land around the SEAL team's position. As he comes within earshot, the man shouts in English, 'Jude Lyon!'

Jude climbs wearily to his feet and moves to the edge of the nearest window.

'What do you want?' he calls out.

'A word,' the man says.

Jude glances at the team leader, who shrugs. It may have been quiet for a couple of hours but even so, none of them have slept.

'I'll huff and I'll puff,' the man shouts. 'Don't make me blow your house down!'

'You want me to call in?' the team leader asks.

'No,' Jude replies. 'I'll just go out and have a chat.'

*What else is there to lose?* Apart from his life.

He steps out into the street with that stomach-flop feeling that comes with a leap into the unknown.

The man is waiting for him in the ruins. As Jude approaches, he plants the flag and sits on the trunk of a fallen palm tree. He lights a cigarette. He offers one along with a brass lighter and Jude, who rarely smokes and always regrets it after, accepts. He sits on a concrete shelf between fingers of twisted steel reinforcing bar, takes off his helmet and runs his fingers through his matted hair. They smoke together without speaking for a couple of minutes. Jude wonders how many snipers are watching him through scopes. It makes the cigarette more satisfying, somehow.

'I have no argument with you, Mr Lyon,' the man says, eventually. He's a Russian, with a broad, pale face that makes him look vaguely like a potato and thin blond hair parted neatly on the side. 'I just want your prisoner. If you give him to me, you and your American friends can have safe passage to the river.'

Jude considers the offer: Mutairi for freedom. A straight swap. 'How do I know whether to believe you?'

'You are fortunate, Mr Lyon,' the Russian says, flicking his cigarette stub away. 'You have a guardian angel. She watches over you. I think you know this. She says not to harm a hair on your pretty English head. She is very specific on this matter. And she has a message for you. She says that you have neglected her and you are fortunate that she is in a forgiving mood.'

Something twists in Jude, regret and a certain bitterness at his employers for prohibiting contact with Yulia and along with it, a large dollop of relief that she doesn't seem to harbour any resentment about it.

'I too think you are lucky,' the Russian says. 'I am not in a position to defy Yulia Ermolaeva. Not if I want my son, who is severely disabled, to stay on in a special school that is able to meet his needs. Which means you can walk out of here any time. Be my guest.' He stares at his boots that are covered in dust. 'But here's the rub, if you want your colleagues also to walk free you have to give us Wahab Mutairi.'

'I need to consult with my team.'

'You have five minutes, maybe less. I can keep my Syrian friends on a leash but the Iranians, frankly speaking, they are not civilised. They are hungry for blood. They will tear your friends to pieces.' He lights another cigarette. 'I will wait here for your answer.'

Jude returns to the building and looks around him. The grimy, exhausted soldiers crouching at the windows surrounded by empty shell cases. The wounded spread out across the room. The empty plasma bags hanging from nails on the walls and spent bullets like gleaming pebbles on the floor.

'They want Mutairi,' Jude says. 'We either give him to them now or they try to take him by force. How much ammunition do we have left?'

The SEAL team leader shakes his head. 'Not much more than a magazine per man. And we're low on water.'

'So, they'll succeed?'

'It will cost them but eventually, yes.'

'If we give him up, they'll give us safe passage to the river.'

The team leader eyes him suspiciously. 'You believe that?'

Yulia has never let him down. 'Yes, I do.'

The team leader shrugs. He's beyond arguing. 'It's your call.'

Jude looks at Mutairi, who is cowering against the wall with the dawning realisation of what is about to happen to him written on his face.

'No,' he says, wide-eyed.

'Get up,' Jude tells him, harshly.

'They'll kill me!'

Together they grab Mutairi by the arms and pull him upright.

'You have information to trade,' Jude tells him. 'Use it wisely. Maybe you'll survive.'

They drag him, kicking and pleading, across the room to the door.

'Ready?' Jude says.

The team leader nods.

They step out into the open.

The Russian in the rubble stands up as they manhandle Mutairi towards him, and the snipers hold their fire.

'You made the right choice,' the Russian tells them, producing a set of handcuffs from his belt. He attaches one cuff to Mutairi's right wrist and the other to a folded-over length of rebar.

'Now shut the fuck up,' the Russian tells him. 'Or God help me, I'll castrate you.'

Mutairi closes his mouth.

'That's better,' the Russian says. He puts his arm around Jude's shoulder and squeezes, his face just inches from Jude's. 'I like it when a deal comes together.' He lets go and turns to the team leader. 'I'll bring a truck up as close as I can. A good solid Kamaz. There will be stretchers in the back for your wounded and your dead. You will have to move them to the truck yourselves. Tell your men to unload their weapons and keep the barrels lowered. We will be watching. And tell your compatriots on the other side of the river, no more artillery.'

He points beyond the piles of rubble and shredded palms to the road leading north to the bridge.

'That way for Kansas,' he says. 'Drive nice and slow. You can keep the truck.'

Twenty minutes later they drive across the metal-framed bridge and back into friendly territory.

# 4

# House call

Jude jolts awake and is momentarily confused – emergency lights flashing, sirens whooping – before realising where he is, and the complaining from every joint and muscle reminds him of the last few days. He aches worse than he did the morning after the helicopter crash. It's after eleven at night and he has fallen asleep fully clothed. He tentatively swings his legs over the side of the sofa and waits for his head to stop spinning.

The door entry buzzer goes. He guesses it's not the first time it's been pressed.

'I'm coming,' he grumbles and levers himself to his feet. The buzzer goes twice more before he reaches the video-phone.

'Hello?'

'Jude, it's Helena. Helena de Leij. Can I come up?'

His shrink, who is charged with ensuring that he doesn't go mad, is standing out on the cobbled street, staring up at the camera from under the bangs of her chin-length bob. She doesn't do home visits, as far as he is aware.

'Hang on.' Instinctively, he doesn't want to let her in, but of course he does. He opens the locks on the steel door and hobbles out into the corridor to wait for the elevator. When the doors open, she unwinds her scarf from around her neck and kisses him on the cheek, which she has never done before.

'You look terrible,' she says.

'Thank you.'

She strides uninvited into his apartment and he trails behind her. She's long-legged and lean, and if she wasn't so perplexingly opaque, he'd likely find her irresistible.

'Quite a place,' she says, looking around.

'It belongs to a friend,' he says. 'I'm looking after it for him.'

'Yes, the absent Sanjay.'

Like every other guest, the gravitational pull of the floor-to-ceiling wall of glass draws her across the living room. He watches her stare out at the ostentatious 'starchitect' towers of the City, London's financial district, with their blinking red pin lights.

'Doesn't it make you feel exposed living here?'

Jude explains to her that Sanjay directed a promotional video for a security company not long after he'd bought the unconverted warehouse space and he'd accepted payment in armoured glass.

'It'll stop anything short of a .50 calibre bullet, apparently,' Jude says. It had been one of a string of videos for cash-strapped start-ups when Sanjay was getting himself established that had resulted in the apartment having top-of-the-range surveillance and entry systems as well as bespoke water filtration and air-conditioning units.

'Where is your friend now?'

'He's in the South Pacific directing a film for Victoria's Secret. And no, he doesn't get paid in lingerie.'

'That's almost funny,' she says, and then in a blandly concerned tone, 'How are you?'

'I feel like I've been in a helicopter crash.' It is astonishing to feel so pulverised without actually having broken anything.

'The third day is always the worst,' she says, knowingly.

'You've been in a helicopter crash?' he asks her.

'Once, a long time ago,' she says. He's heard that there's an encrypted message group that shares conjecture about her previous lives. He wonders if he should join. 'And in yourself?'

*In yourself?*

'Do you mean, how am I mentally?' he asks.

'No flashbacks?' she says, watching his face.

'No.'

'Are you sure about that?'

She purses her lips. She must know how good that looks when she does it.

'Nothing I can't handle,' he says.

'Tremors?'

'No.'

'Hallucinations?'

'No.'

'Sudden anger?'

'No.'

'Sudden fear?'

'No.'

'Okay.' She drifts towards the kitchen. 'You're not the sort of person who gets post-traumatic stress.'

'Aren't I?'

He has sometimes wondered if her real job is to make him ignorant of who he is and what he thinks.

'No, you're more the sort of person who worries about why they haven't got it,' she says.

That's more information than she's ever offered before. 'You think that's abnormal?'

'No.' She looks over her shoulder at him. 'Do you?'

'Why are you here, Helena?'

'They want to send you back into the fray. I'm supposed to decide whether you are ready.'

'Am I?'

'You tell me?'

'Well, I suppose it depends what you mean by fray?'

'I imagine that you'll be mostly in bed.'

'Sounds doable.'

'Have you got anything to drink?' she asks, her immaculate French manicure drumming a beat on the zinc-topped island.

'Whisky?'

He pulls a bottle of Bruichladdich *Classic Laddie* out of a drawer.

'Perfect.'

'Water?'

'Just a splash.'

He pours them both a generous measure and adds water filtered to a thousandth of a millimetre from a copper jug.

They stand either side of the island.

'What are we drinking to?' Jude asks.

She raises the glass to her nose with her eyes closed and takes in the aroma. For a few moments, she appears oblivious to the world. And for another moment she seems on the brink of showing a genuine emotion. Then she smiles to herself, and Jude detects what he thinks is a hint of regret before she puts the glass down.

'I want you to get drunk,' she says, in a blandly assertive tone.

'Why?'

'The hangover will take your mind off the crash.'

'Okay.'

'Good.'

'Are you going to join me?' he asks, knowing the answer to the question.

She takes an envelope from her inside coat pocket and puts it down on the counter.

'Passport, flight details and e-Visa enclosed,' she tells him. 'You can enjoy your hangover in economy class.'

'Where am I going?'

'Istanbul. Your Russian "friend", Yulia Ermolaeva, is all alone in a hotel staring soulfully across the Bosporus.'

'I see.'

So that's what Helena means by 'mostly in bed'. She's sending Jude to Istanbul to sleep with a senior Russian intelligence officer who also happens to be the wife of the Russian military attaché to the UK. Surely she crossed a line and abandoned her duty of care to him when she agreed to this task? He wonders why. Perhaps she has come around to his view that sex is the curative to most if not all of his psychological ills. Perhaps sex goes with drinking in her clinical purview.

'Chuka has asked that you stop by the office and see him on your way to the airport,' she says. 'I imagine that he'll have further information for you.'

Chuka Odechukwu is the new head of MI6.

'Thanks.'

'Take care of yourself, Jude.'

She kisses him on the cheek again. When she has gone, he finishes his drink and pours another. He considers the boarding passes, completed e-Visa and weathered passport with his photo inside but an unfamiliar name. They could have used a better photo. He hobbles to the safe in Sanjay's suit closet, opens it and takes out a burner phone marked with yellow tape. He carries it back to the bottle. He always finds starting conversations the hardest. An apology is due but is likely to be met with derision. Eventually, he settles on a more direct approach:

What are you doing?

It is after two a.m. in Istanbul but Yulia's response is almost immediate.

I'm all alone with little choice but to pleasure myself . . .

She almost never fails to raise a smile. He types a question:

Shall I come visit?

This time her message is a leering face emoji. He is grinning in anticipation as he replies:

I'll be there tomorrow night

Job done; he pours another drink. After all, it's what the doctor ordered.

# 5

# The temple

The following morning, duly hung over, Jude rises in the elevator to the top floor at Vauxhall Cross, the apex of the Inca pyramid that houses MI6. Under the previous incumbent, Samantha Burns, C's office was known throughout the building as 'The Temple of Vesta' and she was Queen Bee. As far as Jude knows, the office and its newest C have yet to earn their own nicknames. It is still too soon after the changing of the guard. The circumstances of Queen Bee's death at the hands of Guy Fowle are too raw.

Jude is escorted smoothly down the executive corridor to the open doors of Control's office and stands for a moment on the threshold. He has to give it to Chuka, the man has impeccable taste. The heavy Victorian furniture has gone, replaced with mid-century modern classics, and the paintings of imperial adventurers favoured by his predecessor have been removed and instead there are a few carefully chosen gems from the Government Collection. There is an achingly vibrant Howard Hodgkin, one of Barbara Rae's haunting Arctic works, and an eye-watering black-and-white Bridget Riley, placed discreetly at the edge of the eye line of anyone facing Chuka's asymmetric desk. It seems to ripple and forces your attention unerringly back to the desk and its occupant.

The first black man appointed the head of the Secret Intelligence Service pauses from the paper he is annotating with green ink and looks up at Jude. He is in shirtsleeves and braces with the curved wall of glass and its expansive view of the Thames behind him.

They haven't seen each other since Queen Bee's funeral. Jude wonders if perhaps Chuka Odechukwu does not care to be reminded that Jude played a greater part than anyone else in

23

exposing her wrongdoing, thereby clearing a path for his meteoric rise to power. Perhaps he would rather view it as an orderly succession than a coup.

'How are you feeling?' Chuka asks, turning the paper in front of him face down. He does not invite Jude to sit.

'Battered and bruised but otherwise okay.'

'You are fortunate that Yulia Ermolaeva considers you useful or I don't suppose that you would be alive today.'

'My relationship with her is obviously useful to you too or I don't suppose I would be here in your office today,' Jude observes, staring over his shoulder. Until recently, in Jude's mind the Westminster skyline had represented a timeless evocation of stability and common sense. But now it seems truth and lies are malleable concepts and 'fair play' has been usurped by deception and digital skulduggery. The union of nations with London as its capital has never seemed more fragile.

From Queen Bee he would have expected a sharp rebuke but Chuka sighs and tugs at his white cuffs, which have scarab beetle cufflinks as large as pebbles. His tolerance for insubordination would seem to be greater than that of his predecessor.

'I assume that Yulia knows you're coming?'

'Yes.'

'Her husband was with her until yesterday lunchtime,' Chuka explains. 'He left the hotel via the service entrance without checking out and took a cab to the airport, where he boarded a plane for Athens using a Swiss passport.'

Valery has gone walkabout. 'What's he up to?'

'Right now, he's sitting in a hotel room near the Parthenon. No visitors other than a female escort who he has used before. She reports that he is uncharacteristically upbeat. So far, he's made only one call. We don't know what was said but the phone is linked to Dmitri Troshev.'

Troshev, known as the Chef, is a former brigade commander in Russian Special Forces and a founding member of Valkyrie, the Russian private military company (PMC) that is actively causing instability and strife in Syria, Libya, Ukraine, Venezuela and parts of central Africa. Before embarked on the mission that would lead him to Guy Fowle, Jude had been running an operation exploring links between Valery Ermolaev of the GRU and PMC Valkyrie.

'The call was received on Pathos at a villa owned by Oleg Solokov.'

Solokov is a pro-Kremlin oligarch who is believed to own a controlling stake in PMC Valkyrie via various opaque offshore entities. He is Chair to Troshev's CEO.

'You think Troshev is at Solokov's villa and our friend Valery's trying to get himself an invite?' Jude asks.

'It's party season on Pathos,' Chuka says. 'We've sent a surveillance team to the island.'

'And you want me back on my old job?'

'You have built an open, productive and mutually beneficial relationship with Yulia Ermolaeva. And judging by the volume of text traffic, she obviously likes you. I take it you enjoy her company?'

'I do.'

'So, see what you can find out.'

'I won't pretend with her or deliberately mislead her,' Jude says, stiffly.

'I don't expect you to. Given the current uncertainties at home and overseas, I see considerable value in a back channel of communication with someone on the Russian side that we both believe to be reasonable in outlook.'

'And if I report that she is uncharacteristically upbeat or even uncharacteristically downbeat, will I be described as a male escort that she has used before?'

Chuka gives him a pitying look. 'That depends on who the report is intended for.'

He has a point. 'I'll do my best,' Jude says.

'Try not to agonise about it, Jude,' Chuka tells him. 'There are precious few enjoyable assignments these days. This one you've earned.'

Again, Chuka has a point. The truth is Jude's looking forward to seeing Yulia.

'I've arranged for a car to take you to the airport,' Chuka tells him. 'We don't want you missing the flight. And remember to buy her something nice in duty free.'

'Message received.'

'Apparently she likes Opium by Yves St Laurent.'

'I know, I wrote her file.'

'Good.' Chuka smiles and jumps to his feet. He walks Jude back to the elevators in his socks and presses the button for him. 'I'm sure I can rely on you.'

# 6

## The bridge of continents

The following morning, Jude is lying naked on a marble slab in the hot room of a private *hammam* in Istanbul with Yulia beside him. Having rinsed and lathered them with soap suds, a male and female masseur are vigorously scrubbing them with woollen washcloths. He feels grateful that his bruises have largely faded to yellow and green.

The *hammam* is in the vault of a high-ceilinged art-nouveau hotel that was a merchant bank in Ottoman times. It is located in the winding, cobbled streets beneath the Galata Tower and since his arrival they haven't strayed far from the bedroom. Her security team is in a neighbouring hotel but, more than anything, they want to be alone together. There is a new timbre to their lovemaking. It's always lacked inhibition but now it's less guarded and clandestine, and more fulfilling. He's less bothered by the fifteen-year difference in age between them. Nevertheless, their relationship is still bounded on all sides by secrets. He has to restrain that selfish tendency that he knows he has to get carried away and speak his feelings in the moment, rather than wait until he's made a more realistic appraisal of the situation and his own state of mind.

After the *hammam* they dress in towelling bathrobes and sit in cracked leather chairs, drinking mint tea. She teases him by opening her knees. She has a neatly edged thicket of jet-black hair between her thighs that fascinates and excites him.

'As delighted and entertained as I am by your presence,' Yulia tells him, abruptly snapping her knees shut, 'I am not naïve enough to believe that I am the only reason that you are here?'

He sits up straight. She's right, much as he'd like to, he can't put it off any longer.

27

'Where's your husband?' he asks.

'Valery is in Athens,' she replies. 'He's meeting the military atta-ché at the Russian Embassy.'

'And if I told you he wasn't?'

Her eyes narrow over the rim of the cup and he glimpses a flash of anger mixed with unease. 'Go on.'

'He is on his way to Pathos to meet with Dmitri Troshev.'

'They were in Chechnya together,' Yulia says, a little too quickly. 'They get drunk and exchange war stories.'

He decides not to push it; they have the rest of the weekend.

Later, back in bed, they watch BBC World News while Yulia rubs hormone gel into her thighs. Westminster is still cordoned off and the Houses of Parliament are wrapped in bright blue protective sheeting because so much asbestos was released inside during Guy Fowle's attack. London Fire Brigade officers in gas masks and HAZMAT suits are seen entering and leaving the building via the St Stephen's Gate. A correspondent by a flower-strewn army barricade on the south side of Lambeth Bridge reports that they are still recovering bodies from Parliament and the deep shaft of Westminster underground station. The death toll has now passed that of the Lockerbie bombing, making it the worst terrorist attack in the UK's history.

'It's so ghastly,' Yulia says, switching it off. 'I can't bear to watch it any more.'

There had been a kind of morbid fascination in following the rolling news coverage in the days that followed the attack. But Yulia's right, it's become almost unwatchable.

'If you hadn't shared information with us, Guy Fowle would have had longer to prepare the attack and many more people might have died,' Jude tells her.

'We don't have to be enemies,' she says. 'It's not written in stone.'

'Agreed.'

They lie beside each other, staring up at the high ceiling from their rumpled bed.

'When I was a child oranges were a rare and precious gift,' she says. 'When we had one my mother and I would peel it and put the strips of peel on the radiators so that the whole apartment smelled of orange. And we'd share it segment by segment, savouring each one. Hoping that it would never end.' She turns and places her palm on his chest. 'You're like a precious segment of orange.'

When he doesn't say anything, she looks up again and sighs.

'I think that my husband is in trouble,' she says, eventually.

'What kind of trouble?'

'Financial. What other kind of trouble is there?'

'Is that why he has gone to see Troshev?'

'I don't know,' she says, 'but yes, if I had to guess, and knowing how injurious it will be to his pride, I'd say he's gone to ask for a loan.'

'And will Troshev give it to him?'

'Perhaps. And perhaps he will want something in return. If you want to know my husband, Jude, you have to understand what it was like for those of us who lived in Moscow in the late nineties and the effect it had on us.'

'Then tell me, please.'

'At that time, Russia was in chaos. No one was getting paid: coal miners, doctors, soldiers, even the workers in the nuclear power plants were going hungry. We lived in a decaying housing block and it was boiling in summer and freezing in winter. We drove a dilapidated Niva and Valery told endless, grandiose stories about his days as a paratrooper in Chechnya. I did things to survive that I would not do again. We both did. For my husband, there was only one lesson from those times: that you must make money to survive. He loves money more than anything. It was his misfortune not to be one of those who grew rich in the chaos. He is bitter about that. He is bitter about many things, including me.'

'And how does he feel about me?'

'No man likes to be a cuckold. You make him very angry.'

He props himself up on one elbow. 'Are you safe?'

She turns to face him. 'I have to be careful when he is drunk but he is always remorseful the next day.'

'And that's okay?'

'Life is not perfect, Jude. It is about compromises, accommodations and alliances. We do the best we can with the materials at hand.'

'I don't accept that,' he says.

'I'm a realist, Jude. I can't afford your idealism.'

'You know that you could come over to us.'

'Oh, my darling, you're so sweet, but please don't project your fantasies onto me.'

'I'm serious.'

'And be hunted for the rest of my life? To die by polonium or novichok? I don't think so. Our president is not a forgiving man.' It's as if a cloud passes across her face that is replaced, moments later, by a more familiar and mischievous smile. She combs her fingers through the fine hair below his navel. 'Besides, I have a deep mole to run. My very own *illegal*. A handsome young British intelligence officer.'

He accepts the compliment with a melancholy smile.

# 7

## The Chancellor's vacation

The excited sounds of the teenagers calling out as they dive-bomb the sea from the rocks at the base of the cliff rise up to where Gabriel and Joth are sitting with their feet up on the whitewashed terrace wall of Joth's Greek villa.

Gabriel is holding forth. 'I ask you, what the fuck am I supposed to do? I'm the finance minister of the fifth largest economy in the world and I have absolutely no control over interest rates or any of the other levers. All it takes is less than a two per cent shift in the bond markets, a correction in the OBR forecasts and that's it, my entire political career is a dismal, fucking failure.' Add to that the stupefying cruelty of the tabloids that regularly taunt him as metropolitan mediocrity, only in office because he poses no threat to the Prime Minister. And add to that the ruthlessness of the PM's special adviser who is probably behind the hostile briefings. It's no wonder he feels beleaguered. He gesticulates at the yachts floating serenely out in the azure bay with a fat, conical joint between his fingers. 'Look at those tossers out there on their fancy boats. Most of them are sitting on more than the GDP of entire nations and not one of them pays any money into my exchequer. No one holds them responsible.'

'Mate, chill,' Joth says. 'It's the weed talking.'

Joth calls everyone *mate*, even minor royals and oligarchs, extending the *a* in a lugubrious, throaty way. He's right. Gabriel hasn't been this stoned since they were at Harrow (or 'the other place' as the Etonians call it). He's never really been that keen on marijuana. When they were in the Bullingdon Club at Oxford ecstasy was the drug of choice but, even then, he was never really at the Bacchanalian end of things. He was always quieter and coyer than his more blue-blooded friends. However, the weed is prime Indica organically grown on the sun-kissed hills of Westmoreland in Jamaica, and he is on holiday with his oldest and most trusted friend. The weed was delivered this morning by bicycle courier to Joth's floppy-haired seventeen-year-old, Xander, who is some kind of digital prodigy. Gabriel drops his feet and leans over the wall to look down at the pool on the terrace below where his wife Charlotte is celebrating a morning of tennis by sharing a bottle of rosé wine with Joth's third wife, Violeta. They are both topless and Gabriel is mesmerised by Violeta's impossible breasts. It's stoned thinking but they look remarkably like nuclear warheads. While he is watching, Violeta reaches out and runs her hand down Charlotte's face in a stroking gesture of incomprehensible intimacy.

He shakes his head, thinking he's imagined it.

Joth is grinning at him. 'You're lucky your wife is still so hot.'

Gabriel feels increasingly uncomfortable discussing sexual desire. It's not as if he's prurient. There was a time when he couldn't sit in a meeting without undressing every woman in the room but since he's been taking anti-anxiety medication, he's found his libido has collapsed. He still has sex with Charlotte but it involves a lengthy build-up, which he usually fills by reading the papers in his red ministerial box as he waits for the Viagra to kick in. It doesn't help that William Gladstone, the Grand Old Man of nineteenth-century British politics, once owned the box. He can't shake the sense that the ghost of his illustrious predecessor is staring over his shoulder in voyeuristic anticipation.

'Don't worry, Gabe, you'll be able to clean up on the after-dinner circuit once you're done,' Joth drawls. Gabriel dislikes being called Gabe even more than he dislikes being called mate. He wonders why he still tolerates it after all these years. You really don't get to choose your friends. 'I'm sure they'll find you a paid board position in one of the extractives, copper, coltan, whatever. Maybe you could run a talk radio station.'

Gabriel frowns. He's spent his entire career within earshot of Big Ben, as a Party worker, an MP and finally a minister.

He's never worked anywhere else. 'What do I know about talk radio?'

'What the fuck do you know about economics?' Joth retorts.

'I resent that!'

They both start giggling and Gabriel recites the twelve times table which he won a competition for at school.

'Pass me the doobie,' Joth says, eventually.

Gabriel hands him the joint. There's no avoiding it: money is the problem; professionally and publicly, obviously, but personally too. He can't keep up on a Cabinet minister's paltry salary. There just isn't enough of it. Not for school fees, Jasmine's cash-sink of a pony or Alfie's extra tuition. Not to mention Charlotte's plush yoga retreats. How on earth does raw food cost so much? It doesn't help that his oldest friend is the scion of a European banking family that dates back to the Hapsburgs. Nor does it help that his wife runs a company selling up-market bath and body products and seems to think that, just because all their rich friends have her Refresh and Relax brands with their blend of bespoke essential oils in their bathrooms, she deserves to live the same life of luxurious hedonism as they do.

'We've been invited to a party tomorrow,' Joth says, gesturing towards the far side of the bay, where villas perch improbably on the sheer cliffs. 'We'll take the Riva across the car park.'

At this time of year, the bay, which Joth likes to regard as his own particular playground in the Aegean, tends to fill up with floating palaces of the global financial elite and he refers to it as the *Klept car park*.

Gabriel shakes his head. 'Whose party?'

'Oleg Solokov.'

'Russian?'

'Yeah and a bit Ukrainian as well. The eastern part. Made his money in copper. He wants to make a donation to the Party.'

'We can't have Russian money, Joth. You know how bad it looks.'

'The whole country runs on Russian money.'

'He's got to be on the electoral roll or run a UK trading company if he wants to make a donation.'

'Oleg Solokov owns a whole portfolio of legitimate UK companies, mate. I'm sure that at least one of them is based up north. He can give you some spending money. British money, kosher as tikka masala.'

'I don't know about that.'

'You should meet him. Solokov's the sort of contact you need for afterwards when it's time to cash in. Courteous for a chap who's bought his own furniture. Get Charlie to give him some of that kumquat bath gel so he can get himself all lathered up in the shower. He'll probably make her an offer she can't refuse.'

'It's Moroccan rose not kumquat.'

'Yeah, whatever.'

'What do you think of the dress?' Charlotte asks, twirling in front of the mirror in their suite. 'Violeta gave it to me.'

'It's quite short,' Gabriel says, looking up from his Jack Reacher novel.

'You used to like my legs.'

'I do like your legs,' he says, his eyes drifting back to the page. 'What will the kids say?'

'The kids? We're entirely invisible to them unless they want money. What are you worried about? Do you really think I'd let some lusty Cossack throw me over his shoulder and drag me off to his super yacht? You'd be wide of the mark there.'

He looks up again. 'I'm sorry?'

She gives him a resigned look that is increasingly familiar, 'Don't worry, Gabriel. It doesn't matter. What are you planning to wear?'

He frowns. 'I don't know.'

Ever since he's been at the Treasury, he's assumed that his daily uniform is a well tailored but unostentatious suit, a reassuringly plain shirt and a suitably sombre tie. Making him ready at a moment's notice to respond to runs, crashes, closures, pandemics, terrorist attacks or any other kind of financial meteorite lobbed at him.

Holidays present a problem. What to wear?

'That Paul Smith shirt I bought you.'

'Okay,' he says.

Joth owns a 1959 Riva Super Florida speedboat with V8 engines and a handcrafted wooden deck and hull that once belonged to a Hollywood starlet. He pilots it across the azure waters of the bay casually dressed in board shorts and a T-shirt, sunglasses and a baseball cap. While Gabriel trails his hand in the cool water, Xander provides a running commentary on the flotilla of 100-metre-plus giga-yachts they pass while hopping between their Wi-Fi networks. Gabriel learns that Xander's skills are not simply limited to buying drugs on the Dark Net but also include hacking sophisticated security systems. He explains how Russian oligarchs, Gulf royals and American tech giants dominate the yacht scene via a complicated network of offshore structures designed to limit liability and preserve anonymity. It's not an absolute sort of anonymity because it's clear that the owners want each other to know what they've got. Xander lists the exclusive features of each yacht that constitute bragging rights in this part of the Mediterranean: infinity pools, helipads, cinemas, dive rooms, leisure submarines, missile defence systems and anti-paparazzi shields that dazzle digital cameras.

'Which house is it we're going to?' Gabriel asks, looking beyond the yachts at the cliff.

Joth points to a modern, glass and steel villa set in gardens on a natural shelf midway up the sheer wall of black rock. A glass-walled elevator runs from the top of the cliff to the sea.

'Part of the house is inside the cliff,' Joth says. 'They dynamited their way in. It was bloody noisy. Chap sent me a case of vintage Dom as recompense and invited me over to have a look-see when the building work was finished.'

Gabriel can see people descending towards the villa in the elevator.

'Put your laptop away,' Joth tells his son as they approach the jetty at the base of the cliff, 'and collect everyone's phones in the

Faraday pouch and lock them in the safe. Unless, that is, our guests want to hand them over to the Russians on arrival?'

Gabriel glances at his wife on the red leather bench opposite but she's whispering conspiratorially in Violeta's ear, her short dress riding high on her thighs.

'Gabe?'

Xander holds out a black nylon bag and Gabriel switches off his private and government-issue phones and puts them inside.

# 8

# The pig and the cleaver

The taxi drops Valery Ermolaev at the entrance to the villa, an undulating wave of twelve-foot-high white concrete that follows the contour at the top of the cliff edge. Beyond the blue-and-white-painted crash bollards there is a brushed-steel door, a camera and an intercom.

Within seconds of exiting the taxi, Valery can feel the sweat running off his forehead and down the back of his legs in his suit trousers. He speaks Russian into the intercom and they keep him waiting for ten minutes while the air ripples with heat rising from the asphalt. Eventually, the door opens with a hefty clunk. He hands over his phone and allows himself to be frisked, before being given the choice of the stairs or the glass elevator. He chooses the elevator.

The descent is stunning: a bird's-eye view of a bay with a flotilla of sleek white billionaire's yachts resting at anchor. The doors open onto a party. There are guests mingling beneath the pergolas and alongside the pool. Bees float above pink and blue azaleas. Amongst the crowd, he recognises a media magnate's eldest daughter speaking to the villa's owner, the oligarch Oleg Solokov. He also recognises a Hollywood action hero from the 1980s flanked by a trio of silicone-augmented beauties, a rabble-rousing Hungarian politician, and a Baron from the British House of Lords with his Brazilian boyfriend.

He stops one of the white-coated waiting staff. 'Where's the Chef?'

The waiter rolls his eyes and nods towards the house. 'He's in the kitchen with his cleaver.'

★  ★  ★

Valery watches the Chef raise the cleaver and bring it down between the pig's head and its shoulders.

*Thock.*

On the television behind the Chef, the Russian Patriarch is warning that social media will hasten the arrival of the antichrist; through the glass wall, the Aegean stretches away to the horizon.

Another chop.

*Thock.*

Valery is a large man but even so, the Chef dwarfs him. He has legs like the Pillars of Hercules and he can roar like a bull moose. He's big like circus strongmen often are, with a huge belly and fat in his limbs, the muscle underneath as thick as the shoulders of the pig on the slab before him.

Valery wonders how many of the bodyguards it took to haul the pig down off the hook on the ceiling and onto the marble counter-top at the centre of the villa's gleaming aluminium kitchen. There are five of them and it's a measure of the size of the room that their presence doesn't make it seem crowded. They watch Valery with predatory interest.

*Thock.*

The pig's head separates from its shoulders.

'Why are you here?' the Chef says, pointing the bloody cleaver at him.

'I have something important to discuss with you.'

'You look like you're going to boil to death.' The Chef turns to point the blade at one of the guards. 'Bring him a glass of water.'

Valery removes his sodden jacket and hangs it on the back of one of the high-backed stools. He sits and a tall glass of water is placed in front of him. Across the table, the Chef resumes butchering the carcass.

Twenty-five years earlier, Valery and the Chef had fought together in the ill-fated battle of Grozny in the first Chechen war. Grozny means awesome and terrible in Russian and so it had been. Both counted themselves lucky to have survived. Since then their fortunes had taken different though not unrelated paths.

Valery had continued serving in Russian military intelligence, the GRU, and the Chef set up PMC Valkyrie, the private military company whose main customer was the Russian state.

The Chef pauses, puts down the cleaver and wipes his hand on his bloody apron. He pours two shots of vodka from an unmarked bottle beside him and gives one to Valery.

They toast. No words need to be said. Valery downs the vodka.

'What do you want, Valery?' the Chef asks, putting down his untouched glass and chopping the pork into cubes and sweeping them to one side in batches, building a mountain of meat beside a stack of iron skewers. Valery is fast gaining the impression that he has been admitted under sufferance and if they hadn't spent New Year's Eve 1995 lying in a ditch on the main road into Grozny, he wouldn't be here at all.

'I have a plan that will make us both rich,' Valery says.

The Chef continues chopping. 'I am already rich.'

'As rich as this,' Valery replies, gesturing around him.

The Chef laughs. 'Do you really think that you can count that high?'

'I can count as good as anyone,' Valery says.

The Chef points the cleaver at the nearest yacht in the bay beneath them. 'You see that boat. She cost a million dollars a metre.'

'And she doesn't belong to you,' Valery says.

'No,' the Chef concedes.

'You could buy one, maybe two,' Valery says.

The Chef grunts sceptically and resumes chopping, breaking up the ribs.

*Thock, thock, thock, thock* . . .

He pauses between blows. 'Did your wife send you?'

Valery feels his face redden. 'No.'

'Where does she think you are?'

'She believes that I have business in Athens.'

'And, where is she now?'

'She's in Istanbul for the weekend.'

'Who with?'

When Valery doesn't answer, the Chef shakes his head. 'Does she know how much money you owe?'

He feels suddenly light-headed. 'No.'

*Nobody is supposed to know how much money he owes.*

'You look like a fucking beetroot,' the Chef says and shakes his head. 'Only fools gamble.'

'I had a losing streak,' Valery protests. 'It was bad luck.'

'I don't believe in luck.' The Chef seems disappointed. 'I'll give you a loan. Just this once, for old time's sake. After that you're on your own.'

'You're not listening to me,' Valery says, his voice rising. 'I don't want a loan. I want to make you money. Big money. Four hundred and eighty million dollars.'

The Chef's eyes roll. 'You want me to rob a bank?'

'No. A prison.'

'A prison?'

'Inside the prison is a prisoner.'

'You surprise me.'

'Inside the head of this prisoner is a password. The password unlocks accumulated cryptocurrency holdings of Islamic State.'

'Where is this prison?'

'London. It will require boldness.'

The seconds tick by as Valery continues to meet his gaze. Eventually, the Chef turns to one of his bodyguards.

'Maksim, bring me Fyodor.'

While they wait, the Chef tosses the cubes of pork into a huge earthenware bowl with a marinade of onions, red wine, pomegranate juice and paprika. 'I cooked this for the president,' he says, 'on the Day of Heroes of the Fatherland. Now I cook for degenerates.'

He looks out across the terrace at the oligarch's guests. The English Baron is standing over a sun lounger by the infinity pool, feeding olives to his boyfriend who is practically kneeling before him.

'I have been naked with this man in the *banya*.' The Chef practically spits. 'He whipped me with birch leaves. Only afterwards, Oleg tells me that he is filthy queer.'

'I could have told you that,' Valery says.

The Chef looks at him, his forearms slick with red wine and pomegranate juice. 'You think I should listen to you more?'

'Yes, Chef, I do.'

'You explain details of your plan to Fyodor,' he says. 'If he likes it, then perhaps we will do it.'

Fyodor? It's not a name that Valery recognises. 'And if you do it?'

'Then you're free of debt and your Chinese friends won't have any reason to cut off your balls.'

'I want more than that,' Valery says. 'I want half.'

'If your idea is viable, and more than just a drunken fantasy cooked up by a desperate man, you'll get a ten per cent finder's fee like everyone else.'

A man steps into the kitchen from a door that Valery had not previously noticed. He is wearing black clothes; black T-shirt, black jacket, black trousers, and black shoes. He is slender with pale skin stretched tightly across his face, swept-back white hair and colourless eyes. There are chunky platinum rings on his fingers and thumbs that make Valery think of knuckledusters, including one with what looks like a curved blade on it.

'Chef?' the man asks, softly. Despite his skinny frame, there is something deeply unnerving about him.

'Fyodor, this is Colonel Valery Ermolaev, the military attaché at our embassy in London. I believe that you are familiar with his work?'

Fyodor smiles, his face a skull. 'I am.'

'Valery, this is Fyodor aka Scary Bear. I know you are familiar with the unique work of the Protean Bears.'

*Scary Bear.*

The world takes a terrifying lurch sideways. There are certain secrets that rely on absolute deniability. Valery realises with utter conviction that he is in the wrong place with the wrong man and that if his superiors ever learn of it, his life will be immediately forfeit.

'The Colonel here has a proposition for us that involves a large amount of money,' the Chef says.

Scary Bear stares at Valery who is rooted to his stool with his heart hammering in his rib cage – it feels like he's having a heart attack.

The Chef laughs, knowingly. 'He is scary, isn't he?'

'I shouldn't be here,' Valery gasps. 'I can't be seen with him.'

The Chef shrugs his massive shoulders. 'No one invited you.'

And then it gets worse.

'Excuse me.'

A cut-glass English accent.

The Chef frowns. Valery watches the bodyguards tense and rise on the balls of their feet.

'Someone spilled red wine on my shirt,' a man says from behind Valery, his voice worryingly familiar.

'Take off your shirt,' the Chef says, in English.

'I was just looking for a sink.'

Valery swivels on the seat and finds himself face to face with Gabriel Morley, the Chancellor of Her Majesty's Exchequer. He has a large red stain on his shirt and he is nervously eyeing the muscle in the room. There is a tall, floppy-haired teenager wearing a Chelsea Football Club top standing beside him.

'Maksim will rub affected area with detergent and warm water,' the Chef says. 'Five minutes or less and everything will be normal. It is best done immediately.'

The bodyguard steps up to the man and holds out his hand.

'Ah, right, thank you,' Gabriel stutters.

'You are minister in British government,' the Chef says, watching him unbutton his shirt.

'Yes. Please call me Gabriel.'

'Gabriel?' the Chef says, as if he is unsure of the name and what it might say about its owner.

Gabriel stands uncomfortably with his arms folded across his bare chest while Maksim attends to his shirt at the sink. The boy beside him is staring at Fyodor as if there is something about him that is familiar.

'Do you eat pork?' the Chef asks.

'Yes.'

The Chef nods to himself as if he is reassured by the news.

'I recognise you,' the boy says to Fyodor.

Silence.

The Chef and Fyodor exchange an incredulous look.

The boy ploughs on, oblivious. 'I knew it. You're Scary Bear.'

Fyodor recoils like a scalded cat.

'Maksim, give Gabriel his shirt back!' the Chef thunders, snatching the cleaver off the block.

The bodyguard thrusts the sodden shirt into Gabriel's hands.

'Put it on outside,' the Chef says. 'It will dry quickly.'

'This way, Xander,' Gabriel says, backing out onto the terrace. 'Xander!'

It's as if the boy suddenly becomes aware of the jeopardy that he is in.

'Right, yeah. Sorry, sorry.'

He bobs out onto the terrace after Gabriel and they hurry away beneath a pergola towards the other party guests.

'How did he know me?' Scary Bear demands.

'I don't know,' the Chef snaps. He gives Fyodor a thunderous look.

'I don't believe this!' Valery says.

'You don't believe it?' the Chef yells. 'You fucking idiot!'

# 9

## Would you rather?

Jude is sitting in the kitchen at his sister's house. Hannah has her laptop open on the island and his nieces are interrogating him at the table. Olivia is putting the questions and Abi is watching carefully, clutching a floppy rabbit named Mee.

'Would you rather always be ten minutes late or ten minutes early?'

'Ten minutes early.'

Abi takes her thumb and the tip of the rabbit's ear out of her mouth. 'What would you do for all that time?'

'Wait and watch,' Jude tells her.

'Would you rather be famous while you're alive and forgotten when you're dead,' Olivia says, 'or nobody when you are alive and famous when you're dead?'

'Nobody when I'm alive.'

'Would you rather be invisible for one day or able to fly for one day?'

'Invisible.'

Abi's eyes widen. 'What would you do?'

'Go and sit next to somebody I like.'

'That's just weird,' Hannah says.

'I'd keep them safe,' Jude says.

'You can sit next to me,' Abi tells him, 'and Mee.'

'I'd like that,' Jude says.

'But you won't know he's there,' Olivia says, rolling her eyes, and resumes the game. 'Would you rather be in a room that is totally dark for four days or a room that is lit up all the time for four days?'

'The dark room.'

'Would you rather sell all of your possessions or one of your organs?'

'I don't have any possessions.'

'What is an organ?' Abi asks.

'Your heart is an organ,' Olivia says.

'Some people think your uncle is heartless already,' Hannah says.

'What people?' Olivia asks.

'Grown-ups.'

'Would you rather lose your left hand or your right foot?'

'Bath time,' Hannah announces. 'No further questions.'

Later they sit at the table sharing a bottle of Picpoul and Hannah raises the Westminster attack. She was the on-the-day editor at the TV news programme where she works when it happened.

'We were in the newsroom, all standing together watching the footage on one of the screens,' Hannah says. 'It came to the bit where an as yet unidentified man, widely but inaccurately reported to be an undercover police officer, shot the woman wearing a suicide vest in Parliament Square and I very nearly said, "That's my brother".'

'I'm glad you didn't,' Jude tells her.

'It would have been quite a scoop,' she says, ruefully.

'If we'd caught them earlier, maybe I wouldn't have had to kill her,' Jude says.

The final exultation of Zeina Hussein will live with him forever: standing with her arms spread wide on Parliament Square, her thumb on the red switch connected to her suicide vest, his finger squeezing the trigger and the bullet striking her forehead.

'Do you regret it?'

'Yes.'

'If you hadn't killed her, even more people would have died.'

'I know,' Jude says, 'but she was a damaged person under the influence of a psychopath.'

'What does your therapist have to say?'

How to explain that his therapist seems more concerned with the effects of the helicopter crash and the overnight battle in the

Syrian town, than she does with the events of the Westminster attack. Or maybe that's Jude reading too much into Helena's recent visit. Maybe he's the one who labours under the illusion that each new event cancels out the previous ones.

'She advised me to get drunk,' Jude says.

Hannah frowns. 'How is that supposed to help?'

'Something about the hangover blunting the memory.'

'Did you?' Hannah asks.

'Did I what?'

'Get drunk.'

'Yes,' Jude replies.

'Did it help?'

He shrugs. 'The jury's out.'

What helped was seeing Yulia.

Hannah fills their glasses.

'Kirsty has been in touch,' she tells him. Kirsty McIntyre was the broadsheet journalist who had helped Jude to uncover the identity of Guy Fowle. For a while they had acted as a team, sharing information that had exposed a cover-up by the intelligence services and led to the downfall of Queen Bee, the former head of MI6. 'She says you told her you were going overseas and you haven't been returning her calls. She says that the only possible explanation for ignoring her is that you must be dead.'

'I was overseas.'

'But you're back now. Are you going to call her?' Hannah sighs. 'She's my friend. I'm responsible for introducing you and, who knows why, she has taken a liking to you.'

'It's difficult,' Jude says, uncomfortably.

'Because you're a spy and she's a journalist?'

'Yes.' Though it's more than that. It's hard for him not to feel that any person caring for him must be making a big mistake.

'You don't have to talk about work.'

'I'm supposed to report the details of any conversations that I have with her.'

'Perhaps you should have thought of that before you kissed her.'

How to explain? There had been no forethought in the kiss, even if it was the culmination of days of simmering mutual desire. They were on a hillside in Greece. He remembers the light in her eyes and the passion of the kiss that followed; the taste of grappa on her lips and the answering need in him.

'I don't know what to do about it,' he says. There doesn't seem to be any way forward for him. As with Yulia, his route to a transparent and meaningful relationship is blocked. To pretend otherwise is selfish.

'Meet her. She deserves an explanation. Remember she has also kept your identity out of the news.'

'Okay.'

'Good. Are you going to Fowle's arraignment?'

The twenty-eight days that the police are allowed to hold a suspect without charge under anti-terror legislation are almost up and Guy Fowle is due in court to hear the criminal charges against him.

'Yes,' Jude says.

'Will he plead guilty?' Hannah asks.

Jude has read the forensic psychological assessment of Fowle that is based on extensive interviews with Fowle's family, a head teacher who is convinced that he burned her school to the ground, the only surviving psychologist who interviewed him as a teenager, a university flatmate who survived an attempt to hang himself, and several of the physically and mentally traumatised soldiers who served under him in the army.

'The psychologist believes that he's deliberately refusing to speak,' Jude tells her. 'Which means the court will be forced to enter a plea of not guilty and it will have to go to trial. Because he's grandiose and narcissistic, it's in his character to crave the kind of attention that will bring. The psychologist thinks he's likely to use it as a platform to deliver some kind of nihilist manifesto and taunt the relatives of the dead.'

Hannah shakes her head in disgust. 'He's a monster.'

'We live in a time of monsters,' Jude says. 'We made him. We trained him and protected him. Everyone from the army, to the security services and all the way up to the Foreign Secretary was more interested in covering up their mistakes and saving their careers than trying to stop him. We brought it all down on ourselves.'

'We?'

'The government.'

'I'm a journalist, Jude. I hold government to account.'

# Behind glass

In the back seat of a police BMW, a family liaison officer is holding out a plastic carton to Katherine Fowle and Jude is watching.

'Put your watch and your jewellery in there.'

The car is heading south over the Thames on the high bridge at the Dartford Crossing. Katherine turns back from staring at the river four hundred feet below and removes her earrings and then her watch, dropping them into the box.

'And take off your sunglasses.'

She has been wearing sunglasses since they collected her from the airport. Jude isn't sure what he expected to see beneath – she has agreed to meet the man who abused her throughout her childhood – but her eyes are clear.

Unreadable.

He can't get the image out of his mind of her brother repeatedly punching her in the stomach in her cot when she was a baby. Katherine's mother had told him that not long before the Westminster attack.

They take the first slip road after the toll, crossing over the motorway and heading west towards Thamesmead and Woolwich.

'Guy is being held away from any other prisoners in the segregation section of the High Security Unit,' Jude explains. 'The HSU is a separate prison within the Category A prison. On arrival, we will all be X-rayed and then escorted there. In the meeting room you will be separated from your brother by an armoured-glass screen. Sit in the chair. Don't approach or touch the glass. I don't know if he's going to speak to you. But if he does, you must tell him that we want the password to his cryptocurrency account. If he gives us that, then he can have access to the books that he has requested in writing that are either missing or not available in the library.'

Katherine nods.

'I will be in the room next door and watching on CCTV. If he says or does anything out of the ordinary or in any way suspicious or threatening, I will terminate the visit, is that clear?'

Katherine nods.

The last time he had seen her, on the island in the Hebrides where she and Guy had grown up, Katherine had urged Jude to kill her brother.

'You're sure you're willing to go ahead with this?' Jude asks.

She nods.

They follow a sign that says *Belmarsh and Courts.*

Guy Fowle is waiting, not a muscle stirring.

He is sitting in a secured enclosure, behind glass that is as thick as a bible. He has his eyes closed and his chained hands are resting palms down on the laminate surface of a desk.

Jude watches on the monitor as the door clicks open and Katherine enters. She is wearing baggy, shapeless clothes, a sweatshirt and sweat pants. She sits in the plastic chair opposite her brother. Fowle opens his eyes. They stare at each other through the glass without expression. Neither speaks.

The family liaison officer shifts uncomfortably beside Jude.

'What are they doing?' she says.

'Wait,' he says.

The gesture is almost imperceptible, and Jude might easily have missed it, Fowle's right fingers flick upwards in a gesture that he interprets as *go away.*

In response, Katherine stands and pulls her sweatshirt over her head. Beneath it she is naked. The family liaison officer gasps.

Katherine's entire upper body is covered in scars, they radiate outwards from her breasts in a complex display. Jude has seen similar markings on the body of Zeina Hussein, one of the Westminster attackers, and read the coroner's report that suggests that they have some secret ritualistic significance for Fowle that may be sexual in nature. Katherine steps forward and presses herself to the glass with her arms outstretched.

Fowle rises to meet her.

'Get it out of me!' she screams.

Prison wardens burst into the room and drag Katherine away from the glass and out of the room.

Fowle stands back, smiling. He looks up at the black sphere that contains the camera and for the first time since he was arrested, speaks.

'Jude Lyon, are you there?'

Jude kneels before Katherine out in the prison corridor. She is wearing a prison blanket across her shoulders, covering her chest.

'He is not going to hurt you ever again, Katherine,' he says.

'You have no idea,' she replies.

'Help me to understand,' he says, gently. 'What is it that you want him to get out of you?'

She looks down at him. 'A demon.'

He doesn't know what to say.

'We shouldn't have asked you to come here,' the family liaison officer says, in an accusatory tone.

'I'm sorry,' Jude says, helplessly.

Ten minutes later, Jude enters the visitor's room and sits on the plastic chair.

This is the fourth time that Jude has been this close to Fowle. On the three previous occasions Fowle could have killed him but chose not to. Jude still isn't sure why. For several minutes they sit opposite each other without speaking. There is something atavistic and unknowable about Fowle. It feels like being in close proximity to a big cat – a lion or a tiger.

Eventually, Fowle raises his chin and speaks without looking at him. 'I see the essence of people. The Hindu word for it is *Atman*. I see it in colour. Only rarely do I see someone who shines. Most barely register. They are indistinguishable from cattle.' He cocks his head. 'How many are now dead as a result of my attack?'

'Two hundred and seventy-seven.'

Fowle is pleased. 'Two more than yesterday.'

It is predicted that the death count from the Westminster attack will rise even higher as those who were most badly maimed when the bomb detonated in the packed concourse of the underground station succumb to their injuries.

'But not enough, right?'

Fowle does not reply.

Fowle's eyes flick upwards for a moment and Jude meets his gaze. What he sees there is so unsettling that it takes all his will-power not to immediately look away.

'I achieved what I wanted to,' Fowle replies.

'We know how you did it. How you used seven accomplices to assist you. We found the decomposed body of the seventh, the forger Underhill, in his antique shop just a couple of days ago. You cut his throat with a knife. The same knife you used to cut the throats of at least five others. What is it about the throat and the knife that appeals so much?'

'It's intimate,' he replies, opening his eyes again.

'But messy.'

'I don't mind blood.'

'Now you're being coy, Guy. We both know you like blood very much. I saw the cuts on Zeina Hussein's body and now the ones on Katherine too. It didn't take long for the coroner to work out what you were up to. You can't help yourself, can you?'

Fowle sighs. 'What do you want?'

'I want to understand.'

'Are you sure about that, Jude?' He smiles knowingly. 'It will lead you down a path that you might not be able to handle.'

'I can handle it.'

'I have to disappoint you, Jude. I know that you want to shine but your aura is too diffuse, too faint.'

'What do you think the press are going to make of it if they find out about the feeding?' Jude says. 'All those corny Dracula comparisons.'

'Are you trying to threaten me?'

'Put it this way, I'm encouraging you to cooperate.'

'And how can I do that?'

'Give us the password for your cryptocurrency account.'

'How very typical,' Fowle says. 'Do you feel insulted that they sent a Jew to ask for money?'

'It's all you have to bargain with.'

'Have your masters told you what they want to spend the money on?'

'No,' Jude replies. 'I think they are more concerned that you don't have it.'

'And if I give you the money?'

'Some of the more lurid details of your sexual predilections are kept out of the press and we let you have the books and writing implements you want.'

'And if I refuse?'

'No books, no pencils and no means of expressing yourself,' Jude says. 'You're left in segregation with nothing to do but spread your own shit on the walls for amusement.'

Fowle leans back and closes his eyes again.

## II

## Sharing savoury custard

On the night before the arraignment, Jude is sitting at a corner table in a small, intimate restaurant in Hoxton with brick walls and a blackboard menu. There is a bottle of chilled Les Crêtes in a wine cooler beside him.

He stands as Kirsty enters and feels something unfurl inside at the openness of her smile. She's wearing a sleeveless metallic maxi dress and silver sandals. They kiss on the cheek and he pulls back the chair for her, before sitting himself.

'Wine?' he asks.

'Do a dog's nuts glisten in the moonlight?'

Smiling, he pours them both a glass.

'You know it's customary to let the woman face the room,' she says, before taking a sip.

'Ah, I'm sorry,' he winces, 'do you want to swap?'

'It's okay. I get the feeling you like to keep an eye on the exits.'

He smiles, ruefully. 'Force of habit.'

It's what he's done all his working life: maintained line of sight on doorways.

She looks around. 'Nice place, to what do I owe the honour?'

'My sister felt it was necessary to prove to you that I'm still alive.'

'I did wonder. I even checked the obituaries.'

The waiter approaches with a blackboard and she scans the menu and listens attentively to his recommendations. She asks him to elaborate on a couple of ingredients and Jude suggests that they share the savoury gorgonzola custard as a starter.

'I'm game,' she says.

They order several other plates to share.

When the waiter is out of earshot, she leans towards him, 'The last time I saw you it was on the television. It was just after the Tube station explosion. You were in Westminster Square pointing a gun at Zeina Hussein. That was quite something, running out into the square and taking on a suicide bomber all by yourself.'

'You make it sound like a question.'

She is examining him closely with her eyes narrowed, as if she is trying to get the measure of him. 'That's because it was.'

'People tend to do things like that when they don't have time to think.'

'Is that what happened to you?'

There is no side to Kirsty. Her face isn't a hiding place, it is her. It is one of the things that makes her so attractive, along with her directness. What is beautiful about her runs all the way through her. It makes it almost impossible to lie to her.

'I didn't have a lot of time to think,' he acknowledges. 'But I had a choice. I could have stayed in cover and maybe survived the explosion. So, no, it wasn't just because I couldn't think of anything else.'

'Why then?'

He shifts uneasily in his chair. 'Lots of ordinary people were going to die. I decided that I wasn't the sort of person to let that happen. I suppose it was a decision about the kind of person I am.'

'Someone who runs towards danger?'

'No, that's not it. It was about doing the right thing. About trying to be a better person and not just doing things because they are easy.'

'Do you need to be a better person?'

He sighs. 'You know what happened. I was complicit in a cover-up. My employer paid protection money to a senior commander in Islamic State to keep Guy Fowle locked up. Who knows how many innocent people died because of the money that was paid?'

'You did the right thing,' Kirsty says. 'It's because of you that the cover-up was exposed and the truth came out.'

'Fowle killed a lot of innocent people in London.'

'And because of your actions and the choices you made, many more people survived and he'll never get the chance to do it again.'

Jude shudders, remembering the interview room at Belmarsh. Katherine Fowle screaming at her brother to get the demon out of her and the maniacal darkness in his eyes.

'What's up with you?' she asks.

'I saw him,' he admits.

'When?'

'Recently.'

'How was he?'

'Unrepentant.'

'It did your head in?'

He nods. 'Yes.'

'He's a psychopath,' she says. 'He's a proper, real-life psychopath. It's a mistake to believe that he's like us. He's other. Don't even bother trying to understand him.'

'That's pretty much what he said.'

'Let's talk about something else,' she says, brightly.

When the custard arrives, it's more of a collapsed soufflé and they scoop it up with crunchy, homemade grissini.

'That's pure barry!' she says.

More dishes arrive, orecchiette with pesto and fiery nduja, tentacles of charred octopus on a bed of lemony potatoes, salads of beetroot and blood orange, and broad beans and celery, and Jude is pleased to see her eat heartily. He orders another bottle of wine.

'So, you studied at Edinburgh?' she asks.

'Yes,' he replies.

'Why Scotland?'

'I wanted to try somewhere new. I fell in love with the place and its people.'

She raises an eyebrow. He winces.

'It's corny, I know.'

'And then you joined the army?' she asks.

'That's right.'

'Why?'

'I come from a long line of soldiers. My grandfather was one and my father and stepfather. My grandfather used to say it was the only way to become accepted, to show our loyalty.'

'Because you're Jewish?'

'That's right.'

'But you were raised by your stepfather.'

'Yes, after my mother died.'

'And he wasn't Jewish.'

'You've done your homework.'

'I'm a journalist.'

'My stepfather was also a soldier. And more of a father to me than anyone else.' There is a pause. He has said as much as he wants to. 'What about you?'

She guffaws. 'I am assuming you've done your homework, spy boy. What does it say on my file?'

He laughs. 'I know that you were born and raised in Glasgow, in Govan. I also know that you're an only child and you love your dad. You're the first in your family to go to university, Glasgow, of course. Your bedroom at your parents' house is just as it was when you left it for London. It's like a museum to the Delgados and Arab Strap. I'm sure John Peel would have been proud of you. I also know you have beaten copper pots hanging from a rail on the ceiling of your London flat.'

She reaches for the bottle and fills their glasses. 'You've been stalking me on the web.'

'You have quite a following,' he observes.

She winces and shakes her head. 'Did I really post a photo of my bedroom in my parents' house?'

'I'm afraid so.'

She rolls her eyes. 'I must have been mashed.'

'It's between one with the caption *Mulk Boatles*, which is indeed a picture of two glass milk bottles,' he tells her. 'And one of a couple sleeping rough in a doorway. You've been interviewing them and cataloguing their lives for three years or so. I've listened to the podcasts. You balance indignation at social injustice with a raucous sense of humour.'

'That's in my file?'

'There is no file.'

'Excuse me?' She looks outraged. 'Why not?'

'Secrets always come out in the end. Interfering in press freedom is a mug's game.'

'I'm not sure you're cut out for government work,' she says.

He sighs. 'Tell me why you chose journalism?'

'Because I wanted to understand the world and help other people understand it too.'

He smiles. 'How's that going for you?'

She gives him a defiant look. 'I got a free education and my parents raised me to believe that you have to give something back. I started out as a trainee on the *Glasgow Herald* back when there was such a thing as trainees, and from there, to London. I feel like it's a real privilege to do what I do.' She laughs at herself. 'That's true, by the way.'

'I don't doubt it.'

They decide to do without dessert and she lets him pay the bill. When they go out onto the pavement, she turns to him expectantly, with her eyes shining. They kiss, with wine tasting lips, hesitantly at first and then passionately. It's even better than it was in Greece. It's hard to know how much time has passed when she gently pushes him away.

They stand facing each other.

'Next time, you can invite me of your own accord and not because your sister told you to,' she says, with the hint of a smile. 'I might even go Dutch.'

They kiss again, and again she pushes him gently away.

'Good night, Jude.'

She turns and walks away.

12

# The arraignment

Jude rises early the following morning and for the first time in several weeks, he runs through a training sequence in *Pencak Silat*, the ancient martial art that he studied as a young man on the Indonesian archipelago. On the mat in Sanjay's purpose-built gym, he raises his left knee and turns his head upward, stretching his arms outward and joining his hands together above his head to greet the sky, as the legendary master Sumaryono taught him. Kneeling, he bows and touches the ground to his left and right to salute the earth. Rising, he stands with his fists together close to his chest, gathering his energy.

First the basic exercises, punching and stabbing with closed and open fists, followed by inward and outward palm strikes. Then elbow strikes: turning and diving, upward and downward. He moves between strikes with bent knees, from zig-zag to dancing eagle step, favouring the low foot stand of coastal practitioners who learn to fight in rice fields and on sandy beaches. Then a flurry of slanted and sweeping kicks aimed at an opponent's knees, chest, chin and temple. He runs through a series of *jurus*, premeditated sets of movements of increasing complexity, incorporating methods of avoidance, deception and attack.

After forty minutes, he opens a drawer inset with weapons and takes out a curved *Clurit*, a simple farmer's sickle. Placing it on the mat before him he greets the sun again before taking it up in his right hand. From a standby position he delivers a series of horizontal, upward and downward cuts, gradually including inward palm strikes and kicks.

Next he takes up a *Kerambit*, a small curved knife resembling a claw with a distinctive finger guard that was originally designed

59

for raking roots and planting rice; a weapon of humble origins perfect for slashing, punching and hooking. Using the sickle in one hand and the knife in the other, he runs through a further series of *jurus*, cutting and slashing, striking and blocking, until finally he is too exhausted to go on.

Returning the weapons to the drawer, he heads for the shower. Half an hour later, wearing a navy-blue tweed suit and a matching blue silk tie he steps out of the elevator onto the street with a slab of buttered toast covered in rhubarb jam.

He heads for Bank, from where the light railway will carry him to Woolwich.

Guy Fowle is escorted in transport chains by four prison officers along the underground tunnel that runs from Belmarsh Prison to Woolwich Crown Court and is brought before a judge in court room one.

The car park outside the court is full of satellite trucks broadcasting across the world, and armed police patrol the pedestrian forecourt and guard the main entrance to the steel-clad building.

Jude is inside waiting, sitting on an oak pew at the back of the packed press area, having passed through a full body scanner. He recognises several of the journalists from their byline photos as well as relatives of the deceased from recent media interviews. Five minutes after he takes a seat, he watches Kirsty enter and take a seat further along the same pew. She glances in his direction and gives him a wink. He grins back at her. Of course, reconciling their jobs will never be easy but hopefully not impossible. The route to the meaningful relationship he wants needn't be blocked. She knows what he is and who he is, and doesn't seem deterred. He feels optimistic that they can find a way to make it work. He wants to kiss her again like he did outside the restaurant.

The judge orders the courtroom doors to be locked and the senior prosecution barrister, acting for the Crown, rises to his feet. He reads out the multiple and varied charges against the accused. Two hundred and seventy-seven counts of murder in the

Westminster attacks and twenty-five counts of murder in the Basra ambush. It takes four hours. Throughout, Fowle stands and maintains what Kirsty will later describe in print as an expression of *sublime expectation*. When the prosecution is done, Guy Fowle is finally invited to enter a plea.

He smiles.

Accounts of what follows are fragmentary and confused, in part because of the types of weapons used in the attack, in part because of the sophistication of the malware attack on the court's CCTV systems, and in part because there are only a handful of survivors. Jude is so fixated on the expression on Fowle's face, that he barely registers the small door behind the judge's dais opening.

Stun grenades come spinning through the air.

Flash-blinded with his ears roaring, Jude drops from the bench to the floor while machine-gun fire rakes the wood-panelled walls above him.

Bodies flail and collapse.

Outside the building a car bomb explodes.

The space between the benches is an obstacle course of the dying and the dead. Jude crawls towards the central stairway. A two-person fire team with a belt-fed machine gun maintain a relentless rate of fire from the judge's dais, sweeping left and right, and up and down.

The next volley of grenades contains tear gas that burns his eyes and mouth, and causes a fit of coughing that makes it difficult to breathe. Scrabbling around in the space between pews, Jude finds a plastic bottle of water. He rolls on his back and pours the contents into his eyes and mouth.

Abruptly the gunfire ceases.

Jude continues crawling. A hand brushes his face and a woman's voice whispers, 'Who's there . . .?'

'Kirsty? It's Jude. Are you injured?'

'No. I don't think so.'

He squeezes her hand. 'Stay low and keep your eyes closed. I'll come find you, I promise.'

He heaves himself over a body beside her into the stairway, curls up into a ball with his hands over his head, and rolls down the stairs through clouds of drifting gas towards the front of the court room. It seems to take forever. At the bottom, he uncurls and scrambles forward to beneath the judge's dais. Eyes streaming, he squints at the dock.

Fowle is gone.

He crabs sideways. Steps strewn with hundreds of scalding-hot cartridge casings lead up to the judge's dais. Keeping low, he climbs the stairs and dashes forward through the door behind the dais and into the judge's private chambers. Closing the door behind him, he gets his first taste of breathable air. Beyond the judge's desk there is another door with an illuminated fire exit sign that leads into a narrow corridor. Opening the door, the first thing Jude sees is the body of a man in body armour and a gas mask with his neck at an unnatural angle, lying on the floor.

Jude scoops up the automatic rifle beside the body and advances with it tucked in his shoulder, staring down the sights but barely able to see. The door to the private car park beyond is hanging off its hinges and police sirens are screaming.

Jude steps out into blinding sunlight and glimpses armed police officers charging around the back of the building and between the ranks of cars towards him. He drops the gun and raises his arms.

Of Fowle and his rescuers, there is no sign.

Jude is sitting in the back of an ambulance feeling bruised and battered while a paramedic rinses his eyes with a mixture of water and sodium bicarbonate, and a female police officer takes his statement. His clothes have been bagged up and he's wearing a white paper jumpsuit.

A message over the police officer's radio informs them that a burning white transit van has been found under a road bridge in Thamesmead on the Eastern Way and it's assumed the attackers have switched vehicles. Automatic vehicle number plate recognition is being used to track all vehicles heading in and out of London.

Jude turns to the paramedic beside him. 'There was a woman alive at the back of the room. Her name is Kirsty McIntyre, do you know where she is?'

'She's in one of the other ambulances.'

'Thank you.'

Jude climbs out the back and walks between two rows of ambulances that run the length of a supermarket car park, looking in the back of each one until he finds her. She is sitting, also in a paper suit, while a paramedic removes wooden splinters from her arms with a pair of tweezers.

'Hey,' he says, gently.

She looks at him and for a moment he isn't sure if she knows who he is. Her eyes are blood-shot and she looks exhausted.

'I can't believe that I'm not dead.'

'I'm glad you're not,' he tells her. He looks at the paramedic. 'Are you done?'

'Nearly.'

'Is there anyone I can call to tell them that you are okay?' Jude asks her.

'No. My editor is dealing with that.'

'Do you want me to take you home?'

She nods. 'Please.'

# 13

# Black Agnes

Kirsty lives in a former council-owned red-brick apartment block in one of the narrow side streets off East London's Brick Lane. A police car drops them outside and he follows her up several stairs and along a landing that overlooks a central court-yard to a back stair, lined with well-tended plants in clay pots, that leads up to two rooftop flats, one of which is Kirsty's. He wonders if its location reflects a desire for privacy in her that matches his own.

Her hands shake in the lock and she grits her teeth in anger before the door finally opens. He hangs back a little and she looks back at him. 'Are you coming in?'

'Only if you'd like me to?'

She hesitates before answering and he's on the point of excus-ing himself when she says, 'Please.'

It's a small, neat one-bedroom flat with an arch separating the kitchen from the living room. The kitchen reflects a love of good food and cooking that is well documented on her social media feeds. Every inch of space is utilised. There are copper pots hanging from the ceiling and rows of spices in labelled jam jars on shelves that climb the walls. Hatched steel handles proud of a wooden knife block and magnets on the fridge that tell the story of states visited in a road trip across the USA. On the wall here's a portrait of Black Agnes, a fourteenth-century Countess of Dunbar, who defended her castle against an English siege and destroyed a notorious battering ram called the 'sow' by dropping a boulder on it from the battlements. Black for her dark hair and olive complexion, looks that Kirsty shares.

'Are you too a brawling, boisterous Scottish wench?' Jude asks, quoting a contemporary ballad.

She looks at him and for a few moments she looks right through him before focusing again. 'I forget you're an art historian.'

'It's actually a picture from a children's book,' he explains.

'You made an unusual career choice,' she says, not exactly coldly but not warmly either.

'It's not a well-trodden path but there are a few precedents,' he says, with a sense that just talking is helping. 'There was Tomás Harris, an art dealer who ran agents in the Second World War and of course, Anthony Blunt, the Queen's art historian.'

'Wasn't he a traitor?'

'There is that,' Jude acknowledges.

'You better put on the news,' she says. 'I'll make tea.'

He finds the remote beside an ikat-covered cushion on the sofa.

*Sky News* is reporting from the Queen Elizabeth Hospital where most of the seriously wounded have been taken, including many in a life-threatening condition. There are still no official figures for the number of dead.

He glances back at her. She is standing at the fridge sniffing the milk. Apparently, it's fine. She brings strong brown tea in matching mugs from the Ceilidh Place, a hotel in Ullapool.

They sit beside each other on the sofa without touching.

Eyewitnesses are describing a plume of white, choking smoke following the detonation of the car bomb outside the courthouse and the sounds of gunfire from inside the building. The only statement issued by the Metropolitan Police confirms that tear gas was used in the attack, presumably to dampen speculation that even more harmful chemicals were used.

She mutes the television. 'He got away, didn't he?'

'Yes,' Jude says.

'You think that he planned this at the same time as he planned the Westminster attack?'

Jude shakes his head. 'I don't think so.'

'The paramedic treating me said that the body of one of the attackers was recovered from the judge's chambers with his neck broken. And from the way the body was found it looked like someone had done it with their bare hands. Did you kill him?'

'No.'

'You weren't armed.'

'I didn't do it,' Jude says. 'He was dead when I got there.'

'But you were the first one there?'

Jude realises that she's goaded him into saying more than he should.

'Fowle killed him,' she says, thoughtfully, when he doesn't respond. 'Which means he was kidnapped and not rescued. Why would they do that?'

Only a very small number of people know the extent of Guy Fowle's cryptocurrency holdings and it's not something that he can share. His black-taped work phone rings.

'Saved by the bell,' she says, as he answers it.

'Jude?'

'Yes.'

It's Gretchen, the talented and idiosyncratic statistical physicist, who is the only remaining member of what passes for Jude's team. Recruited by means of a fiendishly difficult mathematic puzzle chalked on a pavement in Shoreditch, which she answered in record time, Gretchen spent two years as an analyst at GCHQ before being transferred to the Situational Awareness Group, an off-site and rarely acknowledged branch of the Secret Intelligence Service that Jude commands.

'Are you okay?' she asks. Gretchen grew the rhubarb and made the jam that he had on his toast that morning. It feels like a long time ago.

'Yes, I'm fine.'

'Can you talk?'

'I can listen.'

'I understand. I'll talk. The coroner says that the assailant whose body was found in the judge's chamber has a double-headed eagle holding pistols tattooed on his chest.'

Kirsty is watching him keenly from the sofa.

'And you know what that means,' Jude says, carefully.

'Yes, it's a Serb nationalist marking. The National Crime Agency have been informed and Interpol too. As soon as I get a clear face pic, I'll start running facial recognition software.'

'Good.'

'I'll let you know when I've got something.'

'Okay.'

'Get some rest, boss.'

'Okay.'

He ends the call.

'I'm sorry,' he says, uncomfortably.

'It's all right,' Kirsty says but her eyes suggest otherwise. 'I guess you've identified the dead kidnapper?' When he doesn't answer, she says, 'I preferred it when we worked together and were honest with each other.'

As did Jude but there's nothing he can do about that now. He looks down at his paper suit. 'I should probably go home and get some clothes.'

'You can't go out like that,' she says. 'My ex left some gym kit here, sweatpants and a hoodie, which I haven't got around to throwing out. He was about your size. You can have a shower first, if you like.'

'Thank you.'

He turns the shower lever over into the red as far as he can bear it and lets the hot water pummel bruised muscles. When he returns to the living room ten minutes later, he finds Kirsty curled up asleep on the sofa with her face lit by the muted news coverage.

He would dearly love to curl up beside her but his hope earlier that day that they can make a relationship work seems forlorn. She's recovered enough to be left alone and he can't trust himself not to tell her more if he stays. It's only a matter of weeks since they were collaborating to expose wrongdoing at the highest levels of the Secret Intelligence Service and he wouldn't have hesitated to share any secrets with her then. Now he can't. Not until he knows who freed Guy Fowle and whether they were working for a foreign power, and probably not even then.

He finds a blanket on her bed and puts it over her and switches off the news. He considers leaving a note but decides against it. After all, what could it say?

*I'm shutting this down because it's no longer expedient.*

It's a painful insight into an ugly side of himself. He lets himself out without waking her and walks up Brick Lane to Shoreditch and the lonely fortress apartment that passes for home.

# 14

# Sistemnyy sabotazh

Electricity slams through Guy, spasming his limbs and snapping his jaw shut on his tongue. He's been tasered before, his captors in the Caliphate had loved any kind of new toy for inflicting punishment and his current captors have used one on him several times already. He's built up a certain resistance. Even so, it's harsh. His incisors have bitten through his lower lip on both sides. He lies in the boot of a car with a mouthful of blood and roaring in his ears, listening to the scuff of feet on concrete and the booming sound of conversation.

'Give me a hand here.'

He feels himself lifted up and dragged across an open space. He's drifting in and out of consciousness: a jumble of events with blank spaces in between. He has no idea how much time has passed.

'Did you see what happened to Cema?'

'This fucking piece of shit broke his neck.'

He is on the floor and men with Eastern European accents are taking it in turns to kick him in the back and ribs before someone shouts at them to stop. He is hauled up again.

His bare feet thumping on stairs: he can't tell if he is going up or down.

'Hey. Look at this.' A voice crashing in his head and the smell of chlorine in an echoing space, 'Go get Scary Bear. He's coming around.'

He hears footsteps rapidly receding.

He lets his head loll backwards and opens his eyes a fraction. He is sitting on a tiled slope with lights set in the floor. He is naked in an almost empty swimming pool. A metre to his left stands one of his captors in a shiny suit, watching him warily. In front of him there are two wooden chairs. One of them is empty and in the other is his sister Katherine. She is gagged and the left side of her face is a single purple mass of bruising with the eye swollen shut. Behind her is the blue shimmer of water at the deep end of the pool.

Guy keeps his face slack and lets it fall forward again as if exhausted. *Always exaggerate how injured you are.* They have him trussed in a wooden seat like those opposite him and his bonds, like Katherine's, are plastic cable ties. He subtly flexes his wrists but finds little in the way of give.

'Time to pay attention,' the man tells him. 'Scary Bear is here.'

Guy lifts his head with a grogginess that isn't hard to fake and listens to the footfall of a man on the steps at the shallow end and then advancing down the slope towards him. The man crosses in front of him, turns the chair and straddles it. He is dressed all in black.

It's a rare pleasure to look into the face of another apex predator. As a rule, they tend not to encroach on each other's territory. So often humans are as insubstantial as X-rays. He can see right through them.

By contrast, Scary Bear seethes with life.

'Guy Fowle, I salute you,' he says, and smiles. His teeth are bright white and his face is so gaunt he looks like a speaking skull. Only the rings on his fingers shine. 'They say that a murderer does his work not for the sake of hate or silver but just to write what is written within himself. I see what is written in you. The lines of unique code. You understand what few others do. That Britain's weakness has always been its elites with their contempt for the common man and their demand for special privileges. That a judge must have his own private and undefended entrance to a courthouse, or that queuing for security is far beneath peers of the realm. What opportunities it creates. When I saw the Westminster attack on the news, I was truly impressed. The House of Lords was always Westminster's weakest point – the sheer number of people killed, and of course your escape. So much asbestos in the air, they say that you might as well have set off a dirty bomb in Parliament. I had to delete it from my list of targets.'

Guy struggles to speak.

Scary Bear leans forward. 'What's that?'

'You have a list?'

Scary Bear settles back. 'Of course, but now it is an app.' He takes a phone out of his pocket, thumbs the home button to unlock it and stares at the screen, *'Sistemnyy sabotazh* or, in English, Systems sabotage. We call it Grom. It's first generation. It has drop-down menu and multiple scenarios colour-coded for convenience, a timeline, and escalating scale of destruction. In this, it is similar to nuclear football, but for conventional attacks. Can you imagine? No cash, no food in shops, no petrol in pumps, no medicine in hospitals. No clean water, not even in pipes. All institutions of state undermined. The streets running with blood.'

'Why don't you use it?'

'I wish I could.'

'You're a dog on a leash.'

The rush of anger is blinding and for a moment he thinks that Scary Bear will pounce. It is too soon. Guy is not ready. But then the anger subsides. Guy feels the Serb in the shiny suit beside him relax.

'Your problem is that you have no self-control,' Scary Bear tells him. 'That's why you got caught.'

'Prison isn't so bad,' Guy replies, 'and besides, I knew someone like you would come for me, eventually.'

'You are a valuable man,' Scary Bear concedes. He looks to his right. 'Unlike your sister, who it seems has no secrets.' He gets up and crosses to face her. 'She knows nothing about the hundreds of millions of dollars in your X-cash account or the password.'

Scary Bear high kicks Katherine in the chest. She is propelled backwards and the chair tips over, plunging her into the water. Guy watches with interest as bubbles burst around her submerged head. Scary Bear glances at him with raised eyebrows. 'You don't want me to save her?'

He was eight years old when he realised that he was utterly unique, and therefore alone in the world. It was around that time that he started committing acts of violence against his baby sister. He has fond memories of the slap of his fist against her flesh. When she reached puberty, he taught her to cut herself, not too deep but deep enough to tap the blood and leave a scar. He is grateful to her for many things, including not revealing his password, which she, of all people, should have been able to guess. But, at the same time, he is free from sentimental attachment. 'I don't care either way.'

'Which makes her surplus to requirements.'

'If you say so.'

They watch in silence as she drowns.

'I continue to be impressed,' Scary Bear says, when the bubbles stop. 'You are truly a magnificent specimen. I suppose you're now wondering what will happen to you when you are surplus to requirements?'

'Enlighten me?'

'I'll be honest with you. I'd like to let you go. Really, I would. There is so much *sabotazh* you could do. I'd even help you.'

'But orders are orders?'

Every spare second, he can keep Scary Bear talking, counts.

'And these ones come from the top,' Scary Bear tells him, straddling the chair again.

'The Kremlin?'

Scary Bear shrugs. 'Who can tell? Certainly, people close to the leadership.'

'Good to know.'

'The best I can offer you is a painless death if you make the X-to-X transfer. Otherwise it's Goran and his secateurs.' Goran produces a set of hand shears from the pocket of his suit. 'He'll start with your pinkie fingers.' Guy watches as Scary Bear presses his right thumb to the phone to unlock it again and taps on a wallet app. 'I just need your password.'

'What makes you think that there's any money left?'

'Come on, Guy, you think I am a fool? We both know how frugal you were in execution of attack. I mean, given the resources at your disposal it's surprising you didn't attempt something on much larger scale. I think that you let your animosity towards your mother blind you to the potential.'

'Perhaps I'm not finished,' Guy tells him.

'Believe me, you are. It's time to pass the baton, Guy. Now give me the password.'

'No.'

Scary Bear spreads his hands in good-natured exasperation. Goran steps forward, secateurs at the ready.

Scary Bear meets Guy's gaze, almost unwillingly. 'I am sorry.' He nods to Goran.

'It's time.'

The moment has arrived. There will never be a better one.

Guy braces his back and legs and comes up out of the chair, tearing through the cable ties in a spray of blood and lacerated flesh until the plastic snaps across bone. He head-butts Goran, hearing a satisfying crunch over the thunder of his own pulse. The force of the blow enough to drive bone fragments into the Serb's brain and kill him. The adrenalin kicks in and the scene around him slows down. Guy's hands already in motion, scooping up the chair, the blood spiralling down his arms, sweeping it across as Scary Bear rises, smashing it into his face.

Scary Bear collapses.

Guy drops to one knee and reaches under Goran's jacket for his gun. The other man is standing in the shallow end, weapon raised, trying for a shot that won't hit Scary Bear. Guy throws out his arm and fires. The shot hits the man square in the chest. His body falls back against the side of the pool, blood spurting like a high-pressure hose from an artery.

Scary Bear lands hard on Guy, knocking the gun out of his hands. They skid down the slope and into the water. Clouds of blood billow around Guy's head. Scary Bear's jaws open like a shark. Guy's scarecrow hands tighten on his windpipe. The waters churn red as they roll.

*One potato, two potatoes, three potatoes …*

Guy breaks the surface, gasping for air and continues squeezing.

*Twenty-one potatoes, twenty-two potatoes …*

Eventually, Scary Bear stops struggling and Guy stops counting.

He rises, bloody and silent from the water. Whoever else might be in the house will soon be on their way to find out what has happened. Guy drags Scary Bear's body just out of the water and uses the shears to sever the Russian's right thumb. He pockets the thumb along with Scary Bear's phone, picks up Goran's pistol and heads for the double doors at the entrance to the pool.

He is about halfway up the stairs when another man appears in the doorway above. He sees Guy and reaches for the weapon in his jacket. Guy puts a bullet in his chest. A quick glance through the doors with the gun at shoulder height shows an empty corridor beyond with pale orange-pink light streaming in from windows secured with metal grills. A long silk runner and a table covered in a dust cloth midway down.

The wounds in his wrists are starting to have an effect. His vision blurs at the edges and he has to stop and lean back against a wall. He needs to stop the blood loss quickly. He staggers on down the corridor with renewed purpose. He finds a toilet concealed behind the sweeping T-shaped marble staircase that leads to the upper floors and binds his wrists with cotton hand towels, tightening the knots with his teeth.

He returns to the dead man at the top of the stairs and strips him of his suit jacket and trousers. He buttons the jacket across his chest and pulls down the sleeves to cover the bandages.

He walks back to the staircase and crosses the parquet flooring to the front door. He opens it and steps out into a leafy London street not long after sunrise. Traffic is sparse and the air is filled with the early chorus of chattering birds.

## 15

# Blow up

Two hours later, Guy stands beneath a plane tree in a shaded street of mansions broken up into flats in Ladbroke Grove, just north of the motorway overpass. He walked here from Chelsea, taking twice as long as it should, zigzagging along side streets and through parks to avoid main routes and concentrations of CCTV cameras. On arrival, he checks every car in the street and scans the windows of the flats behind him. There is no overt sign of surveillance.

The attic flat of the house in front of him is the focus of his attention. Sixteen years have passed since he walked out the door and headed for Iraq. Candida may have moved. It seems possible that her father, a red-trouser buffoon who made his money in property development, may have sold it out from under her. She might be dead or in prison, or even clean.

Perhaps she will not want to see him. After all, he treated her cruelly and he did not say goodbye.

He steps out from under the tree and climbs the steps to the main door. He presses the button at the top of the list on the entry phone and stands back to wait. That there is no name seems encouraging on several levels.

'Hello?'

He smiles. Her husky voice, redolent of cigarettes and whisky, was always one of her more attractive features.

'It's Guy.'

Silence.

He is acutely aware of the danger of the moment. If she is calling the police, he needs to run now. He starts counting down from ten.

'Are you still there?' she asks at three.

'Yes.'

The door clicks open. He climbs four flights of stairs. The final flight is narrow and leads up to what must have been servants' quarters when the house was built. Candida is standing in the doorway, in a dressing gown tied at the waist. She has long, honey-blonde hair that frames her elfin, once exquisite face. Up close, he can see the damage caused by whatever shit they cut street heroin with these days, and the old scar above her left eyebrow where he hit her with a baseball bat.

'You've got blood on you,' Candy says, worrying her lower lip with her teeth. Her lips have always looked like they've been in a battle. It's one of her more irresistible features. 'What happened to your wrists?'

'Just a spot of bother,' he tells her. It was a saying they had back in the day that covered just about any event, however calamitous. He reaches out to pull her towards him in an act of acquisition, his arm sliding downwards until his bloody palm is stretched across her buttocks.

He moves to kiss her and she lets him, her bruised lips against his: his tongue probing, his penis thickening across her taut belly.

After a few moments, he steps back from her.

'You haven't changed.'

She shakes her head.

He runs his hand over her buttocks again.

'Cosmo is asleep,' she says, her grey eyes unreadable.

'Cosmo?'

'My son.'

He follows her down a narrow corridor with a framed poster of the Michelangelo Antonioni film *Blow Up* with Vanessa Redgrave spread-eagled against a red background, and David Hemmings astride her, pointing a camera at her face. Beyond it there is a door with a KEEP OUT sign and a mosaic of stickers, Black Butler manga characters in various iterations of anger, horror and frustration.

Her bedroom is in the eaves at the end of the corridor. It's as he remembered it. Frozen in time. Candle stubs everywhere, a lava lamp and a statue of the goddess Kali. Rajasthani cushions dotted with mirrors and an Uzbek *Suzani* as a bed cover. Louvred wooden shutters to keep out the light.

He sits on the bed while she goes to the bathroom for her first aid kit. He sees that her old medical text books are still on a high shelf above the door. Against the wall there is a line of shoes in ascending height from sneakers to heeled knee-high boots. He's not accustomed to feeling territorial but there was a time when this was his territory. The discovery that a stranger crept in after he left and now there is a child in the adjacent room does not sit easy with him.

*It's taking the piss.*

When she returns, she kneels before him and the leaves of the dressing gown part, revealing the pattern of scars on her inner thighs. Her gift to him. A glimpse of the unique and arcane mandala that he wrote on her skin. She unties the makeshift bandages and inspects the wounds.

'This is deep,' she says, looking up at him. 'I can see bone.'

'Can you stitch it?'

'I can try.'

'Where's the boy's father?' he demands.

'He disappeared without leaving a forwarding address.'

As suddenly as it came, Guy's anger dissipates.

'Give me a shot,' he says.

She hesitates.

'I've got money,' he tells her, 'more money than you've ever dreamed of.' He can see that she wants to believe him. She never had any money to speak of and it doesn't look like that's changed in the intervening years. 'If you look after me and keep me safe, I'll give you money for whatever you want, forever. I promise.'

From beneath the bed she takes a shoebox with her works inside. He watches as she cooks up with a spoon and a lighter, and then ties off his arm and slides the needle in a vein.

When she is done, he leans back onto the bed with his arms outstretched.

'Fuck, that's good.'

She stands and reties the cord on her dressing gown. For a moment, he wonders if she has given him a killer dose. She has good reason not to believe him about the money. He's lied to her before. And he can tell that she's still angry with him for leaving. It seems a ludicrous way to go after everything that he has been through. But then every death is ludicrous, if you think about it.

'You're okay,' she says, knowingly. 'You won't be hearing the mermaids sing.'

'In my right pocket you'll find a thumb,' he tells her with a smile spreading across his face. 'Put it in the freezer.'

He drifts away.

# 16

# Chelsea offshore

Jude is met by the senior investigating officer, a detective chief inspector from Counter Terrorism Command (SO15), on the cordon at the edge of a garden square in Chelsea. He introduces himself as John Nganga and they solemnly shake hands. They are both wearing white paper suits, white latex gloves and white wellington boots. Nganga is so tall that there is a gap between the cuffs of his paper suit trousers and the tops of his boots.

'I hope you're not squeamish,' Nganga says.

'Not really,' Jude tells him. He signs the crime scene log and ducks under the incident tape.

Together they walk along the pavement between multi-million-pound houses with imposing white porticos on one side and a logjam of police vehicles with spinning lights on the other.

'A local resident walking his dog spotted the open door and the blood trail leading down the steps and across the road to the private garden opposite,' Nganga explains, moving with a rolling stride that suggests he's saving his energy for a sprint. 'An armed response vehicle was on the scene within seven minutes. They found five bodies inside, four men and one woman. We know from the blood trail that someone walked out alive and Lambeth control room are reviewing local CCTV footage, looking for Guy Fowle.'

They stop outside the four-storey house. The ground-floor windows have steel lattice security grills across them.

'Do you know who owns it?' Jude asks.

Nganga shakes his head. 'The neighbours are clueless. It's registered to a shell company in the Cayman Islands. According to the land registry roughly ten per cent of the properties in the borough have anonymous owners shielded by offshore tax havens. The whole area is awash with plundered and laundered cash.'

Jude warms to Nganga's visible sense of injustice. Together, they climb the steps, careful to avoid the blood marks that have been ringed with spray paint. Inside, scenes of crime officers are taking photos and dusting surfaces for prints. Nganga leads him down a corridor to the back of the house. The body of a man in underpants and a blood-drenched white shirt is splayed at the top of a staircase that leads to the basement.

'The blood splatter and the bullet recovered from the wall behind him suggest that he was shot from below by someone climbing the staircase.'

The dead man is large and bull-necked with a shaved head.

'Have you identified him?' Jude asks.

'Not yet,' Nganga replies. 'We did recover a Glock 17 pistol from beside him. We couriered it over to the National Ballistic Information Service, who have already identified it as belonging to the Watson cache.'

'The Watson cache?'

'Grant Watson is a former US Marine who smuggled sixty-three Glocks into the UK from the US through Manchester Airport in 2010. He wrapped the broken-down parts in his clothes in his hold luggage. Forty-two of them were still missing, as of yesterday. Luckily for us, Watson purchased the guns legally with his own credit card, and he test-fired them before travelling. After they caught him, the US Alcohol, Tobacco and Firearms Agency were able to recover the spent bullets from a landfill site in South Carolina. That means we know when we find one but we also know when one has been used.'

Jude kneels and rips open the man's shirt. The wings of a double-headed eagle rise either side of the bullet's entry hole.

'The same tattooing as the victim in Woolwich,' Nganga says.

Jude nods and rises.

'I'm assuming that Fowle stripped him for his clothes,' Nganga says. 'Follow me.'

They go down the stairs. The swimming pool is awash with blood. There is a man's body on the tiles at the shallow end and two more at the edge of the pool of water at the far end. One of them has had his face caved in and the other appears to have drowned. There is a woman, strapped to a chair, still floating in the water. Jude is halfway across the pool when he recognises her. He stumbles and Nganga grabs his arm to stop him falling.

'What is it?'

There aren't any words to describe the sorrow he feels. 'It's Katherine Fowle,' he says, 'Guy Fowle's sister.'

Jude is sitting at the edge of the pool, watching the coroner supervise the removal of the bodies, and John Nganga is down the other end of the room briefing the head of SO15.

He's received a text on his red-taped phone from Kirsty.

Thanks for bringing me home.

He's considering a reply when she sends a second text.

Are you in Chelsea?

His black-taped work phone rings. It's Chuka Odechukwu.

'Give me your analysis,' he says.

'The gang responsible for breaking Fowle out of Belmarsh were after his money and, just like we did, they thought they could use Katherine as leverage to get it out of him.'

'We didn't kidnap or threaten Katherine,' Chuka tells him. 'She went to Belmarsh of her own volition. What happened to her isn't your fault.'

It doesn't feel that way. He'd brought her to London and he hadn't paid sufficient attention to whether she had returned to Scotland.

'We need to tell her parents.'

'That's being handled,' Chuka tells him. 'Your job is to concentrate on Guy Fowle. Where is he?'

'The police are reviewing CCTV footage out to a six-mile radius but I wouldn't get your hopes up.'

'There are half a million CCTV cameras in London, Jude. The average Londoner is caught on camera hundreds of times a day. Fowle is not invisible.'

Simon Conway

'Most of the footage needs to be reviewed in real time and it comes in hundreds of different formats that need to be converted before viewing.'

'I'll speak to the Commissioner and get more people assigned to it,' Chuka tells him. 'In the meantime, where do you think he might have gone?'

'According to the coroner, the injuries Fowle sustained in freeing himself require urgent medical attention. He won't go to a hospital but I've spoken to the police here and they're checking their database of nurses and vets with suspected links to organised crime.'

'Good,' Chuka says. 'And the identity of the kidnappers?'

'Four of them have tattoos that mark them out as Serbian nationalists. Including the one we found dead in the judge's chambers. I'm guessing that Fowle must have killed him during the escape.'

'And the fifth?'

'No distinguishing markings of any kind.'

'The PM's chairing a COBRA meeting in an hour from now. I want you there with your analyst ready to deliver a briefing. See if you can get her to wear something appropriate.'

'I'll try.'

He looks again at Kirsty's text but there is no way he can reply.

# 17

# The fifth man

Sixty minutes later, Jude is in Cabinet Office Briefing Room A in Whitehall.

The Cabinet Secretary is sitting on the Prime Minister's left-hand side and on the right are the three holders of the Great Offices of State: the Chancellor, the Foreign Secretary and the Home Secretary, a trio generally regarded as lacking the skills needed to cope with the complexities they face, bouncing from gimmick to cock-up in an unfocused panic about the consequences.

Chuka Odechukwu is there with Evan Calthorp, the head of the Security Service (MI5), sitting beside him. As ever, Calthorp looks like he's dressed for a funeral. His palms are pressed together and pointing like an accusatory arrow across the table at Mobina Sinha, the Home Secretary, who is small like people of power often are. Whitehall is awash with rumour of a rift between her office and MI5, with whisper of secrets that remain unshared. The Home Secretary is said to have an equally fractious relationship with Jemima Connick, the Metropolitan Police Commissioner, who is sitting flanked by the heads of Counter Terrorism Command (SO15) and Specialist Firearms Command (SCO19), both bull-headed middle-aged men who zealously protect her. Also, at the table is the PM's special adviser, Maurice Hermon, who grew up on the Shankill Road in Belfast, and follows in the footsteps of a long line of insatiably furious political advisers who snarl into their phones from dawn until dusk. Finally, a tall woman with scene-stealing copper-coloured hair that makes Jude think of Elizabeth Siddal, the model for Millais's *Ophelia*. When he catches her eye, she smiles at him before returning her attention to the screen.

The faces of the five-man gang that broke Guy Fowle out of

Woolwich Crown Court are displayed on the video wall. Gretchen is standing beside it in sleeveless dungarees with a tablet in her hands and a 'fuck-you' expression on her face. Chuka's suggestion hadn't gone down so well. Jude is pretty sure that briefing a COBRA meeting isn't what she signed up for when she joined GCHQ.

'Proceed,' the Prime Minister tells her.

'We have identified four of the five members of the gang,' Gretchen explains, defensively at first, but relaxing as she gets into her stride. 'They belong to the *Zemum* clan of the Belgrade mafia that is involved in cross-border arms and drug trafficking, protection rackets and heists. Three of them are former members of a Serbian police unit that was disbanded in 2003 after they were implicated in the assassination of the prime minister. The two youngest served in the French Foreign Legion, seeing active service in Chad and Northern Mali.' She points to the picture in the top left of the wall. 'That is Goran Pjevac whose body was found beside the water at the deep end of the pool. The most recent Interpol report identifies him as a senior member of the *Pink Panthers*, an international jewel thief network, responsible for multiple heists across Europe. He is suspected of being an outside accomplice in a notorious prison break from the *Bois-Mermet* Prison in Switzerland.'

'How did they know about Fowle's money?' Evan Calthorp asks, tight-lipped.

'They didn't need to. They were contracted for the job for their expertise,' Jude replies. 'Pjevac knew about prison breaks.'

'Who contracted them?' the Prime Minister asks.

'This is where it begins to get . . .' She wants to say 'interesting' but catches herself before letting it out. Instead she ducks her head and taps her tablet. The entire wall is filled with an Instagram posting by an account holder named *Cema*: a photo of a large man in an unmarked green uniform, crouching in a trench with a Kalashnikov in his hands. There is an air traffic control tower in the background. 'That's Milorad Stanisic, nicknamed *Cema* or cement. His body was found in the judge's chambers with his neck broken. The photo was taken near to Donetsk Airport in the disputed Donbass region of Eastern Ukraine.'

The caption under the photo reads,

*Dogs bark but the caravan passes. If we want to survive, we must
urgently turn to the East and Mother Russia, anything else is
ruinous for the Serbian people and the country.*

Jude is aghast. 'It's Valkyrie.'

'Explain,' Calthorp hisses.

'Let her finish,' Chuka says.

'Go on,' the Prime Minister says.

'We have intelligence on Serbian nationals obtained from
social media postings and Serbian High Court documents that
show them fighting with various units in the Donbass region of
Ukraine.' Gretchen taps her tablet again and the wall is filled
with a map that shows the relative positions of various military
units spread across the breakaway region of Eastern Ukraine:
the International Brigade, the Seventh Brigade, the Serbian-
Hussar Regiment, the Ural Unit, the Batman Unit, the First
Slavic Unit, the Rezanj Unit and, west of the city of Donetsk
near the strategically crucial airport, the Prizrak or Ghost Unit
of PMC Valkyrie.

'Stanisic was a contractor for the Russian private military
company Valkyrie that was founded by Dmitri Troshev, popularly
known as the Chef.' She taps the tablet again and this time the wall
shows a surveillance video of the entrance to a Greek villa. 'Three
weeks ago, Troshev was at a party at a villa on Pathos in Greece
that is owned by Oleg Solokov, an oligarch with connections to
Eastern Ukraine. He is suspected to be one of Valkyrie's main
shareholders, possibly its principal shareholder.'

She is interrupted by an uncontrolled coughing fit, the
Chancellor of the Exchequer convulsing in his chair. The Foreign
Secretary slaps him on the back and the Prime Minister pours
him a glass of Malvern water.

Gretchen pauses the surveillance footage.

'Sorry,' Morley says, between sips. 'Sorry.'

The Prime Minister gestures impatiently at the screen. 'Go on.'

Gretchen presses play again. A taxi pulls up and Colonel Valery Ermolaev, the military attaché at the Russian Embassy to the United Kingdom gets out. 'Colonel Ermolaev stayed two hours and then left, also in a taxi. The surveillance team remained in place to log the other guests departing. We didn't have full coverage because there is another access point, a jetty at the base of the cliff. However, we did get this.' She pauses, fast-forwards for a few seconds and presses play. A black Range Rover is parked outside the villa. The steel door at the entrance opens and a pale-faced man dressed in black emerges and walks towards the Range Rover. Gretchen hits pause.

'That's the fifth man, whose body was found drowned beside the pool with his right thumb cut off. I still haven't identified him but using facial recognition software, I have found a photo that he appears in.' She taps the tablet again. On the screen there is an image of an outdoor barbecue in a snow-filled glade in a birch forest; a gathering of men, in heavy jackets, standing around a grill. 'The picture was taken at a dacha outside Moscow on an afternoon in December two years ago, at a private event to mark the Day of Heroes of the Fatherland.'

'Oh fuck!' Maurice Hermon says.

Turning the meat on the grill is a smiling Dmitri Troshev and beside him is the Russian president, also smiling. Gretchen enlarges a section of the photo. Standing at the back, with his pale face visible between two others is the fifth man.

'There's no way we'll keep a lid on that,' Maurice Hermon adds.

Jude remembers his final words to the Kuwaiti financier Wahab Mutairi before he handed him over to the Russians in Syria, '*You have information to trade.*'

'Russian military intelligence learned from Wahab Mutairi that he had transferred four hundred and eighty million dollars to Guy Fowle before he left Syria for Europe,' Chuka explains.

'And the reason they know that is because of a botched attempt by us to capture Mutairi,' Calthorp says, glaring at Jude.

'Can we stick to the point,' Chuka says.

'Valery Ermolaev is up to his neck in gambling debts and desperate for money,' Jude says, calmly.

'How do we know that?' the Prime Minister asks.

'Because Mr Lyon is having an affair with his wife,' Calthorp says.

And all eyes are on Jude. The woman opposite raises an eyebrow. Gretchen scowls. It seems that everyone has an opinion on Jude's love life except him. He doesn't know what to think.

'We assume Valery Ermolaev passed the information to his old army comrade, Dmitri Troshev, at Solokov's villa on Pathos,' he explains, 'presumably in return for a cut of the money. Troshev assigned a Serbian gang to the task who had previous form in prison breaks and put them under the management of his associate, the as yet unidentified fifth man.'

'While you were screwing his wife in Istanbul, Valery Ermolaev was selling Guy Fowle to Valkyrie,' Calthorp says.

'This may not have been a state-sponsored operation,' Chuka says. 'If Valkyrie was acting independently, it's important that we don't over-react.'

'I'm going to have to say something to the press,' the Prime Minister says.

'We need to hear from the Russians first,' Nigel Featherstone, the Foreign Secretary says. 'I've called in the Ambassador.'

'If you don't get a straight answer out of him, I'm calling the Kremlin,' the Prime Minister says. 'I'll ask the president a direct question, *Were you behind the prison break?* If I'm not satisfied with the answer, there will be consequences.'

'Yes, Prime Minister,' the Foreign and Home Secretaries say in unison.

'What about you, Gabriel,' the Prime Minister demands, 'you're being uncharacteristically quiet?'

The Chancellor looks pained. 'I don't think that we should over-react,' he says softly. 'We might find ourselves backed into a corner.'

The Prime Minister glowers and consults the room.

'And what about Guy Fowle? Where the hell is he?'

Everyone looks uncomfortable.

'At the Met, we're doing everything we can to find him, Prime Minister,' Jemima Connick explains. 'He's injured, he needs medical treatment and somewhere to recuperate. He hasn't been in this country for more than fifteen years and he has no known friends or associates.'

'You can buy a lot of friends and associates with four hundred and eighty million dollars,' Calthorp says with the hint of a sneer.

'I expect the police and the intelligence services to work together closely on this one,' the Prime Minister says, firmly. 'I shouldn't need to remind you how dangerous he is.'

'Agreed, Prime Minister,' Mobina Sinha says.

'Too fucking right,' Maurice Hermon says. 'The longer Fowle is on the loose, the more you all are going to look even more incompetent than usual.'

'And the more likely it is that there is a terrorist attack,' Calthorp says, dourly.

'We ask our friends in the Secret Intelligence Service for their full cooperation,' Mobina Sinha adds.

'Of course, Home Secretary,' Chuka says. 'My team is at your disposal.'

'A smaller group will reconvene later today,' the Prime Minister says, 'but for now all other matters are of lesser priority. That is all.'

The Prime Minister stands up and leaves the room with the Cabinet Secretary and Maurice Hermon in tow.

Jude is surprised to observe that for a man generally regarded as being 'in a hurry', Gabriel Morley is the last of the politicians to leave and he is sweating despite the air conditioning.

She catches up with Jude in the carpeted corridor that leads to the Whitehall entrance to the Cabinet Office. Her thick mass of red hair frames a face with a creamy complexion and deep blue eyes.

'Hey Jude.' A distinctive Scouse accent, which excuses the corny greeting, and a gold ring on her finger to show she's married. They shake hands formally and there's something about the awkwardness of it that she seems to enjoy. 'I'm Rosanna. I'm heading up the operation for Calthorp.'

Which explains why she was in the room: she's MI5 or Box as they like to call themselves.

'Your boss doesn't like me very much,' Jude says.

She laughs. 'I did wonder.'

'But that doesn't mean we need to be enemies,' he tells her.

'I'm glad to hear it,' she says. 'In fact, I could do with your help. You know Fowle better than anyone. I want to speak to his former colleagues from the army and university. Anyone that might have a clue as to where he might have gone to ground.'

'Sure, anything I can do.'

She cocks her head. 'Something's bothering you?'

'Yes,' Jude replies, surprised that she can read him so easily. 'Why did Fowle take the Russian's thumb?'

# 18

## Does not compute

After his armed protection officers have scouted the café and issued the all clear, Gabriel takes off his tie and puts on a black beanie hat, pulling it down over his ears before entering. An extensively pierced barista with a sneer on his face takes his order and slides the soy-milk latte across the zinc counter towards him when it's made. He sees it has WANKR written on it in black felt-tip pen where the customer name goes. He carries it to the farthest table against an exposed brick wall, where Xander is waiting for him.

'That's quite a disguise,' Xander Foggerel says, eyeing the hat. He glances at the two painfully conspicuous bodyguards sitting at the end of the long central table. They have what looks like an exclusion area around them, several empty seats, then the usual press of students on their laptops and tablets.

'I need to talk to you,' says Gabriel, sitting opposite him.

Xander looks genuinely concerned. 'No offence and I know you must be pretty cut up about what happened. I know my dad is even though he's putting a brave face on it, but I'm staying well out of it.'

'What?'

'I thought Violeta was okay for a stepmum, better than the other ones. You just can't tell, can you? Also, I've stopped dealing drugs, so I can't help you out with that either. Right now, what with everything that happened, keeping a low profile is my first priority. I'm sorry. I know, in your shoes, I'd want to get wasted.'

'I don't want drugs,' Gabriel says, exasperated.

'I think you should speak to your wife.'

'This has got nothing to do with my wife!'

'Okay,' Xander says, puffing his cheeks and running a hand through his hair. 'If you say so.'

'It's about the party.'

'What party?'

'In Greece!' Gabriel realises he is practically shouting. He leans forward and whispers, 'When we were in the kitchen at that Russian's villa. That man who you called Scary Bear.'

'Yeah,' Xander says, looking nervous. 'I can't believe I blurted that out.'

'Who is he?'

Xander looks surprised. 'Scary Bear?'

'Yes!'

'He's one of the Protean Bears.'

'The Protean Bears?'

'Yeah, Scary Bear is like this crazy, anarchist hacker.'

'He's a hacker?'

'That's what I'm saying to you. Protean Bears is this legendary hacking group from Russia that specialises in sequestering malware, worms and phages, that invade and capture operating systems. Scary Bear is a black hat hacker who specialises in boot-record over-writing tools that lobotomise servers, turning everything into a mush of zeros, and also capture tools that target Supervisory Control and Data Acquisition systems which run refineries and power networks and stuff. Everything the Bears build is designed with these constantly shifting codes that evolve to interfere with defensive measures. They have this whole global chaos agenda. Some people say they got co-opted by the Russian state or the oligarchs. Frankly, I'm really fucking worried for my own safety.'

Gabriel stares at him. The idea that a teenager knows more than the combined intelligence services of the United Kingdom is mind-boggling.

'How did you know it was him?'

'The bear claw ring,' Xander says. 'There are supposed to be no photos of him anywhere, not even in the deep dark corners, but the ring is a unique identifier. The story goes that he killed a polar bear with a short-bladed knife. I think it's some kind of symbol of Slavic supremacy.'

'Which hand?'

'Right.'

Gabriel leans back in his chair and stares at the ceiling. The ring that might identify the dead man as Scary Bear is on the missing thumb. Thank God for that.

He snaps out of it. 'You haven't told anyone, have you?'

'No way. I've moved out of my digs. I'm trying my best to be invisible.'

'Good. Good,' Gabriel says, thinking. 'You mustn't tell anyone, even if he appears in the news or wherever. And we didn't have this conversation.'

'Okay,' Xander says, 'I'm cool with that.'

'Good.'

Xander is looking at him strangely.

'Have you been home recently?'

'No.'

When he moved into Downing Street Charlotte had refused to come with him, preferring to remain with the kids at the family home in Westbourne Grove.

'Sorry to ask but when did you last see Mrs Morley?'

Gabriel frowns. 'A week ago?'

'Have you spoken to her?'

He tries to remember. 'Not for a couple of days.'

Something about the home-office printer needing to be replaced. Come to think of it, it's strange not to have received a text. Usually there are several messages a day, though, to be honest, he's not been paying them much attention. Of late, they've mostly been about the weight of the kettle bells that her Brazilian personal trainer is making her do squats and lunges with.

'Have you been back to the house?' Xander asks.

'No.'

'I really think you should get in touch with her. Like, urgently.'

'All right,' Gabriel says. 'I'll call her. I have to go now.'

'Okay.'

'Yeah, look I'm really sorry, Gabe. About everything.'

\*   \*   \*

Driving back to Downing Street in his ministerial car, he deliberately ignores the various missed calls from his special adviser and the permanent secretary and instead follows Xander's advice and calls his wife. Charlotte doesn't answer immediately and when she does, she sounds resigned to a fight.

'Gabriel,' she sighs, 'what do you want?'

'Are you all right?' he asks. 'I haven't heard from you.'

'Didn't you get my letter?'

'No.'

A pause.

'I've left you,' she says.

'You left me a letter at the house?'

She's very diligent about writing thank-you cards, and of course copy for her website, but it's a long time since he remembers her writing an actual letter. There had been flurries of them during their courtship, of course, but that was a long time ago when he was working in the Party's Political Section and she was still interested in politics.

'Yes,' she says, 'but I've also left you.'

'I don't understand, left me what?'

'I don't love you any more. I love Violeta.'

Suddenly, he has this image in his head from *Lost in Space* of the robot saying, *'Does not compute'*.

93

# 19

# Six Kensington Palace Gardens

Ignoring five missed calls from Jude, Yulia puts her phone in a locker in the corridor outside the Ambassador's office and Raisa, his secretary, zealous gatekeeper and occasional lover buzzes her in through the airlock door with a look that could strip paint; poor Raisa with the lustrous eyelashes, who will never fulfil her ambition to replace his current wife.

The Ambassador is a neat and fastidious man. He is wearing a Prince of Wales check suit and steel-rimmed spectacles that are carefully chosen to suggest a shrewd and orderly mind. They have known each other for twenty years, ever since they worked alongside each other in Moscow in the Security Department of the Foreign Ministry. She knows that he is a mostly decent man who, like all of them, has had to make compromises along the way up the promotional ladder. Now he presides over a shrinking embassy with a much-reduced staff due to expulsions and delays in issuing of new visas by the British government.

She has never seen him look so frustrated and ill at ease.

'I have been summoned to the Foreign Office,' he tells her from his desk, with a panorama of Kensington Palace Gardens through the window behind him. 'The British Foreign Secretary is going to demand to know if the Russian state is responsible for the Woolwich attack and the escape of the terrorist Guy Fowle. He is threatening to publicly accuse us of malicious and violent intent towards the UK and its people.'

'What will you say?'

Ignoring her question, he demands, 'Where is your husband?'

'I don't know,' she tells him, truthfully. 'He didn't come home last night.'

'Are you looking for him?'

'Yes, of course I am. I have people searching his usual places.'

'Usual places?'

'The casinos and massage parlours,' she says, coldly.

He takes off his glasses and pinches his nose, as if what he is about to say pains him. 'Is it possible that the GRU was responsible for the abduction of Guy Fowle?'

She grinds her fist into her hip. 'I don't know. Perhaps not.'

'What do you mean by that?'

'I mean that it is possible, even likely, that my husband is involved. But it may not be a sanctioned activity. I think that he may have cooked this up with Troshev.'

'Troshev! That Neanderthal? You're not serious?'

'Valery met with Troshev recently in Greece. The British know this.'

*'Yebat-Kopat!'*

'Valkyrie's little green men may be operating outside Kremlin control.'

'Why?'

She's tired of explaining to men that men do things because of money. Money and sex. It's time they worked it out for themselves.

'The president will have to distance himself from Troshev and Solokov,' Yulia tells him, briskly. 'The West will expect this, at least. The British are less powerful as a result of their isolation but they are more dangerous too, more vulnerable to populist sentiment and over-reaction. On an international scale, if they can prove a direct link through Troshev to the president, which also seems likely, they may seek to invoke Article 5 of the NATO charter which says an attack on one is an attack on all. We will come under closer scrutiny and there will be further sanctions and further expulsions. More US and other NATO troops will deploy to Poland and the Baltics. We will be more vulnerable to proxy attack in Ukraine and Syria, and other places.'

'You think it's that bad?'

'Don't you?'

'This is so ridiculous!'

'It will only get worse if Fowle goes on another killing spree. We will be blamed. The pressure on the British government to retaliate will grow.'

The Ambassador sighs. 'Let's hope they catch him quickly.'

'The British want to hear from me too,' she says.

'You can't say anything to them.'

'Why not?' she says, staring out across the park. 'They already know the truth.'

'I need to speak to Moscow,' he protests.

She gives him a pitying look. 'You know that they will tell you to lie.'

'What the hell do you expect me to do, Yulia?'

'Your Excellency, I expect you to do what is required of you, to lie like all good diplomats do, staying as close to the truth as you can and fudging and fabricating where you have to. But I will not follow your lead in this case.'

'I can't protect you, if you do that,' the Ambassador says.

'Excellency, I mean no disrespect, but if I am forced to rely on your protection, I will know that I am finished.'

She turns on her Louboutins and strides out of his office with her head held high.

She will miss London. It is by far the most varied and amenable of capital cities that she has lived in. And if her marriage is a radioactive disaster with an interminable half-life it has been more than made up for by the finer pleasures on offer. She wonders if there is time for a quick visit to Harley Street to refresh her dermal fillers and Botox her frown lines, and then a farewell glass or two of champagne at the Brasserie of Light in Selfridges.

Looking at her phone, she sees another missed call from Jude. She can't think of anyone she would rather share a drink or a leisurely afternoon in bed with but she knows that it's not a social call and, despite what she said to the Ambassador, she's not ready to speak to him yet. She needs to find her husband.

'Oh, Valery,' she says, gripping her phone tightly to her chest. 'What have you done now?'

# 20

# What the thunder said

Guy wakes to find Candida's fingers dreamily tracing recent and unfamiliar wounds on his torso. Her eyes are paler in the light from the window. She is naked and although her breasts are smaller, her nipples are much larger and darker than he remembers. Nuclei at the centre-point of radial waves of scars. Morcheeba's 'The Sea' is playing on a Bluetooth speaker and she looks like she's in a trance. He smiles and stretches his bandaged arms above his head. She leans in and explores the divot between two ribs where she once knifed him and collapsed his lung. It wasn't long after he'd hit her with the baseball bat and caused several stitches. She could have let him die. Instead, she reinflated the lung.

She had once told him that he would be her soul mate if only his soul was a different shape. He took it as a rare example of self-knowledge on her part. But it is no match for addiction and she is still addicted to him, even after all these years. She has no choice but to follow it down to wherever it takes her. She bends to his penis and takes it in her mouth. He enjoys her abasement. He closes his eyes and lets her bring him to climax.

Finished, he pushes her away.

'Give me your phone,' he says.

She hands it to him and lights a cigarette while he downloads an app and logs on to his X-cash wallet, as the Caliphate's financier Kuwaiti Mutairi had taught him to before he left Syria.

'You're going to make ten different transfers of just under ten thousand pounds to ten different Monex outlets. You get a taxi between them. A different taxi each time. At each place you give a name and you will be asked a question, ten different questions with ten different answers. You answer correctly and they will give you the cash. Do you have a bag?'

'I have a suitcase under the bed. Several, in fact.'

He remembers her collection of vintage Samsonite suitcases, inherited from her mother who died when she was teenager. They stack inside each other like Russian dolls.

'That will do for now but buy some proper duffel bags when you're out. Large and preferably black. Make sure they're the waterproof kind. Do you still have your wigs?'

She smiles. 'They're in a box under the bed.'

It was always a treasure trove under Candida's bed.

'You still wear them?'

'Sure, at parties.'

The first time he'd met her she was wearing a classic white tutu, wellington boots and straight blonde hair that reached her waist. Dyed blue skin. Dancing by herself in the midst of a chaos of ravers in a field in Shropshire, not far from Hereford where he was stationed. He remembers the danger and beauty in her lustrous, knowing eyes.

'Switch appearance between Monex outlets,' he tells her. 'We need to start small until I can find someone who can process a larger transfer.'

'And then what?'

'Buy a car. Whatever passes for unnoticeable these days. Nothing flash. Use cash and spend no more than nine thousand. You know someone?'

'There's an Irish guy who runs a dealership down at World's End who's on the programme.'

'You still go to meetings?'

'Now and then, if I'm clean.'

'Don't share that you've seen me,' he tells her.

'My lips are sealed,' she says. 'Are you in some kind of trouble?'

He could laugh. She's always been so blissfully unaware of the news. The world could end and she wouldn't notice. He hands her back her phone. 'I'll wait here.'

'Make yourself at home.'

He sleeps some more and when he wakes, he feels rested. He washes his face in the bathroom, careful not to get his bandages wet or catch his own eye in the mirror. He wraps a towel around his waist. In the kitchen, he opens the freezer. There is a clear plastic bag with *Thumb!* written on it in black marker pen. He'd always enjoyed Candy's black humour. Scary Bear's phone is charging on the kitchen table with the Glock pistol beside it. He carries them through to the sitting room.

The boy is hunched over a game console, wearing headphones. On the TV screen, a battle is being fought in an abandoned industrial complex. The riflescope traversing back and forth, hemmed in on a collapsing gangway between metal pipes.

The boy pauses the game and turns to look calmly up at him. If he is surprised, he does not show it.

'Hey.'

Guy has never really kept track of the number of children he has had but he tends to know them by their aura when he sees them. The boy is big and his hands and feet are too large as if, like a puppy, he still has to grow into them.

'Why aren't you at school?' Guy asks.

'I've been excluded.'

'Why?'

'I got caught with a knife. Where's Mum?'

'She's gone to buy a car.'

'Why?'

'Because we need one.'

The only place to sit is beside the boy. He puts the freezer bag and the pistol down alongside Scary Bear's phone on the coffee table.

'Is that really a thumb?'

'Yes.'

'Did you cut it off?'

'Yes.'

'Why?'

'I didn't need the rest of him.'

The boy seems to accept his explanation. With a shrug, he returns to the game.

When it has thawed sufficiently, Guy slides off the bear claw ring and pats the thumbprint with a gauze swab to remove any moisture. When it is sufficiently dry, he uses it to unlock the phone. He methodically taps on apps until he comes to one with a large yellow G on a red field called *Grom*. At the prompt, he presses the thumb to the pad again.

Scary Bear was right.

A page of drop-down menus. A list of Cold War enemies and more recent adversaries closer to Russia's borders. He selects the United Kingdom from near the bottom of a list and it offers a menu of vulnerable infrastructure nodes: energy, water, waste, health, material goods, maritime and land-based supply chains, communications and capital. For each node, a packet of data to download. Swiping right reveals the target and the means of implementation: kinetic or cyber. Under kinetic there are lists of illegals and other human assets and under cyber there are lists of specially designed computer worms. All are awaiting activation. A sidebar menu offers bundles of interwoven and escalating attacks with a bar chart to show the timeline from attack to catastrophic consequence.

It is, in a very literal sense, a dream come true: a great, spoked, woven-together weapon of mass destruction. The red-team work Guy was doing for the army in Hereford was child's play in comparison with this. It must have taken years of planning and the level of detail is almost humbling. He feels like laughing out loud.

How the Russians will tremble when they discover that their precious secret weapon is in his hands. He has to assume that it is only a matter of time before someone sends a kill signal and the phone is erased.

He touches the boy's arm, feels the muscle there.

The boy pauses the game.

'I need a pen and paper,' Guy says.

The boy leaves the room and comes back with a black Moleskine notebook.

'It's one of Mum's diaries.'

He takes it from the boy. He flicks through pages packed with neat red writing. It's about a quarter full. 'Do you read these?'

The boy shrugs. 'Yeah, sometimes. They're batshit crazy, man. Are you really my dad?'

'Yes.

The boy considers the news. 'I'm Cosmo.'

'I'm Guy.' He selects one of the bundled attacks and starts taking notes with Cosmo watching him.

'My teacher makes us do that sometimes,' Cosmo says, after a while. 'She says we're going analogue today, like she thinks it's funny.'

Guy slides the bear claw ring across the table to his son.

'We're entirely analogue from here on in.'

# 21

# Evidence of absence

Jude and Gretchen are sitting cross-legged on the floor of the Situational Awareness Group offices surrounded by everything that they have that relates even tangentially to Guy Fowle: cardboard boxes, lever arch files and piles of paper. There is plenty of it. But it's more evidence of absence than anything else. It's possible to track the thoroughness with which Guy Fowle erased his own history by the ragged-edged void it's created, like the tunnelling of a hungry caterpillar. There is no surviving birth certificate or passport, no national insurance number or unique tax payer reference number, no medical or dental records. Instead there are bundled copies of crime reference numbers for unsolved breakins and fire incident reports, and long lists of electronic file deletion notes.

Some of the earliest redactions are by his own hand. Drawings from primary school handed over by Katherine Fowle with Guy's name carefully written by a teacher, and obliterated with furious crayon marks.

'It's more than just covering his tracks,' Jude says. 'It's obsessive from the start.'

'I found an academic paper that describes self-erasure as a specific narcissistic disorder,' Gretchen tells him.

From crayon, Guy graduated to Tipp-Ex and the blade of a scalpel; his name a deleted white crust on school reports and vaccination records. His face scored out on a Rugby team photo recovered from the ashes of one of the succession of fee-paying boarding schools that he attended in Scotland and northern England. Until the age of sixteen, he didn't last long at any one school and his parents were sufficiently well off to keep him moving before anyone joined the dots. Then he changed, he completed his final two years of school and secured a place at university. He became more careful and better at covering his tracks. Without his parents' knowledge, he convinced the Regular Commissions Board to select him for officer training at the Royal Military Academy Sandhurst. Of his army career there is very little beyond a few photos and redacted paragraphs in copies of army operations reports that concern the deployments of the mysterious red-team unit that Fowle commanded at Hereford. The originals are missing along with his personnel file from the national archive in Kew.

As for the journey that followed his departure from the British Army in 2003 and took him to Iraq where he fought for al-Qaeda as *al-Gharib*, the Stranger, there is no evidence. Only hearsay, word from an informant in a camp for captured Islamic State fighters in Kurdish Syria. That in Iraq Guy made an oath of fealty to a near mythological figure known as the *Sheikh al-Jabal* – the Old Man of the Mountain. The Old Man would go on to become one of the founding fathers of the Caliphate, the Islamic State that in its heyday controlled a huge swathe of territory the size of Britain.

The Old Man ordered the mysterious British solider known as the Stranger to kill the crusaders in great numbers and the Stranger obliged. In 2004 Fowle executed a complex ambush near Basra that caused the biggest single loss of life to the British Army in Iraq and contributed to the general disenchantment with the war. True to form, Fowle obscured his own involvement in the attack and made an out-of-work actor post a chilling video claiming responsibility.

Of the period immediately after the ambush, when Coalition forces were engaged in a massive manhunt for the wrong person, there are three phone intercepts that reference the Stranger. They paint a picture of a violent man that even a terrorist movement struggled to handle. In the first, two al-Qaeda commanders in Iraq are disagreeing over what to do after the Stranger summarily executed one of his fellow fighters in Anbar and took the dead man's wife as his bride. In the second conversation, between two Saddam-era intelligence officers who were fighting for al-Qaeda, they discuss the merits of imprisoning the Stranger rather than executing him. One of them, known as Fig, is recorded saying of the Stranger, 'He does what we want efficiently and without conscience, the problem is that he does a lot more of what we don't want'. In the third, an Islamic State foot soldier describes how he helped move a high value prisoner known as The Stranger to a more secure location after he killed two of his guards.

The Old Man could have easily had Fowle killed but as Jude's investigation revealed, the Old Man was not done with him yet. In 2006, the Old Man reached out to Samantha Burns, the head of MI6. He identified Fowle as the real perpetrator of the Basra Ambush and offered a bargain: that he would prevent Fowle from organising any further attacks in return for a generous monthly payment. The Iraq war was deeply unpopular by that stage and Burns was terrified of what Fowle might do. She agreed. And for more than ten years the bargain held until, in the dying days of the Caliphate, the Old Man ordered Fowle to be released and sent him out to kill the crusaders again.

The result was a devastating attack at the heart of British government. The video wall is a mosaic of images, many of them scanned from prints, the negatives long destroyed. Most of them came to light after the Westminster attack and it's hard to be sure that it's Fowle. A face in a line of identically dressed cadets on the parade ground at Sandhurst. A face covered in black-and-green camouflage paint in a huddle of soaked-to-the-skin soldiers in a jungle setting, possibly Brunei. A face caked in dust in the midst of a group of Afghan fighters in turbans, at a guess the Bora Bora Mountains in late 2001. A savage grin beneath a police cap as a man dressed as a firearms officer hurdles the blast barriers outside the Houses of Parliament. Faces that lose definition the more you try and zoom in until they are nothing more than an indistinguishable blur. The more recent prison photos from Belmarsh are more granular although he's never quite looking at the camera, as if he knows that there is some part of his identity that should never be shared. Jude remembers the shock of the first time that Guy returned his gaze. That sense that he was looking into the eyes of the least human of human beings that he has ever encountered.

'It's surprising how fast he moves,' Jude says, holding up to the light one of the X-rays from the comprehensive medical check-up that was performed on Fowle on his admission to Belmarsh. It shows a skeleton knotted with fractures. The deck of photographs beside him show puncture marks of varying sizes, from bullet wounds to needle marks.

'According to the notes, he has a very high pain threshold,' Gretchen says.

The most shocking revelation is the damage caused to almost anyone drawn into Fowle's orbit, like space debris falling into a gravity well. A black hole. A list of classmates, teachers, university students, health professionals, police officers and soldiers, their prospects destroyed and careers forever blighted. Attempted suicide is a common factor with self-immolation a common means. Coroner's reports with depressingly similar photos of charred remains. It's surprising the damage one can do with a can of lighter fluid and a box of matches. There are plenty of other disaster stories. Two school friends drowned in a freak boating accident, several student housemates who suffered complete mental break-downs and have been in and out of psychiatric care ever since, another serving a prison term for heroin smuggling who still maintains his innocence, a succession of soldiers who served above or below him ruined by injury or disgrace.

'Are you hungry?' Gretchen asks.

He realises that he hasn't eaten since before the arraignment. 'Yes.'

She brings a metal bowl covered with a cloth from a shaded corner and puts it down on the carpet. Two forks, two glasses and a metal flask full of water. She kneels and removes the cloth: a salad of golden and candy-striped beets and rocket grown on her beloved allotment, tossed with pomegranate seeds and goat's cheese. He watches her dress it with olive oil and balsamic vinegar.

'How's your friend Kirsty?' Gretchen asks, as she passes him a fork.

'She's okay, I think,' he replies, uncomfortably. He hasn't replied to her messages since he left her asleep on her sofa last night. Their kiss on the pavement in Hoxton seems like an age ago. The thought that it will never be repeated is a depressing one.

'She's lucky to be alive,' Gretchen says. 'You both are.'

She pours them a glass of water each from the flask.

'It's rain water collected from a water butt,' she says. 'I flavour it with slices of cucumber.'

It is delicious, refreshingly free of the metallic, recycled taste of London tap water.

'Somebody is sheltering Fowle,' Jude says, between mouthfuls of beet, 'maybe someone from his past. We need to find out who that might be. Who are we going to talk to first?'

Gretchen hands him a file: an accident involving the partial detonation of an improvised incendiary device on the training area in Hereford and an accusation that the device was maliciously tampered with. A complaint ignored then but revived now because the victim was a member of Guy Fowle's red-team unit at Hereford.

'I think that you should go to Wales.'

# 22

# There is no science without torture

Guy finds a book of multi-coloured Post-it notes in one of the kitchen drawers and uses a pair of scissors to cut the pages into strips to mark entries in the Moleskine. He colour-codes the attacks in yellow, pink, green, orange, purple and blue. Scrolling through the app, he fills the pages with details of the personnel, logistics and funds necessary to complete each task. He carefully copies maps and schematics by hand. Means of ingress and exit. Separately tabbed pages log caches of weapons, vehicles and cash.

While he works, he keeps half an eye on Cosmo who is battling through the levels of the game: from speedboat chases through steep-sided sandstone canyons to scrambling through overgrown jungle temples, to assaulting a snow-covered bunker complex in a boreal forest. Cosmo expends ammunition with wilful abandon and forages for more as he travels.

Guy touches the boy, who pauses the game again.

'What's up, Daddio?'

'I need burner phones.'

Cosmo shifts the ornamental flowers from the fireplace and reaches up into the chimney. He retrieves a plastic bundle taped with gaffer tape. Taking a folding knife from his pocket, he opens the blade and cuts through the wrapping. There are five phones inside, still in their packaging.

'Why do you have five unused phones in your chimney?'

'Mum uses them for selling drugs. You want me to charge them all?'

'Yes.'

Although the paternal instinct fascinates him, particularly when it's a catalyst for violence, Guy has never felt it for himself.

Nevertheless, he feels something approaching satisfaction as he watches his son at work.

'Do you know how to turn the location data off?' he asks, showing him Scary Bear's phone.

'No problem. I can switch off the GPS, location services and Wi-Fi. But if they really want to, they'll know where you are from the phone time zone and other stuff, like air pressure.' He pauses. 'Or roughly where you are, at least.'

'I need to organise a delivery first,' Guy says. 'What's the postcode?'

He looks alarmed. 'Mum doesn't like me to give it out.'

'We're not staying here.'

And alarm turns to excitement, 'Where are we going?'

'On an adventure. That's why we're getting a car.'

The boy gives him the postcode. Guy types it into the drop-down menu and presses SEND. Once it's done, Guy gives him the phone. The boy taps and swipes several times and hands it back to him.

'GPS was off already. Now you're offline.'

Guy returns to the task of transcribing details from the app into the notebook. After thirty minutes he looks up again.

'What's the wind direction?'

Cosmo thinks about it and then taps his phone a few times to download a wind compass app.

'South-westerly?' he says.

'For how long.'

Cosmo scrolls upwards. 'Like, six more days.'

'And then?'

'North-easterly.'

'That should keep us busy.' The doorbell rings. 'Give me your knife.'

It's a Gerber with a moulded nylon grip and a blade just short of three inches that is easily sharp enough to gut someone. Guy carries it with him out into the hall and presses the intercom.

'Delivery for Mr Bakunin,' a voice says.

'Come on up.'

Guy steps out onto the narrow landing with the knife at his side and watches as a man climbs the stairs towards him in motorbike leathers and a helmet with a dark smoke visor. He is holding a padded envelope in his right hand. Guy has to work hard to contain a smile that threatens to spread from ear to ear. The British may have their nuclear submarines skulking under the icecaps waiting for Armageddon but the Russians have an endlessly circling motorbike courier with an envelope full of false identities and nation-breaking malware.

Following the instructions on the app, Guy says, 'The still waters are inhabited by devils.'

'There is no science without torture,' the man replies.

'The belly is full but the eyes are hungry.'

The man hands him the envelope and turns and leaves. Back inside, Guy cuts it open and shakes out the contents over the kitchen table: an assortment of colour-coded USB sticks containing malware and passports of different nations for the exfiltration of deep-cover assets

He looks at the boy. It couldn't be easier. 'We're on.'

Candida returns to find Guy and Cosmo at the kitchen table. Cosmo is reading out the addresses of safe houses and exfiltration routes, and Guy is writing them down.

'Dad says we're on a mission,' Cosmo tells her.

She stands in the doorway chewing her lip. She looks wasted and flushed; there is pain in her eyes compounded of junk and anxiety.

'Did you get everything?' Guy asks.

She stares down at the black duffel bags in her hands as if they are unfamiliar.

'Clothes for you,' she says, wearily, 'and food and money.'

'And did you buy a car?'

'Yes.'

'You need to pack,' he tells her. 'We're leaving in the morning.'

'Why?'

Guy dislikes looking at people as a general rule but he looks into her eyes, engaging the fear he sees there. 'Because the police are looking for me.'

She puts the bags down and rubs her forehead. 'What have you got us into?'

'Dad has a plan,' Cosmo says. 'We're going to help him.'

'You do what I say and you'll both be fine,' Guy tells her. 'You'll have more money than you've ever dreamed of, it's as simple as that.'

'I can never tell when you're lying,' she says.

'Come on, Mum,' Cosmo says. 'We've got it all worked out.'

'And if I say no?'

'It's too late for that,' Guy says, softly. 'It's not just the police. There are other more dangerous people on my trail.'

She doesn't look particularly surprised. 'It's always the same with you.'

Guy has given serious thought to using her as a decoy. He has devised fake errands, all of them plausible. Set in motion, the Russians or the British intelligence services would find her eventually but while they chased her, he would gain valuable time. But there is a chance she might go to the police and he's not ready for that yet. Besides, he's interested in the boy.

'I'm offering you the greatest role you'll ever play,' Guy tells her. 'A speaking part in every scene.'

'It's gonna be massive,' Cosmo says with a wide grin, showing off his platinum thumb ring. He's fully signed up to his role though he doesn't yet know what it will be.

'You'll be the leading lady,' Guy says.

Why not? she's thinking. He can see it in her face. There's nothing else going on in her life. She's scared but interested too. She craves the adrenalin and sense of purpose that he offers. Besides, she's never known how to say no to him. She's an addict and he's her drug of choice.

He smiles.

'You better treat us right,' she says.

'I will,' he tells her. 'We have everything we need in this notebook.'

'Okay,' she says and suddenly, with a shake of the shoulders, she is happy again. 'Who is hungry?'

They both hold up their hands.

# 23

# Paying the price

Yulia is halfway back to her house in the back of the Range Rover, feeling the pleasant buzz of a couple of glasses of champagne, when her phone rings and she decides, with decidedly mixed feelings, to take the call.

'I'm sorry,' Jude says.

It's such a needless apology from a man that she does not consider to be either stupid nor shallow. She realises that he has no idea what to say to her. He is so torn, so compromised, she almost feels sorry for him.

'My husband has disappeared,' she tells him. 'My guess is, he's in hiding. If you find him before my side does, please let me know.'

'I will.'

'Have you found Fowle?' she asks, staring out at the passing traffic.

'No.'

'Do you have any leads?'

'One, maybe,' Jude says. 'He cut off the thumb of one of the kidnappers. The Russian who appeared in the photo with your president. Fowle took it with him.'

'I don't understand,' she says. 'Is it some kind of trophy?'

'I think he may be using it to unlock a phone. But why that particular phone and can you track it?'

'I will try to find out,' she says.

'Good.'

'I'm sorry, Jude. I truly am.'

'I know you are.'

Her phone pulses. Another call. It's Freddie Sultan, one of her husband's drinking buddies, and a close confidant of the Syrian dictator, Bashar al-Assad.

'I have to take this.'

She ends the call and accepts the incoming one. Freddie is drunk and weeping.

'I'm so sorry,' he says. 'I'm so sorry.'

'Where are you?'

'The yacht.'

She barks a new set of instructions at the driver.

The Range Rover races past the old Lots Road Power Station and screeches to a halt in the forecourt of the Chelsea Harbour Hotel. Dima, the head of her protection team, tells her to stay put but she refuses.

They escort her to the marina and bracket her along one of the floating wooden jetties between darkened yachts with their guns drawn. All the lights are out and the only sound is that of buoys knocking against moorings and the wind in the halyards.

They stop at the gangway to the largest yacht.

'Wait,' Dima says in a voice that will brook no dissent. He advances slowly up the gangway with two of her team, while Yulia remains with the youngest, Luka, at the foot of the gangway.

Using hand signals, Dima sends one of the team forward and another aft.

'Freddie?' she whispers into her phone but there is no reply.

They wait for several minutes in silence until Dima emerges from below and beckons her forward.

'Prepare yourself,' he says, gruffly.

It's carnage in the stateroom. There is broken glass and crockery strewn across the furniture and the decking. Freddie is crying into a vodka bottle.

'This way.'

Dima leads her down a narrow wood-panelled passageway and Freddie's bodyguard steps aside to allow them into the master suite.

There is a terrified young woman, naked but for a towel, on the bed. Turning, Yulia sees that Valery is hanging from the coat hook on the back of the hatch with his legs splayed on the floor. She's surprised it carried his weight.

She kneels beside him and takes his cold hand in hers. Like every good Russian soldier, he was stubborn and tenacious: in his work and in his pursuit of her. And he had a flare for drunken melodrama. She had loved him once. For his boldness and the protection that he gave her.

'Where were you when he did this?' she asks in Russian.

'In the shower,' the girl replies, also in Russian.

'Did he say anything to you before he did it?'

'No. He was drunk and emotional but I didn't think, I mean I didn't dream of . . .' She tails off.

'Were you one of his regulars?'

The girl nods.

Yulia reaches out and closes her husband's eyelids.

'I could have you killed,' she says softly to the girl.

'I know.'

Back in the stateroom, she finds Dima standing over Freddie. He has moved the vodka bottle out of reach.

'What did he say to you?' she asks.

Freddie looks up at her. She can see the fear and confusion in his face. She slaps him.

'Why did you do that?' he says, with a hand to his face.

'What did my husband say to you?' she demands.

'He said Fowle has Grom.'

'What is Grom?'

'He said Grom is the end of all things.'

Yulia closes her eyes and composes herself. Grom is obviously important but it can wait. Right now, clearing up this mess is the priority.

'My husband made a mistake and now he has paid for it,' she tells Dima, calmly. 'That's all there is to it. This is an internal matter and not for the local police. I want you to dispose of the body and sterilise the place from top to bottom. Use bleach.'

Dima nods slowly. 'Yes, ma'am.'

'Leave no trace behind.'

'And the girl?'

'Send her back to Russia. Tell her that if she speaks of this to anyone her life will be forfeit.'

'Yes, ma'am.'

'I will take a taxi home.'

'Luka will go with you.'

'Very well.'

The young man sits stiffly beside her, scanning the passing traffic with his hand never far from the holster under his suit jacket, all the way to Primrose Hill. When they arrive, he won't let her get out of the taxi until he has scanned the surroundings and opened the front door.

Inside the residence, she kicks off her heels and heads for the freezer where they keep the vodka. She pours a shot, downs it and then pours another.

She looks sideways to see Luka standing in the doorway with his hands on the frame, looking over-confident. It's the first time that she has ever really looked at him. He is good-looking in a square-jawed kind of way. In the old days he'd have probably been a Youth Pioneer in a white blouse with a red scarf.

'Are you sure you want to drink alone?' he says, with the sly hint of a smile on his face.

She knows it's the testosterone gel talking but she craves the kind of oblivion that a good fuck might offer. Suddenly she is angry: at Moscow, at Guy Fowle, at her stupid, dead husband, and at this callow youth who is deluded enough to imagine he can satisfy her needs and brag about it afterwards. She needs to take charge of the situation. What did Valery mean when he said that Grom was the end of all things? What is Grom? It's time to start asking questions.

'Get out,' she says and watches Luka's ego deflate.

Carrying the bottle up the stairs to her study, she bows to the inevitable and decides to book a flight to Moscow.

# 24

# Burnt man #1

At first light, Jude and the MI5 officer Rosanna – no surname supplied – crouch on the tarmac at the London Heliport in Battersea. In front of them, the rotors have started spinning on a Police Air Service Eurocopter. Jude is surprised to find that, despite his recent crash, he has no qualms about boarding a helicopter again. Maybe Helena was right, rather than being traumatised he's the sort of person who worries about not being traumatised.

The crew chief gestures for them to approach and they run forward under the downdraught and climb aboard. Buckled in, they're up, no dramas, leaving behind the city and flying over lush and verdant countryside, a patchwork of fields, the North Wessex Downs and the Cotswolds, before crossing the Welsh border.

Ninety minutes later, they are driving up a narrow road, hemmed in by stone walls with hill sheep grazing in the surrounding fields and the dark outline of the Black Mountains rising before them, low cloud cloaking the summits. They are catching a ride with a constable named Gwyneth Edwards from the local police station. It's drizzling with rain and they are approaching the Snowdonia National Park.

'Tommy mostly keeps himself to himself,' PC Edwards says. 'He doesn't like people gawping at him. There have been a couple of incidents in the pub when he's had a drink in him, fighting and that, but nothing too serious. People know a bit about his army background and make allowances. Even so, we took his gun licence away.'

Thomas Flynn, formerly a sergeant in the Special Air Service, had served under Guy Fowle in a red-team unit based in Hereford whose job was to play the enemy on complex anti-terrorist exercises, a job that seemed to involve thinking up innovative ways of killing their fellow British soldiers.

'I used to come climbing here when I was at university,' Rosanna says.

'I used to spend a lot of time here when I was in the army,' Jude tells her. He remembers the rain as wrathful and relentless, determined to drown them in their forestry block bivouacs. 'I don't think I've ever been here when it wasn't raining.'

'I brought a psychologist up here,' PC Edwards says. 'Tommy got quite upset about that. Are you going to upset him too?'

'Maybe,' Jude says.

'Well, I'll stay close by while you talk to him, and if he gets out of hand, I'll give him a dose of pepper spray.'

'I hope that won't be necessary,' Rosanna says.

'Then try not to provoke him.'

They turn off into an even narrower track made of hardcore that ends at a cottage beside a stream and a stand of alders. PC Edwards parks her patrol car alongside a Land Rover 90 and they get out. There is a lean-to at one end of the cottage with a stack of split logs and a boxer's punch-bag hanging from a chain. A twist of smoke rises from the chimney.

'Looks like he's in,' PC Edwards says.

They get out of the car and approach the cottage. Half a dozen hens scratch in the mud. The constable knocks on the door and steps back with her hand on her belt. 'Mr Flynn, it's PC Gwyneth Edwards. You know me.'

They wait. After a few moments, the door opens a fraction. It's impossible to make out who's inside.

'There are people here from the security services in London who need to speak with you,' PC Edwards says. 'Will you let us in?'

The door opens and PC Edwards steps inside. 'Follow me,' she says, glancing over her shoulder.

Inside it's neat and orderly. They go down a short corridor into a low-ceilinged living room. Flynn stands beside a fire grate that looks freshly cleaned. He is a short, wiry man with broad shoulders. He ducks his head as if unwilling to meet their eyes. The burns caused by the incendiary device are obvious on his hands and running up one side of his face. He is missing an ear.

'You all sit down and I'll make some tea,' PC Edwards says. 'How do you take it?'

'Milk no sugar,' Rosanna says.

'Same for me,' Jude replies.

'And two sugars for you, Tommy, if I remember correctly?'

Flynn nods his head.

'Can I?' asks Rosanna, gesturing at the sofa.

Flynn nods again. Jude sits beside Rosanna and Flynn sits opposite them, stiff-backed with his hands making fists on his knees.

'You know that Guy Fowle has escaped?' Rosanna says.

'I heard it on the radio,' Flynn says. It looks like the fists are there to stop his legs from shaking.

'We're trying to find him,' Rosanna says.

'He won't come here,' Flynn tells her. 'I'm not worried about that. I told the constable I don't need anyone keeping an eye on me. In his mind, you see, I'm finished business.'

'You seem very sure,' Rosanna says.

'He told me in the hospital that my punishment was proportionate to my crime.'

'And what was your crime?' Jude asks.

'I questioned one of Mr Fowle's orders in front of the men.' He closes his eyes and a tremor shakes his whole body. Once it has passed, he opens his eyes again. 'He didn't like to be disobeyed. So he tampered with the means of initiation of an improvised incendiary device that I had built on the training area. It wasn't a large charge but it went up in my face. Before it was disbanded, our unit had the highest casualty rate in the British Army. Nobody put two and two together though.'

'We're looking for clues,' Rosanna says. 'People that he might have known, someone who might be offering him shelter.'

'He has power over people,' Flynn tells her. 'He sees stuff. The sort of stuff you don't want anyone else to know. It was like he could see right into you. He knew I was frightened of fire. I'd been in a house fire when I was a kid. My mum and I were lucky to get out alive.'

PC Edwards comes back from the kitchen carrying a tray with four mismatched mugs of tea.

'How are you all getting on?' she says.

Flynn nods. 'Okay.'

The constable passes around the tea and then stands in the doorway watching.

'Was there anyone at Hereford, in the unit or the barracks, that he had regular contact with?' Jude asks, gently.

'No,' Flynn says. 'The other officers were just as frightened of him as we were.'

'What about the commanding officer?'

'Fowle had something on him. We were sure of that. The CO was a hard man but around Fowle he was quiet as a mouse.'

'Did you ever see him with anyone from outside the unit?'

'Only once,' Flynn says, staring at his tea. 'We had a dinner in the sergeants' mess and invited the officers and their wives. He brought a woman with him. I sat next to her. She was off her skull. She kept going off to the toilet and every time she came back, she was more wasted.'

'Do you remember her name?'

He shakes his head. 'She had one of those names that only posh girls have.'

'Anything else?'

'She said she was a first-year medical student and she'd just finished her exams. I think she'd driven up from London.'

Rosanna glances at Jude. The investigation into where Fowle might have received medical treatment for the injuries he is believed to have suffered as a result of his escape has yielded no results as yet.

'I don't think she'd known him for long but you could tell she was under the control of Fowle already,' Flynn says. 'She couldn't keep her eyes off him. That wasn't unusual. He was always the centre of attention.'

'What year was this?' Rosanna asks.

He thinks about it for a moment. 'It must have been early summer. A few months before 9/11. A year before he burned me.'

'Do you think you'd recognise her if you saw her again?'

Flynn shrugs. 'She was beautiful. You don't forget someone who looks like that.'

On the train back to London, Rosanna looks up at Jude from her tablet. Her sense of excitement is palpable. 'There are five under-graduate medical schools in London: Bart's, UCL, Imperial, St George's and King's. If she was a first year in early 2001 then she must have graduated four or five years later.'

'I wouldn't assume that she graduated,' Jude says, staring at the passing landscape. It's getting brighter the further they get from Wales. 'First I'd check to see who dropped out or was thrown out. No one survived intact around Guy Fowle for long.'

'I'll get my team onto it.'

She stops typing and looks up again at him a few minutes later. 'You've gone quiet.'

He's not sure what to say to her. That he's been feeling a whole gamut of emotions from exhaustion to fear. He knows that violence is a kind of narcissistic applause for Fowle. In Fowle's mind, some were born to kill, and others to be killed. He knows that the hunt for Fowle will put them both in harm's way and there's a good chance that neither of them will survive.

'We need to find him,' Jude says, 'and quickly.'

## 25

## Without a cat, rats feel free

Candida drives them in a second-hand Corolla east out of Gravesend under a soiled white sky. Between the road and the mouth of the Thames are marshlands criss-crossed with canals and streams with broad muddy banks and sluggish brown water.

They pass a trailer park with three rows of static caravans and a shipping container selling fish-bait from a hatch. Guy tells her to turn off the main road and they follow a single lane of tarmac into the marsh. The road takes a sharp right at an old Anglo-Saxon church with an air of neglect and a gnarled and ancient-looking yew tree in the cemetery. They rattle over a metal bridge. The ragged-edged tarmac ends and a hardcore track leads to a large wooden barn disguised by a wall of poplars. The planks of the barn are bleached as white as driftwood. A sign above the door says *Mr Roxy's Pet Food*. There is a battered pick-up parked beside a caravan and a mud-caked mountain dog on a chain that looks like it could take down a bear.

Candida parks beside the pick-up while the dog tries to fling itself at them. Guy takes a black holdall from the back seat beside Cosmo and gets out.

'Wait here,' he says.

A breeze ruffles the poplars, carrying the smell of mud and rotting vegetation, but he detects a whiff of something sharper coming from the shed.

Across the yard, the door to the caravan opens. A man with a bushy beard and a black hat is holding a shotgun and not quite pointing it at him.

'You're Minkin,' Guy says, sauntering over to him.

'And who the fuck are you?'

The man has what looks like a bad case of acne around the eyes.

Guy says: 'Still waters are inhabited by devils.'

Minkin looks startled. 'Fuck me,' he takes a deep breath. 'Without a cat, rats feel free.'

'The belly is full but the eyes are hungry.'

Minkin shakes his head in astonishment. 'I never imagined the day would come.' He turns on the dog. 'Shut it, Linda!'

The dog reluctantly circles its tail and sits down.

'You better follow me.'

Minkin climbs unsteadily out of the caravan and limps towards the shed, using the shotgun as a crutch, while clouds obscure the sun and plunge the yard into twilight.

'You're not what I imagined,' he says, eyeing Candida and Cosmo in the car.

'What did you imagine?'

'Not a family.'

The irony is not lost on Guy.

Minkin pulls one of the sliding doors open far enough to let them in. There is a concrete floor and a hanging wall of rubber flaps with a cacophony of squealing from within. The smell of ammonia is eye-watering.

'I keep three per cage. A male and two females,' Minkin says. 'But it's not like you can just get them together and they'll go at it. If they don't fancy each other, they'll fuckin' kill each other. Is that my money?'

'It is.'

Minkin pushes through the flaps. It's a rat farm. The shed is packed floor to ceiling with stacks of small cages full of rats in a state of agitation. Above each cage is a chart with a sequence of numbers.

'I used to do a roaring trade with the zoos but then they got picky about conditions,' Minkin shouts above the squealing as he walks down one of the aisles. 'I ask you, when the fuck does a rat think it's too cramped? These days it's mostly private owners, you know people with raptors, snakes and other carnivorous animals.

Just about pays the rent. To be honest, don't know where I'd have been without your generous monthly retainer. It kept the electricity on, which is what matters to you. Keeping your precious little straws safe.'

He looks back and winks.

'My dear old dad always used to say there's money in shit. It's not easy money.' He opens a steel door onto a utility room with rows of waist-high freezers. 'There's real skill in cultivating and concentrating the parasite in faecal matter.' He puts the shotgun down on one of the freezers and lifts the lid on another. Inside, amongst labelled bags of rat carcasses there is a portable nitrogen tank of the sort that veterinary surgeons use to transport frozen animal sperm. He reaches for a pair of thick leather gloves hanging on a nail on the wall and puts them on. 'And the freezing is a tricky business. You got to make the outer walls of the oocysts permeable but you can't let ice crystals form inside or it kills the pesky little fuckers. You have to bleach them and then plunge them into liquid nitrogen at minus 196 degrees.'

He removes the lid on the nitrogen tank and takes out the basket in an icy cloud. In the basket there are thousands of vertically stacked, glass-like straws each one about three inches long but not much wider than a human hair.

'Voilà! My babies,' Minkin says. '*Cryptosporidium Hominis*, single-celled parasites immune to chlorine, coagulation, sedimentation and sand filtration. I added a few nucleotides to give them a bit more of a sting. You got enough there to fuck a whole city.'

Guy smiles. *The future looks rosy.*

'There, you see, I knew I'd get a smile out of you eventually,' Minkin says, replacing the basket and screwing the cap back on. He hangs the gloves back on the wall. 'Did you know the Assyrians were the first ones at it? That's right, they poisoned the wells of their enemies with rye argot. It's a fungus. It fucks you up something rotten. It's like your limbs are burning. Then there was Vlad the Impaler, a chap renowned for being truly fuckin' ruthless, who poisoned his own wells to deny them to the Turks. More recently the Japs poisoned the reservoirs in Manchuria with typhoid. I don't recommend you use a reservoir though. I know Walthamstow would be easy because all they've got there is a fence, but there's too much dilution and the little critters are more likely to get detected. No, your best bet is the distribution network, so a pumping station. And all you need for that is your own pump with the necessary power to overcome the pressure in the pipes and inject the straws in the system. They call it reflux contamination. You know what reflux is? It's like when sick comes back up in your mouth. Fuckin' horrible.' He gives Guy a sly look. 'Have you decided where you're going to do it?'

'Maybe.'

'You have, haven't you!' He wags a dirty finger at him. 'You filthy rotter . . .'

'What will you do?' Guy asks.

'Back to the homeland for me. I'm straight to the airport after this. Remember you've got a few days after you've contaminated the system before the first symptoms will show. And don't forget to stock up on bottled water, unless you want a savage case of the runs, that is. Anything else I can do for you?'

'No, that's it,' Guy says. He gives him the holdall.

He watches while Minkin meticulously counts the money on top of one of the freezers, taking it out of the holdall a bundle at a time and flicking through the notes with a spit-dampened finger. When he's done, he smiles. 'It was a pleasure doing business.'

'It was,' Guy agrees, and pulls the Glock from the small of his back as Minkin grabs for the shotgun. Guy is quicker. He shoots Minkin in the knee, dropping him to the floor.

'Fuck!' Minkin screams.

Guy picks up the shotgun and breaks it open, pocketing the shells before throwing the gun into the farthest corner. He packs the money back in the holdall while Minkin writhes on the floor.

'You fucking bastard!'

Guy slings the holdall over his shoulder. Using the gloves, he lifts the liquid nitrogen container out of the freezer and carries it back down the aisles of squealing rats and out into the car park, where Candy and Cosmo are standing by the car looking worried.

The dog has resumed flinging itself to the end of its chain.

'We heard a shot,' Cosmo says.

'It's fine,' Guy replies.

The money and the container go in the boot beside their bags and he removes a metal jerrycan of fuel and carries it back towards the shed.

'I'll be back soon,' he says.

Back inside, he finds Minkin crawling towards him down one of the aisles, dragging his shattered knee behind him.

'I'll get you,' Minkin yells. 'I'll fuckin' get you!'

When he sees what's in Guy's hand, he starts waving his hands frantically.

Guy stands just out of reach, removes the cap on the jerrycan and douses Minkin with petrol. Then he walks back out again sloshing petrol across the rats in their cages until the jerrycan is empty. He flings it away.

He pauses by the rubber flaps and looks back.

'No,' Minkin pleads. 'No, please.'

Guy takes a brass lighter out of his pocket and thumbs the flint. He holds the flame aloft before touching it to the nearest cage. The flames race down the aisle and engulf Minkin.

Guy turns and sees Cosmo standing wide-eyed by the rubber flaps.

'Sick,' Cosmo says and from the way he says it, Guy understands that he is impressed. Together they walk back out to the car. Without breaking stride, Guy shoots the dog.

# 26

# Burnt man #2

At dusk, John Nganga, the DCI from SO15, stands beside Jude and Rosanna in the taped-off yard looking at the charred timbers of Mr Roxy's barn. They are surrounded by pools of water and churned-up ground left by the Fire Service.

'Forensics recovered two bullets,' Nganga explains. 'One from the corpse in the shed and the other from a dog. Both came from the same weapon that Guy Fowle used to kill two of the men in the Chelsea house.'

'And the identity of the dead man?' Rosanna asks.

'The company Mr Roxy's Pet Food is registered in the name of a sole proprietor, one Levi Minkin, who moved here from Israel in the mid-nineties. His name is not on the electoral register but as far as we can tell he lived over there.'

Across the yard, scenes of crime officers are carrying plastic boxes full of belongings from a caravan to a waiting van. Nganga hands them both a set of gloves. Inside, the caravan smells of sweat, grease and damp. The sink is overflowing with dirty dishes and there are piles of unwashed clothes and invoices on every remaining uncleared surface. The bed sheets don't look like they've been changed for months.

From the midst of a stack of papers on one of the shelves, a SOCO recovers a sepia-stained photograph and hands it to Jude. The picture is of a group of men in fatigues sitting on the edge of a trench on a hilltop fortification. One of the men is holding a shoulder-fired missile above his head like a trophy. An American Stinger, by the looks of it. The sandy-coloured ridges marching into the distance behind them makes Jude think of Afghanistan. Jude shows Rosanna the photo. 'Minkin is a Sephardic surname.

Large numbers of Russian Jews moved to Israel after the Soviet Union collapsed.'

He checks his phone, there is still no response from Yulia. He takes a photo of the men by the trench with his phone and sends the image to Gretchen.

'We'll go through it all and send over copies of everything of interest,' Nganga tells them.

The Situational Awareness Group is a secure annex to MI6 head-quarters, with its own Echelon server, located in a nondescript 1930s office block on Albert Embankment. Its neighbours, above and below, and either side, are mostly not-for-profits, unaware of it hidden in their midst. Jude leads Rosanna from the elevators along a corridor to a brushed-steel door. He presses his thumb and then his fingers to the reader on the wall and the red light turns to green.

'There are only two of us,' Jude tells her as he pushes the door, 'though there's room for more.'

In the hallway beyond, there is scaffolding, exposed overhead cabling and rolls of plastic-wrapped carpeting that give the place an air of newness and impermanence. She follows him through another door and into the brightly lit interior of the incident room.

Gretchen is sitting alone in front of the video wall like a visitor in front of an Old Master at a gallery. Levi Minkin's heavy-browed face fills the screens like Big Brother.

'You were right about Minkin,' Gretchen says, looking over her shoulder at them. She eyes Rosanna suspiciously.

'Gretchen, this is Rosanna,' Jude says.

'You were at the Cabinet Office,' Gretchen says with a hint of accusation.

'I was,' Rosanna replies, raising her eyebrows to Jude.

Gretchen turns back to the wall. 'Minkin was born in Minsk in what is now Belarus in 1964,' she tells them. 'He served with the GRU's 22nd Special Forces Brigade in Afghanistan. In January 1987, he was part of a reconnaissance team in Kandahar that recovered a Stinger shoulder-fired missile. The US were supplying them to the Afghan opposition, the Mujahedeen. That's what Minkin's holding in the photo. He left for Israel in 1989 and moved here ten years ago.'

'Anything from the Israelis?'

Gretchen shakes her head. 'They're not sharing.'

'Anything else?'

'The police sent over his bank statements.' Gretchen gets up and goes over to her desk, which has a burgeoning collection of orchids and bromeliads spilling over onto the adjacent desks. She taps at her keyboard and a cascade of scanned papers light up on the screen. 'For the last three years he has received a monthly stipend from a brass-plate company based in the British Virgin Islands.'

'You think Minkin was a sleeper agent?' Rosanna asks, looking over her shoulder.

'Maybe and maybe they activated him three years ago. We need to know who owns the company to identify the source of the funds. The Metropolitan Police have submitted a disclosure request to the authorities in BVI as part of the criminal investigation into his death. But it could take weeks for an answer.'

'We don't have weeks,' Jude says. 'The more pressing question is what was he doing breeding rats?'

'Rats spread disease,' Gretchen says. 'Leptospirosis, Q Fever, Hantavirus, Haemorrhagic Fever, Salmonellosis, Rat Bite Fever. The list is as long as your arm.'

'But the rats were destroyed in the fire,' Rosanna says.

'I've got more that's new for you,' Gretchen says.

'Go on.'

'Special Collection Services at RAF Croughton intercepted a satellite call two nights ago from Valery Ermolaev to Dmitri Troshev in Solokov's villa on Pathos. Valery is obviously drunk and much of what he says is incomprehensible but at the end he says, "Fowle has Grom". At that point Troshev becomes agitated and terminates the call. We have not identified any other reference to Grom in Russian diplomatic, military or commercial communications. The Greek police have raided the villa but the place has been trashed and Troshev and Solokov are gone.'

'What does Grom mean?'

'Thunder in Russian.'

'Thunder?'

'The Slavic god of thunder is also the god of war and weapons,' Gretchen tells them. 'It could be a weapon.'

'Keep widening the search,' Jude says. 'Any reference to Grom no matter how oblique.'

'Sure, boss.'

He wishes that Yulia would answer his calls. He needs her insight. 'Where's Yulia Ermolaeva?'

Gretchen looks apologetic. 'I should have told you. Border Force report that she departed on a flight for Moscow this morning.'

He's surprised and unsettled. He really hopes that she's gone of her own volition and not been recalled.

'Do you want to get a drink?' Rosanna asks him in a sympathetic tone.

He looks at his watch. It's after nine p.m. He's been awake since dawn but he doesn't feel tired.

'Sure.'

They cross Albert Embankment and go through an arch under the railway viaduct to the park beyond. It was from here that dissident Irish Republicans fired a rocket grenade at the MI6 building in September 2000. On the far side of the grass is a pub long past the daily end-of-work crowd. They find a quiet corner where they can't be overheard and Jude buys a scotch and a gin and tonic at the bar.

'Do you think that there's any chance Yulia Ermolaeva knows more about this than she's letting on?' Rosanna asks, gently.

'No,' Jude says, reflecting back on his most recent conversation with Yulia. 'She told me that she's as much in the dark as we are. I think she may have gone to Moscow in search of answers. I'm hoping that's the case.'

'You like her,' Rosanna says, watching his face.

'It's not about that.' He shakes his head. Although he does like her. 'Everything about the attack on Woolwich reeks of an opportunistic attack. Valery Ermolaev trying to get rich quick. Yulia admitted as much. But this latest murder suggests something else, something that we haven't figured out yet. Think about it. Guy Fowle is kidnapped from the courthouse by a Serb gang that we believe were working for PMC Valkyrie. He then escapes. We presume he finds shelter somewhere and medical attention. He ought to be lying low. Instead, his next stop is a Russian émigré, a former GRU soldier, who breeds rats. Fowle kills Minkin and torches a barn. Why? What does it mean? And what's he going to do next?'

'We can try and figure it out together,' she says.

Jude likes the idea of them working together. There's a quality in Rosanna of determination and understated confidence that he is finding reassuring. But before he can reply, her phone vibrates on the table-top.

She answers and he watches her face light up. She listens and groans in embarrassment. 'Really?' The answer is apparently yes because she holds out the phone to Jude. 'My husband wants to speak to you.'

'Hello?' Jude says.

'It's Charlie Bevan.'

Jude recognises the voice. They attended operational training together at Fort Monckton in Hampshire. He remembers Bevan as an intelligent and confident intelligence officer, an accomplished linguist with Cantonese and Korean.

'You've met my wife,' Charlie says.

'I have.'

'We have an eighteen-month-old toddler called Archie.'

'Congratulations.'

'He misses his mother.'

'I'm sure he does.'

There is a pause.

'Together, you're going to find Fowle?' Charlie says.

'We're going to find Fowle,' Jude confirms.

'Good. Try and keep Rosanna alive for me.'

'I will.'

'Please give the phone back to Rosy.'

He watches Rosanna's face. She listens and says, 'I love you too.'

She puts the phone back on the table.

'Sorry. Charlie's taken a career break to look after the baby,' she says. 'I think he misses the chase.'

Jude raises an eyebrow. 'Rosy?'

'Don't!'

'Why do I feel like I've just been given the gypsy's warning?'

Rosanna smiles, not unkindly. 'You don't have the best reputation when it comes to married women.'

It's Jude's turn to feel embarrassed.

Rosanna's phone vibrates again. She holds it to her ear.

'Candida Taunton,' Rosanna tells him after finishing the call. 'Her parents live near Hereford. She was thrown out of St Bart's in her second year on the back of a conviction for allowing her London premises to be used for the supply of Class A drugs. Since then she's worked as a model and an actress.'

'Do you have an address?'

'Ladbroke Grove.'

'Let's go.'

Thirty minutes later they join an armed police assault team as they break down the door with a battering ram and storm through the flat. Everywhere there are signs of a hurried departure: drawers and cupboards are hanging open, and clothes are discarded on the floor. Two phones are smashed to pieces on the kitchen table, their SIM cards turned to slag in the microwave.

Candida and her son have fled.

# Devils in still waters

London has always been a honeycomb of passageways and voids, and the app guides them to unlit and unmonitored parts of the city that defy all surveillance. Always there are swift means of ingress and egress, and the assets approach from opposite directions. They are cautious, scanning their arcs, fearful of ambush, and their faces are indistinct. Guy exchanges clumsily translated Russian proverbs with them and feels the charge in the air, the excitement that an operation years in the planning is finally under way. He uses a fresh burner before each meet. Afterwards he snips the SIM card in two and crushes the phone under the wheels of the Corolla.

In Lewisham in South London, they back the car up against a water utility van parked beneath a railway arch that is green with moss and running with condensation. Guy passes the nitrogen tank and one of the USB sticks to a man wearing a bright orange uniform with reflective sliver chevrons, his face shadowed by a white helmet.

'When do you want me to do it?'

'The sooner the better,' Guy tells him, handing him a Belgian passport.

'I'll do it tonight.' The man sounds relieved. After tonight, his job will be done. In accordance with his orders, he will wait twenty-four hours and then leave the country.

'I'll see you in the motherland,' Guy tells him. It amuses him to think how bitter the man will be when he realises the truth.

They cross the Thames at Tower Bridge and behind the Mile End Road a thin-faced Somali money dealer passes over a garbage bag full of bricks of cash in a narrow channel between a boarded-up Victorian hospital and the gothic horror of an overgrown cemetery.

When he shows her the contents of the bag, Candy's eyes light up again.

They head towards the Regent's Canal.

The next meet is on the towpath beside the mouth of the Islington Tunnel. Guy sits on a bench beneath a mature chestnut tree and waits with eyes closed, memorising maps from the Moleskine, while listening for movement. Eventually, he hears the soft footfall of a man in sneakers approaching along the towpath from the east. He sits beside Guy and places a black bag on the path between them.

'Still waters are inhabited by devils,' Guy says, opening his eyes and staring at the oily black surface of the canal.

'It is written with a pitchfork in flowing water,' the man replies, with his hands clasped between his knees. He is a disgruntled ammunition technician from the Defence EOD, Munitions and Search School at Kineton and like a succession of quartermasters before him he has been hoarding spare ammunition for years to hide the occasional inadvertent discrepancies in store tallies. The bag between them contains thirty off-the-books white phosphorus grenades that were withdrawn from British Army service in 1997.

'The belly is full but the eyes are hungry.'

Guy hands over a plastic bag containing bundled stacks of used twenties.

The man leaves the way he came, sticking to the shadow of the overhanging trees.

'Where are we staying tonight?' Cosmo asks, leaning forward between the seats, when Guy returns to the car.

'Pick somewhere,' Guy says, passing Candy the Moleskine. 'There's an entire page full of addresses.'

The fourth meet is with an Irishman in a brick alleyway silvery with broken glass and needles near Kilburn High Road. The Irishman is carrying a large brown paper parcel tied with string. Guy has another plastic bag full of cash.

'I've had this under my bed for twenty years,' he says, handing it to Guy.

'Does it still work?' Guy asks. It's heavy, thirteen or fourteen kilos he guesses.

'I've done as I was told and cleaned it thoroughly once a month.'

'Good.' Guy gives him the bag of cash.

'Do me a favour,' the man says before turning and walking back the way he came. 'Kill as many Brits as you can.'

'I will,' Guy tells him.

He puts the parcel in one of the black holdalls in the boot.

'A mews house in Kensington,' Candy says eagerly, when he gets back in the driver's seat. 'Three bedrooms and a basement pool.'

It's what she's always wanted, an entire home of her own.

'One night only,' Guy tells her and watches the disappointment in her face. He knows that it is only a matter of time before whoever designed and built Grom comes looking for its new owner. 'The safe houses won't be safe for long.'

'So, where do we stay tomorrow night?' she asks.

'We keep moving,' Guy tells her, logging on to his cryptocurrency wallet.

They drive east along one of the arterial routes that leads out of the city.

'What next?' Cosmo asks.

'A brush with the law.'

They drive past a solitary line of chain hotels surrounded by building sites and park under a flyover on the northern perimeter of London City Airport. Above them a bridge crosses a marina on the western edge of the runway. Fifty metres away, beneath one of the concrete abutments, a police Trojan armed response vehicle is waiting with its lights off. Guy gets out of the car and walks towards it.

The driver's side window is lowered and Guy hands over a USB stick to a police officer whose face is shadowed by the visor of his black and white chequered baseball cap.

Guy turns without speaking and walks back to the Corolla.

'What now?' Candy asks, when he starts the engine.

'We switch cars.'

They head back into the city, entering a narrow street running alongside a railway viaduct west of Bethnal Green. Guy pulls up in front of a garage in one of the arches and an Asian man wearing a baseball cap with a Captain America shield on it is standing in front of it. He crushes a cigarette beneath his heel before approaching their car. Leaning in the driver's side window, he looks them up and down.

'Hiya, sweetheart,' Captain America says to Candy, ignoring Guy.

'Hiya,' she says. 'I like your hat.'

Guy suppresses the urge to slam his head up and down on the window's rim until his face is entirely pulped.

'Still waters are inhabited by devils,' he says, instead.

'God won't give it away,' Captain America says with an indulgent smile, not taking his eyes off Candy. 'Pigs won't eat it.'

'The belly is full but the eyes are hungry.'

'Your wish is my command.'

He opens up the garage and Guy drives in, parking between a silver Range Rover with tinted windows on one side and an inspection pit on the other.

'Sweet,' Cosmo says, admiring their new car.

'It was recently serviced and it has a full tank of gas,' Captain America tells them, giving Cosmo the keys. 'There is a bag in the boot with a sledgehammer, a crowbar and a pair of bolt cutters as you requested.'

Guy nods and Candy hands over another twenty thousand dollars in cash.

'Thanks, sweetheart.'

Guy steps away to make another call on a burner as they transfer the black holdalls from the Corolla to the Range Rover.

'What will you do with our car?' Cosmo asks, with his back to Guy.

'Break it up for parts, my friend,' Captain America says, in an expansive tone, 'and send them in a thousand different directions.'

Watching them, Guy takes the knife out of the back pocket of his jeans and steps lightly forward. He pulls the man's head back with one hand and with the other slices the blade of the knife across his throat, opening the artery. He steps back and kicks the man into the inspection pit.

Cosmo stands over the pit with blood spatter on his face.

'Why did you do that?'

'He was annoying me,' Guy replies. He picks the baseball cap off the floor and gives it to Cosmo.

'Who's going to break up the car now?' the boy says, petulantly.

Beside him, Candy is chewing her lip.

'It doesn't matter,' Guy tells them. 'We're ahead of the clock. I've speeded up the timeline. We can do whatever we like.'

Cosmo shrugs and gets in the back of the Range Rover.

He could laugh at the wounded expression on Candy's face.

'The boy needs to toughen up,' he says. 'If he's going to survive what's to come.'

They drive west along the Embankment.

# 28

# Angry Bear

Gabriel Morley is feeling glum in the office on the top floor of his family home in Notting Hill surrounded by cardboard inserts like giant mutant egg boxes, folded cables bound with black twist ties, sticky orange tabs used to hold together electronics in transit and enough clear plastic bags to suffocate a toddlers' playgroup. There is a brand-new printer on the desk beside his encrypted government-issue laptop but he can't get the two to talk to each other.

He is alone and in his cups; two-thirds of the way into a bottle of Château Beychevelle claret that he'd been saving for a special occasion. Since such occasions are now likely to be few and far between, why not drink it now? Charlotte is uncontactable at an ayurvedic retreat in Goa with her new love Violeta. She is discovering her 'true self' unencumbered by him. His kids have moved into Charlotte's sister's house around the corner and have made it clear that they do not believe that he has the time nor the inclination to look after them. In the letter that she left for him above the fireplace, Charlotte has insisted on using lawyers as the only means of future communication. And just to add a massive pinch of international jeopardy and by reason of an inadvertently spilled glass of wine, he has accidentally enmeshed himself in the prison break of the worst mass terrorist in British history.

What more could go wrong?

He has to print and sign an engagement letter from a divorce lawyer recommended to him by Joth in a decidedly frosty telephone conversation. Because like Joth's family, the Foggerels, they also date back to the Holy Roman Empire and probably cut their teeth divorcing Medicis and miscreant popes, they insist on physically rather than electronically signed documents.

The problem that he faces is that an administrator password is required to download the printer software onto the laptop, which belongs to the state and not to him. Resigned to a lengthy period on hold listening to Elgar, he calls the twenty-four-hour tech support line at the Treasury. He is answered surprisingly swiftly by a polite man with a South Asian accent who introduces himself as Hardeep. He asks Gabriel for his name. Hardeep gives no indication that he recognises it. He then asks Gabriel to describe the problem, which he duly does.

'Are you happy for me to shadow your computer?' Hardeep asks.

'Yes,' Gabriel says, 'please do.'

Hardeep then asks him to tap on the government's weirdly ontological *Who am I?* question mark icon on his laptop and enter a code in the box, which he reads out to him. Gabriel enters the code and then sits back with his wine glass and watches the cursor moving outside his control across the screen. At least something is working.

A new tab opens.

User name: .\!treasureadmin!
Password: ＊＊＊＊＊＊＊＊＊＊＊＊＊＊＊

'That should be downloading now, sir.'

'Thank you.'

The screen flickers and suddenly he is confronted by a full-screen image of himself stepping off Joth Foggerel's boat onto the private jetty beneath Oleg Solokov's villa.

'Did that work?' Hardeep asks.

He stares in horror at the screen and at the phone.

*Shit!*

'Is there anything else I can help you with?' Hardeep asks, amiably.

*This can't be happening.*

*No! No! No! No!*

'Sir?'

'No,' he says, screaming on the inside. 'That's everything, thank you.'

'Glad to be of service, enjoy the rest of your evening, sir.'

The moment the call ends, the image on the screen is replaced with the head and shoulders of a brown bear.

'Good evening, Mr Morley,' says the bear in a deep, gravelly voice. 'Are you enjoying your wine?'

Gabriel moves fast, pressing his thumb against the laptop's built-in camera.

'Don't be childish, Gabriel.'

The image on the screen changes to one of Gabriel bare-chested in the kitchen at Oleg Solokov's Greek villa with Dmitri Troshev, Valery Ermolaev and the hacker Scary Bear.

Defeated, he slumps back in his seat. 'Who are you?'

'Does it matter?'

The bear is remarkably lifelike, really high-quality CGI.

'Yes,' Gabriel says. 'Of course it matters.'

'Well then, you can call me Angry Bear.'

'Are you serious?'

The bear's voice has a worldweary tone. 'I have evidence that implicates you in the conspiracy to attack Woolwich Crown Court and seize the terrorist Guy Fowle. What was your cut of the Islamic State money going to be?'

'Now hold on a minute,' Gabriel protests. 'None of that is true. It was a complete coincidence that I was in that kitchen. I had nothing to do with the prison break or anything that happened. For God's sake, some oaf spilled wine on me!'

'I know. But do you think that the police or the security services will believe that? Will the Prime Minister?'

Gabriel stares at the screen.

'Is that how your career should end?' the bear asks. 'In abject disgrace?'

'What do you want?' Gabriel says, eventually.

'Guy Fowle has something that belongs to me.'

'The police and the intelligence services are doing everything they can to find and apprehend him.'

'Good. It will be useful to know what steps are being taken to apprehend him.'

'I'm a privy councillor!' Gabriel protests. 'One of the Queen's trusted advisers. I've taken an oath of secrecy.'

'That is good. That is why I am allowing you privileged access to confidential information.'

'What are you talking about? What information?'

'It is possible that Guy Fowle has set in motion a series of events that will have a negative effect on your national economy.'

'What do you mean by negative effect?'

'Frankly speaking, I think he's going to fuck everything.'

'What does that mean?'

'Money, the lights, the water, all the stuff that makes things tick.'

Gabriel is incredulous. 'What? How?'

'It's not so difficult, you know. I strongly suggest that you drink only bottled water. You can no longer trust what comes out of the tap.'

'There's something in the water?'

'I think a lot of people are going to die.'

'What do you mean?'

The screen ripples and reverts to a generic picture of some North American national park.

Gabriel grips his head in his hands. It's so fucked. There's no way that this is going to end well. He should just go and confess all to the Prime Minister. A quiet resignation. Except that's not what it's going to be like. Gabriel knows the PM well enough to know he'll be thrown to the wolves. The PM's special adviser Maurice Hermon will ensure a savage flogging in the press. And for what? It's not as if the infuriating bear asked him for anything specifically. There's no point losing his head. It occurs to him that it might even be a prank. That's what most hackers are, pranksters. With Xander bloody Foggerel as the prime suspect.

His personal phone rings. It's a journalist from the *Mail*. He had lunch with her once. It wasn't as ghastly an experience as he'd expected. She'd written rather a sympathetic piece. No chance of that now, he thinks. Nevertheless, he answers.

'Mr Morley?'

'Yes, Andrea, what can I do for you?'

'Is it true that your wife has left you for the wife of your best friend?'

He has always believed that sensationalist intrusion is an immutable fact of British public life and you just have to live with it. Even so, he surprises himself with the brevity of his answer. 'Yes, that's a fair summary.'

'You don't seem very upset?'

Although Gabriel's suffered plenty of professional adversity, he's never actually suffered any private adversity. He has loving parents, close siblings and an absence of bereavement or serious illness. Not a single divorce in his entire extended family. He simply doesn't know how to react.

'I wish them every happiness,' he says and ends the call.

That's that dealt with, barring the headlines. He takes another sip of wine. Of course, there's the coming to terms with the fact that everyone that he meets for the next weeks and months is going to be looking at him and thinking about what sort of a disaster of a man he must be that his wife left him for another woman. His fellow Cabinet ministers sniggering behind his back.

*Fuck them all!*

He takes another sip of wine. It really is very good. There's an entire case in the cellar.

# 29

# The mews

In the early hours of the morning, Candy parks at the entrance to a cobbled mews in a spiral of one-way streets, just a stone's throw from the great Victorian museums.

'The code for the key safe is 1917,' Guy tells her. 'It should be at ankle height on the right-hand side of the front door.'

Before she gets out, she leans across and kisses him passionately on the lips, whatever doubt she had now dispelled. Cosmo makes a disgusted noise from the back seat.

They watch as she enters the alley, keeping to the shadows at the sides. They wait. Ten minutes go by. Guy grips the handle of the Glock tightly.

Abruptly a rectangle of cobbles is lit up, a pair of wooden doors swinging open and Candy's silhouette beckoning. Guy drives the Range Rover down the mews and into the garage, and Candy closes the doors behind him.

'It's lovely,' she tells them when they get out of the car. 'Even the fridge is stocked.'

She leads them through a door into a kitchen and dining room with sliding glass doors that looks out on a private courtyard lit up with recessed spotlights. They kick off their shoes and feel the warmth of the underfloor heating through their feet.

They follow her up two flights of stairs.

'Get some sleep,' Guy tells Cosmo at the entrance to a bedroom on the top floor. 'This may be your last night in a comfortable bed.'

'I want to play a part not just sit in the car,' Cosmo says.

'You will,' Guy tells him. 'Tomorrow night we begin in earnest.'

★   ★   ★

In an excavated basement, Candida finds a thirty-metre pool. Delighted, she strips naked and dives in, straight as an arrow. She swims several lengths, before treading water.

'Are you coming in?' she asks, playfully.

The last time Guy was in a swimming pool he was spinning in a death roll with his hands clamped around Scary Bear's throat. And the last time he was truly out of his depth was when a boat he was travelling in sank in the Mediterranean. His memories of what followed that event are jumbled and chaotic, he was suffering severe heroin withdrawal symptoms, but he remembers the breaking waves, the bobbing of the lifejacket and the hand on the rope-handle at the back of his neck pulling him through the water.

He shakes his head. 'Not this time.'

She flips over and continues scything through the water.

Upstairs, Guy lays out his belongings. He uses the knife to cut through the string on the brown-paper parcel that was given to him by the Irishman in Kilburn and unwraps it. Inside are the greased parts of an M82 Barrett .5 calibre (12.7mm) semi-automatic sniper rifle and two ten-round magazines. Also, a box of twenty armour-piercing incendiary rounds. He fits the parts of the rifle together. Fully assembled, it is nearly a metre and a half in length. Next, he charges the magazines with the bullets. Each one has a red tip and a ring of aluminium paint. After that, he unpacks the white phosphorus grenades with their distinctive yellow band, setting four to one side and putting twenty-six back in the bag. Then he counts the remaining money: just over two hundred thousand pounds in tightly packed bricks of used twenties. When he is done, he builds a cube out of the bricks. Finally, he tears open the packaging on ten more unused burners. He loads them with pay-as-you-go SIM cards and plugs them into sockets across the ground floor.

When he has finished, he returns to transcribing information from the app to the notebook. Using the search function, he finds a biography and personal details of Jude Lyon. It's all there: full name, parents (deceased) and stepfather (alive), date and place of birth, religion, sexual orientation, and reports that he is stubborn and does not respond well to authority. None of the sexual kinks or addictions that are flagged in his colleagues.

Smiling, Guy writes down the list of Jude's known addresses.

He looks up at the soft slap of feet on the polished floorboards. Candida has emerged from the basement, towelling her hair. He listens as she opens one of the kitchen cupboards and then the fridge. The glug of wine poured.

She crosses the room and stands facing him with her back to the sliding doors and a wine glass in her hand. She is naked and from the tops of her hip bones to the tip of her pubis is a narrow, inverted triangle with the eyelid of her navel midway across its flat line. There isn't an ounce of fat on her. The scars on her body radiate out from it and encircle her breasts. Each one of the women that he has marked carries some elemental part of him trapped in the design on their skin.

'That's a very large gun,' she says, contemplating the sniper rifle on the table.

'It's a beast,' he agrees.

'What's the plan for tomorrow?'

'First, I meet with a Chechen and after that a Nazi. Then we head north on the motorway.'

'And tomorrow night?'

'First strike, it'll be spectacular.'

She sips her wine. She knows he's not going to tell her any more than that.

'Someone must clean this place regularly,' she says, thoughtfully.

'We'll be long gone before they're here.'

'But they'll know we've been.'

'Like I said, we're going to need somewhere else to stay,' he tells her. 'Somewhere with no connection to this phone.'

'Who's after us?' she asks.

'The British police and the intelligence services. And in all likelihood, the Russians. If they're not already hunting us, they will be after tomorrow.'

Her eyes narrow. 'And you think that we can evade them?'

'Of course,' he says. 'Chaos will be our friend, you'll see.'

Later, on a king-size bed on the top floor, she sits in lotus, cooking for two fresh needles. She has changed his bandages and cleaned the wounds. Cosmo is asleep in the room on the floor above them.

'Where were you?' she asks. She means the years he spent in Iraq and Syria, first as a fighter for Islamic State and then, for a decade, as its prisoner. 'I had no way to tell you that I was pregnant.'

'I was locked up,' he tells her, setting the alarm at two-minute intervals on several burners. 'Did you think I would come home and play happy families?'

He sees the hurt in her eyes. It's the most fascinating thing about her – an actor's trick – the way she can express so many different emotions by simply rearranging her face. It's not an exaggeration to say that she did more than anyone else to teach him how to read and understand faces.

'We're going to need more of this,' she says miserably, tapping the end of a loaded needle with her fingernail to expel air bubbles. She hands it to him.

'We have the cash,' he tells her. 'We just need to find a fresh supplier. You've never had any problems with that.'

She nods. They both know she has an instinct for it.

'Come on,' he says.

They tie off their arms and inject the drug.

Once the initial rush has passed, they open their eyes and marvel at each other again. The glow on their skin and the brightness of their teeth. The hypnotic whirl of scars. Their bodies levitating above the quilt.

Her smile widens further and is as mischievous as can be.

# 30

# Grumpy before coffee

Jude wakes from a nightmare to the sound of the pips at the start of the *Today* programme and reflexively pats the bed beside him until he finds his phone. He peers at the screen. No new update from the police or the security service on the search for Fowle. He closes his eyes again and breathes deeply, filling his lungs, ribcage and belly before exhaling slowly through his mouth. His dreams are no longer iterations of crashing helicopters: the last thing he remembers before waking was gunfire, splintering courtroom pews and a burning man rushing towards him with flaming hands.

The news headlines on the radio report that the hunt for the fugitive Guy Fowle continues and that the police and the intelligence services are exploring links between the body of an unidentified man found dead in a Chelsea house and the Russian president. Overnight the Russian Ambassador to the UK tweeted that Russia played no part in the attack on Woolwich Crown Court and the Foreign Secretary will be responding later on the programme. The police are searching for a woman and her teenage son following a raid on a house in Ladbroke Grove and there are unconfirmed reports of a connection between Guy Fowle and the death of a man at a warehouse fire in Kent.

Learning *Pencak Silat* in a jungle camp on the Indonesian island of Sunda, Master Sumaryono had taught him that ordered breathing was as subtle and noble a discipline as the containment of pain.

Some days though, simply breathing is not enough.

Even the gym feels too small to contain Jude's anger and frustration, the weapons too precise. Instead, he opts to run-like-fuck to work. He heads out and runs south to the river with his clothes in a pack on his back, lengthening his stride and picking up speed as he goes. He gives into it when he reaches the river. He sprints full-pelt west along the Embankment with the water shimmering beside him in the early morning light. He crosses on the cable-stayed Jubilee Bridge to avoid the Westminster barricade. As he runs past the London Eye, he sees the ugly blue plastic shroud that covers the Houses of Parliament. With Guy Fowle on the loose, it's hard not to imagine what similar atrocities might be in store.

After St Thomas' Hospital, he stops and walks the last hundred yards to catch his breath with his hands on his hips and his shoulders back. People hurry past him heading for work. It's too early for the white-collar rush hour and they look like the kind of people whose work goes mostly unseen and unappreciated.

Entering the Situational Awareness Group offices, he finds Gretchen sitting amongst her tropical plants, exactly where he left her the night before.

'Have you been home?' he asks her as he heads for the water cooler.

'We got the DNA results back on Candida Taunton's son, Cosmo,' Gretchen replies without answering his question. 'Guy Fowle is his father.'

Jude is not surprised or in any way reassured. Given the pleasure Fowle appears to take in inflicting pain and suffering on his family, Jude doubts that it makes the boy any safer.

'What about Candida?'

'The police have spoken to her parents, who own the flat she lives in. They haven't seen her for months and they believe that she is using again.'

'Using?'

'She's back on heroin. The police are trying to track down members of the Narcotics Anonymous group that she attended, but many of them are difficult to find or unwilling to talk.'

'I'll call Tamar,' he says, tapping on the favourites icon on his red-taped phone.

'Good luck with that.'

*The Saboteur*

'What kind of time do you call this?' Jude's youngest sister demands when she eventually answers.

'We call it morning,' he says. As an undercover officer in the Metropolitan Police he knows that Tamar's life is mostly nocturnal. And she's always grumpy before coffee.

She hawks and spits. 'Damn, my head hurts! What do you want?'

'I'm looking for Guy Fowle.'

'Yeah,' she says. 'You've told me that before.'

She had been there outside Parliament with Jude in the immediate aftermath of the Westminster bomb, and a grenade fragment wounded her in the subsequent fire-fight. 'Why haven't you found him yet?'

'I'm trying.'

'So what are you bothering me for?'

'We believe that Candida Taunton, an ex-girlfriend of his, is on the run with him.'

'I refer you to my previous statement.'

'She's an addict.'

'Okay, that's more promising. What's her drug of choice?'

'Heroin,' Jude replies. 'She's going to need to score at some point soon.'

'Send me her bio and a photo. I'll put the word out.'

Jude is about to say thank you but she's cut the connection. He sighs and looks at Gretchen.

'You have an interesting family,' she says.

'People say that.' He realises to his shame that he knows nothing about Gretchen's family. And now it would be too awkward to ask. 'I'm going to have a shower.'

Ten minutes later he is standing in front of the video wall. Gretchen has highlighted four locations on a map like stars in a constellation: Woolwich Crown Court, the Chelsea house, Candida Taunton's flat and Mr Roxy's Pet Food.

'We need to identify the car that they were using,' Jude says.

'The police are reviewing camera footage in the vicinity of Candida's flat and Levi Minkin's warehouse.'

Rosanna calls.

'Good morning,' she says. 'Did you sleep okay?'

He decides not to share the details of his nightmare. 'Yes, thank you.'

'Have you heard from Yulia?'

He hears what he thinks is a small child burbling in the background and feels a stab of envy. 'Not yet.'

'Are you sure we'll hear from her again?'

'I am.'

'Okay,' she says and he's grateful for the lack of scepticism in her voice.

# 31

## It's hard to be a Chechen

Ruslan Dudayev is sitting in the shadow of a tree with deep pink flowers. It's going to be a sunny day and the park is busy. Everyone around him is busy tapping and swiping, each with the world in their palm and yet oblivious all the same. He has a coffee in a reusable cup in one huge hand and a massive vape with a pistol-grip in the other. With each exhalation, he billows apple-flavoured smoke.

He is in London for the first time in six months and grateful that his arthritis is not giving him pain.

'Still waters are inhabited by devils,' Fowle says.

Ruslan had recognised Fowle the moment he sat down beside him on the bench and removed his sunglasses. He is impressed. He knows the legend of *al-Gharib* – the Stranger – the British psychopath who was too violent even for the Caliphate. Who killed so many British soldiers in Iraq and was then kept locked away in a mountain prison for more than ten years; who escaped at the end, and travelled on the migrant trail across Europe to his home country where he led the attack against the British Parliament.

'That's where the dog is buried,' Ruslan replies and with it feels the satisfaction of a task now within sight of its end. For nearly three years he has waited for this moment, living with the constant threat of assassination. Twice the FSB have tried to kill him. Twice they have failed but he bears the scars of the attempts: a knife wound that has left him with a limp and a face pock-marked from dioxin poisoning.

'The belly is full but the eyes are hungry,' Fowle says.

Across the park, Millennials in gym gear and tabards do squats for an off-duty army physical training instructor.

*And so, it begins . . .*

'I know your face from the news,' Ruslan says. Guy Fowle's intense gaze staring out across the Woolwich courtroom in the seconds before the attack. No hint of what was to come but the suggestion of a smile on his face. 'The papers say you are amused by your own villainy.'

Fowle does not appear to take offence. 'I'm amused by my adversary's incompetence and lack of imagination,' he replies.

'That is our strength, I think,' Ruslan says, 'you and I. That we have imagination.'

He does not believe that Guy Fowle is an instrument of the Russian state any more than he believes that he himself is or ever was its loyal servant. There is a part of him that would like to know how Fowle came by the passwords, to satisfy his curiosity, but it's not necessary. Once the words have been exchanged there is no going back. That is the only rule of Grom. He has money in Panama and he assumes that there is more in the bag that Fowle has put down between them. He has his own extraction route that is known to no one but himself.

He's waited long enough. It's time to do the job and leave.

'Are your believers ready?'

'They are ready,' Ruslan says. 'They are straining at the leash.'

Since their return from Syria, he has moved them from safe house to safe house to keep them hidden from the security services. He has prevented them from speaking with their families or going anywhere near social media. He has cooked for them and gone down on his painful knees to pray with them. He has kept them fit and physically strong. He has nursed them through homesickness and self-doubt, motivating them with talk of their crucial role in the coming Armageddon. He thinks he probably knows them better than their own mothers.

'They are impatient for the end times,' Ruslan says. 'The attack in Westminster inflamed them.'

'Now is their time,' Guy says.

On a visceral level, Ruslan has always found it hard to imagine why anyone would willingly blow themselves up. And yet he has persuaded countless people to do that very thing – in Chechnya, Iraq and Afghanistan. He has sent men and women – zealots and nihilists, the disenfranchised and dispossessed, on foot and by car, blinkered and open-eyed – into oblivion. He has watched the billowing clouds of detonations and felt the satisfaction of watching pawns sacrificed in a larger geopolitical game that they would never, in a million years, understand.

'Is my money in the bag?' he asks.

'It is. And a passport.'

He inclines his head in gratitude though he has no need for the passport. 'Thank you.'

'Will they perform their tasks?' Guy asks.

It would be foolish to promise that not one of them will hesitate when the time comes. No one really knows what's in the mind of a suicide bomber in the seconds before they trip the switch. All of them are traumatised and the youngest, Saif, is more damaged than the others. Who can tell if paralysis may come over them at the final moment? But Ruslan has done everything he can to prepare them for the end.

'Enough will,' he says. 'I just need the target list.'

Guy nods. 'I'll text it to you.'

Ruslan nods and sucks on his vape. He would dearly love to know Fowle's endgame but he knows better than to ask. He exhales a cloud.

'When?'

'The answer is in the wind,' Fowle replies.

Ruslan watches a brindle Staffordshire bull terrier pulling a young woman across the grass. 'I'll move my people to new locations,' he says. 'Places that only I know. We don't want any outside interference.'

'That's wise.'

Ruslan is pleased to see that they understand each other.

Fowle hands him a burner.

'I'll message you on this,' he says. 'Destroy the phone that I messaged you on before.'

'Of course.'

Fowle stands and replaces his sunglasses.

'Do you need anything else?' Ruslan asks.

'I'm good.' Guy strides away.

# 32

# Grom

The dacha is forty kilometres east of Moscow. A two-storey metal-roofed house with rust stains stretching from the gutters to the ground, sitting at the centre of a natural clearing in the forest.

Yulia parks the rental car at the iron gate that always used to be open and walks the rest of the way along a neglected track with grass growing up through it. In the distance, above the wall of birches and firs she can see low mountains ground down by ancient glaciers against a colourless sky.

The door is opened by an old woman that she barely recognises. It is the General's wife, Svetlana. Her face is a mass of wrinkles brightened only by a slash of bright pink lipstick.

Svetlana scowls at her: many years may have passed but it seems that she has no difficulty recognising Yulia. 'Have you come to help look after him?'

'I'd just like to speak with him.'

'I thought not.' In a fit of jealousy, Svetlana had once tried to run Yulia down with a car in a Moscow street. 'He's sleeping, you'll have to wait.'

'Can I come in?'

'I suppose so,' Svetlana says, grudgingly. She shuffles ahead of Yulia through the gloomy house to the General's study. It is much as Yulia remembers it, the parquet floor decorated with an Afghan rug acquired in the raid on the presidential palace in Kabul that started the ten-year Soviet occupation. The shelves of books and on the wall directly opposite the desk a locked metal cabinet that guards his greatest treasure.

'He keeps the key with him at all times,' Svetlana tells her. 'He knows I'd sell it given the chance. Sit down.'

Yulia sits in one of the lumpy armchairs facing the desk and Svetlana shuffles out without offering her anything. There was a time when the dacha was off-limits to his wife, and Yulia and the General used to roam the surrounding forest in nothing but boots or snow shoes. She remembers the laughter and the startling cold in her nipples and thighs.

When he finally appears in the doorway, Alexei the General looks as old and weathered as Russia itself. She rises and they kiss, three times on the cheeks in the traditional way. He smells of camphor and soap.

'You don't look any different,' he says, holding her at arm's length. He's well into his eighties but there is still strength in his large, gnarled hands. 'Age cannot wither her nor custom stale her infinite variety.'

'In London anything is possible,' she laughs, 'for a price.'

He lets go of her and crosses to the desk, taking a set of keys from his pocket. His hands shake slightly as he unlocks a drawer in the desk and takes out a bottle of Old Kenigsberg brandy.

'If I don't keep it locked away, she drinks it. And then she breaks things.. She was never a very likeable drunk. The glasses are over there.'

Yulia fetches them from the sideboard and when she turns, she sees that he has pushed the keys across the desk towards her.

'Open it.'

She unlocks the metal cabinet and opens the doors.

The seventeenth-century icon once belonged to his namesake Alexei, only son of Emperor Nicholas II, the last heir to the Imperial Russian throne, who was shot by the Bolsheviks in 1918. Gesso on wood decorated with gold filigree, it depicts the Metropolitan of Moscow, the spiritual head of the Russian Orthodox Church.

They sit and drink and stare at it. He has never revealed how he acquired it but as with the rug, she suspects that force was involved and people died, possibly in large numbers. Still, it is beautiful. Priceless. And it could so easily have been destroyed in the revolution.

'That bloody fool of a Patriarch was on the television yesterday telling us yet again that we are approaching the terrible reckoning spoken of in the Book of Revelation,' Alexei says.

'Maybe he's right,' Yulia says.

Alexei snorts. 'What's got into you?'

'Tell me about Troshev?'

'He's a thug, fit to command a brigade and nothing higher, like that fool you married.'

'You were taken.'

He laughs and shakes his head. 'You had a lucky escape. I don't see you as a nursemaid to a geriatric who can't zip himself up after a piss.'

'Valery's dead.'

His face creases into a frown. 'I'm sorry.'

'I'm not. How close is Troshev to the president?'

'He's useful,' Alexei says, after a pause. 'The president likes to conduct war by other means. His little green men in Donetsk, Caracas and Benghazi. Because he's not a government employee, Troshev gives the president a fig leaf of plausible deniability.'

'What is Grom?'

He pauses. She's caught him off guard. Suddenly, he is guarded and suspicious. 'Why do you want to know about Grom?'

'It's been stolen.'

Alexei is aghast. 'What?'

'You heard me.'

'Who stole it?'

'A sociopath with an apocalyptic worldview stole it from one of Troshev's henchmen.'

Alexei shakes his head. 'It can't be.' He looks at her, fearfully. 'Then maybe the Patriarch is right after all.'

'Tell me what it is,' she presses him.

He turns back to the icon. 'It's a state secret. I could be shot for telling you.'

'I promise you that a lot more people are going to die if you don't tell me.'

She watches while he finishes his brandy and pours another.

'Grom was designed as an insurance policy,' he says, eventually.

'Against what?'

'A lack of time.'

'What do you mean?'

'The Americans have more than eight hundred and fifty ground- and sea-based nuclear warheads aimed at us. Moscow alone lies in the bore sights of more than a hundred warheads.'

'We have our own warheads. Our own deterrent.'

'But our early warning network is decrepit and our infra-red satellites and ground-based radars are not fit for purpose. No one makes the parts any more. We face twenty-first-century threats with 1970s technology. Satellite launches, missile tests, fighter jets taking off on after-burners, and even wildfires trigger the system on a daily basis. We're at the mercy of false alarms. Our no-more-than-averagely intelligent president has less than three minutes to decide whether it's a false alarm or hundreds of warheads travelling towards us at four miles a second.'

'So?'

'Six years ago, the Foreign Intelligence Service was instructed to create an autonomous operating system for a network of illegals embedded in key utilities in the West. The software would enable a rapid and coordinated cascade of malware attacks targeted at the infrastructure that underpins Western economies. It was designed to be activated in circumstances in which an attack on the homeland was deemed an imminent likelihood.'

'What possible circumstances are those?'

He gives her a self-righteous look. 'A narcissist in the White House, for instance. First strike is still an official American option, Yulia.'

'If it was the SVR's project, what is it doing in the hands of Valkyrie mercenaries?'

'We weren't happy with the lack of safeguards. Why do you think I'm stuck out here and not in Moscow? The design specifications required that it be immune to any attempt by counter forces to seek to thwart it once activated.'

'What counter forces?'

'You should not underestimate the paranoia of our president.'

'And so, you refused to do it?'

'Nobody refuses the president. Not if they want to live. Instead, we stalled in the hope that his attention would be diverted by some other crisis. We created problems and compounded errors. It was a huge undertaking involving existing embedded sleeper agents and more recently coerced or co-opted assets. We hoped to make it impossible to achieve. But the president wasn't having any of it. After three years, he grew impatient and eventually he took it away from us.'

She shakes her head in disbelief. 'And he gave it to Troshev?'

'No, he gave it to the GRU.'

'And they gave it to Troshev?'

'You seem to know more about that than I do,' he replies. 'I was sidelined. Made to retire.'

'Make an educated guess,' she snaps.

He pours himself another brandy, his large hands shaking slightly. When he offers the bottle to Yulia she refuses.

'Troshev was useful to the GRU,' Alexei says, putting the bottle down. 'In the Ukraine, Valkyrie built a network of skilled hackers, mostly criminals and deviants, that the GRU envied but also kept at arm's length. If the GRU wanted to build the operating system for Grom quickly and with deniability, then perhaps yes, they would go to Troshev.'

'And damn the consequences?'

'Yes, damn the consequences.'

'So, what do I do now?'

Alexei stares at her. 'You have to speak to the president.'

# 33

## The reconquest

There's a poster on the door of the club advertising ten fights tonight, three rounds each. Guy Fowle hammers on the door with his fist and stands back. The black painted wall of the single-story building stretches without windows to the street corner.

A large barrel-shaped skinhead with powerfully muscled arms opens the door and stares at him and the bag in his hand, before surveying the street behind him.

'I came alone,' Guy says, 'as arranged.'

The skinhead steps back, allowing him to enter.

Inside there is an octagonal mixed martial arts ring and a bar that runs the length of the room with a bored-looking woman in a bikini top behind it. In the ring a wiry, bare-chested man wearing finger-less gloves is striking blows against the punch mitts of another man to the accompaniment of the kind of portentous music that features in Cosmo's first-person-shooter games. Guy sees that there are two more men sitting in a booth on a leather banquette watching them. On the wall closest to the ring there is a yellow and black sign that says *Stop Grooming Girls, British Girls Matter*. On the other walls there are posters with slogans that say *Harden your hearts and sharpen your swords* and *One of you is worth any number of them*.

The music stops.

'Put the bag down and take two steps to one side,' says a man from the booth. 'Got your gloves on, Jon?'

The skinhead holds his hands up to show he is wearing black leather gloves.

'Open the bag, mate,' the man says.

The skinhead kneels, draws the zip the length of the bag and turns back the flap.

'Fuck me,' he says, looking inside. 'You should see this, boss.'

The bare-chested man walks out of the ring towards them, removing his gloves. There is a runic SS sign tattooed on his chest. He looks down at the white phosphorus grenades in the bag and up at Guy.

'I recognise you,' Tommy says. 'You're Guy Fowle. The lone wolf.'

'And you're Tommy Shield.'

According to Grom, Tommy is a former member of National Action, a banned neo-Nazi group.

'Take your clothes off,' Tommy says.

Guy strips naked and stands with his legs parted and his arms hanging loosely at his sides while Jon searches his clothes for a wire. If the intention is to make Guy feel vulnerable it does not have the anticipated effect.

'No phone,' Jon says. 'No weapons.'

'Still waters are inhabited by devils,' Guy says.

'Your elbow is close,' Tommy replies, 'yet you can't bite it.'

'The belly is full but the eyes are hungry.'

They are both smiling now.

'Follow me,' Tommy says and leads him to the occupied booth. One of the men there is slim with preppy clothes and a side parting and the other has a meaty build and a pallid complexion. He is wearing a White Rex T-shirt with crossed hammers on it that barely contains his gut. Tommy and Guy sit opposite each other, trapping the other two between them in the semi-circular booth.

'You struck a blow for the race war that will soon engulf Britain,' Tommy says, loudly enough that everyone in the room can hear him. 'I admire you for that. Killing all them fat, greedy Jews in the House of Lords and making the Muslims take the fall for it.' His eyes are gleaming. 'This may surprise you but I tell my boys to read the Koran and to learn from ISIS, their propaganda and their structure and strategies. You know why? Tell him, Renfield.'

The preppy one with the side parting leans forward with his hands clasped together and speaks earnestly, 'Because we need our own white jihadis for the reconquest. We need our own spectacular attack. The sort that makes the world stand still and take notice. Only then can we can stop the great replacement and make our country white again.'

According to Grom, Renfield is a paedophile, a habitué of child-grooming sites, though his compatriots do not know it.

'Jess, bring us four lagers,' Tommy calls out. He drums his fingers on the table-top. 'What is it you want from us, Mr Fowle? Will it be spectacular? I do hope so.'

'It will,' Guy tells him. 'Soon the city will grind to a halt. The police will be helpless and your enemies unprotected. That's your opportunity. Check your PayPal account.'

Tommy snatches a phone off the table and swipes through the screens before pressing the app. He whistles under his breath.

'That's a lot of money.'

'Payment for your foot soldiers,' Guy tells him. 'Withdraw the cash as soon as you can. On my word, I want you to firebomb mosques and synagogues. Also shopping centres and petrol stations, places that your enemies work or congregate. I'll send you a list.'

The barmaid arrives with a tray full of tall glasses of Hungarian lager. In addition to the bikini top, she is wearing tight denim shorts and three-inch heels. She puts beer mats branded *'Reconquista will make Europe great again'* down and the glasses on top of them.

'Anything else, Tommy?' she says.

'No, that's sweet, Jess.'

The pallid man beside Guy leans forward to watch the sway of her ass as she walks back to the bar. His name is Miller and according to Grom he is not what he seems.

They clink glasses and Miller takes a long gulp before putting his glass down in front of him.

'There'll be children in those places,' he says, hesitantly.

'Vermin are vermin,' Renfield replies.

'It's total war,' Tommy agrees. 'We can't afford to be squeamish.'

Guy puts a companionable arm around Miller's shoulders. 'Exactly.'

Miller shifts uneasily.

'When will we know to strike?' Tommy asks.

'Forty-eight hours from now. You'll know because everything will be fucked.'

Tommy nods. 'It's tight but feasible. We'll get word out and distribute the grenades.'

'Good.'

'Is there anything else?'

'As long as there have been fascist parties in Britain, they've had spies inside them,' Guy says. He strikes, pulling the top of Miller's head back with one hand to extend the neck vertebrae and twisting his jaw sideways with the other hand until they snap.

He lets go and Miller's head strikes the table.

'Wow!' Tommy says, sitting back in his seat.

'He was a police officer,' Guy explains. He slides up out of the booth and saunters over to his clothes with everyone watching him. He starts to get dressed. Ordinarily, Guy wouldn't give the time of day to Tommy or the scum around him. For all their talk of total war, he can see that they lack the discipline for real fighting. Not like the Chechen and his carefully nurtured jihadis. But if Guy's plan is to work, it must be given a nudge. Destroying London's infrastructure and bringing the city to its knees is not enough: the British public are too docile, too easily curfewed and too eager to heed the smack of firm government. They must be goaded into civil unrest. And that's where Tommy comes in. If nothing else, his men can be relied upon to lob a few grenades through a few selected doorways in return for cash.

While he is buttoning his shirt, Guy says, 'Don't worry about the body. Soon the city will be full of them.'

# 34

## All cats are black in the dark

Jakub Wojick's day starts much like any other with a cup of tea. It's brought to him by his wife Rachel, who is still in her pharmacist's white coat. With her is their eldest son, little John, fresh from primary school. It's his namesake big John, Rachel's father, who always says, 'It's a well-known fact that a good cup of tea can make a morning, on these shores at least.'

That last bit for Jakub, his Polish son-in-law.

'You don't have a monopoly on tea,' Jakub always tells him. 'Poles have been drinking tea for hundreds of years.' It's a ritual like the tea-drinking itself. He likes tea. Even when it's not morning but afternoon, and he's on night shift. And he likes to be woken up by his eldest son's smiling gap-toothed face.

Coffee will come later when he is in the control room.

'How's Abel?'

Their youngest is named for Jakub's father. Little John and Little Abel.

'He's asleep in the hall,' Rachel says.

Jakub imagines him still harnessed in the car seat, mouth open and eyes closed, exhausted by nursery.

'I'll get the dinner on,' Rachel says, shooing little John out after her.

Fifteen minutes later, Jakub comes down the stairs, freshly showered. In the kitchen/dining room of their modern home, Rachel is sitting beside the high chair acceding to Abel's idiosyncratic eating choices. Tonight, it's strawberries and cubes of salami. John is blowing on a piece of fish finger.

He stares longingly at his wife's glass of wine on the countertop. One more night in the control room and then three nights off when he can have a drink.

Unexpectedly, his phone rings in his pocket.

*Unknown.*

Probably a cold caller asking if he's been in a recent road traffic accident. He answers and an unaccented English voice says, 'Still waters are inhabited by devils.'

Earth-shattering silence.

He steps out of the kitchen and into the small snug where he keeps a desk, and his framed degree certificates on the wall. He closes the door and leans against it.

The voice repeats its message. 'Still waters are inhabited by devils.'

When the words come it is as if by rote. He says, 'All cats are black in the dark.'

'The belly is full but the eyes are hungry.'

The call ends. Jakub can feel the weight of gravity pressing him down the door to the carpet. He nearly gives in. But he knows if he does that, he will never get up again. Instead he returns to the kitchen, where Rachel furrows her brows. 'You look like you've seen a ghost.'

'Family trouble,' he says.

'Your father?'

'No, one of my cousins.' He has many cousins, unruly types from the south-eastern corner of Poland near the border with Belarus. A place so undistinguished that he has successfully persuaded her that it is not worth visiting.

'Will you have to go back?' she asks. She doesn't like him to be away.

'Maybe. Let's hope not.' He summons a smile. 'What's for dinner?'

Later, after the kids are asleep and not long before he goes to work, they make love. She is getting ready for bed. Going through the nightly ritual of cleansing and moisturising. He takes her by the hand and leads her to the bed. There is an urgency to his love-making that surprises and delights her.

'What's got into you?' she says, afterwards.

He stares at the ceiling.

It's hard to imagine that he will never see her again.

★    ★    ★

Jakub is walking from his front door to the car when an unfamiliar teenager swoops past on a bicycle and throws a package at his feet. It is a padded manila envelope with a USB stick inside. He pockets the stick and puts the envelope in the wheelie bin.

After that, it's a short drive to the oil depot. On a clear day you can see the industrial ranks of storage tanks from the house. Usually he listens to the radio, not tonight though.

He's waved through the barrier and parks in the duty supervisor's parking bay. He uses a regular swipe card to enter the main headquarters and the combination of a code and the card to enter the control room.

He conducts a brief handover with the day supervisor, assiduously shakes hands with the two night-shift operators and assumes his position at the command console. From the console with its eleven flat-panel monitors, allowing him to run multiple software applications, Jakub is responsible for one of the largest oil depots in the UK storing petrol, kerosene and aviation fuel with pipelines to Humberside, Merseyside, and Heathrow and Gatwick airports radiating from it.

At ten thirty p.m. the terminal's gates are closed and from his seat he checks the levels in the sixty functioning storage tanks. Unleaded petrol is still flowing into three of the tanks at a rate of nine hundred cubic metres per hour from a refinery at the mouth of the Thames.

Nothing out of the ordinary.

Except the stick in his pocket. He knows that it contains a computer worm that will infect and update computers across the company's network while preventing detection of its presence. The main payload of the attack will make the gauges indicate an unchanging level in the fuel storage tanks while they're still filling, and at the same time override the emergency switches which should detect that the tanks are full and automatically shut off the supply.

It's the moment that he was trained for. Five years he has waited. In that time, he has carefully solidified his cover. He has married and had two beautiful English boys, John and Abel.

Rachel wants another child and although she will never say it out loud, he knows she would love to have a girl. They have made friends; people that would describe him as quiet and self-contained but kindly. His work colleagues will say that he was not given to joining in with the usual banter in the control room but not against it either.

His name is not Jakub. He's not really Polish and his father's name is not Abel. He is Russian and he has another wife in Rostov and by cruel coincidence two boys. They are older and they miss their father. The only time he gets to see them is on remedial 'family' visits to Poland, when he slips quietly across the border into Belarus and from there to Russia.

If he inserts the USB stick, he will be reunited with them. If he does not, he will undoubtedly be killed.

When conversation between the operators turns to the televised statement by the Prime Minster that afternoon, accusing criminal associates of the Russian president of being behind the attack at Woolwich Crown Court, he inserts the stick. Within two hours of inserting it, the three tanks start to overflow. Hundreds of tonnes of fuel spill out through the roof vents. Much of it evaporates, creating a thick fuel-air vapour that rolls out amongst the other tanks and over the containment walls, trapped by an inversion layer of warmer air above.

As the minutes tick by without anyone realising what is happening, he becomes increasingly agitated. It is his patriotic duty. It is what he is trained for. But somehow, he never expected this to actually happen.

At three thirty a.m., with the cloud of vapour several metres deep, Sanjip, one of the shift operators says, 'It's getting really foggy out there, boss.'

Jakub opens a narrow drawer and takes out a sharpened pencil. He walks over to the operator's console with the pencil held tightly in his fist. He looks over Sanjip's shoulder at the CCTV footage: the blurred sodium lights and indistinct shapes of the tanks. He counts the seconds, waiting for comprehension to come.

'Shit,' Sanjip breathes. 'We've got a leak . . .'

Jakub clamps his left hand over Sanjip's mouth and with his right he stabs him in the eye with the pencil, driving it deep into his skull.

He steps back from the shuddering body and looks right.

Michelle, the other night-shift operator, is staring at him with her mouth open. He should kill her too. But she's pregnant. It's only been a week since her first ultrasound scan.

'Fly away, little bird,' he tells her.

Jolted into action she runs for the door. He lets her go. He hopes that she will find somewhere to take cover but it seems unlikely.

He should be running too. There is a carefully planned extraction route: a safe house on the Essex coastline and a waiting submarine. Instead, he returns to his console and rings Rachel to wake her.

'Jakub?' she says, sleepily.

'I'm so sorry, darling.'

'What is it, Jakub?'

'You have to put the boys in the car and drive north on the motorway. Right now, darling. They're fine in their pyjamas. Best you go right now. You're not safe.'

'You're frightening me, Jakub.'

'Do what I say. Promise me you'll just go.'

'I don't understand.'

'I love you. Goodbye.'

He switches off his phone.

A few minutes later he watches on one of the monitors as two police cars with flashing lights pull up at the front gate. The barrier is swiftly raised and the cars accelerate towards the main building.

Jakub watches Michelle running through the petrol fumes towards them.

# 35

## Candy and Guy

They watch the explosion from the grassy ramparts of a stone-age fort ten miles away. Even at that distance they recoil from the blast wave and feel the wash of heat on their faces.

'Wow!' Cosmo says, mesmerised.

Guy smiles indulgently with his arm around Candy's waist, and she kisses him hungrily. It's better than any firework display. For half an hour they stay where they are, Candy's head resting on Guy's shoulder, watching huge bursts of fire erupting in the sky.

'Now the Russians will definitely come,' Guy says.

'That excites you?' she says, searching his face.

'It increases the stakes for everyone.'

'How many more things are we going to destroy?'

'We've only just started,' Guy says. 'Come on. We need more weapons.'

They walk back down the path from the fort to the car park, their way lit up by the ongoing explosions. In the car, Cosmo pulls a coat over his head and, within minutes, is snoring noisily.

'Adenoids,' Candy says, rolling her eyes.

'He did well tonight,' Guy says.

'He wants to impress you,' she says. 'It's only natural. You're his father.'

They sit in silence as Guy navigates narrow lanes that rise gently through pale moon-lit beech woodlands to a chalk escarpment.

'When I shared at meetings, I used to tell the room that Cosmo's father was dead,' Candy says, when the silence gets too much for her. 'But I never believed it. I always thought you were alive somewhere and that I'd see you again. That you'd meet our son. I prayed for it to my higher power.'

'When the job is done, we can go somewhere far away,' Guy tells her. 'Somewhere safe. Just the three of us. We'll be rich and no one will be able to touch us.'

'I want a garden in the tropics,' she says, 'with orchids and two green parrots.'

'A view of the ocean,' he says, genially.

'Yes,' she says, eagerly. 'I'll get clean and do yoga every day at dawn and then we'll swim in the sea.'

'I'll teach Cosmo how to hunt.'

'I want that so much.'

Guy is careful to disguise his true intentions from her. He knows how important these ludicrous daydreams are to bolster her sense of gnawing self-doubt. For now, he'll keep up the pretence.

'We've got a lot of work to do before we can go away,' he tells her.

'I'm with you all the way,' she says. 'Whatever you need.'

They continue driving south-west across the ridgeline, avoiding main roads, driving through medieval flint-walled villages, following the remnants of an Iron Age trackway. There's only one woman that he would take with him to a secret hideaway. Setting aside the fact that he killed her husband and her grandfather, he has no idea if she is even alive.

He should find her, he thinks. When this is over.

Eventually, they join the motorway heading south-east.

Cosmo sits up and rubs his face.

'Where are we going?' he asks.

'London.'

Not long before dawn, Guy follows a fox across a park in Shoreditch, giving a wide berth to a group of youths standing under a street lamp with knotted trainers hanging from it. He goes through a graffitied concrete underpass and across waste ground hemmed in by barbed steel railings and overrun with thickets of buddleia. He crosses a red-brick footbridge, the sides of which have been raised with corrugated iron. The fox trots past a stocky, thick-set man wearing a baseball cap who hands Guy two reassuringly heavy black holdalls, and in return accepts a sealed envelope containing Scary Bear's phone.

Back at the car, Guy places the holdalls in the boot beside the other two. He unzips them and looks inside. One of them contains two modern AK-12 rifles and two PL-15 pistols both manufactured by Kalashnikov Concerns. There are suppressors for the pistols and paper cartons of 5.56mm and 9mm small arms ammunition. The other holdall has four disposable Russian-made rocket launchers, two with armour-piercing warheads and two with incendiary warheads.

Satisfied, he takes out a pistol and suppressor and one of the boxes of 9mm ammunition. Back in the car he hands the empty magazine and ammunition to Cosmo and tells him to fill it.

An hour later, they park in the shadow of one of four high-rise council-owned tower blocks in South London. Accessing the electoral register, Guy has identified a single-occupancy flat near the top floor. The lifts are out of order and they climb the stairs, Guy and Cosmo carrying two holdalls each.

On the sixteenth floor, they go down a narrow corridor between rows of doors and near the end Cosmo and Guy position themselves either side of a door with the bags beside them. Guy has a suppressed pistol in one hand. Candy stands in front of the door and presses the buzzer.

They hear feet shuffling towards them inside.

The door opens on a chain and an elderly woman's pinched face peers out through the narrow gap between the door and the frame.

'What is it?'

'Is that Mrs Beattie?'

'Yes,' the woman says, timidly.

'I'm Candida, from social services.'

'You're not the normal girl.'

'She's off sick,' Candy says. 'Are you going to let me in?'

'I don't know if I should.'

Guy steps in front of Candy, sticks the pistol in the gap and pulls the trigger. The noise of the shot is muted. The woman hits the carpet with a louder thump. Using the bolt cutters, Guy snaps the chain and they are in.

Stepping over the woman's body they go through into a living room shaded by lace curtains. There is a door that leads out onto a balcony with geraniums growing in window boxes on the ledge. From the balcony, there is an unobstructed view of the east tower.

Guy sits in a plastic chair and puts the holdall down beside him. Candy lights a cigarette.

'What are we waiting for?' she asks.

'We're going to take a look at the opposition,' he says. 'I'm guessing there'll be fireworks. Why don't you get some sleep while we wait?'

'Okay.'

'Can I watch the television?' Cosmo asks.

'Sure,' Guy tells him. He unzips the holdall and takes out the transit pack containing the two RPO-Z rocket launchers with the incendiary warheads. He unclips a tube and lifts it to his shoulder. With one hand on the fore-grip and the other on the trigger, he looks through the optical sight at the east tower.

Presently he can hear the sounds of detonations from the oil depot on the television news and Cosmo's excited commentary.

'We did that! Fucking, yeah!'

Then silence.

'Dad?'

Guy carefully puts down the rocket launcher. He steps into the living room, where pictures of the three of them are displayed on the screen.

## 36

## Fighting the fire

Cabinet Office Briefing Room A is as full as Gabriel has ever seen it. He is sitting to the right of the Prime Minister with the Cabinet Secretary on the PM's left. Beside Gabriel are the Foreign Secretary and the Home Secretary, and other assorted ministers. Facing them, on the other side of the table, is what the PM's special adviser dismissively refers to as the 'Blancmange' – senior members of the civil service, the police and the security services.

For everyone else, it's standing room only.

On one of the screens, the Chief Fire Officer for the county is briefing from a Gold command centre hastily established eighteen miles from the seat of the explosion in the headquarters of the local constabulary. On the screens either side of him, rolling straplines on muted news channels are reporting the initial detonation as the largest explosion in Europe since the Second World War.

Angry Bear's judgement on Fowle is ringing in Gabriel's ears, *'Frankly speaking, I think he's going to fuck everything.'*

Forty fire engines, plus twenty support vehicles and more than three hundred firefighters are on the scene, tackling the blaze. Assets from sixteen regional fire brigades are assisting. Gabriel is finding it hard not be mesmerised by the images of the fire, its flames a hundred feet high, and the fresh explosions each time a new tank goes up. A plume of smoke, visible across the whole of south-east England, has risen nine thousand feet in the air.

'We're requesting extra foam supplies from all across the UK,' the Chief Fire Officer says. 'But we are going to need more.'

'We've already put in a request to the French and the Dutch, Prime Minister,' says the Minister for Fire and Resilience in the apologetic tone reserved for Anglo-European cooperation these days.

'How long before the fire is out?' the Prime Minister asks, ashen faced.

'It's too early to tell,' the Chief Fire Officer says. 'Every time another tank goes up, I have to withdraw my firefighters.'

'How many tanks are left?'

'Twenty-seven.'

He explains that the public exclusion area has been widened twice already and now includes the M1 motorway, the main arterial route north from London which usually carries more than a hundred thousand vehicles per day.

'Give me an estimate,' the Prime Minister demands.

'Forty-eight hours at least before it's under control and we can begin to think about opening the motorway.'

'And casualties?'

'Provisionally, we believe that as many as a hundred people were killed in the initial blast and thousands wounded. But we won't know for sure until we have the fire under control.'

'Bloody hell!' the Prime Minister says.

'The hospital closest to the seat of the explosion was evacuated and casualties have been distributed across five hospitals in neighbouring counties. Because it happened in the early hours, the industrial park adjacent to the terminal complex was largely empty, otherwise the immediate death toll would have been much higher.'

'That's something to be thankful for,' the Prime Minister says with characteristically misplaced bravado.

'Of course, Prime Minister,' the Home Secretary Mobina Sinha says, at her most oleaginous. 'Unfortunately, the industrial park contained major delivery depots for DHL, DPD and Amazon. All have been completely destroyed. Worse still, it included the national data centre and its cloud services platform. That means the loss of the single largest IT services provider to the public sector.'

'And the consequences of that?'

'The websites for the Department of Work and Pensions, HMRC and the NHS are all down,' the head of the National Cyber Security Centre explains. 'That means no universal credit or pension payments, no tax and no hospital operations or screening results. In addition to that, the websites of most of the political parties and the terrestrial news channels are down. In summary, large portions of the domestic web have disappeared.'

'Whose bright idea was it to put the national data centre next to an oil terminal?' says Maurice Hermon, the PM's special adviser.

'Frankly speaking, Prime Minister,' Mobina Sinha says, 'the impact is worse than a full-on cyber-war.'

The bear had said, *'a series of events that will have a negative impact on your national economy.'*

'Gabriel?' the Prime Minister says.

*It's all coming true!*

'Gabriel!'

'The Securities and Exchange Commission suspended trading on the stock exchange before it opened,' Gabriel replies, hurriedly, 'but we're already taking a hit on the currency markets in Asia.'

'How long can we keep the stock exchange closed?'

'Under section twelve of the Securities Exchange Act, the SEC can suspend trading for up to ten days to protect investors.'

'Surely to God we don't need ten days?'

'That depends whether there are further attacks to come,' Evan Calthorp says, 'and how we respond.'

Unnerved, and unwilling to engage with him yet, the PM looks down the table at the Transport Secretary. 'What about Heathrow and Gatwick?'

'Both have run out of fuel, Prime Minister. The airlines are diverting flights to regional airports where feasible but their fuel stocks are limited and a large number of flights are being cancelled.'

'I'm talking to the CEOs of the major airlines after this meeting,' Gabriel says. He is expecting an earful and the usual demand for a bailout. They are furious that so many of their planes are grounded. 'And the Petroleum Industry Association.'

Another earful.

The news channels are already reporting cancelled flights at the nation's airports and lines of cars queueing at gas stations in anticipation of parts of the country running out of fuel.

Finally, the Prime Minister looks at Calthorp.

'And you're sure that this was a deliberate act of sabotage?'

'Yes, Prime Minister.'

'You had better tell me about it.'

'I'd like to clear the room first,' Calthorp says.

The Prime Minister stares at him without understanding his meaning.

'For reasons of national security,' growls Gavin Samson, the head of Counter Terrorism Command.

The Prime Minister nods, grimly.

All that Gabriel can think is, *What about the water?*

# 37

## Ship in a bottle

It's a small, tense group that gathers around the conference table.

'The duty supervisor was a man named Jakub Wojick, originally from Poland,' Gavin Samson tells them, his large red face barely containing his outrage. 'As far as we can tell, he's a clean skin. Married with two children. According to the company's human resources database, he holds a Master's in chemical engineering from the Faculty of Drilling Oil and Gas at the University of Science and Technology in Krakow. He moved here five years ago and has been employed at the oil terminal throughout that time with consistently favourable performance appraisals. One year ago, he was promoted to shift supervisor.'

'What exactly happened?' the Prime Minister asks.

'The size of the explosion suggests a major fuel oil leak over several hours,' the Chief Fire Officer replies.

'The only way for that to happen without tripping alarms at the company's national control centre is by the use of sophisticated rootkit malware,' the head of the National Cyber Security Centre says. 'Once inside the system the rootkit will have released its payload like a ship unfolding in a bottle, infecting the programmable logic controllers which act as an interface between physical machines like electrical switches and digital command signals. Because the control system is sealed, the malware would have had to be directly inserted into the control system, probably via a USB stick, and act autonomously thereafter.'

'And Wojick is the only one who could have done that?'

'Two 999 calls were received immediately before the explosion,' Gavin Samson says. 'The first was from one of the night-shift operators, who reported that Jakub Wojick had murdered the other duty operator in the control room. The second was from Wojick's wife, who had received a call from her husband telling her to drive their children far away as quickly as possible.'

The Prime Minister's eyes scan the table and settle on the head of MI6.

'We're talking to the Polish Internal Security Agency to confirm Wojick's identity,' Chuka says in response.

'And I've reached out to the Americans to help with identifying the malware and its source,' the head of the National Cyber Security Centre adds. 'They're sending a Tailored Access team from Darmstadt.'

'Let's not beat around the bush here,' Calthorp says. 'The malware was Russian and Wojick was a deep-cover Russian agent. A so-called illegal. We know they are the only other nation with the capacity to design the kind of malware used. They've been using Ukraine as a Petri dish for these kinds of attacks for years now. Be in no doubt, this represents a dramatic escalation. Frankly speaking, an act of war. In which case we need to explore options for retaliation.'

'You want to start a war?' Maurice Hermon says, incredulously.

'The Russian Ambassador assured me personally half an hour ago that the Russian state was not behind the attack,' Nigel Featherstone, the Foreign Secretary, says. 'He was absolutely adamant.'

'He would say that, wouldn't he?' Calthorp says. 'He's a liar.'

'Hang on,' Featherstone says.

'The Russians lie,' Calthorp says, witheringly. 'They regard disinformation as an entirely legitimate diplomatic tactic. Just as we do, if the circumstances warrant it. If you haven't worked that out, you haven't been paying attention.'

'If it's not the Russians, who the hell is behind the attacks?' the Prime Minister cuts in, before Featherstone can respond.

Nobody says anything for what seems like an age.

'I think it's Fowle,' says one of the intelligence officers who is standing with his back to the wall.

And everyone is staring at him. Gabriel remembers him from the COBRA meeting following Fowle's prison break.

'What makes you say that, Mr Lyon?' the Prime Minister asks.

'He's loose and he has motive.'

'And where's he getting the resources from?' Calthorp demands, angrily. 'You think he had Jacob Wojick in his contacts book?'

'I believe that he has a phone with him that belonged to a senior commander in PMC Valkyrie,' Jude Lyon replies, calmly. 'So yes, maybe he did. And maybe he has other similar contacts too. This may be the start of a campaign.'

'What do you mean?' Gabriel asks, though he's pretty sure he knows the answer.

'I mean that if Guy Fowle has stolen from Valkyrie the identities and means of activation of a network of Russian deep-cover assets in the UK, there is every reason to believe that he will activate them. If subsequent attacks resemble this one, then we need to consider the vulnerability of critical infrastructure including power, transportation, water, banking. All the highly complex machinery that we take for granted.'

*All the stuff that makes things tick,* Gabriel thinks while Jude pauses to let the gravity of his words sink in. He's glad that Jude mentioned the water. There's bottled water at the table, he really hopes they're all drinking bottled water.

'I've been warning you since I walked through the front door of Downing Street,' Maurice Hermon says, with a dismissive gesture across the table at the 'blancmange'.

'Oh, yes,' Calthorp says, scathingly. 'In your incomprehensible blog.'

Gabriel tried reading Hermon's blog once but Calthorp's right, it really is gobbledygook. A mishmash of terms like 'non-linearity' and 'controlled skids', all of it peppered with quotes from Bismarck and Clausewitz, like the ramblings of a pretentious sixth-form student.

'You've done fuck all to prepare for these kinds of system shocks,' Hermon snarls. 'You're a train wreck waiting to happen.'

'Gentlemen, please,' the Prime Minister says, turning to Jude. 'If you're right, Mr Lyon, you had better find Fowle quickly and stop him.'

'Yes, Prime Minister,' Jude replies.

'In the meantime, I want to see a list of options for a proportionate response if we establish that it was the Russians behind the attack.'

'It will be on your desk by lunchtime,' Calthorp tells the Prime Minister.

'Find Fowle and that phone.' the Prime Minister says, rising from the table. 'I have to brief the President of the United States in twenty minutes and after that the Secretary General of NATO.'

Gabriel rushes back to his office in the Treasury and tells his staff that he is not to be disturbed under any circumstances. He draws the curtain behind his desk before sitting and opening the laptop. He puts his earphones in and clicks on the question mark icon.

The screen ripples and fills with the face of Angry Bear.

'What the hell is on that phone?' Gabriel demands.

'I warned you that it was dangerous.'

There is something about the bear's expression that is infuriating.

'I thought it was a joke!' Gabriel says, practically shouting. 'I thought this whole bloody thing was a hoax.'

'I don't make jokes. And now you know that this is not a hoax.'

*This is all so bloody insane.* 'Fowle is really going to fuck everything?'

'Why wouldn't he?'

'Where is he?' Gabriel demands, plaintively. 'You must know.'

The bear stares at him.

'Perhaps,' the bear says, eventually. A thought bubble opens on the screen beside its head with a South Kensington address on it. 'The key code of this property was activated at an unscheduled time early yesterday morning. Fowle may be using it as a safe house.'

Gabriel looks at the address. 'What do you expect me to do with that?'

'Call it in,' the bear says and cuts the connection.

Gabriel stares at his desk and the piles of paper that he should be reading. The reassuring calls he should be making to foreign finance ministers and heads of international industries: *Nothing to worry about. UK PLC is resilient. We've weathered worse before. Keep calm and carry on. Blah, blah, blah …*

He slams the laptop shut, pulls out his earphones and closes his eyes.

It doesn't help.

With a worldweary sigh he reaches for his private phone and calls Xander.

'Gabe? That's pretty intense about the explosion, man. You guys must be really freaking out. You think it was Guy Fowle?'

'I need a burner phone,' Gabriel says, 'and something to disguise my voice.'

'Okay?'

'I need you to get me them and meet me in St James's Park. Now.'

'Right now?'

'Yes. It's a matter of national security!'

## 38

## Fail-deadly

Out on the street in Whitehall after the meeting has broken up, Jude sees five missed calls from Kirsty on his red-taped phone. It's no surprise if she's drawn a connection between Guy Fowle's escape and the oil terminal explosion. Deciding it's best to ignore them, he texts Yulia instead, on his yellow-taped phone:

It's not written in stone. You said it yourself. We don't have to be enemies.

He's convinced that Grom is a weapon, or at least a trigger for activating Russian illegals in the United Kingdom, and it is on the phone that is now in Fowle's hands. Only Yulia can confirm that and she has gone silent.

Rosanna joins him on the pavement. 'You know how to bring a room to a halt.'

'It needed saying.'

'Have you heard from Yulia yet?'

'No.'

He is still holding on to the hope that Yulia is trying to find out the truth about Grom and that's why she has gone to Moscow. And if she can't communicate with him, it's because it would put her in danger to do so.

'Walk with me,' Rosanna says. Together they head north on Whitehall to the edge of the army cordon. 'Do you really think Fowle is acting alone?'

'I can't be sure,' he says. 'But what's in this for the Russians?'

'They can smell blood in the water,' Calthorp says from immediately behind them where he has been eavesdropping. 'We're on our own, Europe is divided, the Americans are increasingly isolationist and Russia sees an opportunity. Fowle is just a convenient

182

tool, a means to achieve an end.' He steps past them, glances back at Rosanna and says, 'Best you don't get too entangled with Mr Lyon.'

They stop and watch as he passes through the concrete barricade and steps off the pavement onto Horse Guard's Avenue, raising his hand for an approaching taxi.

'Prick,' Rosanna says, under her breath.

'He wins no points for charm,' Jude concedes.

'It's also rather presumptuous.'

And suddenly, because his mind is prone to such tricks, entanglement is at the forefront of his thinking. She is striking, beautiful even, with her lustrous red hair. And it occurs to him that he wouldn't have to hide anything from her. It's a long time since he's been able to be completely open with someone, if you discount his shrink, with whom his main effort is directed towards the opposite – a concerted attempt to avoid revealing anything significant about himself. In many ways, Rosanna is exactly what he's been looking for; it's a bloody shame that Charlie Bevan got there first.

'I don't think he meant it literally,' he says, awkwardly.

'Really?' When she sees the look on his face, she laughs and rolls her eyes. 'Would you be more comfortable if we talked about work?'

'Definitely.'

They fall silent as they navigate the exit to the cordon, nodding to the armed police at the barricade.

'It's long been suspected but never proven that the GRU have a network of Russian illegals across the UK,' she says, when they are out of earshot again.

'We may be about to find out.'

'You really think that this is the beginning of a campaign of attacks?'

'If the network exists and Fowle has access to it, then yes I do.'

'If you're right and this wasn't a Russian-sanctioned attack but one that used their assets, why won't the Russians just stand them down?'

'I'm not sure,' he admits. 'Maybe they don't want to sacrifice their illegals and they're gambling that we won't retaliate. Or it may be something to do with the way the illegals are activated.'

'What do you mean?'

'I mean if Grom really is a weapon that allows whoever controls it to activate every illegal simultaneously, that's a pretty damn apocalyptic scenario. You'd only ever use it in time of war. In those circumstances you'd be worried about losing your command and control function. You might design it to prevent anyone stopping it once it's been activated.'

'You mean the opposite of a dead hand?'

'Yes, a "fail-deadly" system that operates even if the higher authority has been destroyed.'

'So, what do we do?'

'I think that the Prime Minister was pretty clear,' he says.

'Find Fowle and stop him.'

'Exactly.'

'My team are working on that.' She holds her hand up for a taxi. 'You coming?'

As one slows to meet them, he says, 'Where are we going?'

'Your office.' She is smiling. 'I hope you don't think its presumptuous but we moved in.'

'That is kind of presumptuous,' he says, opening the door for her.

'You have the space.'

'I do.'

Sitting on the back seat of the cab with Rosanna beside him, Jude thinks that it is the best news that he has heard since he opened his eyes that morning.

'Your friend Gretchen is enjoying the company,' Rosanna says.

The idea of Gretchen enjoying, rather than suffering, another person's company is a novel one.

# 39

# The Church of the Robe

It takes Yulia a few minutes to realise that the church has emptied of other visitors. She has been sitting despondently in a pew far beneath the single golden dome of the fifteenth-century Church of the Robe, feeling flushed and by turns tearful and angry, wondering why there isn't an emoji for the menopause and who the hell would she send it to anyway?

Not to Jude whose last message was a simple question:

What is Grom?

She is convinced that she has wasted a morning, just a couple of hundred metres from here, sitting in anterooms and hallways in the Kremlin, watching rolling news coverage of the London explosion while worried young things scurried back and forth between offices, and the apparatus of Russian government refused to speak with her. She seemed to be the only one paying attention to the TV screens. The men who would not see her – naturally they are men – are all beneficiaries of the president's largesse and his unlikely rise to power. They form an interlocking, neo-feudal court that has learned to write its own rules and suborn those who should enforce them. Naturally there is a Russian word for it – *proizvol* – the abuse of power at every level and jurisdiction. But they are vulnerable too. As a result of foreign election tampering, many of them are on the American blacklist. Confined to Russia, they can no longer travel to their London residences or their holiday homes in Spain and the Caribbean. Their financial affairs are under close scrutiny by the FBI. She fears that it has created a bunker-like mentality. They lack the imagination to understand how much danger they are in and the resolve to do anything about it.

Her beloved Russia is suffering from a degenerative illness. Its president and his cronies, who personify threat abroad, have come to symbolise its debilitation at home.

She glances at her watch on her damp wrist. It's lunchtime and the place should be packed but the tourists are gone. She is about to look back towards the door when she sees movement in one of the side bays that contains the famous icon depicting the journey of the Virgin's robe from Palestine to Constantinople where it miraculously prevented the city from being conquered by an invading horde.

Two bodyguards in black suits and ties and crisp white shirts appear out of the shadows and take up protective positions. Behind her, footsteps echo in the high chamber: a sizeable entourage approaching.

'Keep your eyes on the altar, *Baba*,' a bodyguard calls out.

Of course, he means it in the usual derogatory sense as the wife of a peasant but she has always preferred to think of herself as the character in Nekrasov's poem, *Baba Yaga*, a woman who can stop a horse at full tilt with a stare.

Someone sits in the pew behind her.

'It is interesting to me that you have chosen a church that celebrates the intercession of a woman in a great battle. Was it deliberate, Yulia Ermolaeva?'

She is always surprised by how reedy his voice is. How lacking in depth or authority. The last time she heard the president speak it was at his annual address to the Federal Assembly and she had thought him wooden and rushed. Ill at ease with domestic matters and the country's elemental grievances. For too long he has relied on a promise that is now wearing thin: the recovery of collective self-respect in exchange for personal subservience.

'I could not know you would come, Mr President,' she replies.

'Nevertheless, I am here.'

'Thank you.' She bows her head in acknowledgment, feeling the sweat pooling between her breasts.

'What is on your mind?'

'I was thinking that a leader would have to show great will and confidence to take command of a situation as dangerous as this,' she tells him, 'to exercise independent judgement and brake a runaway train.'

'You seek to flatter me?'

'I would not presume to do that.'

She can't help but remember what Alexei the General, her mentor and former lover, once said of the president: 'He is the unremarkable only child of an unremarkable working family. He is an absolutely average man. He has an average personality and average intelligence. You could go out the door and find thousands and thousands of people in Russia, all of them just like him.' It's hard to believe that the future of the nation that she loves and does everything to protect rests with this unremarkable man.

'Do you think that the Americans don't have their own version of Grom?' the president says.

The brittleness is there, the contempt for those who would deny Russia its rightful place in the world. It is almost as if the Soviet Union had coughed up, from the great mass of its populace, this average exemplar, with his aggression, his ignorance, and his nostalgia for the way things were.

'I do not question its necessity.' Though, of course, she does. How could he be so foolhardy as to build such a weapon? And to make matters a thousand times worse he allowed it to be handed over to that venal oaf, Troshev. She fights back the sudden, heedless urge to turn and confront him. One of the downsides of the testosterone that she's taking to suppress the worst effects of the menopause is that it also suppresses the better effects, like not giving a damn. 'Grom has fallen into the hands of someone who would gladly see the whole world burn. You saw what happened in Westminster. We have given him a deadly weapon and he is sure to use it.'

He remains silent for a while and then says, 'What would you have me do?'

'Send a kill signal. Disable the phone.'

'That is not possible.'

With a sense of sudden foreboding, she realises that the president doesn't have full command of the app.

'Where is Troshev?' she asks.

'He is in custody. He has told us everything he knows.'

'And the hackers who built Grom?'

'We are hunting them.'

She stifles a gasp. It is even worse than she thought. 'You have no choice but to come clean and cooperate, Mr President. Give them everything you can, even if it's not everything there is. I urge you to hand over lists of targets and the names of sleeper agents to our counterparts in the West.'

'I will not give up one of the foundation stones of our national defence.'

'Even if it leads to the very war that it is designed to prevent?'

'We cannot let that happen, Yulia,' he tells her. A tall dark-haired man slips silently into the pew beside her. 'This is Yuri Gregorovich. He commands a covert team from the Main Directorate that will travel back to Britain with you to stop Guy Fowle and recover the phone.'

'And if that doesn't work?'

'You will not thrive.'

'I understand.'

'I hope you do, for your sake. I am told that your husband was a fool but you are not.'

'I have my orders, Mr President.'

He stands and pauses briefly to squeeze her shoulder. She feels her skin crawl at his touch.

'Good luck, Yulia Ermolaeva.'

She listens to him leave with his entourage and the bodyguards recede into the shadows again.

The man beside her is staring boldly at her. He has a narrow lupine face and green eyes, framed by jet-black hair that falls to his broad shoulders. Typical bloody GRU, puffed up with arrogance.

'The plane is waiting,' he tells her. 'We have located the phone. We can be there by midnight.'

# 40

# One step behind

The Situation Awareness Group is a hive of unexpected and purposeful activity. Every work station appears occupied. Casually dressed twenty-somethings are moving back and forth from the glass-walled offices that flank the operations room. He sees that even the windowless room with foam-covered walls, which Gretchen refers to as the Black Room, is occupied.

As Jude crosses the open space in Rosanna's wake, he catches sight of Gretchen smiling at him across the top of a dividing wall. It seems that Rosanna's right and she's with her tribe. The number of orchids and bromeliads has multiplied tenfold.

Rosanna stops in the middle of the room and says to no one in particular, 'Can we get a briefing?'

The whole room stops and Jude is impressed by her effortless authority. A curly-haired man in sneakers and a white sleeveless cricket jumper with a Blue Peter badge on his left pocket grabs a tablet from one of the work stations.

'Jude, this is Dan,' Rosanna says.

Jude nods and they shake hands.

'The police found the car they were using,' Dan explains. 'Candida Taunton purchased a seven-year-old Toyota Corolla with cash two days ago from a used car dealer called Ray Ridley in World's End. That's the same day that Levi Minkin of Mr Roxy's Pet Food was killed and his barn burned to the ground. We made the connection through the Narcotics Anonymous meetings that both Candida and Ray attend on an irregular basis. Ray was uncooperative at first but when SO15 explained he was likely to be charged with terrorism offences he quickly changed his mind. Three hours after its purchase, number plate recognition places the Corolla heading east out of Gravesend in the direction of Mr Roxy's Pet Food. And an hour later heading back into London.' Dan touches the tablet screen and the video wall shows a map of north and east London with red data-pins marking the locations where the vehicle was logged by CCTV and road-rule enforcement cameras. 'The gaps between sightings suggest that the vehicle was stationary on at least five occasions. We have been reviewing video footage in these locations but so far we have not identified Guy Fowle, Candida Taunton or their teenage son Cosmo.'

'Quite the family,' Rosanna says.

'We lost all track of the vehicle at two a.m. in Bethnal Green,' Dan continues. 'There are no further sightings of the Corolla so I think we have to assume that they switched vehicles. The police are looking for abandoned and burned-out cars that match the Corolla's description. They are also talking to registered scrap dealers and garage owners, but we've had no luck yet.'

'What about the malware used in the oil terminal attack?' Rosanna asks.

'We can't examine it because we don't have a copy. It was destroyed in the explosion. However, we do know that it was communicating with the company's national control centre right up until the moment of the first detonation,' a woman says from the door to the Black Room. She's wearing a vest and her arms are fully sleeved, even more intricately tattooed than Gretchen's. 'Analysis of the data suggests that the malware recorded the settings on the tanks and the valves before it released its payload. It then sent the recording on a loop, tricking the control centre systems into thinking the tanks were filling normally when in fact they were already full, the safety valves were open and fuel was spilling out.'

'What about the Americans?' Rosanna asks. 'Have they seen this kind of behaviour in malware before?'

'They believe so, in the Ukraine. The NSA are sending a team from the dagger complex at USAF Darmstadt. They'll be here this afternoon.'

'Good.'

The woman nods and goes back into the Black Room.

Rosanna leads Jude to his office and closes the door. She walks over to the window and looks around impatiently.

'Fowle's the father of her son, I understand that, and he went to her for medical treatment but Candida can't have seen him since she was pregnant. Why would she willingly put herself and her son in danger like this?'

'He's controlling her,' Jude says. 'That's what he does. A mixture of coercion born of fear and something else that I don't fully understand but seems a lot like possession.'

'Possession?'

'If you apply for a disclosure order of her medical records, I think you'll find she's scarred in the same way that Zeina Hussein and Katherine Fowle were. Fowle cuts complicated patterns in their skin that seem to have meaning for him and the women he marks. Katherine said that he had put a demon inside her.'

Rosanna frowns. 'I am Legion?'

The biblical image of a herd of demonically possessed swine throwing themselves off a cliff strikes a chord. He will never forget the expression on the face of

Zeina Hussein in Parliament Square before he shot her. 'Something like that.'

Dan sticks his head through the door. 'We've had an anonymous tip-off. An address in South Kensington.'

'Let's go,' Rosanna says.

They arrive just as the police are sealing the entrance to the mews and follow the assault team as they break down the door of the house with a battering ram and spread out through the building. They find a maid from the Philippines in the basement laundry room, pulling freshly washed sheets out of the machine.

Again, they are too late.

They quickly establish that the house is owned by an offshore company based in the British Virgin Islands. It is maintained and the fridge restocked on a weekly basis by a property management agency that receives a monthly payment by bank transfer from

Lichtenstein. The maid reveals that in five years of looking after the house it is the first time that she has known anyone to spend the night.

Jude and Rosanna stand out on the cobbles and watch while scenes of crime officers enter and begin the painstaking business of gathering evidence.

Rosanna's phone rings.

'The tip-off came from a burner phone used somewhere in St James's Park,' she tells him when she's finished the call. 'They're reviewing video footage from the park entrances.'

'There are no cameras here,' Jude says, looking the length of the mews, 'plenty of intruder alarms though.'

'I guess the owners value their privacy.'

'Not one of them is occupied.'

'This is really beginning to piss me off,' Rosanna tells him.

Her phone rings again. He watches her face light up.

'They think they've found the missing phone,' she tells him.

Jude remembers his concern that the hunt for Fowle will put them both in harm's way. Judging by Rosanna's expression, that's nowhere near the forefront of her mind and he wonders if maybe it should be.

# 41

# God is the Streets

'We've been using cell tower triangulation to locate unregistered mobile phones with their GPS disabled in the vicinity of the Chelsea house where Guy Fowle was held after he was broken out of Woolwich and subsequently in the area of Candida Taunton's flat in Ladbroke Grove,' Gretchen explains to them as soon as they reach the Situational Awareness Group's offices and before Jude can fully scan the room. 'Cross-checking has revealed a specific unregistered phone with a call history that shows clusters of activity including communication with other burner phones at the Chelsea house in the period prior to Guy Fowle's escape and subsequently at Candida Taunton's flat. The user switched off the phone not long before the Corolla drove east to Mr Roxy's Pet Food. The phone was switched on again early this morning in Shoreditch. Location data currently places it in a housing estate in Barking in South London.'

'Our search of CCTV and traffic camera footage within a two-hundred-and-fifty-metre radius of the location where the phone was switched on this morning has yielded one significant result,' Dan says. He taps his screen, and the wall fills with a screen grab of a man passing a kebab shop. He's wearing a baseball cap but looking off to one side with his chin raised and his face lit by the headlights of a passing car. 'We're ninety-five per cent sure that the man in the image is known as Pato. He belongs to an Albanian organised crime group that is subject to an ongoing police investigation named Operation High-Rise. As you can see, he's carrying two large black holdalls. Fifteen minutes later we see someone of the same build and wearing the same baseball cap returning but without the hold-alls. Instead he's holding a much smaller package.'

'We need to speak to the head of the police unit conducting the investigation,' Rosanna says.

'Here,' says a familiar voice. Jude turns to see his sister Tamar swinging her scuffed boots on one of the work tables at the back of the room. She has a blue-and-white police lanyard around her neck.

'This is Detective Inspector Tamar Lyon,' Dan says, by way of introduction. 'She's from Serious and Organised Crime Command.'

'Hello, big brother,' she says looking from Jude to Rosanna and back again with a raised eyebrow.

'Ah, I see,' Rosanna says, momentarily embarrassed.

'I've been given instructions to assist you in any way I can,' Tamar says, hopping down off the table and walking towards them. 'Which I'm really hoping doesn't involve me getting injured again.'

She isn't going to let Jude forget about the piece of shrapnel from a grenade that wounded her during the Westminster attack, that she maintains was meant for him.

'We'll do our best to prevent it,' Rosanna says, briskly. 'Now what can you tell us about Pato?'

'He's retail,' Tamar says. 'A courier who belongs to a small, close-knit East London gang of Albanian origin that call them-selves God is the Streets and operate out of a housing estate in Barking. They answer to the Mafia Shqiptare, the Albanian organ-ised criminal syndicate which now pretty much controls the Dutch and Belgian ports, and is on its way to a near-total takeover of the UK's cocaine market. We believe that the syndicate has also been discreetly trafficking weapons into this country for the use of its network of Albanian and affiliated gangs. That's where Operation High-Rise comes in. We are focusing on disrupting a pipeline from the Balkans for weapons and ammunition, includ-ing assault rifles, diverted from military and police stores. We have already identified five gangland murders attributed to them. Our biggest concern is that they may be used in a future terrorist attack.'

'It's fair to say the black holdall contained weapons?'

Tamar nods. 'They don't sell weapons to just anyone but as long as Fowle has some means of introduction to the gang and the syndicate approves, it's a reasonable assumption.'

'And the phone is now in a high-rise on the estate that God is the Streets operate from,' Gretchen adds.

'Exactly. It's the same high-rise that we believe they are using to store weapons for the syndicate,' Tamar says. 'Right now, it's a no-go zone but we have it under surveillance.'

'We have to recover that phone,' Rosanna says.

'What if it's a trap?' Jude says.

Rosanna looks at him. He can sense the impatience in her. 'Go on.'

'Why would Fowle hand over a phone to the Albanians?' Jude says. 'And why switch it on before doing so? He's advertising its presence. He wants us to charge into a building that's full of weapons and gangsters.'

'I need to speak to Calthorp,' she says and heads for the privacy of one of the glass-walled offices.

Tamar watches her go and looks across at Jude. 'She makes an impression.'

'Give it a rest.'

'You like her?'

Jude sighs. There's nothing more irritating than a younger sister. He watches Rosanna walking back and forth on the far side of the glass talking to the head of MI5. Tamar's right, he does like her. And she's beginning to worry him too.

'What happened to the journalist?' Tamar asks.

'I couldn't make it work?'

'I think I warned you about that at the time.'

'I'm sure you did.'

'And your married Russian friend?'

'She's gone back to Moscow.'

'You never learn, do you?' Tamar says.

'I need you to do me a favour,' Jude tells her, changing the subject. 'Check your informants. The chat rooms and messaging services that you have penetrated. Anything out of the ordinary. It doesn't matter how small or tangential. It may be a clue.'

A couple of minutes later, Rosanna steps out of the office.

'Our orders are to find out what's on that phone,' she tells them. 'We're going in.'

# 42

## The east tower

On the eighteenth floor, Agron and Pato are staring at the phone on the table and beside it a clear plastic bag containing a severed thumb. Behind them on the wall, a bank of monitors show CCTV imagery from inside and outside the flats.

'This was not part of the agreement,' Agron says. He's been furious ever since Pato brought him the package. 'Our instructions were to hand over the weapons, nothing more.'

'Call the client,' Drita says from across the room, where she is scrolling through her Instagram feed beside a table stacked with bricks of cocaine. 'You have a number.'

'And say what?'

'You can start with what the fuck is it with this thumb?'

Agron takes out his phone, consults his list of contacts and dials a number never before used, 'It's connecting.'

On the table the black phone rings.

'Shit!' Agron immediately terminates the call.

He's staring at the phone like it's a bomb.

'What the hell do we do now?'

Drita gets up and walks across the room towards them, her heels clicking on the rough concrete floor. She picks up the plastic bag and looks at the thumb inside.

'What are you doing?'

'Seeing what's on the phone.' She opens the bag and they all recoil from the smell. She hands it to Pato. 'See if that unlocks it.'

Struggling to disguise his distaste, Pato presses the thumb to the button and the phone's screen lights up.

'Give it here,' Drita says. She scrolls right, scanning the apps until the phone beeps. She looks at Agron. 'Somebody just sent a message.'

'What does it say?'

She looks at him. 'It says *they're coming.*'

Yulia is sitting in the back of a transit van full of men in black with an assortment of shotguns and assault rifles fitted with noise suppressors secured between their knees and backpacks full of equipment at their feet. She is dressed for combat, wearing black cargo pants and black Air Force One sneakers, a tailored black flak jacket and beneath it a black cashmere rollneck. It has been many years since she was this close to the sharp end of an operation and she's feeling anxious.

'The phone is on the eighteenth floor of the east tower,' Yuri says with his back to the driver's partition, all eyes on him in the cramped space. 'First we take down the lookouts at the base of the building. Then we go in through the service entrance and then up the stairs, securing each floor as we go. Assume anyone inside is a hostile and shoot them on sight. We recover the phone and we leave. Understood?'

'*Da!*' they respond in unison.

They pull on balaclavas. Yulia's is too large for her and she imagines that along with the helmet it makes her look like an owl.

'Go!'

The van's doors open and they jump out, fanning out into fire positions. Yulia stays close to Yuri as they approach the housing estate across an expanse of waste ground.

Four aluminium-clad tower blocks rise in the darkness above them.

Jude is standing in front of a wall with schematics of the east tower block taped to it and rows of screen grabs of identified members of the gang with their names written in black marker pen beneath them. They are in a command centre on the tenth floor of the west tower. At the window on the far side of the room, a firearms officer is staring through a tripod-mounted night-vision camera at the tower block opposite.

'The gang controls the entire building,' Tamar explains. 'Effectively using the residents as human shields. They have a network of teenage lookouts surrounding the tower and on the lower floors and armed guards at the entrance to the elevators and in the stairwell. A steel door blocks access to the stairs beyond the fifteenth floor. Our sources suggest that the floors above that are used for storing drugs and guns and the whole operation is run from a command centre on the eighteenth floor.'

'Explain the plan to me,' Rosanna says.

'First, an outer cordon will go up preventing all vehicular and pedestrian access to the estate,' the tactical firearms commander, a Detective Inspector named Gorman explains, 'then two assault teams will deploy. Assault Team One will surround the building, arrest the lookouts and secure the exits. Assault Team Two will enter the building and make their way from floor to floor managing the evacuation of residents. Lethal force will only be used if there is immediate danger to the life of my officers. Once we have fully evacuated the residents and isolated the fifteenth floor and above, you can enter into negotiation with the gang to recover the phone.'

Tamar rolls her eyes. 'And if they won't cooperate?'

'We can cut off the water and electricity at any point. If necessary, we can pump the whole building full of tear gas. We're ready for a siege.'

'Is that cladding what I think it is?' Nganga asks.

'Yes,' Tamar says. 'It's aluminium. If someone starts a fire the whole building could go up.'

'We have the London Fire Service on standby ready to deploy when the cordon is in place,' Gorman says.

There's nothing about the operation that sits right with Jude. He retreats to the back of the room and squats down with his back to the wall. Tamar joins him. They watch Gorman standing beside the night-vision camera, talking to his teams on his throat mic.

'Are you thinking what I'm thinking?' Tamar says.

'That this is a bad idea? Yes, of course.'

Rosanna glances back at them. Jude can tell that she's determined to go in.

Tamar's phone rings.

'Shoot,' she says.

He watches her listening. There are times, particularly when she is concentrating, that she reminds him so much of their father. The same single-minded determination.

'Keep looking,' she says and ends the call.

'We've lost contact with a confidential informant inside a white supremacist group,' she says, 'The group have abandoned the gym they use as a headquarters and we're not having any luck at their home addresses.'

'Boss,' the watcher at the window says, 'someone's just taken out the Albanian lookouts.'

Gorman immediately replaces him at the camera.

'What's going on?' Tamar says.

'We're not the only people who want that phone,' Jude replies.

'All stations, this is control,' Gorman says into his throat mic, 'we have unknown armed assailants approaching the building. Seal the outer cordon now.' He looks back at Rosanna. 'Whoever they are, we'll trap them inside.'

Rosanna nods.

'Assault Team One, standby,' Gorman says.

'We should wait,' Jude says.

Gunfire echoes across the estate, the sound snapping back and forth between the towers.

# 43

## Conflagration

The Russians suffer their first fatality when one of the Albanians in the lobby on the ground floor lets off a burst of fire before being cut down. Yulia steps over her comrade's body, careful to avoid the spreading pool of blood, skirts the dead Albanian beside the elevators and follows Yuri through a door to the base of the stairwell. His men are climbing the stairs with their rifles raised like medieval archers. Others follow behind, their guns pointing downwards.

Just ahead of her on the sixth floor a man rushes through one of the doors and is dropped with a suppressed round.

'We're being watched,' Yuri says. There are cameras on every landing, overlooking the stairs. They continue to rise, shooting the cameras as they go.

Another burst of gunfire, this time from several floors below. A voice in her earpiece tells her that the attacker has been killed.

Abruptly, the lights go out. Yuri and his men tip down their night-vision goggles and switch them on. They continue to rise.

In the east tower control room, Agron is staring at the CCTV monitors when the lights go out and the screens go blank.

'You better call Tirana and tell them that we are under attack,' he tells Drita.

He can hear Pato breathing beside him in the darkness. He stifles the urge to smash the fool's head on the floor. They are under attack and punishment will have to wait.

'Issue the heavy weapons and take the men down to the fifteenth,' he commands, reaching into his daysack, which contains a head torch.

He drops the Grom phone onto the floor and by the light of the torch he crushes it with the heel of his boot until it is destroyed.

Jude watches from the window as the darkened tower is lit up by flashes of gunfire.

'They're inside the building,' the watcher at the window says.

'You think it's the Russians?' Rosanna says.

'We'll know soon enough,' Jude replies. He texts Yulia again:
We need to talk, now!

'What are your orders?' Gorman asks.

'You can surround the building and secure the exits,' Rosanna says. 'Do not enter.'

Gorman nods. 'Assault Team One, go!'

Seconds later, the tower is rocked by an explosion that blows out the windows on the upper floors.

Yulia becomes separated from the others after they use shaped charges to blow the steel door and the wall of sandbags behind erupts. It's impossible to see. The air is full of sand billowing in every direction. Gunfire crackles in the stairwell.

She stumbles down a corridor, bouncing from wall to wall, while somewhere behind her a grenade explodes. She feels a sharp sting in her thigh and falls against an unlocked door and through onto bare concrete. The sand and dust follow her in, rolling over the top of her like fog. She grips her thigh with both hands and curses as she feels the blood oozing between her fingers. With her other leg she kicks the door shut.

A further explosion echoes through the tower and for the first time she hears the wail of approaching sirens. Even in the midst of the battle, she realises what an epic disaster this is, and how it is going to take all her powers of persuasion and coercion to contain the damage. She turns and drags herself, hand over hand, away from the door. Her helmet butts up against a table leg, which shakes and dislodges a rain of bricks on her helmet and flak jacket. One of them splits open and showers her with powder. She tastes cocaine.

She pulls herself through a doorway onto ceramic tiles, and using her good leg hooks the door closed behind her. Gasping at the pain, she lifts herself onto a toilet seat, removes her helmet, balaclava and body armour and drops them on the floor. Using a toilet roll, she makes a thick wad of toilet paper and presses it against the wound on her thigh, which she fastens with her scarf.

Letting her head rest against the wall, she rests for a few moments before reaching for her phone. She sees the message from Jude and immediately replies:

Help me

Are you in the building?

Yes

What floor are you on?

I don't know. I'm in an apartment.

You need to get out now. The building is on fire. I'm coming.

Yulia switches on the torch on her phone and using the door handle pulls herself upright. She limps out, heading for the stairwell.

Jude rises against the tide of residents evacuating the building, scanning their blackened faces desperately looking for Yulia amongst them. He's soaking wet from the fire hoses that are already pummelling the outside of the building.

Above him in the stairwell, pairs of firefighters weighed down with breathing apparatus are also making their way upwards, at times forced to stop because there are too many people for them to pass. There is still gunfire coming from the upper floors.

It's getting harder to see and the floor numbers are indistinguishable. As he climbs, his hands slide across a hot film of grease on the walls. A firefighter passes him going down with a baby cradled in her arms. All the traffic is downwards now. He starts coughing. The heat is almost unbearable.

He stumbles to a halt and falls into a corner of the stairwell to avoid being in anyone else's way. More firefighters pass him,

*Simon Conway*

carrying people away from the fire, then a police firearms officer from the first assault comes stumbling down with his gun swinging on its sling and rattling against the balustrade, and the gas mask making a skull of his face. Then there's nothing above Jude but smoke, dense black smoke. He can't move. It's too hot. He can only stare upwards.

Seconds later two firefighters with their breathing alarms sounding appear out of the darkness carrying someone between them. He pulls himself upright and staggers towards them. One of the firefighters steadies him, sliding his arm under Jude's shoulder, and he leans in recognising Yulia by torchlight. He touches her face. Her eyes open and briefly focus before closing again and, in that instant, he sees the ghost of a smile.

Together they descend, retreating from the heat and the smoke.

They pass armed officers in protective positions on the sixth floor and reach the bridgehead on the fifth where a white-helmeted watch manager is overseeing the rapid transfer of casualties to the ambulance crews. Two paramedics carry Yulia down to the ground level and Jude follows.

Outside it is raining debris and the sides of the building are roaring like a burning gas main. Several cars are on fire. He sees a blur of movement and a thud as a body strikes the play park beside him.

Guy watches through the sniper scope from the south tower as Jude Lyon staggers out of the burning building towards a taxi rank of waiting ambulances. With him is one of the initial attackers, who Guy guesses must be a Russian intelligence officer. She is injured. He is sorely tempted to pull the trigger but it's better to know your enemies and there isn't time to learn new ones. After all, Jude Lyon has the advantage of being predictable. A reassuring mediocrity.

Guy lowers the rifle and looks at Candida and his son standing in darkness, bathed with firelight. They both seem equally entranced by the conflagration.

At his feet is the disposable launch tube that he used to fire an incendiary warhead at the east tower shortly after the first explosion. Overkill perhaps, but he has learned that when starting fires maximum effort is always best.

They need to keep moving.

'Let's go,' he tells them.

# 44

## Yulia's choice

Yulia perches with one buttock on a cushion in an otherwise spartan interview room with a rough blanket around her shoulders and mascara stains running down her cheeks. A fragment of metal has been removed from her thigh and the wound stitched and bandaged. It's still numb from the local anaesthetic which was all that she would allow them to give her.

Jude and an intelligence officer who introduced herself as Rosanna are sitting on the far side of the table. A tall black police officer is standing with his back to the wall.

'I have diplomatic immunity,' she says.

'That's not going to work,' Rosanna says.

She sighs. 'Go on then.'

'Why were you in the tower, Mrs Ermolaeva?'

'I was recovering stolen property,' she replies.

'A phone?'

'Yes. But you knew that already.'

'And what was on the phone?'

She looks at Jude. She wants to reach out and tuck a stray curl of hair behind his ear. He needs a haircut. And a shower to wash the smell of smoke from his skin and a change of clothes and a good night's sleep. He conjures such tenderness in her, with his concerned expression and his selfless desire to do what's right.

'We can offer you protection,' he assures her. 'Somewhere safe.'

'And are you willing to join me there?' she asks. 'Now that you have saved me from a burning tower. Will we live together in an idyllic country cottage and grow hollyhocks and rambling roses?'

He looks so sad and embarrassed. He'll risk his life for her but he will not commit to her. It's not that she wants him, exactly. After all, she's finally free. It is irritating nonetheless.

'You are in serious trouble, Mrs Ermolaeva,' Rosanna says, coldly, 'as is your husband.'

'My husband is dead,' she says. 'He did something very stupid and rather than pay the price for it he chose to end his life.'

'I'm sorry,' Jude says.

She can't stand his pity. 'I'm not.'

'What is Grom?' Rosanna asks.

*A means of retribution for a humiliated nation.*

'When you were little and your friends were all deciding who was going to "be" a Disney princess, were you always Ariel?'

'I never played princesses,' Rosanna replies, stone-faced.

'Then maybe you can't understand,' she says, 'neither of you can. We have a word in Russian, *"obida"*, it means resentment. Anger at being denied what is taken for granted by others. You can motivate an entire nation with resentment.'

'What is Grom, Yulia?' Jude asks, sadly.

'I need to speak to my president.'

'And what will you say to him?' Rosanna demands.

'I will tell him that if he doesn't want to start a war, he needs to hand over the names and location of every illegal and other GRU asset embedded in the critical infrastructure of this country. And he needs to do it now. Does that satisfy you?'

Yulia watches Jude and Rosanna exchange a look and is jealous of the expression on Jude's face. It explains the earlier embarrassment, at least. Perhaps Jude has finally found what he is looking for, this beautiful spy with the pre-Raphaelite hair and the subtle detailing in the cuffs of her fitted white shirt. Someone he can openly share his secrets with.

'We will need to consult with a higher authority,' Rosanna says.

'Would you like some tea?' Jude asks her.

'No, I don't want any fucking tea, Jude.'

\*  \*  \*

An hour later at Downing Street, a small group that includes Jude and Yulia huddles around the Prime Minister's large mahogany desk. They both reek of smoke. The Russian president is on speakerphone and Yulia is explaining the failure of her team to recover Grom while an interpreter whispers softly in the Prime Minister's ear. Calthorp is there and Maurice Hermon, the PM's special adviser. The Chancellor, Gabriel Morley, is there too, staring at the phone with the anxiety of a compulsive gambler, waiting for the dice to land.

When she is done there is silence on the other end of the line.

The Prime Minister leans forward over the desk and speaks in a measured tone. 'Mr President, I cannot countenance what your intelligence services are responsible for but I can assure you that any response will be measured and greatly influenced by the assistance that only you can provide.'

The PM sits back and they wait.

'Prime Minister,' the president says eventually, in English. 'Thank you for bringing this matter to my attention. Of course, it is unfortunate that rogue elements of our intelligence services have taken it upon themselves to build this weapon that is named Grom. Just as it is unfortunate that your intelligence services took it upon themselves to cover up the existence of the international terrorist Guy Fowle who is responsible for initiating these attacks and so many others.'

Across the table, Evan Calthorp is shaking his head. The PM shoots him a warning look.

'Mr President, we urgently need your help to stop these attacks.'

'Prime Minister, let me assure you that I recognise the urgency of the situation. Those responsible for the design of Grom will be arrested and prosecuted. Recognising the gravity of the situation, I am sending information that will prove useful to deter future attacks. It will be delivered to Yulia Ermolaeva by personal courier. I ask your assistance with the facilitation of the flight plan and any other matters necessary to ensure that she is able to give you the information that you need.'

'Thank you, Mr President.'

The call ended, Gabriel Morley slumps in his seat and says, 'Thank fuck for that.'

Maurice Hermon scowls at him, 'What's got into you?'

'It's the economy, stupid,' Gabriel retorts.

A police convoy from SCO19 with blue lights flashing delivers them on the motorway to a Stansted Airport hotel where an entire floor has been taken over for them and armed police are stationed at the elevators and in the stairwells.

Yulia sits on the counterpane of a double bed with Jude beside her and without thinking he switches on the news. The tower block fire is still raging, burning gobbets of aluminium cascading from its upper storeys. A correspondent says, 'The question people are asking of the government tonight is this, are we under attack and if so by whom?'

'Switch it off!'

'I'm sorry, that was thoughtless of me,' he says.

She stares at the empty screen. 'I'm thirsty.'

He brings them both bottled water from the fridge.

'I argued for full disclosure from the beginning,' she tells him, 'as soon as I learned the nature of Grom.'

'I believe you.'

She starts crying. 'I thought I was going to die.'

He puts his arm around her. 'You got out. It's okay.'

She shrugs him off and rubs the back of her hand across her face. Looking across the room, she sees herself in a mirror for the first time since entering the tower block.

*Baba Yaga.*

One look from her could definitely stop a galloping horse.

'I need a shower.'

'I'll leave you to it.'

'Yes, you better run off to Princess Ariel.'

'I don't think she's going to enjoy being called that,' he tells her.

'I don't think she's going to sleep with you,' she retorts.

'That's not what I want.'

'Please,' she says. 'You can't hide your feelings from me. You never have been able to. Now, leave me alone!'

She closes her eyes and waits for him to leave.

Rosanna is leaning against a wall in the corridor outside. She looks up from her phone when he emerges from the room. He wonders if she has been talking to her husband.

'How is she?' she asks.

'Exhausted.'

Leaning against the wall beside her, Jude realises that he's not far off exhaustion himself. She hands him a key card. 'Have a shower and get some sleep. There's a room for you next to hers.'

'What will you do?'

'Wake you when the plane lands.'

'Are you not tired?'

'I didn't charge into a burning building tonight.'

'There is that,' he concedes.

'Is it true that you met Yulia on a dating site?' she asks.

'It was a fishing expedition,' he says from the doorway. 'I was just the bait.'

'I must have heard a different version of the story.'

'It's true that there are different opinions on the outcome,' he says. 'So, if you didn't play princesses what did you play?'

'Dinosaurs.'

'Right.'

'I can do a mean T-Rex impression.'

He believes her.

# 45

## The mermaids singing

Guy opens a spiked iron gate and they approach a dilapidated Georgian townhouse set back from the road. The soot-stained brickwork is shrouded in wisteria and the wooden shutters are drawn on the ground-floor windows. Candles flicker in the upper windows.

The brass door handle is a clawed hand. Guy pauses before knocking. Inside, a man is shouting in English and another in French. The French-speaking man is shrill.

'*Chatte!*' he cries. '*Chatte!*' They hear a door slam and a glass break. Guy knocks on the door and the sound echoes like a gun shot in the overgrown courtyard.

A small man with shoulder-length grey hair and large round sunglasses opens the door. He is wearing tartan trews, a red threadbare velvet smoking jacket and a spotted cravat. He waves a glass of red wine at them, sloshing some on the steps.

'Are you from a proselytising religion?' he says. 'I don't appreciate pointless interference in the quiet of other people.'

'Mr Arbuthnot,' Guy says. 'It's Guy Fowle.'

The man removes his sunglasses. His stoned, red eyes are rimmed with kohl. Recognition dawns and with it an expression in equal parts of fear, surprise, excitement and lust.

'My darling boy. My ragged claws. You were a ball of light in my hands. And look at you now! Big as Caesar. You great big tart, come and give me a kiss!'

'This is Candida and Cosmo.'

His gaze flicks past Candy without registering her presence and lights up as he sees Cosmo. 'Well, well. Progeny.'

'*Chatte!*' the other man shouts from inside.

'Are you going to let us in?' Guy asks.

Arbuthnot waves them in with a drunken flourish. He kisses Cosmo clumsily on the cheek as he passes.

They enter a wood-panelled hallway decorated with gaudy oil paintings of street transsexuals. From the floor above comes another explosion of French rage.

'Be quiet!' Arbuthnot shouts. He rolls his eyes at them. 'Street trash.'

A narrow-hipped young black man wearing a polka-dot bandana around his neck comes down the wooden stairs, buttoning his wine-red leather trousers. He is in high heels and totters uncertainly on them as he descends.

'Wow,' he says. *'Une famille si heureuse.'*

He gives them all the finger as he walks past them and out the door. Guy grabs him by the collar and hauls him back inside.

'Not so fast,' he says.

The youth stumbles and falls in a heap on the floor.

*'C'est quoi ce bordel?'*

Guy turns the key in the lock and pockets it. Arbuthnot seems to find this hilarious.

'Shall I open another bottle?' he says.

'That would be a good idea,' Guy agrees. He picks up the young Frenchman and pushes him towards the stairs. They climb in single file past paintings of naked men wearing puppy ears and a landing halfway up with a window that looks out on a back garden as verdant as a jungle. On the first floor, they enter a large L-shaped room. There is a stained chaise longue and two armchairs with the stuffing coming out around a glass-topped coffee table with a pile of white powder on it and the usual paraphernalia, a debit card and a rolled tenner.

They look at an enormous painting above the fireplace. It is an acrylic of two men wrestling on a bed, one face down and the other on top of him.

'Do you like it?' Arbuthnot says, selecting a bottle of red wine from a rack. 'I like it.'

'It's very you,' Guy says.

'You always said the nicest things,' Arbuthnot tells him. He sits on the chaise longue and pats the place beside him. 'Come on, Cosmo, don't be shy.'

Cosmo sits, looking uncomfortable.

The Frenchman flounces over to a window seat and curls up in it.

'I heard you've been rather naughty,' Arbuthnot says, opening the bottle.

'I've been killing the right people,' Guy says, sitting opposite him.

'Yes, very good,' Arbuthnot says, leaning forward excitedly. 'The modern artist must live by craft and violence.'

'His gods are violent gods,' Guy says.

'I have always thought the suicide should bump off at least one swine before taking off for parts unknown,' Arbuthnot says.

'I have to go out and score,' Candy says. Looking up, Guy can see the need in her face. They have run out of heroin and she must have more.

'That's a very good idea,' Arbuthnot says with his hand on Cosmo's knee. 'We'll have a party.'

Weighing the risk, Guy decides to let Candy go. He gives her the key. 'Come straight back,' he says.

'Of course.'

'The boy stays here.'

He sees the disappointment in her eyes. 'Your son.'

'Our hosts want to hear the mermaids sing,' Guy tells her, meeting her gaze.

She nods slowly.

'And don't pick up any surveillance.'

'I know what I'm doing,' she tells him.

When she has gone, Guy turns to Arbuthnot. 'This place must be worth a packet now?'

'As you know, it was Mama's,' he replies. 'Of course, I've had to borrow against it to maintain a certain standard of living. After that unpleasantness in Scotland it seemed prudent to give up teaching.' He smiles, conspiratorially. 'Not everyone was as willing as you.'

He pours them both a glass.

'Here's to happier times.' They clink glasses. 'Do you mind if I?' Arbuthnot asks gesturing at the cocaine on the table.

'Of course,' Guy replies, genially.

When Candy returns, Arbuthnot is holding forth in front of the fireplace and Guy is listening to him with an expression of amused contempt. Cosmo has fallen asleep on the chaise longue and the Frenchman is helping himself to another line.

Candy unpacks her works on the table. In addition to heroin she has brought fresh syringes and needles still in their packaging.

'Is that what I think it is?' Mr Arbuthnot says, staring wide-eyed at the plastic baggie with off-white powder inside.

'You better believe it,' Guy says.

'*Oh, la, la,*' the Frenchman says, kneeling in front of the coffee table. Arbuthnot joins him. Both of them stare at Candy in wonderment as she cooks up using a spoon.

To Guy, all it needs is some farm animals to resemble a nativity scene.

'Who's first?' Candy asks, looking over their shoulders at Guy.

'*C'est moi,*' the Frenchman says, greedily.

Guy steps forward and takes the loaded needle from Candy. He ties off the Frenchman's arm with his bandana. He uses the vein in the crook of the youth's elbow, a burst of bright red rising in the valve before he presses the plunger. When he takes the needle out, the Frenchman slumps at the foot of the chaise longue.

'Who's next?' Candy says.

'Got to be you, Mr Arbuthnot,' Guy says.

Candy cooks up again.

Arbuthnot shrugs of his jacket and offers his arm. Guy tenderly rolls up his teacher's sleeve pausing to kiss him on the lips before undoing his cravat and using it to tie off the arm. Candy passes him the needle. Beside them, the Frenchman has gone very pale. His pupils are pinpricks and there is foam around his mouth.

'What's the matter with him?' Arbuthnot says, with a hint of panic.

Guy's hand tightens on his arm. 'He's overdosing. It's time to murder and create. Don't you want to hear the mermaids sing?'

Arbuthnot begins to struggle but Guy's grip is unbreakable. He shoots the load into Arbuthnot's vein and catches him as he slips backwards, gently lowering his head to the floor. 'And we drown . . .'

He looks up at Candy who is chewing her lip and staring at the heroin. Cosmo is awake and has been watching.

'It was necessary,' he says to them both. 'Cheer up.'

Cosmo nods and Candy forces a smile.

'You've got a busy day tomorrow,' Guy tells Candy, 'and you've got homework to do.'

He grips the Frenchman by the ankles and drags him across the floorboards to the top of the stairs.

'I'll put them in the coal hole.'

# 46

# Cosmo

When Dad kills it's so matter of fact. He's never in a rush or angry. He can be gentle like with the paedo who owns this creepy house and his annoying twink. Gentle and with a soft voice just like the lady from the vet surgery when Orpheus the cat was given the needle, like you know Dad's done it lots of times before. Not so gentle afterwards though when he was dragging them down the stairs. Lying in bed on the top floor, Cosmo can still hear the wet, crunchy sound their heads made as they hit each step on the way down to the kitchen.

Dad can be fast too, like when they were switching cars and that guy in the garage showed him disrespect and he just walked up to him and cut his throat and sprayed bright red blood everywhere, everywhere, before kicking him into the pit and giving him his cap.

And you just know he can be much, much faster than that in combat when it's all reaction times and hand-eye coordination and racking up kills. Cosmo can't wait to see that happen. It'll be awesome.

Mum told him to never look Dad straight in the eyes. She says it's for his own protection. Like Dad might cut his throat too, even though he's his own flesh and blood. But of course, he's watched him when Dad doesn't know he's looking. An' fuck, yeah, they're freaky. But not because of something wrong with them. They're not darting this way and that like a mental person. They're intense and focused. He is a man who does what he wants like there's no gap between thought and action, like a samurai, a black ninja.

His eyes have zero feelings to hide. Maybe that's what scares people so much.

Mum is definitely scared of him but she loves him too, so, so fiercely. And you can tell they are a good team. They're in the bedroom on the floor below, probably having sex with each other right now. Everyone at school tells him how hot his mum is and how she should do porn and be really famous. Cosmo wonders if this is how he was made, in someone's random house with dead bodies lying around and weapons and drugs and stuff everywhere. That would be cool.

He's definitely going to ask Dad to show him in the morning how to use the rockets and other military grade stuff in the black bags he's been collecting. How can it be harder than a game console?

More than anything Cosmo wants to learn from his father and become a ninja too. When he said that to Mum when she was saying good night, she did that thing where she chews her lip and her eyes fill with tears. And she said he wasn't old enough yet and he had to wait. It was too dangerous. And he told her that was bullshit and this was his big chance and she shouldn't get in his way.

'We'll talk about it tomorrow,' she said but he knew she was just putting it off and he knew he'd get the same answer tomorrow. And what made it worse was that he knew that she was going to play a role in taking them to the next level and he was just going to have to watch.

Mum is a strange woman, one minute all loving, the next full of bitterness, and the stories she tells are sometimes true, sometimes made up, and sometimes a mixture of the two. He's read everything she's ever written in her secret notebooks and like he told Dad, most of it is batshit crazy. Sometimes she writes about Dad like he's some kind of demon or fallen angel from a game or Netflix, or an old book like the Bible. Of course, that means she feels special too, like she's some kind of chosen one. And you only have to see the way she dresses at Halloween to know that she has it in her to be the Devil's bride. Other times she curses Dad for ruining her life and never being happy and needing to take drugs and sell them, and tell lies and sleep with random guys for money, all just to forget about him.

Cosmo prefers to think of his dad as a warrior who knows every short cut and work-around in the game, tooled up and fast enough to kill hordes of enemies, adept enough to navigate every level and wipe out every other player, and reach the final level.

Really it should be a fiery end.

Dad loves fire more than anything else. It's like slippery magic in his hands. It was so cool when he touched the Zippo lighter to the rat cages and the blue-and-orange flames raced down the aisle and covered the disgusting ogre who lived in the caravan.

The fat ogre waving his burning arms and legs like a spaz.

And then the next level: the explosion at the oil terminal which Cosmo played wing-man in, delivering the packet to the Russian secret agent who worked in the control room. The packet with the USB that knocked out all the safety switches and the alarms and stuff. Standing on the really old hill watching the explosions as the tanks went up one after the other, it was like a huge dragon roaring with its mouth wide open.

On the third level, firing the rocket at the tower block and watching it melt the metal and the whole building turning into an inferno in no time. Dad's eyes may not have changed, standing there on the balcony watching burning Albanian gangsters falling from the top floors like orcs, but he smiled. He grinned. And Cosmo grinned along with him and Dad even put his arm around Cosmo's shoulder and it felt like they were truly a father and son team. Even Mum looked happy.

Then they had to scarper.

He knows that they are going to have to keep moving between levels, staying in different places every night. Sometimes they have to kill people just to keep them quiet. Dad must do his work undisturbed. Some nights there won't be a bed but that doesn't bother him.

It'll be worth it to reach the final level. He knows what's up there. He's sneaked a look in the Moleskine.

The Saboteur

The big red button: press it for the apocalypse.

Radioactive ash in the air and on the surfaces of everyday things.

He hears police cars racing down the street with their sirens wailing.

# 47

# Homework

Lying on the four-poster bed, surrounded by hand-printed toile drapes decorated with junkies and vagrants, Guy listens to the police cars go by. He has little doubt that they are hunting for him. He has questioned Candy closely about her drugs purchase. She has described everyone she saw on the street in detail as he taught her when they were a couple. And she has described the route she took on her return and the evasive tactics used. He is as satisfied as he can be that she was not followed. Cross-legged beside him, she is doing her homework for the following day: reading the pages of the Moleskine that are not ruled out of bounds and tied off with a rubber band.

Guy has used his cryptocurrency wallet to purchase from a free classified ads site a rigid-hulled inflatable boat with a 60 horse-power engine, which he is due to collect from a boatyard in Kent in the morning. And he has spent himself in Candy's willing mouth.

'This one's not an ideologue,' Guy says, staring up at a painted ceiling covered in leering cherubs and copulating satyrs. 'That's his big secret.'

'I get it,' she says, studying the written biography. She's wearing reading glasses and nothing else. 'Simon Devereux. He behaves like he's some kind of yogi but at his core he's venal.'

'And our friends the Russians were with him at start-up and on every rung up the slippery ladder, providing capital and neutralising competitors.'

'Neutralising,' Candy says, 'that's an interesting metaphor.'

'The Russians were nothing if not thorough.'

'And such eclectic sexual tastes.'

'Yes,' Guy agrees, eyeing the pale scars radiating outwards across her body from her breasts and pubis. 'The Russians find reassurance in kompromat.'

She sees what he's staring at and raises an eyebrow. 'So tomorrow is about switching off the cash machines?'

'And all financial transactions.'

'Could be interesting.'

'Yes.'

'I can see you're looking forward to it,' she says.

'Yes.'

She cocks her head. At times her movements are exaggerated and coquettish. They remind him of a marionette. She's had her fix and heroin is pulling her strings.

'Where will it all end?' she asks.

'First, we bring the infrastructure of the city to its knees,' he replies, matter-of-factly. 'Then we seal the people in their little boxes.'

'Boxes?'

'Their homes.'

'I get it. And then?'

'We destroy the city.'

She rolls on her tummy and runs a finger along his clavicle, feeling the knots where it's been broken and reset multiple times. The way the tips of the stag's horns tattoo on his chest ripple across the breaks. She loves to touch the battlefield of his body. 'And do we form a part of the final attack?'

'Don't worry,' Guy says. 'We'll merely be bystanders, but I'll make sure that you and Cosmo have a ring-side seat.'

'And what will we see?'

He turns his head so that his mouth is just inches from hers and whispers, 'It's a secret.'

She reaches for the knife on the nightstand. She hands it to him, hilt first. 'You've waited long enough.'

Her eyes shine brightly as he takes the blade to her skin.

It's a bright morning with clear blue skies and the police have not found them. Candy is standing at the centre of the living room while Guy circles her, looking her up and down. She's wearing a tight-fitting Roland Mouret dress and Manolo Blahnik booties with crystal trim around the ankle.

'You look good enough to eat.'

'Honey, you say the sweetest things.'

The clothes were hand-delivered by motorbike courier along with Theo Fennell jewellery and Charlotte Tilbury make-up and a collection of other parcels for later usage: black chest webbing, red-lensed torches, range-finding binoculars.

'It's important to grab his attention,' Guy says.

'I know.'

She shimmies her shoulders in anticipation, her blow-dried hair cascading down her back. A glimpse of her old, defiant self. He can tell that she's excited to be playing a starring role again.

Across the room, Cosmo is sitting at the coffee table where they killed Arbuthnot the previous night. He's eating a bowl of cereal and practising taking the end caps off an RPG 22 and extending the launch tube, as his father has shown him.

Guy leans in to Candy's shoulder, his hands roving up and down her slim hips and across her rib cage, stroking the plasters beneath the fabric and pinching her nipples to make them stand proud. 'You're the brash, brassy fund manager representing a high net worth from the Gulf who is interested in stashing his cash in London. That's enough to capture Devereux's attention. It's up to you to intrigue him and arouse him. Then remind him who his masters are.'

'I know my lines.'

Guy glances across at Cosmo. 'Pack that away. You're heading out with me.'

'Cool, Daddio.' Cosmo collapses the tube and puts the end caps back on before returning it to one of the black holdalls. There are four of them, an arsenal of weapons, in a row in front of the fireplace.

'Take care of him,' Candy says, softly.

'Of course. He's my son.'

She kisses him on the cheek and uses a piece of tissue to wipe the lipstick off his skin.

'Are we coming back here?' Cosmo asks.

'No,' Guy tells him.

'Let's go then.' He picks up two of the heavy bags and staggers with them towards the stairs. Guy takes the other two.

Candy follows them to the landing. Looking back at her from the front door, with the light from the window behind her, Guy thinks she looks as exotic and doomed as a pharaoh's bride.

'You won't see me until we meet at the boat on Ragpicker's Wharf,' he tells her. 'But I'll be watching you from the rooftop the whole time.'

# 48

# Grom redacted

Jude, Rosanna and John Nganga are standing outside the private jet centre, flanked by a fifteen-strong specialist team of armed officers from SCO19 that is commanded by a police sergeant. There is a convoy of armoured Trojan BMWs fitted with state-of-the-art satellite navigation and communications gear on the taxiway beside them. Above them, the sky is black with rolling clouds of smoke and the air is heavy and still as if it is congealing. They can taste the residue from the burning oil terminal on their tongues.

'What are you thinking?' Rosanna asks.

'That Guy Fowle has been ahead of us at every turn, right from the very beginning. We need to take back the initiative.'

'Let's see what the Russians give us,' Rosanna says. 'Maybe we can stop him in his tracks.'

'Maybe,' Jude says with more enthusiasm than he feels.

His red-taped phone rings. It's Tamar.

'A woman matching Candida Taunton's description purchased heroin in Bethnal Green last night,' she tells him.

'Fowle is still in the city,' Jude says.

'And I still can't find the missing neo-Nazis. It's making me nervous.'

'They may have dispersed in preparation for an attack,' Jude tells her.

'Dammit!' She ends the call.

'The plane is approaching,' the police sergeant informs them.

They hear it before they see it. An unliveried white Lear jet that lands out of the smoke. It turns at the end of the runway and taxis to the waiting convoy. Behind Jude, a car door opens and Yulia emerges. She limps over to stand beside him.

Together, they watch as the steps unfold and a man in black suit and white shirt emerges. He is carrying a black suitcase. They watch him as he walks past them and opens it on the bonnet of the lead vehicle.

He turns to them.

'Yulia Ermolaeva?'

She limps over and they watch as the man removes a black phone from a recess in the foam padding, switches it on and holds it up to capture an image of Yulia's retina. He waits for a moment and then nods, apparently satisfied. He places the phone back in the briefcase, closes it and hands it to Yulia. He looks across at Jude.

'Any attempt to tamper with the software will cause it to immediately erase the contents.'

'Understood,' Jude tells him. He puts an arm around Yulia and ushers her towards the convoy.

Jude watches in the rear-view mirror as the plane takes off into the midday darkness, heading back the way it came. They race down the motorway.


Gretchen is sitting in front of a monitor in the situation room at the SAG offices with a revolving diagram of the phone's memory cache open on the screen and the video wall. She's scanning the Grom app with Yulia sitting on a pillow beside her and Rosanna, Dan and Jude standing over her. The rest of the room are watching the video wall from their work stations.

'Much of the data is locked and by the looks of it can only be unlocked remotely,' Gretchen says, 'presumably from Moscow.'

'Can you crack the code?' Jude asks.

'Eventually maybe, but even with the processing power that we've got it'll take time,' Gretchen says, looking up at him. 'And there's the risk that tampering will cause erasure. I think that they're going to be selective over what they release to us.'

Rosanna shakes her head. 'Dammit!'

'I'm sorry,' Yulia says.

'What do we have?' Jude asks.

Gretchen's fingertips dance on the keyboard. 'Downloading now.' A new window opens and a string of addresses scrolls down the screen. 'It's a list of safe houses. Forty in total, spread across the Midlands, Yorkshire and south-east England . . .'

'We need armed police at all those addresses,' Rosanna tells Nganga. 'And if there aren't enough police use the army.'

'I'm on it,' Nganga says, with his phone clamped to his ear.

The screen goes blank.

'Dammit!' Gretchen says.

Yulia accesses the phone with her retina and the screen wakes up again.

'The Russians unlocked another directory,' Gretchen says, reading a cascade of pop-up windows on the screen. 'It's Levi Minkin of Mr Roxy's Pet Food. His undergraduate degree was in biochemistry. He was harvesting cryptosporidium from rat's faeces. It's a water-borne disease that causes diarrhoea, vomiting and fever. There's a drop-down list of water pumping and testing stations across the capital. Also, the contact details of a Thames Water employee. Tomas Jankowski.'

'I'm calling Thames Water now,' Rosanna says, stepping away from the work station.

'I'll inform the Communicable Disease Surveillance Centre and activate the Drinking Water Inspectorate emergency plans,' Dan says. 'They'll arrange for the testing of water samples.'

'I'll speak to DEFRA and the Health Protection Agency,' Gretchen says. By now everyone is standing and Dan is allocating tasks.

Rosanna looks over from her phone. 'Jankowski's not reported for work for the last two days.'

'We're too late,' Jude says, his voice carrying across the room. Everyone has stopped and is staring at him. 'We need to focus on the next target.'

'I have one more accessible directory,' Gretchen says. 'Financial services, banking infrastructure.'

A further cascade of windows. Gretchen scrolls down complex strings of number and letter combinations in a screenshot of a Command Prompt window.

'What are you looking at?' Jude demands.

'Passwords,' she says. 'Administrator credentials recovered from operating system memory after the installation of database management systems.'

'What does that mean?'

'Whoever controls the passwords has access to the hosts that control ATMs, interbank transfer and card processing systems, and payment gateways for all the major high street banks. Jesus! They could have put anything in them.'

The screen goes blank. Again, Yulia wakes it up with a retina scan.

'We've got a name and a photo,' Gretchen says. A head-and-shoulders shot of a man of indeterminate age. He's wearing an open-necked white shirt with a double-layered collar. 'Simon Devereux. He owns a cyber-security company based near Tower Bridge called Currency Technologies that specialises in analysis of banking security systems. He does consultancy work for all the major high street banks.'

'Let's go,' Rosanna says.

'If Fowle is there he may be expecting us,' Jude says.

'We'll put in a wider cordon and trap him inside it,' Nganga says.

# 49

## The yogi of the firewall

Currency Technologies occupies the second floor of a former warehouse at Ragpicker's Wharf, just east of Tower Bridge. Candida gives her name and is processed through building security by a six-person team in smart black suits. She says goodbye to all her freshly acquired jewellery as they place it in a safe box mounted on the wall. She is invited to choose her own four-digit password.

Six, six, six, obviously, like the tattoo on her ankle. And another six for luck.

Then she is pointed at the body scanner and asked to remove her shoes.

A West London girl in a black hijab runs a detector wand along her arms and down her legs and briefly between them. She turns with her arms still raised and watches as her shoes emerge on the far side of the belt.

'That's all good, Miss.'

A couple of minutes later and she is ascending in a leather-lined freight elevator with a cast-iron gate. The gate-keeper waits for the car to come to a juddering halt before pulling the gate. Candida emerges to find a concave wall of glass bricks diffusing sunlight. A young man with a beard greets her. 'Candida?'

'Yes.'

'I'm Archie. This way please.'

She follows him into a gallery with cast-iron uprights and brick walls. Devereux's office is a glass-enclosed cubicle on the far side of an encampment of sofas and bean bags that looks like it's ripe for a sleepover. Fashionably dressed millennials look over from a coffee machine to watch her pass.

Simon Devereux is standing barefoot in the doorway. Slim and tanned with a linen shirt and dove-white hair that curls behind the ear, his only adornment is a recycled plastic wristband promoting a worthy cause.

'I don't think we've met,' he says as they shake hands, in a manner intended to leave her in no doubt that he would remember her if they had.

'You're right,' she tells him, maintaining eye contact, her pupils deliberately dilating. 'But I've read a lot about you.'

'It's nice to know somebody reads the trade magazines. Tea or coffee?'

'I'll have an espresso and do you have anything to eat?' All this moving around is making her hungry. 'Biscuits. I don't want nuts or fruit or seeds.'

He raises an eyebrow and glances at Archie.

'I think Sasha has some Hobnobs.'

'Good man,' Devereux pats him on the arm. He turns his attention to Candida. 'I was intrigued by your message.' He gestures at a chair, a mid-twentieth-century classic. 'Please sit.'

She sits and crosses her legs, the dress riding up her thighs.

He closes the door and smiles at her.

'I love your dress, by the way.'

'Yes. Thank you.'

He sits behind an empty desk. They stare at each other.

'As I'm sure you know, our systems penetration work has been exclusively for domestic and European clients up until this point,' he tells her.

'But you are open to widening your customer base?'

'Yes, if the circumstances are right.'

He smiles at her. You can tell that the smile is never far from his face.

'Obviously, the gentleman that I represent would be a potential gateway for you to the re-emerging banking networks in the Middle East region,' she says.

'That is attractive,' he acknowledges.

She lets that hang for a while. 'But I have to admit that since I arrived, I have been wondering whether it's a good time to invest here.'

His smile takes on an oleaginous quality. 'Why ever not?'

'Have you seen the sky?'

'Of course I have. It's full of smoke. All the more reason to utilise my services.'

'You think so?'

'Your client wants reassurance that his money will be safe and secure in London. I can offer him an independent analysis of the security of the network operating system of any bank here.'

'And the banks will let you do this?'

'I have a client list just as you do. My clients are also banks. They want reassurance as much as you do. The only condition that a bank will demand, apart from a non-disclosure agreement of course, is that I share the specific findings of the evaluation with them first and work to fix any identified vulnerabilities. All you have to do is sign the NDA and name the bank.'

'All of them.'

'All the banks?'

'Yes.'

'You want a full evaluation?'

'I want more than an evaluation,' she says.

His smile widens. 'Okay.'

It's a question more than a statement.

She says it. 'Still waters are inhabited by devils.'

It's wondrous to see. His whole face sags, as if the filler in his cheeks and jawline can no longer support it. Suddenly he's aged twenty years.

'Spit it out,' she hisses.

'It was smooth on paper,' he says, stumbling over the words, 'but we forgot about the ravines.'

'The belly is full but the eyes are hungry.'

He's shaking his head. 'I didn't expect this.'

'You must have known that it was a possibility,' she says, 'we invested a lot of capital in your start-up not to mention the actions we took against your rivals.'

'You'll destroy the nation's entire banking network.'

'Yes, that's the idea.'

'It's all kicking off,' he says, incredulous.

He must be watching the news. Candy doesn't mind events but she does find twenty-four-hour news irritating. Guy's obsession with it is the least attractive thing about him.

Archie backs into the room, without knocking. He is carrying a tray with an espresso in a small white cup, a mug of what looks like herbal tea and a saucer with three Hobnobs.

'Dark chocolate,' she says. 'My favourite.'

'What if I refuse?' Devereux says, when Archie has gone.

'It's a bit late for that.'

'I could give myself up.'

'You've systematically infected the operating system of every major bank with zero-day malware. A loading programme for unused attack simulations ready to be switched on. You can't plead ignorance, Simon. And even if you cooperate, you're going to prison for an awfully long time. And of course, we'd make sure that your experience in prison was an unpleasant one. But that assumes that we give you the choice. I have a sniper with a .50 calibre rifle loaded with armour-piercing rounds on a nearby rooftop. It's excessive, really. You have a large window and your glass is ordinary. I just have to raise my hand. Should I?'

He gulps, a genuine fish-like gulp. 'No.'

She almost feels sorry for him.

'Good. I'm glad that we understand each other. In recognition of your service you will be allowed to live out the rest of your life in splendour in a Gulf State that has no formal extradition treaty with the UK. No more hassle with your ex-wife. We can't do anything about your low sperm count but we have put fifty million dollars in escrow pending transfer to your cryptocurrency account, as of twenty minutes ago.'

He glances at his screen and taps at the keyboard to open the escrow wallet.

'Fuck!' he whispers. Then his eyes light up with greed.

'It's time to sing for your supper,' she says, taking an Emirati passport out of her clutch and placing it on the desk between them. 'You know that these are like gold dust.'

He looks at her.

'When?'

'Now.'

'Right now?'

'You want the money, don't you?' she says.

He takes a deep breath and faces his screen. It's remarkable how few keystrokes it takes to send out a message that activates the malware embedded in processing centres across the banking network.

'Now what?'

'I take the stairs and get the fuck out of here, pronto.'

'And what about my money?'

'What about it?'

She raises her hand and Devereux's head explodes. The rest of him lands on the floor with a thump.

She kicks off her Blahniks and runs for the emergency exit.

# 50

# The battle of Ragpicker's Wharf

They race east across the city with blue lights flashing. Rosanna and Jude are wearing Kevlar vests in the back of the lead vehicle in the first convoy and Rosanna is speaking to her husband on the phone.

On the police Airwave radio two separate specialist firearms units from SCO19 are coordinating their approach from the east and the west. Out at Battersea a Eurocopter is preparing for lift-off and on the north bank of the river another firearms unit is heading for the Marine Policing Unit at Wapping where fast ribs are being prepared.

On the car radio, Mobina Sinha, the Home Secretary, is giving the daily briefing. She announces 'Operation Temperer', a plan under the Civil Contingencies Act to redeploy a thousand armed police officers from across the country to the streets of London with the additional deployment of more than five thousand troops to protect key installations. Following the Home Secretary, the Chief Medical Officer issues a warning to Londoners not to use water straight from the tap and boil it instead.

'You can't let the baby sleep for three hours in the morning, Charlie,' Rosanna says, exasperated, 'he won't sleep through the night. Shit! I'm running out of power.'

They turn off Jamaica Street into a narrow street between former Victorian warehouses, the sirens echoing in the canyonlike walls. Currency Technologies is in a yellow-brick warehouse ahead of them at the end of the street.

Rosanna is leaning down into the footwell for a battery charger when an armour-piercing round strikes the windscreen. It punches through the armoured glass, bursts the driver's head like a popped paper bag, pierces his headrest and the Kevlar-strengthened upholstery of the seat above Rosanna's left shoulder. They veer into a row of parked cars, ripping through them like a tin-opener, before bouncing back into the centre of the road.

Jude and Rosanna are thrown back against their seats and then forwards as the BMW behind collides.

Two more shots follow in quick succession. Jude pops both their seatbelts and pulls Rosanna down into the footwell. They are both showered with blood.

Guy runs to the far side of the building with the Barrett rifle in his hands and Cosmo following. He hadn't expected the police to get here so quickly. He is prepared nonetheless. He rests the bipod on the chest-high parapet that surrounds the roof, aims at the second armoured convoy, which is approaching from the east, and shoots the driver of the lead vehicle. It swerves hard right and rolls, tumbling on its side and coming to a halt on its roof. The vehicle behind ploughs into it and the rest of the convoy skids to a halt. Firearms officers abandon their vehicles.

Guy collapses the bipod and slings the rifle over his shoulder. He runs midway across the roof to where one of the black holdalls is open. He grabs an RPG 22 rocket launcher and carries it to the other side of the roof where the first armoured convoy has come to a halt. He kneels behind the parapet, takes off the end caps and extends the launch tube. He thumbs the pop-up sight to 250 metres and hefts it on his shoulder. Rising and turning to face the street, he aims at the third vehicle in the convoy, which has stalled at ninety degrees to the road. He fires the fin-stabilised projectile and it strikes the side of the BMW, lifting it into the air and bouncing it off one of the high brick walls. He drops the launcher and runs back to the bag for another. He's midway across the roof when he realises the danger he's in and throws himself down. The searing back-blast from a rocket launcher washes over him. He springs up to see Cosmo beaming back at him from the parapet with an empty launch tube on his shoulder.

'I did it!'

He's hit one of the cars from the second team.

'Get down!' Guy shouts.

Too late. A bullet from below lifts the boy with his arm outstretched and the launcher in his hand. He seems to hang in the air. It reminds Guy of the Robert Capa photo of a falling soldier from the Spanish Civil War. He had a flatmate named Jerry at university who had a copy of it on the wall. It hadn't taken that long to persuade Jerry to take his own life.

He watches as the boy tumbles onto the roof. Irritated, he runs forward and kneels beside him.

Dead.

He had not planned for Cosmo to die this way, not before the final attack.

'We're sitting ducks here,' Jude says, with their faces right next to each other. Rosanna's eyes stare out at him from her bloody face. He reaches up between the seats to retrieve the driver's pistol from its holster. 'Follow me.'

He turns in the cramped space, pulls on the handle and kicks open the door. They roll out onto the tarmac one after the other and run to the cover of a recessed doorway. Reaching it, they hunch against the side wall. Jude looks back at the burning hulk of the third BMW and through the smoke to the two others stalled behind it. He watches as firearms officers debus and take up fire positions behind their vehicles.

John Nganga rolls out of the second vehicle and joins them in the doorway.

'Are you wounded?'

Rosanna shakes her head. 'No, it's not our blood.'

The police sergeant commanding the armed officers joins them. Via his chest-mounted radio, the second team are reporting that the shooter is on the roof of an apartment block close to the Bermondsey Wall. They take a quick tally of casualties, the injured and dead.

The helicopter sweeps overhead, the pilot reporting a body and two discarded launchers on the rooftop of a building at the intersection at the end of the street.

'Go! Go! Go!' the police sergeant says.

The remainder of the team run up either side of the street with their weapons raised. Jude looks at Rosanna who nods and they set off after them.

Guy darts out of one of the exits of the building and over a bridge across a moat of pea-green water. He has the Barrett rifle slung like an unwieldy spear across his back and he is carrying a Kalashnikov on a sling. His tactical vest is loaded with magazines and white phosphorus grenades. Currency Technologies is straight ahead of him on the far side of the road and he needs to cross it. He lets the carbine fall on its sling, pulls the pin on a grenade and lobs it underarm onto the street. It bounces across the tarmac and explodes.

Blinding gobbets of phosphorus arc in every direction followed by a billowing cloud of dense white smoke.

Guy runs forward using it as a screen. Midway across the street he drops to one knee and fires a burst into the smoke, in the direction of the firearms unit to the east, which is using the crashed vehicles as a makeshift barricade. He runs past the entrance to the warehouse and into a narrow alleyway that leads to the back of the building. He reaches it just as answering fire chews up the road behind him.

He runs through an archway in the Bermondsey Wall and out onto a pontoon that's beginning to lift off mud as the tide rises. It leads towards a shanty town of forty or so ageing Dutch barges, tilting against each other in the mud as the tide rises. Soon they will be entirely afloat. Midway to the barges a helicopter flies right over the top of him.

He fires a burst at the cockpit and rakes the length of it. In response, the chopper banks and peels off towards the spires of Canary Wharf. He continues firing until the magazine is empty. He jumps up onto the red-painted steel deck of one barge and runs across to another that leads to another that is overgrown with bushes and trees. He pauses to reload in the shadow of an alder.

'Candy!'

'Here,' she calls, from somewhere ahead of them in the maze of interlocking barges. Guy turns back to the pontoon that connects the barges to the shore and fires a burst, hitting the first police officer who comes through the archway.

Guy runs beneath the forest canopy from one barge to another. He finds Candida crouching beneath one of the trees. Her eyes are wild and her face is so pale that Guy wonders for a moment if she has been shot.

'Get up,' Guy growls.

'Where's Cosmo?' she asks.

'He's dead.'

'No!' she screams and launches herself at him.

He clubs her to the ground with the butt of the rifle. He was tiring of her anyway.

Jude sprints out onto the pontoon with John Nganga and five other armed police officers. They hurdle the body of the police officer who Fowle has just killed and run for the nearest barge. Jude has never felt more exposed than he does charging across the deck towards the tangled copse of bushes and contorted trees that Guy has disappeared into.

They reach the treeline without being fired at and spread out to sweep forwards, more carefully now, keeping as low as they can.

Jude spots Candida lying beside one of the trees with a bloody wound on her head. He kneels beside her and quickly checks her pulse to confirm she is still alive. Looking up, he glimpses Guy moving like a shadow through the trees.

He sees him break cover and run across the deck of one of the outer barges.

Running across the barge towards the deeper water at the centre of the river, Guy passes a hatch covered in tarpaulin. At the stern, a rope ladder leads down to where the rib is bobbing in the water.

He crosses to the downriver side. Three police fast ribs are approaching. He drops the AK and unslings the Barrett. He extends the bipod and lies down on the deck. He looks through the sight and aims at the nearest rib, the officers bunched behind the windshield at the raised prow. He fires two shots in quick succession. After the second shot the boat overturns, tipping the surviving police officers into the water. Guy swings the barrel right and sights on the second rib just as it accelerates behind the barges and out of sight onto the mud bank at the shore. He swings left and fires at the third rib which is already turning away in a broad arc. He fires twice more before the rib disappears around a curve in the river.

He rolls on his side and listens to the police calling to each other as they converge on him. He sees movement in the trees and spots Jude amongst them. Shots from one of the warehouses that overlook the river strike the deck beside him. There's no time to use the ladder. Leaving the rifles, he scrambles away and drops over the side into the Thames.

Piercing cold and darkness.

He sinks, bubbles drifting upwards from his mouth and then he kicks his legs and shoots upwards, surfacing beside the rib that he had bought the night before and piloted up from Kent that morning. He pulls himself aboard.

It takes the boat only a few seconds to cross the river. He veers around the heritage moorings and beaches on the mud beneath the Blitz Memorial.

## 51

## Gabriel is elevated

Gabriel has always believed that a politician's greatest asset, above even intellect and charisma, is judgement. Sitting at his desk in the Treasury, watching the images of chaos in shops and supermarkets following the failure of ATMs and chip-and-pin transactions on one screen and the plunging pound across Bloomberg's data service on another, he understands the colossal error of judgement he made in not owning up to being at Oleg Solokov's party on Pathos or revealing that his laptop has been hijacked by an unknown Russian hacker.

He goes and lies down on one of the red sofas beneath the disapproving gaze of the last Chancellor to King Charles I, kicks off his shoes and puts a cushion over his face, holding it down with both hands.

London is utterly fucked. And so is he.

His phone rings. Reluctantly he gets up to answer. It's the Downing Street switchboard with a call from the Cabinet Secretary.

'Put him through,' Gabriel says, with a sinking feeling.

'Chancellor, your presence is urgently required in the Prime Minister's office.'

'I see.'

'Straight away, if you don't mind.' The Cabinet Secretary's tone is sufficiently grave to brook no refusal.

They're on to him. They're going to stab him with a shitty stick.

'On my way,' Gabriel says, trying to sound cheerful.

He puts on his shoes and his suit jacket and pauses to straighten his tie. He might as well look his best for the executioner's block.

⋆    ⋆    ⋆

Gabriel stands on Downing Street and stares up at the white window frames and the black colourwash on the eighteenth-century brickwork. Ahead of him is the black door of No. 10 and its lion's head door-knocker. He is convinced that the end of his career is at hand.

He steps towards the door and as he does so, a custodian opens it for him. Inside, he finds the country's most senior civil servant standing waiting on the black-and-white tiles in reception.

'This way please, Chancellor.'

Gabriel follows the Cabinet Secretary up the main staircase, past black-and-white portraits of previous Prime Ministers on the yellow walls. On the first floor, he opens the door to the Cabinet Room and ushers Gabriel inside, closing the door behind them. The Cabinet Secretary leads him over to the white pillars at the end of the long table.

They are alone.

'The Prime Minister is in his flat being cared for by a paramedic team,' the Cabinet Secretary says, calmly and quietly. Gabriel has always been envious of his immaculately polished shoes. 'He will shortly be transferred to hospital. He has asked that you deputise for him in his absence'

Gabriel is surprised. 'I thought that was the Foreign Secretary's job?'

'That is customary practice, but there is no legal statute. Therefore, the final decisions rest with the Prime Minister and he was clear in his wishes. Whilst he was still conscious, that is.'

'He's unconscious?'

'That is correct.'

'What happened?'

'He is severely dehydrated and displaying the signs of a particularly virulent form of cryptosporidiosis. We believe that he asked for and was given a glass of tap water during a nursery school visit this morning.'

'Fuck!' Gabriel says.

'I will now take you to the Prime Minister's office where you will receive a phone call from the Monarch, who is at Balmoral. I

suggest that you don't swear. After that you will be joined by a
military aide who will brief you on the authentication codes for
the independent nuclear deterrent. When that is done you will
record a video message to the nation from a desk that we placed
in the Pillard Room. I will have a draft of the speech with you in
the next twenty minutes and notes for the press briefing that will
follow the broadcast.'

'That's not really what I expected.'

'You want to draft your own speech?'

'No. That's not what I— Oh, forget it.'


An hour later at the Home Office, Evan Calthorp leans across a
table and jabs an accusatory finger at Jemima Connick, the
Metropolitan Police Commissioner, with his small, mean mouth
churning: 'The country is facing an existential crisis and you're
worrying about a terrorist's rights?'

Sitting between them, the Home Secretary looks exhausted, her
forehead shiny with sweat. And on the screen on the wall, Gabriel
Morley is informing the nation that the Prime Minister has been
hospitalised.

'Candida Taunton's refusing to speak,' Connick says. Since her
arrest, she has been held at Paddington Green police station.
'She's going into withdrawal.'

'Give her to us,' Calthorp demands.

'And what are you going to do to her?' she says, looking from
Calthorp to Jude and Rosanna, who are standing by the wall. They
have washed their faces but their clothes and hair are still spat-
tered with blood.

'That's our business,' Calthorp replies. He turns on Mobina
Sinha, who is doubled up with stomach cramps. 'Are you going to
make a decision?'

'Take her,' she replies, through gritted teeth. 'Do what you want
with her.'


Gabriel's government-issue laptop arrives bubble-wrapped in the
hands of the Prime Minister's private secretary.

'Thank you, Chris.'

When he has gone, Gabriel carefully unwraps the computer and plugs it in to charge. He checks that the doors to the room are closed. Then he puts on earphones and clicks on the question mark icon. The bear's face fills the screen.

'Congratulations, Prime Minister.'

'I'm not actually the Prime Minister,' he protests, trying to keep his voice down.

'But soon, perhaps. If the Prime Minister does not recover.'

'Is this what you wanted, to put me in No. 10?'

'Don't be stupid. It's a fortunate coincidence. Have they given you the nuclear codes yet?'

Gabriel freezes.

The bear laughs. A gravelly, hacking sound with its mouth open and its teeth bared. It is the first time that Gabriel has seen it do that and it is deeply unnerving.

'It's a joke, Gabriel,' the bear says when it has stopped laughing. 'You have enough on your plate. Yes?'

'What do you want?' Gabriel pleads desperately.

'Oh, Gabriel,' the bear sighs. 'I suppose I should let you in on a secret.' Gabriel thinks that the last thing he needs is another secret in his life. 'Grom is not a finished product. It is a prototype. It is still at the system and acceptance testing stage.'

'Acceptance testing?'

'We are seeing interesting and unanticipated gain of function outside the laboratory in a real-life testing scenario.'

'Gain of function?'

'In biochemistry is positive mutation.'

'Mutation?'

'New and enhanced activity attributable to accelerated time-line and autonomous nature of the methods and means of attack.'

'This country is not a test case!'

'Nevertheless, you have to admit it is interesting.'

'What am I supposed to do to stop it?' he yells.

'Find this man who stole it.'

The door opens, the Prime Minister's private secretary takes one step into the room. Gabriel shuts the laptop and pulls the earbuds out of his ears.

'Can I help you, Chancellor?'

It has been made clear to him that the title Deputy Prime Minister is for public consumption only and he retains his current rank as Second Lord of the Treasury with the emphasis on *second*.

'Everything is fine,' he says, though of course it isn't.

'Mr Hermon is here to see you.'

The Prime Minister's Svengali, Maurice Hermon, strolls into the office and perches on the edge of the desk. He's as thin as a whippet and filled with elemental energy.

'What about you, Gabe?' He pokes Gabriel's laptop with a bony index finger. 'Who were you shouting at?'

'You think that you have a monopoly on shouting?' Gabriel retorts.

'Good point, well made! As long as you weren't shouting at your wife.'

'Of course I wasn't shouting at my wife.'

*I was shouting at a bear.*

'Do you think she'll go to the press?' Hermon asks.

'My wife?'

'Yes, you know kiss and tell.' He makes quote marks in the air. 'How my glamorous lesbian lover gives me better orgasms than my uptight husband.'

'Of course not!'

'You know her well, do you?'

'I am married to her!'

Hermon looks unimpressed by his answer. 'It's important that you project authority in this role. Particularly now.'

'That's what I want to talk to you about, what's going on in the here and now! The firebombings! The looting! We've got no fuel or money, and the water is poisoned!'

'Oh, you mean the complete fucking disintegration of the city? How could I forget?'

'What am I supposed to do?'

Hermon gives him a pitying look. 'You're going to announce an immediate lockdown and mobilise the army. We've got two-thirds of a three-line slogan, "Stay Home" and "Stay Safe". Then we need to protect something for the last line. What do you suggest?'

Gabriel thinks about it. 'Protect the nation?'

'The Scots and the Welsh and the Irish will howl.'

'Protect the city?'

'The rest of England will howl too.'

'Protect lives?'

Hermon sighs. 'I suppose it will have to be.'

# 52

# Hideaway cottage

Crossing the city, they are forced to divert the police convoy to avoid a burning mosque. Jude stares out through armoured glass at an angry crowd of worshippers gathering in the surrounding streets. Further on, they pass looters spilling out of ransacked shops. Jude knows that London is no stranger to rioting, every generation or so rioting in the capital has resulted in running battles between the people and the police, but this is especially shocking. This rebellion has no moral or political grievance behind it, only an indiscriminate urge to destroy.

His sister Tamar calls.

'We picked up a nasty little scrotum called Edward Renfield,' she says. 'He is singing. Fowle handed twenty-six white phosphorus grenades and a target list to a neo-Nazi called Tommy Shield.'

'What was on the list?'

'Renfield says he doesn't know but it included mosques, synagogues and shopping centres.'

'Damn,' Jude says.

'There aren't enough police to defend them all,' she says.

He hears an explosion in the background on her phone and the whistle of debris.

'What was that?' he asks.

'Fuck!'

'Are you okay?'

'Yes, I'm fine. I need to go.'

'Tamar,' he says, but she's ended the call.

At Paddington Green, the convoy meets an HM Prison Service van with black-and-white checked markings, and they escort it out of the city with blue lights flashing. From the elevated express-way, they see clouds of dense, black smoke rising into the air.

They change vehicles in a high-walled road policing unit compound beyond the truck stop of a motorway service station on the M4. Candida is escorted in handcuffs from the cramped cubicle of a prison transport cell to a line of three unmarked black Range Rovers with opaque windows. She's lifted into the back of the middle vehicle with female police officers in stab-vests either side of her. Jude gets in the front passenger seat and looks back at her, seeing her twisted face sheened with sweat.

She's not the only one. Half the police detail is looking feverish, though for different reasons. He knows that they are in a race against time before most of them are incapacitated by cryptosporidiosis.

Their final destination is a honeysuckle-clad thatched cottage in a gloomy corner of a privately owned estate on the banks of the Thames near Henley. They drive past a gate house and across rolling parkland before turning off on a gravel track that leads through a beech wood to the cottage.

Pulling up in front of it, they are met by a slim grey-haired woman in a cardigan.

'I'm Diana,' the woman tells Jude. 'I've prepared a bedroom for the prisoner upstairs.' He nods and the two female police officers escort Candida inside. Rosanna joins them.

'Your delivery is due in the next hour,' Diana says. She looks over their shoulders and tuts at one of the armed police officers, who is throwing up in a flowerbed.

'There's only one bathroom so tell the police that they can shit in the woods and bury it afterwards. There's a spade in the shed and a bunk room in the outhouse.' She looks Jude and Rosanna up and down. 'You two are in the cottage. You look like you both need a shower and a change of clothes.'

Sitting on the sofa in the low-ceilinged living room in front of a log fire, Jude and Rosanna watch the news. They are dressed from a cupboard of neatly folded clothes left by previous residents of the safe house that smell of moth repellent. Rosanna is towelling her hair.

On the television they see clouds of tear gas fired by ranks of helmeted police at looters across the city and a special briefing to the press by Gabriel Morley from the wood-panelled dining room at No. 10 announcing an immediate curfew. The firebombings and widespread looting are hampering attempts by the army to deliver fresh water.

Gretchen calls. Jude mutes the television and puts her on speakerphone.

'How are you both?' she asks.

They look at each other, confounded. It's the first time someone has asked them that since Ragpicker's Wharf. And then they're both thinking the same thing: that if Rosanna hadn't been reaching forward into her bag when their vehicle was hit by an armour-piercing round she'd be dead. Her brows furrow. She grips the towel tightly and stares intensely into the middle distance.

'We're okay,' Jude says with a questioning look. Brought back to the moment, Rosanna nods at him and forces a smile.

'Go on,' Jude says.

'The malware used against the banks was an overwriting tool that erases control systems. In that respect it is different to the malware used against the oil terminal, which hijacked rather than destroyed the control systems.'

'What about the water?'

'The Drinking Water Inspectorate has confirmed very high levels of cryptosporidium in London's water,' Gretchen tells them. 'They're expecting a city-wide cryptosporidiosis outbreak anytime now.'

'What about Fowle?'

'Recovered fingerprints and DNA from the mews house in South Kensington confirms that he was there with Candida and their son two nights ago.'

'And since then?'

'No sign that they've used any of the other safe houses in London but we've found an abandoned silver Range Rover in

Limehouse, on the opposite side of the river to Currency Technologies. We have placed it in the vicinity of the Kensington safe house, the oil terminal at the time of the explosion, and close to where the Corolla was last spotted. We found an unused incendiary rocket in the boot.'

'We have to assume that Fowle's found another vehicle or he's on foot,' Rosanna says. 'Any reports of vehicles stolen in the vicinity of where it was found?'

'The police are overwhelmed.'

'Dammit,' Rosanna says.

'What about the anonymous caller in St James's Park who tipped us off about the safe house in Kensington?'

'We have found one person of interest. Alexander Foggerel, the nineteen-year-old son of a London-based merchant banker, Joth Foggerel, who owns a villa on Pathos on the other side of the bay to Oleg Solokov. He was captured on CCTV entering the park just before the call was made.'

'Can you find him?'

'We're looking for him. There's no sign of him at his student accommodation and he has absolutely no social media presence. However, he did publish an article in the *London Review of Books* recently titled "How to buy stuff on the Dark Web". So, I'm guessing the social media hole is deliberate.'

'Keep me informed about efforts to find him. Is there anything more from Grom?'

'Nothing.'

'How is Yulia?'

'Bored and antsy, I think you should call her.'

'Okay.' He's surprised that she hasn't been texting him.

Outside they hear a motorbike pull up in front of the cottage and a wash of blue lights crosses the window.

'Got to go,' Jude says, cutting the connection.

They go out to where a policeman in motorbike leathers makes Rosanna sign for a sealed evidence pouch.

She hands the pouch to Jude. 'When do we do this?'

'When she's really hurting,' Jude says. He sighs.

'I better phone home,' Rosanna says, and walks away across the grass towards the trees.

Jude decides he'd better call Yulia. He dials her number.

'How are you?' he asks, when she answers.

'Darling, I have an overworked eyeball and a pain in the ass,' she says, wearily. 'How the hell do you think I am?'

'Are they looking after you?'

'Your tattooed friend has found me a passable Chablis.'

'I'm sorry.'

'I don't think that my government is going to release any more information to you. I think they've given us everything they've got. Let's hope Candida Taunton knows something useful.'

'We'll see,' Jude says. It seems unlikely that Fowle has told Candida anything revealing but he has to try nonetheless.

'How is Princess Ariel?' Yulia asks. 'Has she succumbed to your charms?'

Jude looks across the grass to the edge of the treeline where Rosanna is talking into her phone. 'She's speaking to her husband.'

'Darling, we both know that the fact of a marriage has never deterred you. You prefer your intimacies seasoned with secrecy, taboo and an absence of emotional attachment.'

'I can't do this right now,' Jude says.

She terminates the call.

# 53

## Truth serum

At midnight, Jude, Rosanna and Diana climb the stairs to the bedroom. One of the female police officers is standing outside the door.

'How is she?' Jude asks.

'Not good.'

'I'd like you to step outside the cottage,' Jude tells her.

When she is gone, Jude looks at Diana.

'You ready?' he asks.

'When dealing with Russians and their proxies, I have never had any problem with sacrificing scruples for expediency,' Diana replies, tight-lipped.

Candida is leaning over the edge of the bed and vomiting into a bucket with a police officer holding her hair away from her face. She is bathed in sweat and her whole body is shaking.

Jude sits at the end of the bed and asks the police officer politely to join her colleague outside. Rosanna closes the door when she's gone and stands against it with her arms folded. Diana rips open the sealed pouch and removes the bag of confiscated white powder inside. She sets it on the counterpane beside a fresh set of works: a half-inch needle with an orange cap and a 1 cc syringe, a metal bottle-top cooker and lighter, a ball of cotton wool, a bottle of sterile water, a packet of alcohol swabs and an elastic tourniquet.

Candida backs against the headboard, staring wildly at them and the powder.

'Where's Cosmo?'

'They shot him.' Jude says, softly.

Her face scrunches up and she starts uncontrollably sobbing.

'You murderers!'

'Guy Fowle is the reason your son is dead, Candida.'

'He was just a child.'

'Guy used children as suicide bombers in Iraq and in London. Do you really think the fact that Cosmo was his son would have stopped him?'

'I didn't have a choice.'

'You always have a choice,' Jude says, angrily. 'People are dead because of you. If you don't cooperate with us the Crown Prosecution Service will seek the maximum sentence under the Terrorism Act. However, if you choose to cooperate, it will be taken into consideration. You have the chance to stop any further attacks. Do you understand what I'm saying to you?'

She rubs her blotchy, make-up-smeared face and nods.

He gestures at the heroin laid out in front of him.

'You want this, don't you?'

She nods, miserably.

'You have to tell me everything you know.'

'Give me a shot,' she pleads. 'Then I'll tell you.'

'No.'

'You bastard!'

'Tell me.'

It spills out of her. Guy Fowle's careful transcription of the details of a cascade of attacks into a Moleskine notebook, the moving between rendezvous points exchanging malware, weapons and cash – the police car from an armed response unit under the bridge by London City Airport, the un-named Chechen in a London park, the white supremacists in the gym and the oil terminal engineer, the address of Fowle's former teacher's house and her role in destroying the banking network. But of the final target she has nothing more to say than that it will involve the destruction of the city.

'That's it?' Jude asks.

'I'm telling you the truth.' She looks defeated and desperate enough that he believes her. 'He wants everything to burn. Everything!'

Jude nods to Diana, who cooks the shot and draws the liquid into the syringe through the cotton wool. She taps out a bubble. With her thumb on the plunger, she pushes the liquid to the tip of the needle.

'Open and close your hand,' she says, wiping the crook of Candida's elbow with an alcohol swab. She puts the tourniquet on her upper arm to make the vein more pronounced and smoothly injects the drug.

Candida's head falls back and her eyes roll upwards.

'Stay with her,' Jude tells Diana and steps out of the room onto the landing to call Gretchen. Rosanna is heading down the stairs, already on the phone to Evan Calthorp.

Fifteen minutes later when he walks back into the living room from the garden, Jude finds Rosanna on her knees putting a log on the fire. The flames light up her face and make her hair shine like burnished copper. She stays as she is and he wonders whether she is aware of him watching her.

'I've asked Gretchen to review camera footage from around the park where Fowle met the Chechen,' he tells her.

She sighs and sits back on her heels. She glances at him. 'When I told Calthorp about Fowle passing a USB stick to a police officer in an armed response unit Trojan he asked me if I felt safe here.'

'What did you say?'

'I told him that most of the police here are sick. So they're unlikely to be illegals. Plus you're here. But he didn't seem to find that very reassuring. So I'm going to sleep with my pistol under my pillow.'

'Sounds sensible.'

'Have you thought about telling John Nganga?' she asks him.

'We don't know who to trust,' he says, uncomfortably. It shames him to think that he now has to consider whether a man that he has grown to like may be an illegal.

'Do you really think that Fowle is going to try and destroy the entire city?'

'Probably.'

'Calthorp said Morley will continue to divert assets from across the country and try and turn the city into a fortress.'

'I think that's what Fowle wants,' Jude tells her. 'He said as much to Candida. *We seal the people in their little boxes.*'

'Then we have to keep looking for him.'

He sighs. 'We do.'

'I didn't tell Charlie about what happened today,' she says. 'How I nearly died. I've never done that before.'

'I'm sorry.'

'Diana's made up a bed for me upstairs,' she says with a sigh.

'I'm sleeping here,' he says. Diana has left him a pile of blankets.

'At least you'll have the fire.'

She gets up and puts a comforting hand on his shoulder before she leaves. 'We did what we had to,' she says, 'to get Candida to talk.'

He turns out the light and sits on the sofa, staring into the heart of the fire.

# 54

## The pinnacle of success

Gabriel's had been a swift and brutal education in politics. After demonstrating guile and cunning as an attack dog in the Political Section of the Party, he had graduated to the role of special adviser in the Home Office, watching a succession of hapless ministers come and go mostly as a result of immigration cock-ups, and adding a tolerance for being on-call more or less permanently to his skills. From there he was selected for the prestigious task of delivering the morning press briefing to the Prime Minister. Every day at three a.m. he'd arrive for work and read the papers. Then, when his more senior colleagues arrived, they would produce the Party's official line on the day's stories. At six a.m. he would walk across Westminster to Downing Street to brief the Prime Minister in the adjacent flat to the one that he is living in now. The Prime Minister was usually in his pyjamas, with his wife asleep in the next room.

From that moment Gabriel had schemed, networked, spun and strategised to become the one on the receiving end of the briefing and that day has finally arrived. He is wearing a pair of navy-blue cotton pyjamas with white piping, that he has kept in their wrapping since he first conceived the ambition. The special adviser sitting opposite him on the sofa looks as unfeasibly young as Gabriel must once have done. It's not exactly as he had envisaged it. He is only Deputy. The actual Prime Minister remains in intensive care. And given the calumny the country faces, can he really be said to be running anything? He does his best to look stoical as the young man describes the catastrophe unfolding in the capital and the litany of scorn heaped on the government by the press. Turning to the financial markets, the UK's FTSE remains suspended but there is turmoil across the globe. In the US the

Dow Jones and S&P 500 are posting sharp declines in response to rising tensions with Russia, and gold – that bellwether of uncertainty – has reached a new high.

The young man pauses. Gabriel knows what's coming. On one occasion, Gabriel had to tell the then Prime Minister that he was accused of sticking his penis in a Black Forest gâteau in a tearoom during his days at Oxford.

'The story about your wife is getting remarkably little coverage,' the special adviser says. 'Though the *Guardian* has pointed out that Joth Foggerel's villa is across the bay from the one owned by Oleg Solokov where Guy Fowle's prison break was planned.'

'It's a large bay,' Gabriel says. 'What does the headline say?'

The young man looks embarrassed. 'The jet set that dines and sleeps together.'

Gabriel grunts. Behind him, his laptop buzzes on the kitchen counter, an unwelcome sound.

'That will be all,' Gabriel tells the young man, rising from his armchair. When he has gone, Gabriel locks the door to the flat and returns to the living area. He stands in front of the laptop and takes a deep breath before tapping the question mark icon.

The bear's face duly fills the screen. He looks even more angry.

'I'm meeting the heads of the intelligence services in thirty minutes,' Gabriel says. 'And I'm not dressed yet.'

The bear growls, menacingly.

'What's the matter?' Gabriel asks.

'That fool in the Kremlin has moved against the Bears.'

Gabriel shakes his head, confounded. 'What has that possibly got to do with me?'

'I want retribution.'

'So?'

'You must have a list of options.'

'Options?'

'For retaliation.'

'I can't just start a war with Russia because you say so.'

'Not a war, stupid. Something more precise. Something that hits them where it hurts.'

'Are you serious?'

'Do I look serious?'

'You're an angry bear, of course you look serious.'

There's a knock on the door.

'Someone's here,' he tells the bear. 'I have to go.'

'Remember, if you want to survive this you need to do what I say.'

'How can I forget,' he practically spits.

Another more impatient knock.

'Coming!' Gabriel shouts.

'And find out where that bitch Yulia Ermolaeva is,' the bear says.

'Fine.'

Gabriel closes the lid on the laptop and rushes to the door to the flat. It's Evan Calthorp, the head of MI5. He looks disapprovingly at Gabriel's pyjamas.

'I'm running a little late,' Gabriel tells him. 'Press briefing ran on. Come in.'

He leads Calthorp through into the living area.

'How's Mobina?' Gabriel asks.

'The Home Secretary is incapacitated,' Calthorp replies.

Gabriel worked with Calthorp when he was a special adviser at the Home Office and he is well acquainted with the powerful emotions that lurk beneath the spymaster's dour façade. Calthorp despises the current Home Secretary, considering her unfit for office. Having her out the way will suit his intentions.

'Help yourself to coffee while I get dressed,' Gabriel says.

Gabriel rushes through to the bedroom, not bothering to close the door behind him and pulls a suit from a rack of identical suits in the wardrobe. No time for a shower. He strips naked and pulls on a pair of boxer shorts.

'The *Guardian* are sniffing around Joth Foggerel's villa,' Calthorp says, from just out of sight.

'Yes,' Gabriel replies, pausing as he puts on a sock. 'I heard that.'

Calthorp doesn't speak again for the time it takes Gabriel to put on the other sock and step into his trousers and when he does, it's with a question. 'Were you at Oleg Solokov's party, Chancellor?'

'Joth has a lot of friends,' Gabriel says, zipping his fly. 'We went to a lot of parties. It's hard to remember.'

'Perhaps you should try harder.'

Calthorp is so bloody relentless. Gabriel knows that he won't give up until he has the answer. Best to just brazen it out.

'Yes, I was there,' he admits, as he buttons his shirt. 'But I didn't see anything. It was just a party with a smattering of C-list celebs. Joth said Solokov wanted to donate to the Party. I knew it wouldn't wash. I told him that. We didn't stay long.' Silence from the other room. 'Evan, I didn't say anything because I didn't see any of them, Ermolaev or Troshev or . . .' He nearly says Scary Bear but stops himself in time. '. . . or the other one. I was humouring an old friend.'

He walks out into the living area and stands, straight-backed, tying a Windsor knot. Calthorp views him sceptically. Either Calthorp has spoken to Xander and knows the whole truth, in which case Gabriel's fucked, or Calthorp hasn't and this is all a fishing expedition. It is slightly worrying that Xander hasn't been answering his calls for the last two days but Gabriel doubts that even Calthorp would keep him locked up for that long without revealing his hand.

'I think we need to take decisive action,' Gabriel says.

Calthorp cocks his head. 'What do you have in mind?'

'A retaliatory strike. Something tactical that leaves the ordinary Russian unscathed.'

'As you know we prepared a range of options at the Prime Minister's behest,' Calthorp says, 'including cyber-warfare.'

'Good,' says Gabriel. 'I like that. Cyber-warfare. Play them at their own game.'

'Shall I walk you down to the briefing room?' Calthorp says with the hint of a smile. 'Then we can get started.'

# 55

# Outbreak

Jude rises through layers of sleep like a diver kicking upward from the depths. When he opens his eyes, he is tangled in a knot of blankets and Diana is standing over him with a cup of tea.

'Your colleague is sick,' she says. 'She spent most of the night in the bathroom. The police team are in similarly bad shape. I've run out of rehydration salts and Imodium, and so I'm going out for more. Do you need anything?'

'I'm fine. How's the prisoner?'

'She's grieving. One of the police officers is sitting with her but I don't think she's a flight risk.'

'Thank you,' Jude says.

On the news, footage of burning mosques and synagogues, and clashes between police and looters, have been knocked off the top spot by scenes of chaos in the capital's hospitals. The cryptosporidiosis outbreak means that many of the city's inhabitants have spent the night wracked by alternating bouts of vomiting and diarrhoea. The elderly and immuno-deficient are the most vulnerable and make up the majority of the reported fatalities but the acuteness of the outbreak means that the functions of government have all but shut down. Transport for London has closed down the Underground and the buses. A much-depleted Metropolitan Police has given up control of areas of the city until further reinforcement arrives, and most resources, including three Challenger tanks from the army, are concentrated in the vicinity of an expanded Whitehall cordon that reaches as far as Trafalgar Square.

In a televised address from outside the door of 10 Downing Street, Gabriel Morley announces that the threat level in London has been raised to Level Four. He points the finger of blame at the

Russian state and informs the world that a targeted cyber-offensive has been launched in retaliation by GCHQ.

Gretchen calls and Jude mutes the news.

'How are you feeling?' he asks.

'You know I only drink rain water.'

'Yes, of course.'

'GCHQ hit the banks used by the people closest to the Russian president with an advanced persistent distributed denial-of-service attack,' she tells him. 'They used botnets from multiple different global networks with forged IP addresses to flood the banks' operating systems and disrupt financial transactions.'

'In plain English?'

'The president's men have no access to their money.'

'For how long?'

'Given the power and bandwidth of the attack it could be weeks before they see it again. A lot can happen to a bank in that time.'

'I can't help but feel this is exactly what Fowle wants,' Jude says.

'I do have something for you,' Gretchen says.

'Go on.'

'An overnight trawl of cameras in the vicinity of the park where Fowle met with a Chechen has identified a suspect, a dissident named Ruslan Dudayev.'

'What do we know about him?'

'Dudayev was granted asylum here six years ago. According to our records, he is an opponent of the Russian regime and there have been at least two attempts on his life by the FSB. Yulia has confirmed this. After the last one he was given a new identity and relocated to West Yorkshire. The last recorded police contact with him was two years ago.'

'He doesn't sound like a Russian asset,' Jude says.

'On the face of it, that's true but I think I may have found a link. A number of the safe houses raided by police are in the same area of West Yorkshire that Dudayev was relocated to and show signs of long-term habitation. One of them has only recently been abandoned, literally within the last couple of days.'

'Shit!'

'What is it?' Gretchen asks.

'If you're planning an attack and you're concerned about operational security it's a precaution to move your team immediately beforehand.'

'You think that another attack is imminent?'

'I think it's a possibility. Can you please put Yulia on.'

He waits.

'Jude?' He can tell from her voice that she's angry with him.

'What can you tell me about Dudayev?'

'The FSB hate him. They won't be happy until he's dead.'

'So, what is his connection to Grom?'

'Dudayev may not be aware that he is doing the work of Russia or if he is, he may have no choice or he may not care.'

'Thank you.' He searches for something to say that will make things good again between them. But there's nothing. 'Please put Gretchen back on.'

'Boss?'

'What are we doing to find him?'

'I've already informed West Yorkshire Police and they've despatched an armed response unit to his address.'

Jude looks up to see Rosanna standing in the doorway, looking pale and sleepless.

'Call me if anything comes of it.'

Rosanna collapses on the sofa beside him.

'How are you feeling?' he asks her.

'Ghastly.'

'Do you want anything?'

She shakes her head. When she doubles up with a stomach cramp, he rubs her back and afterwards she rests against him. Gradually her head falls forward and he gently catches it and lowers it to his lap. On the muted news, there are images of Eurofighters patrolling the skies over the Baltic States and a meeting of North Atlantic Council members above a rolling strapline announcing that NATO is debating a request by Nigel Featherstone, the Foreign Secretary of the United Kingdom, to invoke Article 5 of its charter, confirming that an attack on any one country is an attack on all.

When he hears the crunch of gravel on the drive outside announcing Diana's return, Jude eases himself out from under Rosanna and carefully rests her head on a cushion. Outside, the morning air feels cold and clean on his face. Two members of the firearms unit are standing on the drive and the rest are on camp beds in the bunkhouse, being tended to by Diana. The police sergeant that commands the unit is one of the most severely affected and the constable that has replaced him gives Jude a quick update. Only three members of the team, two men and one woman, are able to function. He explains that he has asked for reinforcements but SCO19 are stretched to capacity and there are other more urgent priorities.

'That's okay,' Jude says, warily. 'I don't think Guy Fowle will come after us here. Send a message that we don't need any more police. I'm going back to London.'

He's had an idea. Someone he wants to speak to about Dudayev.

'You want me to send someone with you?' the constable asks.

He shakes his head. 'Watch the prisoner. Let me know when your team is up and functioning again.'

The constable gives him the keys to one of the Range Rovers. 'Good luck.'

# 56

# The chameleon of the Caucasus

Motorway traffic into London is down to a single lane, with soldiers in camouflage watching from beside armoured fighting vehicles canted across the other lanes with their canons raised. Two police officers in fluorescent jackets are marshalling the traffic. Easing slowly forward in line, Jude sees that several lorries have been pulled over and are being searched by soldiers with dogs.

Beyond the roadblock, the traffic speeds up again, but only briefly, before reaching central London where he sees the first signs of looting and becomes aware of smoke rising from multiple fires. Heading north of the Westminster barricades, he drives through Knightsbridge, passing cars and vans crashed into the showrooms of luxury stores and swathes of shattered glass on the road.

The streets are mostly empty of people, though he glimpses a few hurrying down side streets with their heads down and he passes a man in a hoodie in Mayfair pushing a shopping trolley with a widescreen television in it. Twice he has to change his route and divert further north because the streets are blocked with the burned-out hulks of cars. He pulls over to allow a convoy of fire engines to pass. They drive straight past the fiercely burning Marble Arch synagogue, heading for some other higher priority task. The only large concentration of people that he passes is in the vicinity of University College Hospital, which has spilled out into the surrounding streets to form a dense tent city with water points, rows of portaloos and a cordon of armed police.

\*　　\*　　\*

Jude parks on the south side of a garden square close to the British Museum. At this time of year, the square would usually be crowded with students but now it is empty. He walks across the square and past Senate House, and enters the main building of the School of Oriental and African Studies. Dr Falchikov's office is tucked away at the end of a long, nondescript corridor. He knocks on the door.

'Come.'

He opens the door and steps into the Orient. A large high-sided Knole sofa covered in kilim fabric faces an imposing desk piled high with papers tied together with string. The walls are lined with floor-to-ceiling bookshelves packed with books in Caucasic and Kartvelian languages and propped against them everything from curved knives, drinking horns and pottery shards to a gesso and gold icon of the Virgin Mary. In the corner there is a birdcage with a parakeet inside and beside it a mahogany plant stand with a silver samovar on it.

Dr Falchikov stares up at him sagely from behind the pile of papers. She's wearing the same thick tweed suit as the last time he saw her in his offices what seems like an age ago. Back before he'd ever heard the name Guy Fowle.

Her eyes twinkle. 'Mr Lyon, if my memory serves me correctly?'

'That's right.'

'You are not sick,' she observes.

'No, thankfully not.'

'Me neither. We are made of stronger stuff, I think? Please sit.' Explaining to her that his apartment has a water filtration system with an absolute pore size of less than one micron seems unnecessarily detailed.

He sits on the sofa.

'I don't drink water as a general rule,' she says. 'Would you like some tea? I have read that you must boil for at least one minute. I have been assiduous in this.'

'Yes.'

She pours black tea into a glass from the samovar and adds some fresh mint leaves from a saucer propped on a stack of papers.

'Sugar?'

'No, thank you.'

She passes him the glass and pours herself one before returning to her seat behind the desk.

'We live in extraordinary times.'

'We do.'

'Do you think that there will be a war with Russia?'

'I'm trying to prevent it,' he replies.

'Good. Therefore, I assume that this is not a social visit?'

'You're right.'

'How can I help you, Mr Lyon?'

'I was hoping that you could tell me about a Chechen named Ruslan Dudayev?'

She adds sugar to her tea and stirs it with hypnotic slowness. 'It is some years since I heard that name,' she says, eventually. 'Dudayev is a chameleon, I think. A man of many colours. Here he claims to be a pacifist but before he was many other things. Perhaps your government was a little too hasty to offer him asylum. There are unexplained gaps in his history. There is a saying: the enemy of your enemy may also be your enemy.'

'We have received intelligence that suggests that he is an enemy and if so, he may be preparing an attack. Is it possible that he is working for the Russians?'

'He is no friend of the FSB, that's for sure,' she says, sipping her tea. 'But could he be a tool of some other branch of Russian intelligence? These days anything is possible. The president is surrounded by spies all vying for his patronage. And your own Moscow Rules say that everyone is potentially under opposition control.'

'And if he was?'

'He is said to be a persuasive man. I am told that in Chechnya he had quite a following amongst young and impressionable men of criminal intent. He had a knack for repurposing them for violent and destructive means. After Putin crushed the resistance in Chechnya he dropped out of sight. At that time many of his peers travelled to Afghanistan and then later Iraq. I cannot say for sure, but perhaps he also made that journey? If you want to find him, I suggest that you begin with those disaffected characters that exist on the fringes of certain marginal communities. If I had to guess, I would say that you might begin with those who have returned from foreign wars, Syria or Iraq, for instance.'

'Thank you,' he says.

She shrugs her shoulders. *'De nada.'*

He stands up and places the glass on the only free space he can find.

'Thank you for the tea.'

'I hope you find him. This city has suffered enough.'

Back out on the street he calls Gretchen. 'Contact the Extremism Coordination Unit. We're looking for connections between returnees from the Middle East and the Yorkshire safe houses. I'm heading up there now. Can you put Yulia on?'

He waits for a moment.

'What do you want?' she says.

'Can you find out from your contacts in Syria if they set up a rat run for returning jihadis from Syria? If so, we need their names.'

'I'll ask.'

He terminates the call and immediately phones the head of MI6.

'Speak,' Chuka says.

'We're facing the imminent threat of multiple attacks.'

'I'll inform Morley.'

By the time Jude leaves the city heading north, he sees that the canons on the infantry fighting vehicles are pointing directly at the traffic.

# 57

# The gentle cartoonist

It is late afternoon when Jude parks the Range Rover behind a police van at the edge of a litter-strewn football field in an industrial town in West Yorkshire. From the top of the hill, identical rows of back-to-back terraced houses slope downwards and are mirrored on the far side of the valley, where they rise steeply out of the shadows towards the abandoned hulk of a red-brick Victorian cotton mill that dominates the skyline.

On one side a group of Asian youths have stopped playing football to watch him park. It's not so discreet as vehicles go. On the other side, two council workers in overalls are painting over a St George's Cross with *Behead all Muslims* written beneath it in foot-high letters that has been sprayed on the terrace end wall. From the car's front-seat compartment, Jude takes a pair of plastic gloves and snaps them on.

A police officer is standing at the entrance to a narrow passage that separates the brick-walled backyards of two terraces. He takes Jude's details for the crime scene log and lifts the tape for him to pass.

About midway down the passage, Jude passes a young Asian boy standing watching him from a backyard filled with bed sheets hanging out to dry. He offers something brightly coloured in his palm.

Jude kneels to take a look. It is a piece of orange paper skilfully folded into a long-necked swan.

'Take it.'

'Thank you.' Jude lifts it in his palm, as carefully as he would a real bird trapped in a house. The boy turns and disappears amongst the sheets.

Jude continues. There is another police officer at the rear entrance to the safe house. If he has an opinion on the paper bird cupped in Jude's hands, he does not show it.

Asha, the diminutive local representative of MI5, is standing in the kitchen wearing a white paper suit and a midnight blue Turkish-style hijab.

'I saw the graffiti on the end wall,' he tells her.

'Yeah, it's the local English Defence League. It'll be back up soon after its painted over. At least, with all the practice, they've finally learned how to spell behead properly.'

He puts the origami swan carefully down on the table, which is dusted with fingerprint powder.

Asha frowns. 'Where did you get that?'

'Local kid gave it me.'

'Where?'

'Out there?'

'In the ginnel?'

'The passage.'

She rolls her eyes. 'Yeah, the ginnel. You got to work on your northern vocabulary, brother.'

'What have you found?' Jude asks.

'The whole house is full of explosive residue,' she tells him. 'It must have come from their clothes because they didn't cook the explosives here. Going by the number of beds there were six people living here.' She wrinkles her nose. 'And judging by the state of the place I'd say they were definitely men. It's the same at another house three streets away. Identical set-up and the same number of people. Both houses were abandoned two nights ago, sometime after midnight. The locals aren't exactly trusting of the police but one of the neighbours has confirmed that a man matching the description of the Chechen visited roughly once a week with groceries. The inhabitants stayed in all day and only went out at night. There's a TV with a Wii in the front room and one of the upstairs rooms has been converted into a gym. The smallest weight is twenty-five kilos so they must all be built like gorillas.

A SOCO in a white suit enters the kitchen. 'Can you look at something?'

Asha and Jude follow him up a narrow staircase to a room with double bunk beds. One of the mattresses has been pulled aside on a lower bunk. The SOCO points with a torch at the corner of the timber frame, where a delicate line drawing has been carved in the wood with a sharp knife.

A bird.

'It's Salem al-Futuri,' Asha says, looking at Jude. 'Little bird. He left for Syria in 2013 along with his two older brothers.'

'That's a bit Batmobile,' Asha says, when she sees the Range Rover.

'I borrowed it.'

'Check your privilege, white boy. It must be nice to borrow something and not be locked up for stealing it.'

She hops up into the passenger seat and he starts the engine.

'Where to?'

'Just follow my directions.'

'Tell me about Salem,' he says as he pulls out of the parking space.

'Really?' she says, with a caustic edge to her voice. 'You really want to go there?'

'Yes.'

'First thing, get yourself back on the dual carriageway.' She looks away from him and out the window. 'Everyone seems to think these kids get their heads filled with hate in the mosques but that's not even a fraction of the story,' she says. 'People need to understand the role played by racism, police neglect and the failure of the system for protecting vulnerable young people.'

'You make him sound like a victim.'

'That's because he was. Salem was a talented kid. He drew cartoons and got them published in the local paper. He wrote satirical rap lyrics. He had secured a place at art college. He was well liked and amusing. He wasn't the sort to cause trouble.'

'What happened?'

'The family was systematically targeted by racists. The National Front, the English Defence League and Casuals United had a go at them. Ibrahim and Abdallah, the older brothers, were beaten up on their way to school by men wearing balaclavas and had death threats issued against them on social media.' She snaps directions at him in pauses in her commentary. 'The windscreen of the family car was routinely smashed, and one night a mob gathered outside their house and threw bottles, bricks and stones, breaking several windows. At first, the family went to the police. There were some arrests but no one was charged. CPS said that it wasn't in the public interest. On top of all that, there were allegations that their father was violent towards the boys, including whipping them with electric cables. The father was arrested but the child protection plan wasn't enforced. The father repeatedly broke his bail conditions and visited the house. He cut the landlines and made the boys withdraw their statements.

'Eventually the boys and their mother fled. Their emergency accommodation was riddled with damp and the walls ran with water when it rained. They continued to be targeted by racists. In total the family was moved four times in three years. And then the brothers started to fight back. They won a series of street brawls with their former bullies and they formed a gang. They began with mugging passers-by for their mobile phones and within a few months the police were describing them as a "one-family crime wave". With the father no longer there, the brothers seized control of the house from their mother and started moving other members of the gang in with them. It became the go-to place for police looking for missing teenage boys. It wasn't just their mum Ibrahim and Abdallah bullied and abused; it was Salem too.

'He became introverted. One night, he was filmed in the town centre drunkenly yelling abuse. A crowd gathered around him. According to the recordings posted online, one of the more coherent things Salem said was: "When the day of reckoning comes, you'll all go to hell."

'In the autumn of 2012, the three brothers flew from Luton to Istanbul and from there took an overnight bus to Gaziantep. They crossed into Syria and enrolled in Jabhat al-Nusra, an al-Qaeda affiliate. Within a month of learning that the three brothers were in Syria, the local police had identified a group of twenty young people, all of them under eighteen, who had travelled to Syria. We know from online postings that Abdallah was killed by a sniper in Idlib and Ibrahim in the final battle for Raqqa, the capital of the Caliphate. As for Salem, we have nothing. No record of him returning here or of any contact with his mother for more than three years.'

Jude's phone rings. It's Yulia.

'I spoke to my contact in Syria. He believes that Valkyrie facilitated the transport of a dozen British nationals from there to the United Kingdom after the final battle of Raqqa,' she tells him. 'Salem al-Futuri amongst them. I have given the list of names to Gretchen, who has informed the police.'

'Thank you.'

They turn onto a street of terraced houses not very different from the one that they had left behind twenty minutes before.

'Pull over here on the right,' Asha says.

Jude parks outside a house with a blue door.

'This is Salem's mother's house,' Asha tells him. 'I'll do the talking.'

# 58

# Day of reckoning

Salem drives a seven-and-a-half-ton truck packed full of home-made explosives and 'shipyard confetti' – nuts, bolts and other metal scrap – south towards London on the motorway. The trigger is taped to the steering wheel and within reach of his thumb.

He is ready for death. He has been for some time.

He had expected death in Syria, in Raqqa in the prophetic final battle at the end of historical time when the Caliphate would emerge victorious, and democracy, secularism, nationalism and all the other garbage ideas of the West would finally be destroyed. But it was not to be.

'The Prophet died one and a half thousand years ago but the struggle continues,' the leader told them before they climbed aboard the buses that would carry them out of the besieged city in a deal brokered with the Kurds. 'They can kill us but the promise won't die. We may lose one or two rounds but the fight is not over yet. No matter how many weapons they have and how many planes are bombing us, we will win this war. We are fighting for the sake of God. But they have no cause to fight for.'

Salem rode defiantly with his fellow fighters on top of one of the buses. The convoy stretched for six kilometres. For three days they could hear the American drones buzzing like wasps above them and at night the warplanes flew overhead dropping flares which lit up the convoy and the road ahead with that weird white light that always made him think of Bonfire Night. But they would not attack because of the women and children.

When they reached the Turkish border, the foreign fighters were separated from the rest and broken down into groups by nationality. There were a dozen from England, five of them from his hometown. It was there that he first met the Chechen who introduced himself to them as Ruslan and told them that he had fought the crusaders in Chechnya, Iraq and Afghanistan, and that he would sort passage for them back to England with new passports and new names.

The alternative was to get arrested on arrival.

'I'm offering you the chance to turn the tables on your enemies,' Ruslan told them. 'To redeem yourself and punish the crusaders by using the skills and knowledge that you have learned here against the society that forced you to suffer. We need to make the whole world understand that the Caliphate has no borders or map. What you do in your own homeland will be better and more enduring for us than anything you can do here.'

He explained that on their return they would be permitted no contact with their families or friends, or any aspect of their former lives, and that they would not be able to make any ties or form any friendships. They would constantly be on the move to evade the British police and their informants. And when the time came, they would be expected to sacrifice their lives for God in order to kill as many crusaders as possible.

He remembers them looking at each other and seeing the matching resolve in each other's weary, famished faces. All they wanted to do was go home.

But they would not give up.

It wasn't easy. The journey across Europe was a nightmare. They were treated worse than animals, packed into tiny spaces and barely fed. The criminals that transported them behaved like monsters. One night, the youngest, Saif, was gang-raped.

To give him credit, Ruslan was furious when he heard about that. Back in England, conditions were better but the homesickness was worse. They were moved by van at night between houses. They laboured in subterranean spaces enclosed in plastic sheeting. Lack of contact with their families further sapped their morale. He thought how much his mother must be worrying about him. He asked for drawing materials but he was told it was forbidden. He took to folding paper and carving signs in hidden places.

They mixed batches of chemicals, acetone and hydrogen peroxide, under Ruslan's guidance. At times, the need to speak to his mother made him feel physically sick. They made several tonnes of the explosive known as the 'Mother of Satan'.

Tri-acetone triperoxide.

He is driving a truck packed full of it.

Salem notices that ahead of him on the motorway the overhead signs are flashing a reduced speed limit of 50 miles per hour. The traffic is beginning to slow down and he wonders what is ahead. He glances at his phone. The other drivers in the WhatsApp group have reported their locations within the last half hour. All heading towards London from different directions. His target is where a three-armed Christmas tree-shaped transmission tower delivers high voltage power lines to one of the six super-transformers that supply the city. Since the oil depot explosion and the closure of the M1, he has had to revise his route and is now heading south on the M40.

It's the first time that he's had access to a phone for nine months and he's been fighting the almost unbearable urge to phone his mother and say goodbye since it was given to him by Ruslan this morning.

The next sign announces road lane closures ahead. A highway maintenance truck with a flashing sign is channelling the traffic into two lanes. Cars start cutting in front of him from the fast lane and the traffic slows gradually to a crawl. A police car with blue flashing lights speeds past him on the hard shoulder, heading south.

On WhatsApp, Khaled and Jaffar both report motorway lane closures.

A low-flying police helicopter sweeps overhead, also heading south. They receive a message from Ruslan telling them to get off the motorway and find alternative routes. Salem is several miles from the nearest exit. Ahead of him the motorway is down to a single lane and the cars in front of him are all indicating to feed into it.

Within minutes, he's stuck. The motorway is gridlocked.

When people start getting out of their cars, he realises that he is never going to reach the target. It's only a matter of time before they find him. He feels a crushing sense of disappointment and failure. To have come all this way, to have seen so much, to have made so many sacrifices and seen so many of his friends die on the battlefield, but not to be able to fulfil his destiny is more than he can bear.

His phone buzzes. It's Khaled:

I can see the target.

Salem smiles. Khaled has reached the transformer. The task will be completed. There are two trucks for each transformer. Only one of them needs to detonate to succeed.

With joy in his heart, he phones his mother.

'Who is this?' It's the first time he's heard her voice in three years and she sounds frail and fearful.

'It's Salem.'

'My darling,' she says, her voice trembling. 'Where are you?'

'It doesn't matter, Mama. I just want you to know I love you.'

'I know you're here,' she says. 'I know what you're doing, I'm begging you please don't. You don't have to die.'

'It's too late, Mama.'

'The police are here. I love you, Salem, I love you.'

A woman's voice replaces his mother's. 'Salem, my name is Asha. I'm from the same place as you. I'm with your mother. She's not in any trouble. We need you to tell us where you are.'

Salem can feel the tears running down his cheeks and he grips the steering wheel.

'I have to finish,' he says.

'It doesn't have to end this way,' Asha tells him. 'Your mother has lost two sons. Don't make her go through the pain again. Remember the beautiful pictures you used to draw. You can do all that again. You can live.'

In the distance he can see the flashing lights of the police cars as they race up the hard shoulder towards him.

'I saw the beautiful swan that you gave to the child. Allah is beautiful and He loves beauty.'

There is no beauty left in the world, just the cacophony of sirens.

Police cars screech to a halt.

'There is still hope in you, Salem.'

He gave up hope long ago. It was foolish to have given the boy the swan.

Men in black pointing guns are advancing towards him.

'Think of your mother, Salem.'

'I'm sorry, Mama.'

He presses the trigger.

# 59

# London's burning

Jude flies south lulled by the vibration of the helicopter's airframe.

Beneath them the empty motorway is a ribbon of orange light in the midst of velvet darkness. Before they reach the city they approach the site where Salem detonated his truck. Jude sees the spinning blue lights of emergency vehicles and burning flares on the horizon and then, as they pass over, he glimpses human shapes moving amongst the wreckage of vehicles, and the fierce white light and cascading sparks of an oxyacetylene torch cutting open cars.

After several miles of abandoned cars, they fly over an army checkpoint, one of the posts in the 'ring of steel' that now defends London. He can't decide whether it's a pointless display of military hardware or worse, the soldiers unwitting collaborators in Guy Fowle's plan to trap the populace in the city. He's angry with the Russians for building Grom. He's angry with himself for not locating the suicide bombers in time to stop them. And most of all, he's angry with Guy Fowle for causing so much devastation.

He wants, more than anything, to find Fowle and kill him.

One of his phones vibrates in his pocket. It's the red-taped one, a message from Kirsty:

I NEED to speak to you

He cannot answer. He cannot bear the thought of lying to her.

The chopper flies above the expressway and skirts past the burning carcass of the largest shopping centre in England before heading south-east towards Westminster. Areas of the city are blacked out with fires raging out of control but, despite the absence of the Monarch, the lights are defiantly on in Buckingham Palace. The chopper crosses St James's Park, circles and sets down in Horse Guards Parade, alongside two Apache Longbow attack helicopters.

Jude drops to the gravel and runs out from beneath the rotor wash to where an air marshal in camouflage is holding two fluorescent red batons. There are two armed soldiers kneeling either side of him who escort Jude across the parade ground and through the arch to Whitehall.

The chopper lifts off behind him.

The Cabinet Office smells of bleach with an underlying tang of vomit and faeces. As he makes his way down the corridors, he senses heads turning in his wake. His notoriety is spreading amongst those few who are attempting to maintain some form of governance over the city. There is only one politician inside the cordon, the remainder of its occupants are beleaguered civil servants and members of the security forces, many of them curled up in sleeping bags in the corridors. The Prime Minister is in a coma, the Cabinet Secretary is sleeping and Gabriel Morley is running the country.

Inside the COBRA complex, Jude finds Morley and Evan Calthorp sitting together watching the news feeds. Calthorp is as pale as a cadaver, with dark hollows under his red-rimmed eyes, and Morley looks frayed, like a man who has achieved his life's ambition and found it to be a nightmare.

'They destroyed five of the six high-voltage transformers that deliver electricity into the city,' Calthorp says, turning a pencil over in his fingers. 'We've only got one route left for power into the city and we've had to introduce rolling blackouts to distribute the load.'

'And Fowle?'

'The zero-day malware released into the banking systems is spreading into other networks and erasing data,' Calthorp continues. 'The GPS tracking system for locating police cars, fire engines and ambulances just died.'

'And Fowle?' Jude repeats.

Calthorp looks at him as if he's an irritation and shakes his head. 'Nothing since Ragpicker's Wharf.'

'He hasn't finished,' Jude says.

'Then you had better find him and stop him,' Calthorp snaps. Beside him, Morley stares at the table with his face slack.

Angry and in need of fresh air, Jude goes out through the airlock onto Whitehall and walks across the street to stand beneath the bronze monolith commemorating the women of the Second World War. There are traffic cones scattered haphazardly on the road.

He phones Gretchen.

'Anything on Grom?' he asks her.

'Nothing. And the period between the phone going to sleep and it requiring a retina scan to be woken again has increased to five hours, which suggests that they're in no hurry to release new information.'

'You think that the Russian government have stopped cooperating?' he asks.

'Maybe. Or as Yulia says, they've already given us all they've got.'

'How is she?'

'Climbing the walls.'

'You have my sympathy,' Jude says.

A fox trots by, indifferent to Jude's presence. He watches it heading down the empty street in the direction of Parliament Square.

'I've made some progress in identifying the so-called fifth man,' Gretchen says, 'the one who was found in a basement swimming pool in Chelsea with a thumb missing.'

'Go on.'

'He is a hacker who goes by the name Scary Bear.'

'Scary Bear?'

'Chinese hackers are pandas. Russians are bears.'

'Right.'

'Until recently there were no known photos of Scary Bear but, according to certain forums on the Dark Web, he wore a distinctive platinum thumb ring with a polar bear's claw mounted on it.

We found one that matches its description on the thumb of Cosmo Taunton.'

'Fowle cut off his thumb and gave the ring to his son.'

'Yes. I believe that the fifth man is Scary Bear and we now have a photo of him at Troshev's barbecue with the Russian president.'

'Keep digging around,' Jude tells her. 'He can't have built something as complex as Grom on his own. There must be other bears. If we can find his associates then maybe we can find a way of switching it off.'

He ends the call and immediately calls Rosanna.

'Jude?' She sounds groggy and confused.

'Did I wake you?'

'It's fine. I saw the suicide attacks on the news. Where are you?'

'Whitehall.'

'How is it there?'

'Nobody seems to be in charge.'

She groans. 'I feel so bloody helpless.'

'It's not over,' Jude tells her. 'Something else is coming. I wish I knew what.'

'You sound tired,' she tells him. 'Get some rest.'

'There's no time.'

'Have a shower and change your clothes.'

He heads back towards the Cabinet Office in search of a car from the protection pool. He's decided to take her advice and head out beyond the barricade. Thirty minutes later, two Challenger tanks reverse to create an opening for his Trojan to drive through.

## 60

# Xander comes clean

A bulldozer has cleared a path through the traffic jam that stretches from the Tower of London to Aldwych, pushing piles of mangled and torched cars up onto the pavements. Arriving, Jude parks the police car on a yellow line in the cobbled cul-de-sac outside Sanjay's loft and walks towards the door with his keys in one hand and the Glock in the other. As he does so, he sees a boy in his early teens jump on a bicycle and cycle away at speed.

There's light in the stairwell, which means the electricity is on, but he doesn't risk the lift in case of a blackout and climbs the stairs, past three floors of darkened software start-ups without any staff. It's the first time he's been back at the loft for several days. He lets himself in through the triple-locked door and is confronted with a view of the Gherkin on fire and huge billowing clouds of black smoke above the City. He strips as he watches the flames rising up the building.

He stands under the shower with his palms on the tiles, letting the hot water pummel his body. He is towelling himself when the door buzzer goes.

It's Kirsty standing out in the street with a skinny young man beside her wearing a Chelsea football shirt. He's older than the youth on the bicycle earlier. Jude checks a couple of the other cameras in the cul-de-sac to check that there's only two of them and then reluctantly buzzes them in. He is standing waiting for them with the towel knotted around his waist and the Glock behind his back when the lift door opens.

'Wow, those are quite some bruises,' she says as she slips past him into the loft with the young man following.

'I was in a car crash yesterday,' he says, following them.

'A car crash?' she says, sceptically. She's wearing black cargo pants and a blue T-shirt with *Smooth Life* written on it in red lettering, which seems somewhat at odds with the truth.

'What happened to the Gherkin?'

'Someone firebombed the Bevis Marks synagogue and it spread west. The Fire Brigade are holding a line at St Mary Axe.' She cocks her head. 'Is that a gun or are you just pleased to see me?'

'It's a gun.'

The young man beside her takes off his earphones and looks around. 'Cool digs.'

'Who is this?' Jude asks.

'Xander Foggerel.'

'I see.'

He recognises the name. Alexander is the eldest son of Joth Foggerel heir to the merchant bank Foggerel & Co, who owns a villa on Pathos on the opposite side of a bay to Oleg Solokov, the principal shareholder of PMC Valkyrie.

'You should reply to my calls instead of neglecting me,' Kirsty says. 'Do you have some coffee?'

'The fridge is full of it.'

She opens the fridge door and whistles at the stacks of silver cans. 'Wow! Your flatmate loves coffee.'

'I'm going to get dressed,' he tells them. 'Try not to steal anything.'

He returns five minutes later, in jeans and a blue linen shirt, with the *Kerambit*, the claw-like knife in a sheath on his belt and the Glock tucked in the waistband in the small of his back. She has got the coffee machine working and made them all double espressos.

'You look like you need it,' she says, handing him the cup. 'Do you always dress in navy?'

'Sometimes I wear black.'

'You're embarrassed or ashamed about something,' Kirsty says, searching his face. 'Are you thinking you should have answered my calls?'

Xander is looking back and forth between them. 'Are you two an item?'

'Strictly professional,' Kirsty says with the merest hint of a smile.

Jude takes a sip of espresso and it's like an immediate jolt to the brain. 'How come you're not sick?'

'I only just got back in the country.'

'How?'

'I paid a fisherman in Calais to run me across the English Channel.'

'That figures. Where have you been?'

'Pathos,' she says. 'I was following up on a link between the Serbs who broke Fowle out of prison and PMC Valkyrie. The Greek police were very accommodating. They let me have a look around what's left of Oleg Solokov's villa. The place was trashed. The computer servers in the mountain were molten slag. A neighbour reported gunfire and explosions the night after Guy Fowle's escape from the house in Chelsea. By the time the Greek police arrived, there were five dead bodyguards and no sign of Solokov or Troshev. I'm assuming they're back in Russia now, facing the music.'

'Which suggests that you think the Russian president is not responsible for the attacks?' Jude says.

'Everybody assumes the Russians lie,' she says. 'Like it's in their DNA. But what if the Russian president isn't lying? Maybe this isn't a deliberate state-sponsored attack. Maybe the people responsible for designing the attacks went rogue. If that was the case, wouldn't you want me to get that news out there? It might stop a war.'

'I didn't see too many people queuing for newspapers.'

'The United Kingdom is not just London,' she says, indignantly, 'and, by the way, the whole world is watching.'

She's right, it was a cheap shot. 'As far as I can tell, the Russian president did not initiate the attack,' he tells her, in reparation, 'but there is no doubt that Russian assets under deep cover have been activated and are attacking our infrastructure, physically and with sophisticated malware.'

'Now we're getting somewhere,' Kirsty says with a smile. She looks at Xander. 'See, I told you he'd come clean.'

'And what about you?' Jude says to him.

'I've been keeping a low profile,' Xander says. 'I had no idea who might be looking for me, you know, potentially some very serious Russians. But you can't stay on the run forever.'

'So, you contacted Kirsty?'

He rolls his shoulders. 'Yeah, well you know, she broke the whole Guy Fowle story. I was worried about what he might do next.'

'You sent the anonymous tip-off from St James's Park about where Fowle had been staying,' Jude says.

'I provided the phone and the voice scrambler,' Xander replies, 'but I didn't make the call.'

'Who did?'

Xander looks to Kirsty who gives him an encouraging nod. He stares at the ceiling and winces before looking at Jude again. 'Gabriel Morley.'

Jude experiences a brief and unwelcome out-of-body sensation. 'The Chancellor?'

'It's a humdinger of a story,' Kirsty says.

'I think you better explain,' Jude says.

Jude stands watching him while Xander tells them the story of what happened at the party at Oleg Solokov's villa in Pathos. How a guest spilled red wine on Gabriel's shirt and they went in search of the kitchen to try and get the stain out. How they inadvertently stumbled on a meeting between Dmitri Troshev, Valery Ermolaev and the hacker named Scary Bear. Xander explained that he hadn't realised who Troshev or Ermolaev were until later when he saw their faces on the television but that he had identified Scary Bear by his distinctive thumb-ring, which features a real claw from a polar bear mounted in platinum.

'You found his body along with a bunch of Serb gangsters in the basement of the Chelsea house that Guy Fowle escaped from,' Kirsty adds. 'It was his phone that Fowle stole. The phone that is behind the attacks.'

'Keep going.'

'Scary Bear belongs to a Russian hacking team known as the Protean Bears,' Xander says. 'They're the ones behind the malware attacks on the oil terminal and the banking system. And it would make sense for them to have built the app, an operating system for pairing traditional physical attacks and cyber-attacks.'

'How can you be sure?' Jude says.

'One of the bears is talking to Gabe, I mean Mr Morley. This one is called Angry Bear. It took over his laptop. That's how Gabe knew about the missing phone and it's how he found out where Fowle was staying. I delivered him a burner so he could call it in. He was trying to help.'

'Fowle was long gone when we got the tip-off,' Jude says, dismissively. 'The hacker was playing with Morley.' He glances at Kirsty. 'When are you planning to break this news?'

'It's ready to go online. All it needs is my say-so.'

'And if I asked you to wait?'

'I'd say, are you having a fuckin' laugh?'

'I need you to come with me to Westminster,' Jude tells Xander.

'He's not going anywhere without me,' Kirsty says.

'And if I let you come too, would you hold the story?'

'I might.'

Sixty minutes later, Xander Foggerel is standing in front of the Prime Minister's desk flanked by Jude Lyon on one side and a grim-faced Cabinet Secretary on the other. Barred from the meeting, Kirsty is fuming in an anteroom.

'You're buffering, Gabe,' Xander says.

It is true that Gabriel Morley's face has frozen as if the recognition of the folly of his own actions, neatly summarised in a few curt sentences by Jude, has deprived him of the ability to function. His eyes have glazed over.

'He's had a shitty time recently,' Xander says. 'He's not used to it.'

'We've all had a shitty time recently.' Jude is feeling short of sympathy. He raps his knuckles on the desk. 'The police are waiting.'

Gabriel refocuses.

'Shall I draft your resignation letter for you?' the Cabinet Secretary asks.

'That would be very kind,' Gabriel replies.

# 61

# Bear trap

If it's true that all political careers end in failure, and he's never seen any evidence to refute this, Gabriel's has ended more spectacularly than most. He is sitting in his soon-to-be-vacated Downing Street apartment in crumpled pyjamas at four a.m. with the prospect of a lengthy prison sentence for treason on his mind. The Foreign Secretary has decided to remain in Brussels at NATO HQ in a further effort to get Article 5 invoked. And downstairs the Queen is talking to the Welsh Secretary, Owen Evans, who was the only able-bodied and available member of the Cabinet within a short helicopter ride of Whitehall, and has appointed him Deputy to the Prime Minister in Gabriel's stead.

It's not quite over for him yet and there is some possibility of at least partially redeeming himself. He has his laptop open in front of him and whilst the backdrop behind him is unchanged, the rest of the room is full of stacks of electronics unpacked from aluminium flight cases; computers, monitors, humming water-coolant radiators and a full rack of blinking servers. Add to that a cast of characters that appear to have strayed out of a sci-fi movie.

'The internet is a place of proxies, misdirection and geographic uncertainty,' says a large black American from Darmstadt named Hardcastle. He is wearing a black coat and sunglasses despite being inside. The other members of the NSA's Tailored Access team defer to him as if he's the leader of a cult. 'All of those play against us. What we're looking for is the command-and-control server that the malware on the laptop is communicating with. We should expect the communication to be bounced through several different staging servers and it's going to take time for us to follow it to the source. If we're successful in reaching it, we will deliver our own payload including a web-shell which will give us a foothold in our opponent's computer and allow us to snatch and grab its contents. From the moment the bear connects, and we start tracking the reverse channel, you have to keep him talking for as long as you can.'

'Understood,' Gabriel says.

'From what you've been saying, the bear likes to brag. Encourage that.'

'Will do.'

'And try to relax.'

He nods, though it's rather easier said than done given that his entire gilded fucking life is in ruins. He refrains from saying that.

'When you're ready.'

'Right.' Gabriel takes a deep breath. All eyes are on him. Jude Lyon is tight-lipped, while beside him Evan Calthorp scowls.

'Here goes,' Gabriel says.

He double clicks on the question mark icon and after a few seconds the screen ripples and is filled with the face of the bear.

'Mr Prime Minister,' the bear says. 'Are you having a sleepless night?'

'Yes, actually.'

'It must be hard for you,' the bear says, 'to have it so starkly demonstrated that your control is dependent entirely on electronic data. Noughts and ones. And if I take it away from you, you are nothing more than a dumb cow.'

On the screen on the other side of the room, a digital line arrows south across a map of the globe from London to a staging server in Lagos.

'Are you satisfied?' Gabriel asks.

'Shouldn't I be?' the bear responds.

'You've shut down an entire city.'

A line jumps from Lagos across the Atlantic Ocean to a server in Panama City.

'We have proved that it works,' the bear says. 'A new type of hybrid assault that blends kinetic and digital to devastating effect. It's a transformative moment. No less significant than the Roman shield-wall, the English longbow, the German machine-gun, or the American bomber. It's the beginning of a whole new era in warfare.'

Crossing the date line, from Panama City to Macau.

'And the civilians that have died?'

The bear shrugs its massive shoulders. 'If you chop down a forest, splinters will fly.'

'If you have proved the concept, surely now you can stop?'

Macau to the tri-border area where Argentina, Uruguay and Brazil meet.

'It's not in the power of anyone to stop Grom, Gabriel. Once set in motion, it cannot be undone. That is the beauty and the horror of Grom. Its autonomy.'

'But you must know the targets?'

From the tri-border area to Damascus.

'There are many targets,' says the bear. 'Many menus and many attacks. Its strength is flexibility and unpredictability. Who can tell what Fowle wrote in his book?'

Gabriel tries another tack. 'Fowle wants to trap people inside London. Why?'

Damascus to Paris to Port Moresby.

'Surely that is obvious? Because he wants to kill as many of them as possible.'

'How?'

'Last week maybe I would have told you,' the bear says, 'but this week Angry Bear thinks fuck English people.'

'Please.'

Port Moresby to Helsinki to Bangui.

The American Hardcastle raises a thumb. Gabriel can feel the surge of excitement in the room. He glances up at the network of lines criss-crossing the world and ending right in the centre of Africa.

'What's the worst thing?' the bear asks. 'For a dinosaur, a meteorite. For a human. I ask you? What do you think?'

Gabriel stares at the screen. 'I don't understand you.'

'What don't you understand?'

'Why do you want this?'

'Maybe I don't think you deserve privileges that you have.'

'I'm not sick,' Gabriel replies. 'I don't need cash to eat and I have electricity from a generator. How am I being punished?'

'You don't have any power or authority.'

'That's politics,' Gabriel tells the bear. 'Power comes and goes arbitrarily.

At the bear's end, an alarm is sounding.

It growls.

'You have found me.'

Another screen has a satellite image of a cluster of compounds in a distant city. The cameras zoom onto a flat-roofed building with a satellite dish on it. Hardcastle looks forward and says into one of the monitors, 'I can see you.'

The bear roars.

The screen in front of Gabriel ripples and goes black.

Hardcastle leans back in his chair, removes his sunglasses and pinches his nose. 'Well?'

'We have a photo,' one of his team says.

A screen fills with the head and shoulders of a young woman with shoulder-length blonde hair. Her face lit up by a monitor.

'Behold Angry Bear,' Hardcastle says. 'Let's find out who she is. What about associates?'

'We sent out a network ping from her computer and we got only one in return,' another member of his team says. 'We're pinpointing it now.'

'And the grab?'

'We're reviewing the haul now but it looks like Grom self-erased.'

'And response?'

'The nearest drone in the air is six hundred miles away over Chad,' one of his team says. 'It would take ninety minutes to arrive.'

'We have to assume she will have vacated by then.' He claps his hands. 'That's it, people. The fun is over. Let's get to work figuring out what we've got.'

# 62

# It's darkest before dawn

Jude watches Gabriel Morley being led away by two police officers. He's too tired to feel angry with Morley for his stupidity. He stands up and squeezes between the stacks of electronics, navigating the cabling snaking across the floor and out the flat. He heads down the stairs with Gretchen following, past the cartoons and caricatures of previous Chancellors on the walls and out the door into the fresh pre-dawn air of Downing Street. He feels frustrated beyond measure.

'We're no nearer to finding Fowle,' he says.

'If the Americans can identify the malware, there's a hope of finding a counter to it.'

'How long's that going to take?'

'Too long,' Gretchen concedes.

Jude raises his face to the sky. 'I can't stand this.'

'You need some rest,' she tells him, gently.

'I need to go and speak to Kirsty and Xander.'

They're waiting in the Cabinet Office, after the Americans denied them access to Morley and the bear-trap operation.

'Promise me you'll get some sleep after that.'

'Sure.'

'I've also hit a brick wall and I need a chance to clear my head,' Gretchen says. 'Yulia's demanding to go somewhere green. Can I take her with me to the allotment later this morning? Just for a couple of hours. We'll have the security detail with us.'

Jude hesitates.

'Nobody is looting vegetables,' she tells him. 'Not yet anyway. We'll turn straight around if it's not safe or if there's another incident. Rosanna's team are reviewing the evidence we have on

Fowle, looking back over it to see if we've missed anything. They weren't hit too hard by the cryptosporidiosis outbreak.'

'Okay.'

'Thank you.'

She heads towards the armed police officers at the gate.

'Say hi to Yulia,' he calls after her.

She looks back at him and sighs. 'I think she's expecting more than that from you.'

'Send her . . .' he is at a loss, 'I don't know . . . tell her that I hope she's okay.'

Gretchen looks unimpressed. 'Let's hope she doesn't bite my head off for delivering that.'

Jude goes back inside and takes the stairs down to the basement and follows the service corridor that connects No. 10 to the Cabinet Office. There are soldiers gently snoring on cot beds with their rifles, body armour and helmets stacked beside them the entire length of it. He climbs the stairs at the other end and enters the carpeted corridors of the COBRA complex.

Kirsty and Xander are sitting in a room adjacent to Briefing Room A. They look up as he enters. He can tell that Kirsty is fuming.

'They've traced Angry Bear to Africa,' Jude says, 'and they've got a photo of her.'

'Where in Africa?'

He shakes his head. 'That's all I'm authorised to tell you.'

'After all I've done for you,' she says, standing up.

'What about Gabriel?' Xander asks.

'He's been arrested.' When he sees the expression on Xander's face, he says, 'He was very cooperative. We wouldn't have found Angry Bear without him. I'm sure they'll take that into account.'

'I wanted to say sorry to him.'

'When this is over, I'm sure you can see him.'

'And when is this going to be over?' Kirsty demands.

He doesn't have a satisfactory answer to that.

'When are you going to find Fowle?' she presses him.

He doesn't have an answer to that either.

'I've organised for a police car to take you home,' he tells her.

'That's it?'

'For now. Yes.'

'I'm going to break the story.'

'I know. Thank you for waiting.'

'You're not going to try and stop me?'

He shakes his head again. 'No.'

'Where's the fight in you?'

He sighs. It's a good question. He's never felt more helpless. Fowle is out there somewhere with a notebook containing the details of who-knows-how-many illegals just waiting to be activated and a series of meticulously designed attack-plans, including one of a scale sufficient to destroy London. And it feels like there is nothing that Jude can do about it. He is deprived of all the usual tools of surveillance and detection – the rioting has torched a significant proportion of the city's cameras and large parts of it remain lawless territory. The police and forensics teams are seriously depleted by illness. His only surviving human asset, Candida Taunton, has given up what little she knows. The Russians have stopped unlocking information.

There's no trail of bodies to follow. No obvious clues.

Fowle has gone to ground.

# 63

## The Englishman's widow

Not long after sunrise, Pilar Allan picks her way carefully across the shingle of a Suffolk beach, with the dog ranging ahead of her with his nose to the ground. She greets the plants like one might greet old and familiar friends: sea campion and lady's bedstraw, sea kale and sea holly. There is a sedum, the sea pea, that lives further up the beach towards the marsh.

Abruptly the Cocker Spaniel raises his head to the sea and spots the fast-approaching boat.

'Ghillie!' she calls, knowing he won't listen. He sprints to the shoreline. The first of the marines to disembark kneels in the surf to scratch him under the jaw and behind the ears. It's the tall gap-toothed one who always has a scrap of something edible in his pocket and has earned Ghillie's absolute love.

'Sorry!' she calls out.

They wave off her apologies. The marines are large and unfeasibly young, apparently impervious to cold water, and their eyes sparkle with good-humoured enthusiasm. She watches as they run the rib up the beach to their bivouac, with the dog bounding along beside them, yelping with excitement.

The distinctive white dome of the nuclear reactor is visible above the dunes beyond their camp. When she first arrived here she had been beset by dreams of the radioactive core exploding but it has been a feature of her daily routine for so long that she had grown impervious to its presence, until the soldiers arrived to protect it. She now looks at it with fresh eyes.

Once the boat is under cover, their commander approaches with his rifle slung across his back. He's Cornish, with jet-black hair that suggests a dash of Iberian blood, not exactly handsome but confident with a rakish glint in the eye.

'Good morning, Sergeant Wyllow,' she says.

'Pilar.' He'd only just stopped calling her 'missus'.

She wonders what he sees in her: a lean, spare widow in her sixties with bright blue eyes and long grey hair in a ponytail. Hair that was once as black as his. A handsome face with the evidence that she was once beautiful. If only he knew the anger, that even after all these years, still burns inside her and is as fierce as the reactor behind him.

'It's going to rain later,' she tells him.

He nods, looking out towards the North Sea. 'It'll get rough out there. *Water can flow or it can crush. Be water, my friend.*' In response to her questioning look, he smiles shyly. 'Bruce Lee.'

'Ah!' Of course, a martial arts icon would be his source of guiding mantras. 'Will you go out again?'

'Once more before we're done for the day, I reckon,' he says.

'Stay safe,' she tells him, about to set off again, but then stops. 'Oh, and I forgot, I got you something in town.' She gives him a bottle of *piri piri* sauce from the pocket of her frayed Barbour jacket.

'Makes boil in the bag bearable.' He accepts it with a grin on his face. 'The boys will be pleased. Thank you.'

'I'll see you soon,' she says. 'Come on, Ghillie!'

Eventually the dog rejoins her and they head back the way they came, past the power station before turning left on the bridleway and following the path towards the wooded copse on Goose Hill. At less than ten metres and surrounded by wetlands it is the highest point for several miles and affords a good view of the causeway known as Sizewell Gap, which is the only road through the marshes to the power station complex. The paratroopers have placed their command point there, an interlocking group of tents with camouflage netting slung like spider's web between the trees and surrounded by two-man trenches. The paratroopers are not as friendly as the marines and she finds it harder to disguise her loathing. She calls Ghillie to heel and slips the lead on him, before skirting the base of the hill and rejoining the path in the woodland beyond. She lets Ghillie free again but he stays close.

Her bicycle is posed against a wall by the old abbey. Of the directional fragmentation mines that she set out with before dawn, four are still in the basket with a dishcloth covering them. Each one of the mines contains a concave explosive platter of C4 explosives with a layer of seven hundred steel ball-bearings embedded in epoxy resin. Looking at them fills her with anticipation of the coming battle.

She inhales and exhales, letting her breathing calm the disorder inside her. When she is sufficiently composed, she mounts the bicycle and Ghillie keeps pace with her as she pedals sedately between the hedgerows. She rides south and then east along a poplar-lined avenue towards Sizewell Gap, slowing to speak to Mrs Emory at Hope Cottages who is in her garden, weeding.

'Morning, Pilar.'

'Morning, Joan,' she replies, with one plimsole on the ground. 'How are you?'

'Could be better,' Joan says. 'I had the revolving lights on the ceiling of my bedroom all night.'

The police roadblock on the Gap is fifty yards away. Two armed response vehicles are parked across the road and there are policemen with guns standing on the tarmac.

'I have eye shades somewhere,' Pilar tells her. 'I'll drop them by before tea. Got to go.'

She pedals along the Gap and then slows again for the roadblock until she recognises Sergeant Rozier; it's only two weeks since the baptism of his youngest son. She did the flowers for the church that day. He waves her through. 'Go on, Pilar.'

At the road end she turns onto the bridleway again and heads south-west across the Walks with its maze of footpaths towards the Aldringham estate.

Anthony is waiting for her on the steps of the manor house, wearing faded pink corduroy trousers.

'Ah, Pilar of the community,' he says, gleefully.

She coasts to a halt and hops out of the seat.

'Anthony, your jokes are as old and frayed as your cuffs,' she tells him, propping her bike against the stone newel post at the foot of the stairs. A former director at a merchant bank, Anthony wears his wealth lightly. She climbs to greet him with Ghillie wagging his tail beside her. A chaste kiss on the cheek in case of watchers.

'I'm surprised they let you though the gate given your exotic heritage,' he says.

The two paratroopers at the entrance had shown not the slightest interest in her, though one had run his hands across Ghillie's back as he trotted by.

'I'm old enough to be invisible,' she says.

'Not to me,' he tells her.

As soon as he has closed the door behind them, they kiss passionately. When they break from the clinch, she leads him up the stairs to his bedroom.

'You're eager, today,' he says.

'I have an itch,' she tells him, laughing. 'It needs a scratch.'

She's been feeling this way since she looked up from deadheading her roses two nights ago and saw Guy Fowle standing at the gate of her cottage. He was filthy, and without belongings but nonetheless beautiful, a vision of power and strength, like Achilles taunting the Trojans.

The fulfilment of a promise made to her long ago by the Russian from the embassy in Buenos Aires who recruited her.

'Still waters are inhabited by devils,' he said.

She remembers what followed in exquisite detail: standing and pulling off her gardening gloves by the fingers, feeling the leather sliding across the backs of her hands. The butterflies in her stomach. Ghillie submitting. She replied in a clear voice: 'A spoken word is not a sparrow. Once it flies out, you can't catch it.'

And he smiled, though his eyes remained as sharp as those of a bird of prey. 'The belly is full but the eyes are hungry.'

'You'd better come in and I'll show you to your room,' she told him and led him into the cottage.

She had waited so long for this moment.

\*     \*     \*

Anthony and Pilar strip facing each other on the Persian rug beside his four-poster bed with Ghillie curled up outside the door. Anthony is in his early seventies but apart from a slight thickening around the waist he is in pretty good shape for his age. Pilar is proud that her body shape hasn't changed significantly in the last twenty years. He is a generous lover, thoughtful and considerate, and never in a hurry. He seems genuinely pleased when she climaxes.

'Oh my,' she says, astride him as it happens.

She was thinking of before breakfast yesterday morning, on the landing of her cottage when she met Fowle standing bare-chested outside the bathroom with the magnificent stag's horns tattoo on his chest.

'You first,' he'd said.

Closing the door behind her, she sat on the edge of the bath and felt a flush of excitement.

'That was quick,' Anthony says, when they are done.

She kisses him more passionately than she intended and he is thrilled.

'You know you're always welcome here,' he tells her.

She slips out of bed and puts on one of his wife's dressing gowns and drifts towards the window. She had grown up in a house this size. Back when her father belonged to the Jockey Club of Buenos Aires and knew everybody, or at least that small segment of the land-owning population of Argentina that considered itself to be everybody. Before the coup and the war and economic collapse robbed her of everything that meant anything to her. Before a sympathetic Russian offered her a pathway to revenge. Before the long journey to the Suffolk coast.

She's been coming here to make love to Anthony once a week, regular as clockwork, for two years. It started with an invitation to ride his wife's horse. She'd been dead six months and Pilar could tell he was lonely and in need of a friend. From a coffee in the kitchen after a morning gallop on the beach to leisurely lovemaking in his bedroom had not seemed such a difficult transition.

Looking out, she sees movement beyond a Cedar of Lebanon at the furthest edge of the lawn, a soldier moving between the trenches.

'How many of them are there?' she asks, casually.

'A platoon of thirty or so soldiers here,' he tells her from the bed, 'and another on Goose Hill. They've promised to fill in the trenches when they're done. And they've offered compensation, though I've told them I won't accept it. We all have to do our duty.'

'Our duty,' she muses.

'Matthew's in Cumbria,' he tells her, proudly, 'defending Sellafield. He says it hasn't stopped raining since he arrived.'

Anthony's son, Matthew, is a newly commissioned officer in the Scots Guards. She hasn't met him and she has no desire to do so. The Scots Guards killed her only brother Carlos and her fiancé Gustavo on Mount Tumbledown in the Malvinas on the night of 13 June 1982.

'The major in charge of the paras has accepted my invitation to come to dinner tonight along with the sergeant from the marines and Charles Fletcher,' Anthony says. Fletcher is the inspector in charge of the Nuclear Constabulary unit that guard the power station. An uncompromising man of few words. 'Promise me you'll come.'

She looks back at him from the window.

'Please?' he says.

'Okay, I'll come.'

He has the kind of smile that under different circumstances might have thawed the ice in her heart.

# 64

## Blow back

Watching the press conference on a tablet at Gretchen's allotment with a stoneware jug of rainwater flavoured with sliced cucumber on the bench beside her, Yulia can see the barely contained anger in the Russian president's face as he responds to the increasingly strident questions of the international press corps. It would have been so much easier in Stalin's time. The censors would have simply erased the inconvenient offenders from the image of the president at a winter barbecue to celebrate the Day of Heroes of the Fatherland. But the internet cannot be purged of embarrassing evidence. The body of the hacker Scary Bear is on a slab in a London morgue and the CEO of PMC Valkyrie, Dmitri Troshev and its principal shareholder, the oligarch Oleg Solokov, have their faces plastered across the news.

From a podium in the Kremlin Palace's grandiose Andreyevsky Hall, the president announces the establishment of a commission to investigate corruption and wrongdoing in the Russian intelligence services, and follows it up by announcing immediate and punitive action against PMC Valkyrie and its shareholders, and the arrest of Dmitri Troshev, Oleg Solokov and several senior members of the intelligence services who were 'co-opted' by Valkyrie.

He dismisses the accusation that Russia facilitated the transport of British-born jihadis from Syria to the UK as a ridiculous fiction, drawing attention to the suffering of the Russian people at the hands of Islamist terrorists, and denounces the UK attack on the Russian banking network as a reckless stunt. As for the news that the Atlantic Council is discussing the invocation of Article 5 of the NATO charter, he urges the council members to think very carefully before taking a step that could only be interpreted as unwarranted aggression against Russia.

'Violence breeds violence,' the president says, before walking out between the colossal gold doors that make a dwarf of him. 'If we are attacked again, we will respond.'

Speaking from Red Square, one of the BBC's international correspondents describes it as a remarkable event, particularly given that some of those senior figures arrested have risen with the president from his beginnings in the St Petersburg offices of the KGB, suggesting either a high-level coup attempt has been foiled or a massive cover-up is underway.

Yulia snorts audibly at the ludicrous idea of a coup attempt and the plainclothes police officer standing by a six-foot tower of flowering sweet peas glances in her direction. Kleptocrats are not the sort to organise halfway successful coups. For that you need actual believers.

'A president whose position once seemed unassailable is now looking more vulnerable than at any time since he assumed the highest office,' the correspondent says in his pompous voice.

From outside the new live position in front of the barricade that seals off Whitehall, an assistant political editor describes a government lacking a Prime Minister and paralysed by illness, fuel and food shortages, transport chaos and looting, with no apparent response to Russian aggression.

'The higher the barricades are built around Whitehall, the greater the impression that the government, or what remains of it, has abandoned the rest of the population to their fate.'

The news returns to the aftermath of the simultaneous attacks in London. The southbound lanes of the M40 motorway remain closed following the detonation of a truck filled with explosives in the midst of stalled traffic. Police marksmen killed an attacker on the M3 before he got a chance to detonate his payload and the remaining trucks reached their targets, destroying five of the six super-transformers that supply electricity to the city. The immediate effect was a blackout followed by six hours of civil disorder before the supply was ramped up through the only remaining route for electricity into the city. A city already in chaos after the cryptosporidiosis outbreak, and the failure of cash withdrawal and payment systems.

The next report is from the capital's hospitals that have been overwhelmed and are closed to new admissions. There is shocking footage of abandoned bodies in hospital corridors and overflow tents. Then the oil depot fire, which is still raging out of control, partly as a result of the diversion of Fire Brigade assets to London to put out fires caused by widespread rioting and the deliberate firebombing of places of worship and shopping centres.

Heathrow and Gatwick airports remain closed. The country is running low on fuel.

There is an announcement from the Polish government of an investigation into doctored records at the University of Krakow, where tutors claim no recollection of a student matching the description of Jakub Wojick.

'The true identity of the night-shift manager responsible for the oil terminal explosion is as yet unknown,' the Security Correspondent says from the BBC Scotland studio at Pacific Quay in Glasgow, which has been anchoring national coverage since the lockdown, 'but given recent events, the finger of blame is inevitably pointing at Russia. If he is Russian, then the pressure for a response from the government and our NATO allies will undoubtedly further increase. It remains to be seen whether the Russian president's actions today will be enough to satisfy them.'

Yulia removes the earbuds from her ears. She remembers Alexei the General telling her that the most hopeful thing about the president was the palace on the Black Sea that he was building. That the president was confident enough to believe that he might one day retire rather than be torn limb from limb by a mob that forced their way into the Kremlin and overpowered his guards. To Yulia, he does not look like a man ready to retire.

She calls Alexei at the dacha using the phone that she was given by Jude. It takes an age for it to be answered.

'Who is this?' his wife Svetlana says. She's drunk and slurring her words.

'It's Yulia.'

'Bitch.'

'I want to speak to him.'

'You can't.'

'Put him on the phone. Wake him up if necessary.'

'He's gone. They took him.'

'Who took him?'

'Who do you think? The FSB. This is your doing. You ruined our lives.'

Yulia ends the call and beats her chest with the phone. When she has calmed down sufficiently, she calls the Russian Ambassador on his mobile.

'Who is this?'

'Yulia.'

There is a pause. 'Where are you?'

'Watching vegetables grow,' she says, staring at the grey sweep of sky above a wooded hill. 'Did you know that they arrested Alexei?'

'Is this line secure?'

'No,' she says, 'but then we don't have any secrets any more, do we?'

'What do you want from me, Yulia?'

'Guy Fowle is trying to provoke a war. We can't let him succeed.'

'Have you told that to your new friends?'

'Of course. And they are listening, for now. But they need to know that there is nothing else that has not been revealed. All it would take is one more attack. Please make sure that the president understands that. If Troshev knows something, you need to share it. We need to tell them where this is going . . .'

'I will pass on your message,' he tells her. He pauses. 'When are you coming back?'

She realises that he wants to know whether or not she has defected. 'When this is done and we are safe, I will report to the Embassy.'

'They will be pleased to hear that,' he tells her. 'Take care, Yulia.'

'I will,' she says and ends the call.

Gretchen walks over to the nest of pillows that she has constructed for Yulia on the bench outside the wooden shed that holds her tools. She is wearing sleeveless blue overalls and a red headscarf. Yulia watches her wipe her hands on her overalls and take the phone out of her pocket.

'How are you feeling?' she asks.

Yulia sighs and holds out her hand for the phone without answering. Holding it up to her eye, she unlocks it. She hands it back to Gretchen, who swipes and taps.

'Anything new?'

Looking at the app, Gretchen shakes her head.

'I've told them to release every piece of information,' Yulia says. 'I've warned them of the consequences of another attack.'

'I'll tell Jude when he calls,' Gretchen says, pocketing the phone and returning to her digging.

Yulia can't tell if Gretchen believes her. Surveying the allotment, which slopes towards the base of the hill, she sees a few people moving amongst the maze of sheds, canes and net-covered fruit bushes. In the adjacent allotment, an elderly man with a white St Nicholas beard and a Breton cap looks up from between rows of lettuces and smiles at her.

She sighs and against her better judgement texts Jude.

I want to see you!

# 65

# In the wind

Jude receives Yulia's text as he is being escorted along a corridor at a short-term holding facility near Gatwick, with a buff envelope in his hands. He has just arrived and the helicopter that brought him swiftly here from Whitehall is waiting on the grass beyond the fence. By his side is an officer from the Border Force in a navy-blue uniform. She uses a swipe card to open a series of identical doors marked by yellow and black chevrons.

'We detained him at the foot passenger terminal in Dover ferry port,' the officer explains. 'We found a printed e-ticket for a flight to Panama City in the lining of his suitcase.'

She opens a plain grey door midway down a stretch of corridor and he follows her into a viewing room. On the other side of the one-way glass, a man is sitting at a table in an over-lit room, wearing the blue tracksuit and flip-flops of an inmate. There is another Border Force officer standing between him and the locked interview room door.

'That's him,' Jude confirms.

He texts a quick reply to Yulia:

We've got Ruslan Dudayev. Once I'm done with him, I'll come find you

'Has he said anything?' Jude asks.

'Not a word,' she says.

Dudayev looks up at Jude as he enters the room, and follows his movements with dark, expressive eyes. He has huge fists clenched on the table with so much hair on the backs of his fingers it looks like it has been glued on.

Jude sits opposite him and places the envelope on the table

between them. He politely asks the officer to leave the room and waits for the door to lock before speaking.

It's not like looking into Guy Fowle's eyes, there isn't that sense that he is other than human, but there is something unusual, hypnotic even, about Dudayev's liquid brown eyes – a compelling mixture of sorrow, sympathy and cruelty. For Jude, it provides the beginnings of an answer to the question of how he persuaded vulnerable young men like Salem to kill themselves.

'Your Russian friends have given you up,' Jude tells him.

Dudayev shrugs as if it is in the nature of people to behave in such a way.

'We know that you met with six young men who survived the battle of Raqqa, the last stand of the Caliphate,' Jude says. 'You arranged illicit transport for them from Turkey to the UK. We have forensic and witness evidence that places you at the safe houses where you kept them out of sight and it's only a matter of time before we find the bomb factory where you cooked the explosives. You did all of this for the Russians, your greatest enemy.'

'Who are you to believe such fantasies?'

'And they paid you a generous monthly stipend into an offshore account in Panama for your services.'

'Prove it.'

'You think we can't? The Americans are all across your finances already, Ruslan. There's no pot of gold at the end of the rainbow for you, any more. It's ironic, really. You made a big mistake in not using the passport the Russians gave you. I understand why but we don't have those numbers. Only the hackers who designed Grom have them and they are nowhere to be found. Of course, you realised that your attack was part of a larger plan and that made you suspicious. That's why you arranged for your own passport. It's just unfortunate that you were sold one from a consignment that was stolen on its way to being pulped. The serial number showed up on our computers as destroyed. Somebody fucked you over, Ruslan, and there's nothing you can do about it.'

'What do you want?' Dudayev practically spits.

'I'm curious, you claim to be a patriot, weren't you worried about starting a war and the effect that might have on your people?'

'They will hide in the mountains like they have always done. And when it is over, they will be free.'

'You knew that Fowle was acting alone and without the sanction of the Kremlin?'

'Of course.'

'And you helped him?'

'We Chechens are not bound by any circumstances, or anybody,' Dudayev says with a defiant shrug. 'We will continue to fight as it is convenient and advantageous to us and by our own rules.'

'There's no more fighting for you,' Jude tells him. 'And your circumstances are dire. The only thing that will help you now is if you give us something that helps to find Fowle.'

Dudayev shakes his head. 'What makes you think that he revealed anything to me?'

'Frankly speaking, I doubt he told you anything,' Jude says, 'I think you were just as much a tool for him as you were for the Kremlin.'

'I'll tell you what I know,' Dudayev says, leaning forward, his face shining. 'He's not going to stop. He's going to go on killing people until either you kill him or there's nobody left to kill.'

Jude stares back at him. 'Have you finished?'

Dudayev leans back and crosses his arms. 'I want a lawyer.'

Jude taps the envelope on the table.

'There's a deportation order inside signed by the Home Secretary. She's so sick I had to hold the pen in her hand. We're sending you back to Russia.'

Dudayev's mouth hangs open. 'You wouldn't.'

'There's a charter plane waiting on the runway at Stansted. I imagine they'll have quite the reception party waiting for you in Moscow.' Jude picks up the envelope and stands. He looks at the mirrored glass and for a moment has the disturbing feeling of not recognising himself. The person staring back looks exhausted. His cheeks are hollowed out and there are dark rings around his eyes.

To the watchers on the other side, he says, 'You can take him now. Send him to Russia.'

He heads for the door.

'Wait,' Dudayev says. He stands abruptly, tipping his chair onto the floor. 'There is something.'

Jude looks back at him. 'What?'

'If I tell you, then I'm not going back to Russia?'

Jude shrugs. 'You have my word.'

Dudayev laughs helplessly. 'Your word, Englishman?'

'Best offer you'll get. You tell me now or you're on that plane.'

They stare at each other. It's like staring at a dog, Jude thinks, you can't look away first.

Dudayev blinks and looks down.

'I asked Fowle about the timing of the attack. He said the answer is *in the wind*.'

'The wind?' Jude repeats.

'Yes.'

Maybe, just maybe, it's significant.

Out in the corridor, Jude hands the envelope to the Border Force officer. She opens it and stares at the blank sheet of paper inside, before looking up at him.

'Send him to Belmarsh,' Jude tells her.

He phones Gretchen but the call goes to voicemail. Next, he calls Yulia. Same result. Concerned, he phones John Nganga.

'What can I do for you, Jude?'

'I can't get through to Gretchen or Yulia.'

'I'll check with the protection detail at the allotment and call you back,' Nganga says.

'I'm heading there now,' Jude tells him.

# 66

# Death on the allotment

Yulia looks around the side of the shed at the entrance to the allotment at the top of the slope. A police car has pulled up outside the gates with its lights spinning. The plainclothes officer assigned to them is frowning.

An unexpected arrival.

'What's going on?' she asks.

'Stay there,' he says, walking up the path towards the entrance with his hand on the holster on his belt.

Yulia glances back at Gretchen who has stopped with her foot on a spade. Their eyes meet.

Yulia hears the police officer's question, 'Sir?'

Then the crack of a bullet.

'Run!' Gretchen screams, brandishing the spade like it's an axe.

Yulia comes up off the bench and is on the move before the pain in her thigh where a piece of shrapnel struck her kicks in. She is surprised that the man from the neighbouring allotment with the St Nicholas beard is sprightlier than he looks. He has his hand out and grips hers. Together they run.

She hears three shots and then, a few moments later, two shots in quick succession that strike the side of a shed as they pass it. She feels the prick of flying splinters. St Nicholas keeps low and tugs her after him, dodging between the maze of sheds, polytunnels, trees and fruit bushes. There are three more shots in quick succession. The pain in her leg is searing but the adrenalin is carrying her through it. They reach the bottom corner of the allotment where St Nicholas kneels and pulls apart a tear in the chain link fence and urges her through into the wooded area beyond.

'Follow the path to your left and it will lead past the pond to the road,' the man says in a rush. 'When you get there, flag down a car. Find somewhere safe.'

She sees that he is holding a pistol in his hand. It seems, he too has been watching over her.

'What are you going to do?' she asks.

'What I can. Go!'

She squeezes through the gap and onto the path on the other side. She part runs, part limps down a path beside a wooded slope and into a narrow passage between shoulder-high walls of nettles.

She hears five shots in quick succession.


The helicopter hovers above the patchwork of allotments while the pilot looks for somewhere to land. Jude can see the bodies from the air with police officers standing around them. They are uncovered due to the shortage of forensics tents and blankets, and there is no sign of a coroner's van or scenes of crime officers.

They land on the lawn outside the allotment gates and Jude runs out from under the rotor blades towards the entrance where John Nganga is waiting for him.

'I'm so sorry,' he says.

They walk together through the gate and down the path past the body of the plainclothes policeman, which is being photographed by another police officer, to where Gretchen is lying on the ground with the spade beside her, its blade shattered. Jude stares at her body. Three ragged holes in a line across her Dead Kennedys T-shirt, and her dyed-blonde hair spilling from beneath her headscarf across the freshly turned earth. Her out-flung arms decorated with lightning flashes, mandalas and stars. Honest dirt beneath her fingernails.

'I've spoken to the informing officer, who is on his way to the parents,' Nganga says, gently.

'Who did this?' Jude asks, shaking with anger.

'According to Ms Ermolaeva the attacker arrived in a police car and was known to the plainclothes officer assigned for her protection,' Nganga says. 'He called him sir. The attacker killed three of them including the undercover officer whose body is over there at the bottom end of the allotment.' He points to where a police officer is kneeling beside another body. 'He died covering Yulia's escape.'

'Who knew on your side that they were here on the allotment?'

'A very limited number of people,' he replies. 'I'm investigating that now.'

'And the police car?'

'We've got it on local camera footage but the plates are fake and we've had no access to GPS data since the system went down.'

'What about the Grom phone?'

'No sign of it. I assume the attacker took it with him. If he is an illegal embedded in the police, then perhaps he was concerned that he might be identified by a further release of information? He also took Yulia Ermolaeva's phone. She left it behind when she ran. Which means whoever took it has your number amongst others.'

'When did you get here?' Jude asks, more aggressively than he intended.

John Nganga frowns. 'About twenty minutes ago. Why?'

They stare at each other in silence.

'I didn't kill your friend, Jude,' John Nganga tells him, gently.

'It's my fault,' Yulia says. They are sitting side by side in the back of a police car. Yulia has a foil blanket around her shoulders. 'I suggested that we get outside somewhere. I was going stir-crazy cooped up inside. She mentioned her allotment so I said why not go there.'

'This could have happened anywhere,' Jude says. 'And I author-ised it.'

'She was an evangelist for cucumber water. Full of anti-oxidants and good for your skin and bones, she said. She showed me nothing but kindness and I was rude in return.'

Yulia's chest heaves and she starts to sob. Jude puts his arm around her and feels his anger quickly escalate beyond rage to fury.

# 67

## The predator waits

A marsh harrier floats above the reeds, quartering its hunting ground for prey. The bird's range extends across a thousand hectares of creeks, lagoons, mud flats and barriers of reeds with the power station and its distinctive white dome at its southern edge.

Guy watches as it flushes out a flock of lapwings, their alarm calls causing thousands of waders and wildfowl to explode into flight. The harrier plunges into the maelstrom with its talons outstretched and snatches a starling.

Guy has always been fascinated by predators. As a solitary child in the Scottish Hebrides he spent hours in carefully constructed hides, much like the one he is in now, watching raptors and other flesh-eaters at work, learning the principles of stealth and sudden attack. The harrier is not the only predator stalking the marsh. Guy has already spotted the sleek body of an otter slipping down a mud bank into the shimmering water to hunt for fish. He has always felt a greater kinship with animals than humans, for their greater purity of purpose and their lack of paralysing sentiment. But unlike most animals he does not simply kill for food but rather for pleasure. In that, he is admittedly human. But more than human in the scale of his ambition and the range of his talent.

And he has prey in sight.

Using range-finding binoculars, he has been watching the movement of the paratroopers in their platoon harbour on Goose Hill to his south-west. He has all the defensive positions marked on the Ordnance Survey map beside him and his phone has multiple tiles open, showing the view from battery-powered Wi-Fi cameras discreetly placed by Pilar on the trees that lead to the

*The Saboteur*

police checkpoint and the army command point. He has watched the comings and goings to get a feel for the rhythm and direction of their movements. He has noted their stand-to positions in the trenches at first and last light. He has identified the company commander from the arrogant swagger of his step and the deference shown by those around him. He has decided that he will enjoy killing him when the time comes.

Last night he pulled back at dusk before they sent drones out over the marsh searching for intruders with thermal imaging cameras. Given the dark clouds rising from the sea like an anvil on the horizon, it's unlikely that they will be able to put them up tonight. And even if they do, he'll knock them out of the sky.

He has everything he needs. He may have arrived with nothing more than a handgun but thanks to Pilar he now has an arsenal of weapons.

On the day of his arrival, Pilar showed him the cellar under the stairs and handed him a sledgehammer. Moving several boxes to one side, she pointed at a section of roughly mortared brickwork. Three blows were enough to make a hole large enough to reveal the hidden storage area beyond. He dragged four shock-resistant plastic cases out onto the cellar floor.

In the first foam-lined case there was a man-portable variant of the *Krasukha* electronic-warfare system: a high output Russian military jammer with range of about fifteen kilometres that transmits an inhibitor signal across HF, Wi-Fi and cellular frequencies.

He just needs to switch it on to knock out all communications.

In the second, an olive-drab shoulder-fired missile launcher with a bulbous ultra-violet and infra-red homing sight beneath the launch tube. Beside it, four identical surface-to-air missiles with high explosive warheads, designed to knock out fixed- and rotary-wing aircraft, missiles and drones, out to a range of about six kilometres.

In the third, forty-eight Claymore-style directional fragmentation mines, and in the fourth, a cornucopia of infantry weapons: two rail-interfaced M4A1 fully automatic carbines with forward hand-grips.

'Do you know how to use one of these?' he asked her, as he lifted a carbine out of its foam insert and passed it to her.

'I was raised on the pampas,' she replied, confidently. He watched her point the carbine at the floor, clear the breech and press the trigger on an empty chamber. 'My father taught me to shoot wolves. Later, during my training, I used a version of this weapon to hunt wolves in Siberia. It didn't have so many extras in those days.'

In addition to the underslung grenade launcher, there was the choice of a red-dot close combat gun sight or a night-vision scope to go on the Picatinny rail and a noise suppressor for the end of the barrel.

'That's good enough for me,' he said. The box also contained bandoliers of 40mm rifle grenades and cardboard boxes of 5.56 ammunition. Lifting out the cartons of ammunition, he reflected that she was a better accomplice than Candida could ever have been.

From his vantage point in the marsh, Guy concludes that there is nothing in the movement of the soldiers that suggests that they have received any recent communications or are aware of the imminent threat of attack.

Everything is ready. He has watched the news. London is on its knees. Its inhabitants are weak and vulnerable. Trapped and unable to escape, they will die in radioactive agony in the hundreds of thousands.

A gust of cold wind ruffles the reeds around him, and a few spots of rain strike the backs of his hands. The storm is at hand and soon the marsh will fill with floodwater. It's time to go and prepare for the night ahead. If everything goes according to plan, he will gladly accept credit for the greatest terrorist attack of all time.

The thought fills him with quiet satisfaction.

He eases himself backwards and begins the slow, careful return to Pilar's cottage.

# 68

# The sword

By the time he gets back to the cottage, it's raining hard. Guy stands in the kitchen dripping on the clay tiles while Pilar makes him tea. She is fresh out of the shower, after taking the dog out on another circuit of the power station. He sees that there is an unfamiliar phone on the table.

'That's for you,' she says, careful not to look straight at him but watching him nonetheless. 'Charles Fletcher dropped it off. It belongs to Yulia Ermolaeva, a Russian traitor who is working with the British. It's been unlocked.'

Sitting and scrolling through the messages he sees the exchange of intimacies between Yulia and Jude. It helps explain why the Russians and the British are cooperating. He sees the exchange between them after he fired an incendiary rocket at the high-rise during the three-way battle between the British police, the Russians and the Albanian gang in South London. Jude ran into a burning building to rescue Yulia. Guy realises that he should have killed them when he had them in his sights after they emerged from the building. He has foolishly underestimated both of them.

'Anthony is going ahead with his dinner tonight at Aldringham Hall,' Pilar says, putting a mug of hot tea on the table in front of him. Her hands linger as if she wants to touch him, to draw on the strength in his muscles and sinews. 'I've said I'll go.'

'Good.' He thinks they have a few more hours. 'Have you placed the claymores?'

'Of course.'

From above the rim of his mug, Guy watches Pilar drying dishes with a cloth and placing them in cupboards. She moves with lissom economy, her dance training apparent in every step. She may be outwardly calm but he can see the disturbance in her aura, the excitement bristling like electricity beneath her skin. She knows that she is within a few hours of fulfilling her destiny.

He is so pleased that she has an aura.

Not for the first time, he is impressed by the care and attention given to the design of Grom, the manner in which the illegals are carefully chosen for their ability to act autonomously and without further instructions from Moscow. Their elemental grievances. He wonders at what seems like a mischievous quality in the designers' work.

He likes Pilar.

He is fascinated by her ability to have maintained a pathological hatred of the British for four decades and then to have kept it hidden whilst living in the midst of the enemy. He knows how intense bitterness and resentment can be, and he knows something of the epic tragedy of her personal and family history from the psychological profile written by her Russian handlers that is copied in his Moleskine.

Her father shot himself following the death of her fiancé and her only brother in the ludicrous misadventure that was the Falklands War. Pilar and her mother struggled to survive through the decade of stagnation that followed. They lost all their savings during the hyper-inflation and had the last of the family land seized just before the International Monetary Fund forced Argentina into bankruptcy. Pilar lost her job as a dance teacher and was evicted from her apartment. Her mother died of pneumonia. Pilar was in her early forties, homeless and penniless, and utterly broken. She was not the only woman in similar circumstances that turned to prostitution.

Her saviour was an intelligence officer from the Russian Embassy, always on the lookout for potential recruits, and, judging by the report he sent to Moscow, a keen eye for attractive but vulnerable women. Moscow acted with uncharacteristic haste, and within months she was in Russia being trained by Directorate

S as an illegal, with the promise of one day striking a blow against Britain.

After three years in Russia she returned to Argentina where she was directed to seduce an Englishman on holiday named Roger Allan, a metallurgist, fifteen years her senior, who had retired in the vicinity of the nuclear power station that he had helped to build.

'I know you're not working for the Russians,' she says with her back to the Aga. 'I knew it as soon as you arrived.'

They stare at each other. 'And you don't care?'

'I lost faith in the Russians a long time ago.'

'But you agreed when they approached you about using the cottage as a weapons cache?'

'Yes, and for a while I thought they might make good on their promises but that was two years ago now.'

'And yet you stayed here?'

'There was nothing for me back in Argentina. My husband received a generous pension. When he died, I felt free.'

'Why are you helping me?'

'I have got something for you,' she says. 'A gift.'

He follows her up the stairs to her bedroom. She gets down on her knees and pulls something out from under the bed. A long, narrow wooden box about three feet long. She sets it on the counterpane and releases the catches. Inside there is a sword in a lacquered sheath. It's a Japanese *Katana*. She passes it to him across the bed.

Guy slides the *Katana* out of its sheath and inspects the single-edged blade that he judges to be just short of thirty inches. It has been recently oiled and appears well looked after.

'It's made of traditional *tamahagane* steel,' Pilar tells him. 'My husband designed the blades of the turbines at the power station. And he loved fine steel.'

He turns the sword in his hand and as he does so, a stray beam of sunlight streams in through the window and flashes on the blade before being extinguished by the racing clouds.

Pilar gasps and Guy points the sword at her chest.

'What do you want me to do with it?' he asks. He would like to cut her with it, to capture her rage in a pattern of scars but he doubts there is time.

'Kill them all.'

# 69

# Threat Level Five

Ahead of Jude in the corridor, the PM's special adviser Maurice Hermon is brandishing a Diet Coke and telling anyone who cares to listen that the Secretary of State for Wales, whose political fortunes have waxed and waned across four successive governments, and is now the Deputy Prime Minister and therefore in charge of the country, shot down every approaching plane during an exercise in the use of anti-aircraft missiles in the build-up to the London Olympics.

'Owen Evans can't read a brief or stay on message and now the trigger-happy fucker has his finger on the nuclear button,' the Ulsterman says. Hermon isn't sick. It seems believable that he doesn't drink tap water and exists entirely on caffeinated drinks.

'How are you?' says a familiar voice from Jude's shoulder.

Jude turns to see the shaved head and uncompromising jawline of Brigadier Giles Munro, the Director of Special Forces, who once commanded him in Helmand and has just arrived from the SAS barracks in Hereford by helicopter.

'I'm well, sir.'

'I'm glad you're here,' Munro says. 'We need clear-eyed thinking at the table.'

Inside Briefing Room A, the news footage on the screens shows a city eerily calm but strewn with debris. Rolling straplines announce that the M25 is closed and the city is ringed by military checkpoints preventing all non-essential traffic entering or leaving the city. International airlines are now routinely avoiding British airspace.

'I'm deeply sorry about the loss of your friends and colleagues and I am troubled by the news that the attacker was one of those

319

charged with the security of this nation,' the Cabinet Secretary says, surveying the room. 'I will chair this meeting with the Secretary of State for Wales joining by video link in his role as Deputy Prime Minister.' He nods to one of his sickly-looking staff and the face of Owen Evans replaces the news grid, a man who has achieved a level of authority that he is ill equipped for. The wall behind Evans is anonymous grey concrete. It has never seemed truer that politicians are not as impressive as they used to be.

'Mr Evans, are you happy for me to continue?'

Evans blinks. 'Yes, absolutely, go ahead.'

The Cabinet Secretary turns to Evan Calthorp. 'Am I right in saying that with the loss of the phone containing the Grom app, we have lost the ability to identify further targets, accomplices or means of attack?'

'That's right,' he says.

'And the Russian president is refusing to speak us?'

'That's right,' Chuka says.

'Why not?' Evans asks, from the screen.

'Because he says you are a warmongering fool.'

Evans splutters and falls silent.

The Cabinet Secretary looks at Chuka. 'And what about our allies?'

'Neither our European nor our American allies are willing to take any further steps which may be interpreted as aggression,' Chuka says. 'They're taking the Russian president's threat seriously.'

'Basically, we're on our own,' Evan Calthorp says. 'The Europeans are still furious about the divorce and the Americans are terrified that they're about to be hit by their own version of Grom. Nobody thinks that the Russians did this for just one country.'

'What about your contacts?' the Cabinet Secretary asks Yulia. If he feels uncomfortable about having a senior Russian intelligence officer attending a COBRA meeting, he does not choose to show it.

'They have either been arrested or are not accepting my calls,' she replies.

'Why won't they talk to you?'

'Because Grom is out of their control. They don't know how it ends or the means by which it ends. Of course, the president will not admit that and so he is doing the only thing he can do under the circumstances, which is prepare for war.'

'Your views are noted,' the Cabinet Secretary says grimly and turns to Gavin Samson, the head of Counter Terrorism Command, who has John Nganga sitting beside him. 'What progress in apprehending Guy Fowle?'

'There has been no sighting of him for forty-eight hours,' Samson admits. 'We lost a lot of CCTV coverage during the riots.'

'Which means that he has had two days to prepare another attack?'

'That's correct.'

'And you believe that he is planning another attack?'

'Yes,' Evan Calthorp says. He reaches forward and taps the tablet on the table in front of him, relegating Evans to a small window in the bottom corner. The screen now shows a map of the south-east of England with key infrastructure facilities highlighted: electricity, oil and gas, water and sewerage. A network of pipelines and power lines connecting reservoirs, processing plants, refineries, depots and power stations all providing London with vital services.

'You're certain that the target is going to be London?'

'That's what the mother of Fowle's child told us and it would fit the pattern of the attacks so far, which have disabled key infrastructure in the capital,' Evan Calthorp says, 'causing chaos and costing lives but also trapping much of the populace in their homes.'

'Are you saying that trapping the populace is Guy Fowle's intention and we have played into his hands?'

'That is possible,' Evan Calthorp says.

'And the only clue that we have suggests that the wind may play a part in a future attack?'

'We should not assume that it is accurate,' Jude says. 'Or that by acting on it we make ourselves any safer.'

'You don't trust Dudayev?'

'That's irrelevant,' Jude says. 'The only reason that Fowle shares information is if it suits his purposes as part of a larger plan. This is chess to him. He's giving up pawns for a larger prize. If he told Dudayev, Fowle must have factored in that we might capture him. It was the same with Candida Taunton. He could have killed her on Ragpicker's Wharf but he didn't. He knew that she saw him passing something to a police officer in a Trojan armed response vehicle and that we would get the information out of her eventually.'

'He is giving you crumbs that are designed to cause confusion and chaos,' Yulia says, 'and set you against each other.'

'He's fucking aced that,' Maurice Hermon says.

'Nevertheless, it is the only intelligence that we have,' Chuka says. 'What does it tell us?'

'The prevailing wind in the UK is from the south-west,' John Nganga says, 'but it may blow from any direction for sustained periods of time. The meteorological office is currently tracking the tail end of a storm from the Atlantic that has moved around Scotland and down the English coast. As we speak it's making landfall on the coast of East Anglia. That means that a wind-borne vector released north-east of London would quickly contaminate the city.'

'What kind of vector are we talking about?'

'What's the worst thing?' Jude says, staring at his hands. 'That would cause the most casualties?'

They all look at him.

'A nuclear explosion,' Yulia says, softly.

That brings Jude's head up. He looks at the map, his eyes drawn to the bulge of East Anglia jutting out into the North Sea, searching for a target large enough to satisfy Guy Fowle's ego.

'The nuclear reactor at Sizewell B.'

He lets the enormity of that sink in.

'You should evacuate the city,' Yulia says.

The Cabinet Secretary cuts through the clamour of raised voices with a simple command, 'Stop!'

The room is quiet again.

'Mr Evans, I suggest that you raise the threat to Level Five.'

Evans looks startled. 'Right, yes . . . okay.'

'I will arrange for you to be immediately transported to a safe location outside the danger zone,' the Cabinet Secretary says.

Which means, Jude thinks, that wherever they've got Evans stashed can't be far from where they are sitting now. He wonders if the decision to physically exclude the Deputy Prime Minister from the meeting was deliberate and, if so, is Jude now a co-conspirator in what seems suspiciously like a coup?

'Everyone else in the room is to reconvene in the Pindar complex in fifteen minutes,' the Cabinet Secretary says. 'Move!'

# 70

# Talking Chernobyl

Its official name is the Defence Crisis Management Centre but it's known in Whitehall as 'Pindar' after the Greek poet whose house was the only one spared when the Macedonians destroyed the ancient city of Thebes. It's an airlocked complex of tunnels and rooms several storeys down beneath the Ministry of Defence from which the leaders of the country are supposed to respond to a nuclear attack. It has a spartan 1990s feel about it, including wooden desks and rooms with bunk beds that remind Jude of boarding school.

On one screen there is a map that shows the high-voltage transmission lines that converge on the city like the spokes of a wheel. Only one of them is lit up. A direct line from Sizewell B to the working transformer in north-east London. On another screen there is a gallery view of remote participants.

Sitting at the head of the table beneath the screens is Professor Dame Ruth Sieff, the child of Jewish refugees who fled Czechoslovakia on the *Kindertransport*. She is the Chief Scientist at the Ministry of Defence and current chair of SAGE, the Scientific Advisory Group for Emergencies. Sitting beside her is the response team leader from the Nuclear Accident Response Organisation.

Maurice Hermon leans forward across the table towards her. 'You better tell us how much shit we're in?'

'The pressurised water reactor at Sizewell B is currently running at full power with both turbines operational. That's an electrical output of more than a thousand megawatts,' she tells them. 'That level of power generation is necessary to make up for the shortfall in available power in London as a result of the destruction of five of the six transformers.'

'Which is exactly what Fowle intended,' Jude says.

'Can it be shut down?' the Cabinet Secretary asks.

'Yes, it is possible to use the Emergency Boration System but if the reactor is shut down it will cause the frequency of the grid to fall below an acceptable level,' Professor Sieff explains. 'In turn, that will set off a cascade of automatic disconnections.'

'Which means we lose power across the whole fuckin' city?' Maurice Hermon says.

'Yes,' she says, as if she is calming a recalcitrant teenager.

'For how long?'

'In certain areas, days or even weeks,' she replies. 'Refrigerated and frozen foods will quickly spoil and the ability of much of the populace to boil water to make it safe from cryptosporidium will be significantly reduced.'

'We've already lost the capacity to police large areas of the capital,' says Jemima Connick, the Police Commissioner. 'If we lose power for an extended period, we will lose the rest.'

Hermon stares at them with his mouth open. 'So we protect Sizewell?'

'You switch it off or you defend it,' Ruth Sieff says. 'That's the decision you must make.'

'The site is secured by the Civil Nuclear Constabulary and supported by additional military personnel.' Gavin Samson, the head of SO15, scowls. 'The nuclear reactor is protected by a concrete containment vessel that is 1.4 metres thick and lined with 2,000 tons of steel. It is designed to withstand catastrophic events.'

'Which Fowle will also have factored in,' Jude says. 'How do we know that the integrity of the operating system is not already contaminated by malware? For all we know there may be undercover Russian operatives in the control room as we speak and the reactor may already be running out of control.'

'All the control room staff have been extensively vetted,' Samson says. 'And both the National Grid and the operating company are reporting from their respective control rooms that there is nothing to suggest that the reactor is in any way compromised.'

'Which will be the entire point of the malware,' Jude tells him. 'To send out a message that the reactor is functioning normally. It was the same at the oil terminal.'

'Jude is right,' says Giles Munro, the Director of Special Forces. 'We have to work on the basis that the reactor is either already under enemy control or soon will be.'

Silence as everyone takes that in.

'So we should switch it off remotely,' the Cabinet Secretary says.

'If you do that, we let them know we are coming,' Munro tells him.

Jude nods. 'And if the reactor control system is already infected with malware, we will have no way of knowing whether it has actually switched off.'

'What progress in identifying the malware used in the oil terminal attack?' the Cabinet Secretary asks, turning to their American guest.

The room turns to Hardcastle who has been sitting with his hands flat on the table. 'We're disassembling malware seized from the hacker Angry Bear's computer that we believe is designed to infect industrial control systems but it's going to take time. It's scrambled with alternating layers of compression and encryption and we can only find the key to each layer after decoding the layer on top of it.'

'Well, thanks for nothing,' Maurice Hermon says. He looks at Professor Sieff. 'What's the worst-case scenario?'

'Uncontrolled fission in the reactor causing an explosion that breaches the containment vessel,' she says, calmly.

'Basically, you're talking Chernobyl in these green and pleasant lands?'

'It was a different type of reactor but yes, an uncontrolled leak of radiation.'

'Covering London?'

'Yes, if the wind is blowing in that direction.'

'Which it is,' Jude says.

'Fuck!' Hermon slams the table.

The Cabinet Secretary closes his eyes and they wait while he considers their collective future. With a sigh, he opens his eyes again, and looks to the representative of the Home Office, a young man who looks barely out of his teens. 'Operation Sassoon?'

'There is a plan for the orderly evacuation of up to seven million people to rest and reception areas in the Home Counties via trains and buses,' the official says, nervously. 'But we don't have enough soldiers, police officers or transport staff in place who aren't sick to coordinate or manage it. And we don't have sufficient electricity for the trains or fuel for the buses.'

'If we announced an evacuation the results would be chaos,' Samson says.

'It'd be a fucking disaster,' Maurice Hermon snarls.

'There's no point anyway,' Jude adds. 'The Home Counties would be in the contamination zone.'

'We had better find another answer then,' the Cabinet Secretary says.

'If I may,' the Chief Constable of the Civil Nuclear Constabulary says from a control room in Oxfordshire. 'Since Operation Temperer was enacted and armed police officers were diverted to London, the CNC operation support unit at Sizewell is operating at less than half strength.'

'Is he fuckin' kiddin'?' Hermon says to the room.

The screens are filled with a 1:50,000 Ordnance Survey map showing the power station and the surrounding terrain in detail.

The Chief Constable continues: 'Although their jurisdiction stretches out to five kilometres, the commander requested permission to concentrate the unit at a vehicle checkpoint on the approach road known as Sizewell Gap. No one is going in or out of the control room or the containment vessel without being thoroughly searched. For wider protection they have been reinforced by two platoons of 3 PARA, which is headquartered in the forestry block on Goose Hill to the north-west of the power station, with one platoon covering the marshland approaches and the second to the south on the Aldringham estate. The seaward approach is being patrolled by a troop from the Royal Marines. They have deployed drones in the air.'

'We can send the CNC unit at Sizewell into the control room to secure it,' Samson says, 'until we have a response team in place to operate the system.'

'How soon is that?' the Cabinet Secretary asks.

'We've had a team on standby here in Whitehall since the Civil Contingencies Act was invoked,' the nuclear accident response team leader explains. 'That includes a command control team and a reactor team with HAZMAT suits and self-contained breathing apparatus. You just need to get us there.'

Jude reaches across the table and mutes the gallery. He looks directly at Samson. 'The CNC uses Trojan armed response vehicles?'

'Yes,' Samson concedes.

'We know from Candida Taunton that Fowle met with someone in a police Trojan,' Jude says. 'How do we know that the Nuclear Constabulary team at Sizewell are not illegals? And you want to send them into that control room?'

Samson glowers at him across the table.

'There is an alternative,' Professor Sieff says.

'Please,' the Cabinet Secretary replies.

'After the Fukushima disaster in Japan, a review was conducted into safeguards at Sizewell B and an emergency response centre was built near the power station with back-up generator and control systems to enable operators to control the station remotely if necessary, as well as emergency equipment, high-pressure pumps and vehicles that could be rapidly deployed in the case of an extreme event. We can switch operational control to there and start running diagnostic checks to ensure the reactor is functioning as intended.'

'So, we take control of the emergency response centre,' Samson says to the room. 'I can have armed officers from SCO19 and the nuclear accident response team on site within two to three hours.'

'We can't risk using the police,' Jude says, meeting Brigadier Munro's gaze across the room.

'You're trusting the word of a drug-addict,' Samson says. 'There is no evidence that the police have been infiltrated by the Russians.'

'The man who murdered my friend and colleague was a senior police officer who was recognised by one of your own officers before he was killed.'

'And the only evidence for that is the word of a serving member of the Russian intelligence services,' Samson says, glaring at Yulia Ermolaeva.

'You're not helping your case,' the Cabinet Secretary tells Samson.

'I have an SAS sabre squadron on standby on the helipad at Hereford,' Brigadier Munro says in a voice that cuts across the room.

'Fowle came from Hereford,' Samson responds. 'You made him what he is. How do we know your own squadron isn't infiltrated with Russians?'

'I know my team,' the Brigadier replies, dead-pan.

The Cabinet Secretary looks from Munro to Samson and back again.

'May I speak?' Yulia says.

'Please,' the Cabinet Secretary replies.

'Can I have a pointer?'

Jude passes her the remote and she points it at the map, a red pin light appearing on the screen. Tracking west from the approach road to the power station known as Sizewell Gap, the red dot passes into an area marked as The Walks on the map and stops at a cottage by itself near an intersection of footpaths less than a kilometre from the reactor.

'That is Rose Cottage,' she explains, calmly. 'In it lives a woman named Pilar Allan. She is an *illegal*, a deep-cover agent who trained in Russia and has been embedded in the community for more than a decade.'

'Fuck!' Hermon yells.

'I was recently asked by Moscow to shred the hard copy of her file,' Yulia says. 'I believed that it was a routine request to protect a long dormant and now retired asset. I was wrong. The designers of Grom were seeking to disguise her activation.'

'Fowle may already be inside the defensive perimeter,' Samson says. 'We need to warn them.'

'We can't,' Munro says. 'If our own forces there are already compromised, we will lose the element of surprise. It's the same as trying to shut down the reactor. They could respond by accelerating their actions, causing the reactor to melt down before we have the opportunity to intervene.'

'You better blow that fucking cottage to kingdom come,' Hermon says.

'We will,' Munro replies.

An aide passes Samson a phone. He looks down at the screen and swears under his breath.

'What is it?' Hermon demands.

He looks up, pale-faced. 'The officer who died on the allotment once served under the officer in command of the Nuclear Constabulary at Sizewell.'

'Which is why he recognised him,' Jude says.

'You better blow that fucking checkpoint up too,' Hermon snarls.

'We use the SAS to seize the emergency response centre and SCO19 to seize the power station,' the Cabinet Secretary says. He turns to Professor Sieff. 'I need you there giving direction to the response team.'

'Of course.'

'I will brief the Deputy Prime Minister when he arrives at RAF Northwood. That is all.'

Jude is standing in front of the sinks in the men's toilet, tightening the waist straps on a black Kevlar vest over a long-sleeved black fleece. On the shelf below the mirror is his Glock pistol and *Kerambit* blade, two spare magazines and his various phones, each one in a waterproof zip-lock bag.

The door opens. 'Mr Lyon?'

He turns and Ruth Sieff is standing there, looking up at him.

The stalls are empty and they are alone together. 'Yes?'

'I'm sure your father would be proud of you.'

Jude has no way of telling how his father would feel.

'I knew him,' she adds.

Jude stops what he's doing and stares at himself in the mirror. It has been a long time since anyone said that to him.

'He very kindly invited me to your house for *seder* at Passover,' she says. 'You were just a boy. I was a recently divorced single mother of two children and I didn't have anywhere else to go. I see you don't remember.'

He doesn't know what to say. He barely remembers his father and when he does think of him selfishness rather than kindness is the attribute that comes to mind. A not uncommon accusation from the child of a suicide.

'It's all right,' she says, touching his elbow. 'You have two sisters, am I right?'

'Yes.'

'Are they here in London?'

'Yes.'

She leans in, as if she was speaking as one survivor to another, and uses a voice that does not rise above a whisper but nonetheless will brook no dissent, 'They should leave.'

# 71

# Last supper

The sound of a car horn is Pilar's cue to step into her wellington boots, zip up her yellow sou'wester and pull up the hood. She leaves Guy in the sitting room with the curtains closed and his weaponry spread out across the room, and runs out into the rain to Sergeant Wyllow's waiting Land Rover.

'Welcome aboard,' Wyllow says, when she hops into the passenger seat alongside him. There is water running down from the rubber seals around the windows and the windscreen and pooling in the footwells. He rolls his eyes. 'Not the comfiest nor the driest ride but it'll get us to dinner.'

She sees that he is wearing a headset with a stalk microphone that is connected to a radio at his belt. He reports his approach to the checkpoint. They slow when they reach it and Wyllow winds down the window to speak to the police officer from the Civil Nuclear Constabulary standing there in full waterproofs with water splashing off his peaked cap.

'We're going up to the hall,' Wyllow tells him, 'be back in ninety minutes or so.'

'The major from the paras went through ten minutes ago,' the police officer tells him.

'Great. See you later.'

They drive down the empty road towards the power station with the windscreen wipers swishing back and forth, passing the turn-off for the newly built emergency response centre, before turning up the tree-lined avenue towards the gate at the entrance to the estate. The soldiers wave them through from beneath a bivouac rigged up from a poncho.

There are two Land Rovers bristling with antennae parked

outside the front of the hall with the two drivers sheltering in the lead vehicle. Wyllow parks behind them and together they run up the steps and let themselves into the Great Hall. They hang their dripping coats on the hooks next to a camouflage smock.

'Ah, there you are,' Anthony says when they enter the drawing room, and shakes Wyllow's hand before kissing her on the cheek. 'One of my special gin and tonics? The men are on duty and slaves to their radios, so it's only us retired folk who can have a drink.'

'Of course,' she says.

While he fusses at the drinks trolley, she shakes hands with the officer from the Parachute Regiment who is standing by the French windows, which are being lashed with rain. He is a short, prematurely balding man in tight-fitting combat fatigues who introduces himself as Major Rogers. She wonders what it would take to get these men to reveal their first names. Perhaps they have forgotten them. Like Sergeant Wyllow, he is wearing a headset with a microphone. She watches as Wyllow salutes him before removing his beret.

'I was hoping to have drinks on the terrace at dusk,' Anthony says, handing her a large glass with pink grapefruit and peppercorns floating in it. 'The garden is lovely at this time of year but the rain has beaten us to it.'

'My men have been admiring your garden and of course the house,' Rogers says. He has a noticeable tic that causes his nostrils to flare when he speaks. 'How old is it?'

'The oldest parts of the house are Elizabethan and there were later additions during the Jacobean period and then after the Civil War,' Anthony explains. 'Pilar has been helping me to restore the Elizabethan garden.'

'Pilar?' Rogers looks at her speculatively. 'That's an unusual name.'

'Pilar is from Argentina,' Anthony says, protectively.

'And what brought you here?'

'I married an Englishman,' she tells him, with a disarming smile. 'A metallurgist. He persuaded me to come here and I fell in love with the place. After he died, I considered going back but this is home now.'

'The village is lucky to have you,' Anthony says.

Charles Fletcher, the inspector who commands the Nuclear Constabulary detachment at the power station, enters in his police uniform including body armour and a radio on his chest rig. His shaved head gleams.

'Ah, Inspector,' Anthony says. 'You've met everyone?'

He nods, grim faced. 'I have.'

'How was London?' Rogers asks.

'Not good,' he says.

'And the man they're saying is responsible?' Anthony says. 'Guy Fowle?'

The policeman shakes his head. 'He's still loose.'

'And the Russians are helping him?'

'They deny it.'

'If I may,' Rogers says. 'The considered view is that he couldn't be causing this much havoc without state help.'

'I can't believe that NATO haven't invoked Article 5,' Anthony says. 'What are they playing at?'

'They're waiting to see what happens next,' Rogers says.

'Will Fowle come here?' Anthony asks.

'All I can say is, let him try,' Rogers replies. 'My men are ready.'

'I'm sure there are easier targets,' Pilar says.

The housekeeper opens the door to the dining room.

'Dinner is ready, Mr Wigram.'

'Thank you,' Anthony says, and turns to his guests. 'Simple fare but I think you'll find Mrs Emory's cottage pie is distinctly more-ish. Isn't that right, Pilar?'

'It's renowned throughout the parish,' she agrees, with a twinkle in her eyes.

'Shall we?' Anthony says.

They move through into the Jacobean wood-panelled dining room where Mrs Emory has lit a fire that throws flickering light across the room. She serves them generous helpings of cottage pie with carrots and fat broad beans from the kitchen garden before leaving through a small door beside the fireplace that leads to the kitchen.

'Please tuck in,' Anthony says.

For a few minutes the only sound is the occasional crackle of the radios as sections on the perimeter send their status reports.

Wyllow winks at Pilar. 'All's fine.'

'I'm glad to hear it,' she tells him, putting a hand on his forearm. He actually blushes. Rogers looks on disapprovingly.

The door in the corner opens and Guy Fowle steps into the room with the suppressed Glock in his hands. He raises the gun and shoots Wyllow and then Rogers in their seats; the only sound the dull thump of the rounds hitting them and their knives and forks clattering across the table and onto the floorboards.

Guy crosses the room, nods to Fletcher and stands at the other end of the table to Anthony.

'Pilar?' Anthony says, looking between them, as if he is afraid to know the answer.

Ignoring him, she says, 'Give me the gun.'

Guy hands it to her and she points it at Anthony.

'You're one of them,' he says with horror on his face. 'I don't understand. Why?'

'The Malvinas,' she says and shoots him in the chest.

Guy takes the jammer off his back and puts it on the table. He adjusts two dials and switches it on. The disembodied voices on the radios abruptly cease. They look at their phones. No signal.

'Take the control room,' Guy tells Fletcher. 'Put up a green flare when ground forces arrive.'

He puts the backpack back on and looks to Pilar. 'Are you coming?'

They exit the house through the kitchens, stepping over Mrs Emory's corpse, into the walled garden, running between the raised vegetable beds in lashing rain. A small door leads out to a riot of rhododendrons and a sunken path that goes through a wood and over a footbridge towards Rose Cottage and beyond it, Sizewell Gap.

# 72

# Rosanna returns

Jude is standing at the entrance to Horse Guards, calling his sister, while a helicopter approaches from the west. Across the road on Whitehall there is a convoy of armed response vehicles with police officers in tactical gear moving between them as they prepare to leave.

'Where are you?' Tamar asks, when she finally answers.

'Whitehall.'

'It's all right for some,' she says, breathlessly. He can hear the crackle of gunfire in the background. 'I've got most of the capital's organised crime groups using what's going on to make merry hell, not to mention a bunch of neo-Nazis trying to launch a race war with phosphorus grenades. Make it quick, dear brother.'

When she stops, he says, 'I need you to do something for me.'

'Were you not listening to me?'

'I need you to get Hannah and the kids out of the city. You need to head north. Use back roads and avoid the checkpoints. Get them as far away as you can as fast as you can.'

'Jude, I'm in the middle of something here.'

'Sounds like you're making progress.'

'Ha, bloody, ha.'

'Listen to me, none of that is going to matter if you're dead.'

She goes quiet.

'Please, Tamar,' he says.

'Okay, but if you're fucking with me, I'm going to have your ass.'

'Thank you. Make sure you go with them.'

'Yeah.'

'I mean it. Head north. Get as far away as you can.'

He ends the call. He stares at his phone. He calls Kirsty.

'Now you call?' she says, sounding pissed off.

'Are you in London?'

'No. I'm in Yorkshire sitting in the living room with the mother of one of the young men who blew themselves up in the truck-bomb attack. Judging by her description you got here first.'

'You have to stay there. Don't travel south.'

She is defiant. 'Why?'

'For your own safety.'

She considers this for a moment and then says, 'How many people did you phone before me?'

'My sister.'

'Anyone else?'

'No.'

'That suggests that you're serious.' There is a grudging accept-ance in her voice. 'But if there's a story in London I need to be there.'

'You may not be able to tell it if you're in London. I promise you I'll explain in the next few hours. Until then you need to stay out of the city.'

'I'll think about it,' she says, 'but it will be easier if you tell me why?'

'I can't do that.'

He ends the call and turns to find Rosanna watching him from the archway that leads to the parade ground. Her face is pale and there are dark smudges under her eyes.

'Shouldn't you be in bed?'

'Calthorp thinks you're overly sentimental. Is he correct?'

'Probably. What about you?'

'I phoned an ex-boyfriend. He's a wanker, but it seemed like the right thing to do. He lives on a canal boat and so he knows the tow-paths. I figured that gives him a better chance than most of getting out.'

'What about your family?'

'Charlie is staying put.'

They stare at each other in silence.

'I guess we better succeed then,' Jude says.

'I think so,' she says, grimly.

'Are you sure you're up to this?'

'I'm held together by Imodium and Nitazoxanide. If you're lucky, I won't throw up on you or shit myself. When are we leaving?'

He glances through the archway at the helicopters. There are now two Apache gunships and the Eurocopter that he presumes Rosanna arrived on being refuelled on the parade ground.

'You want to fly or travel by road?'

'Do I have a choice?'

'Sure. Two and a half hours in a car or about forty minutes by helicopter. The cars are leaving any minute, the helicopters from Hereford with the SAS on board are on their way. They will meet up with the Apaches and the nuclear accident response team here and follow on.'

'Car. I really don't think my insides could cope with any more time in a chopper.'

'Okay, follow me.' He leads her to the second last vehicle in the convoy, an unmarked armoured Range Rover, and puts her in the back with Professor Sieff before getting in the front passenger seat.

The cordon opens and they race east along the Embankment and the Highway, passing north of the eerily darkened towers of Canary Wharf and through Newham past the Olympic Park before leaving the city, heading north-east across the Essex flatlands.

'What is the greatest vulnerability at Sizewell, Doctor Sieff?' Jude asks, looking at her in the rear-view mirror.

'It's a pressurised water reactor,' she replies. 'It relies on a constant supply of deionised water, which is pumped under high pressure to the reactor core where it is heated by the energy released by nuclear fission. The heated water enters a steam generator where it transfers its energy to a secondary water system before being pumped back into the reactor core. The steam from the secondary system powers turbines that spin an electric generator that is connected to the National Grid. The biggest risk is a loss-of-coolant accident. If the coolant pumping system fails and the turbines trip but the emergency cooling system doesn't activate and no water flows into the reactor, the heat can increase to the point where the nuclear fuel and its cladding liquify and fall to the bottom of the reactor pressure vessel. That's a core melt-down. If the reactor vessel ruptures, the core will become exposed. This in turn will cause the release of hydrogen gas, which may cause an explosion. If it does and breaches the containment vessel it will result in a major radioactive leak.'

'All callsigns this is Gold Commander,' Samson says over the Airwave radio from Briefing Room A. 'We have lost all communications with the units defending Sizewell and the reactor control room.'

They are driving into the unknown.

# 73

## Ambush

At ten kilometres out, the clipped reports on the police Airwave radio cease and are replaced with a persistent sibilant hiss and their phones show no service.

The convoy pulls over on the hard shoulder and John Nganga runs back down the line of vehicles in the pouring rain. The Range Rover's armoured windows won't wind down so Jude opens the door and Nganga leans in.

'We're being jammed,' he says, water pouring off his chequered baseball cap. 'We have no communications with Gold command centre and the special forces assault teams. Our actions on loss of communications are to proceed to the target, working on the premise that the power station is under hostile control and they are using electronic counter measures. If we are engaged, we are authorised to respond with lethal force. Once we are through the vehicle checkpoint, the convoy will split in two. The first six vehicles will proceed to the power station emergency assembly point to corral the engineering staff and secure the reactor and the operations buildings. The rear six vehicles will deliver Professor Sieff to the emergency response centre to switch control. Any questions?'

Jude looks at Ruth Sieff, who shakes her head. He looks back at Nganga.

'And if we're driving into an ambush?'

'We've got Apache gunships as top cover,' Nganga says.

'Let's hope that's enough.'

Six helicopters swoop overhead, heading east into the wind.

Guy sees them before he hears them, four troop-carrying Pumas with two Apache gunships flying directly towards him, skimming the nap of the earth. They've been ejecting decoys since crossing into the communications blackout zone but by switching between infra-red and ultra-violet, the target-acquisition sensor on the missile launcher is able to distinguish between the chaff and the helicopters. At just over four kilometres out he fires the missile. The solid fuel rocket propels it at 500 metres a second towards the target.

*One two three four five six . . .*

The high explosive fragmentation warhead detonates and shreds one of the Apaches, which plunges into the ground.

They keep on coming.

Guy is already running, putting as much time between himself and the firing point, before the second Apache launches a volley of 30mm canon rounds from the chain gun, which strike the stand of pines behind him, snapping them like twigs. He runs the length of a paddock, alongside a panicked pony, and down the back of a brick stables on a path that leads to a row of cottages beside a single-track road that is running with water. He kneels beside a flint wall and shrugs off his backpack. He takes out another missile and slides it into the launch tube.

Lifting the loaded weapon onto his shoulder, he sees the remaining Apache rising in a spiral beyond the flight ceiling of the missile. Switching his attention to the heavier Pumas, he sees them also rising but at a slower rate. He chooses the lowest, aims and fires.

The missile detonates on proximity to its target. The Puma snaps in half and tumbles down in flames.

Guy is already running. He has vaulted a fence and is running along the edge of a field parallel to a wooded stream when the remaining Apache responds, firing two Hydra rockets from five kilometres up. They strike one of the cottages, and it explodes, raining brick and flint debris in the field behind him.

Stalemate.

They may be out of range but equally they can't approach to land.

A flare rises above the nuclear reactor and then slowly descends by parachute, lighting up the huge dome in luminous green. It's the signal from Fletcher that a vehicle convoy is approaching.

Guy vaults another fence and is on a single-track tarmac road beside a stone bridge. He slides down the bank beside the bridge into a dense thicket of stinging nettles, feeling the exhilarating crackle of the histamine on his hands and face, before landing in the water. It's only about a foot deep but rising fast. Standing beneath the bridge he switches off the jammer and uses his phone to access the Wi-Fi cameras. He sees the police convoy heading for the checkpoint on the road to the power station's main entrance. He uses the radio-controlled exploder to send out an arming signal to the claymores attached to the trees on the road.

He watches the convoy heading towards the checkpoint with his thumb stroking the firing button.

Just after the second helicopter tumbles in flames out of the sky, the communications come back on.

'All callsigns this is Gold,' Samson says from the COBRA complex. 'The enemy have breached the perimeter. Fall back to the reactor entrance. Fall back.'

'November Charlie this is Trojan One,' Nganga says, hailing the Nuclear Constabulary checkpoint ahead of them on the Airwave radio. 'We are acting on the authority of the Secretary of State. We are approaching your location. Stand down and let us pass. Over?'

'Trojan this is November Charlie,' the checkpoint responds, 'stop your vehicles and identify yourself.'

Gold Commander orders a missile strike on Rose Cottage. 'A Hellfire through the letterbox.'

'November Charlie this is Trojan One,' Nganga growls, as they turn the corner into the tree-lined straight and accelerate towards the checkpoint. 'Enemy forces control the power station. We need immediate access to the emergency response centre and we are authorised to use force against you. Stand down. Repeat Back. Stand down.'

They are passing an open field full of curved-steel pig arcs on their left and a row of cottages on their right. Two lines of transmission towers cross the road ahead of them, heading into the marsh.

'This is Trojan One. Stand down. Repeat back. Stand down!'

There is no response from the checkpoint.

Jude's phone vibrates. A message from an unknown number:

Welcome to hell

Simultaneously, the Apache launches two Hellfire missiles from far above, which strike Rose Cottage, and the claymores attached to the trees on either side of the approach road to the power station detonate. Thousands of steel darts travelling at a velocity of more than a kilometre a second strike the convoy broadside. Laminated glass spiderwebs and spalls, rubber shreds and unravels, hardened steel buckles, Kevlar-strengthened fuel tanks burn. The lead vehicle somersaults, landing on its roof. The second vehicle bounces off it and plummets down the grass bank between two trees into the ditch. The third vehicle spins 360 degrees and the rest concertina into it.

The Range Rover slams into the back of the vehicle ahead and is rear-ended by the vehicle behind.

The next thing Jude knows, he is staring at a snowstorm of armoured glass with steel fragments lodged in it. Yellowish smoke is curling up from the remains of the collapsed airbag in his lap and there is white dust everywhere. It feels like he has been punched in the chest and there is a burning sensation in his forearms. He can taste blood in his mouth.

He looks around. The driver is groaning, his broken forearms crossed on his chest. In the back seat, Professor Sieff's head is thrown back against the headrest and her eyes are closed. Beside her, Rosanna is shaking her head slowly back and forth.

The windows are completely opaque but the armour held.

He reaches for the radio handset but it's making the same hissing noise as before.

Seconds later there are two loud explosions, one after the other, somewhere ahead of them, which he guesses are the Apache taking out the checkpoint on Sizewell Gap.

'She's alive,' Rosanna says, with two fingers to Professor Sieff's neck. 'But she needs medical attention.'

Jude closes his eyes and curses. He has to get out. The choice is left or right, either the ditch to his left or the row of cottages to his right. He'd prefer to go right and reach the cover of the buildings but he doesn't know if the enemy occupies them. He can hear gunfire but he can't see anything through the fragged windows.

Left.

He releases his seatbelt and unlocks the front passenger door.

'Wait here.'

He has to kick the buckled door a couple of times before it opens. Then he rolls out and across the tarmac to the nearest tree, coming up to a crouch with the Glock out of its holster. Raking fire from beyond the vehicles strikes the tree trunks above him and he spins around and slides down the grass bank into a ditch that is waist-deep in freezing cold water.

# 74

# Out of the ditch

Looking down the length of the ditch that runs alongside the road, Jude can see a knot of police officers on the bank shooting between the gaps in the vehicles at the cottages. There are more officers sheltering in the running water, many of them wounded. In the distance, towards the coast, he can see flames and smoke rising in rain-lashed tatters from an industrial building south of the power station.

A series of detonations, like a string of firecrackers, light up the base of the hill to the north where one of the platoons of paratroopers is situated. More claymores. Seconds later there is another string of back-to back explosions from the direction of the other platoon to the south. Looking at his black-taped phone in its clear plastic bag, Jude sees that communications are still down, so the claymores must have been tripwire-initiated, which means the platoons probably ran into them as they pulled back towards the power station.

'I need a medic,' Jude calls out, in the pause after the explosions.

John Nganga slides down into the water beside him with another officer, both of them carrying G36 carbines. 'Are you all right, my friend?'

He can hear several people screaming in the distance.

'I'm fine but my driver is injured and the chief scientist is unconscious,' Jude says. 'We need her if we're going to figure out what's going on in that power station.'

Nganga turns and calls back. 'Weir, on me.'

A police officer leaves the wounded and wades towards them, carrying a trauma kit on his back.

'We've got a shooter in the cottages opposite,' Nganga says. 'We think only one. But they're using a suppressor and we don't have good enough eyes-on to see the firing point. An Apache took out the checkpoint ahead and that's the emergency response centre burning in the distance.'

So much for the plan to grab control of the back-up control room. Jude looks up at the helicopters circling far above. 'What about the SAS and the response team?'

'We can't talk to them,' Nganga says. 'But I don't think they'll come in while someone is out there firing surface-to-air missiles.'

'We're on our own,' Jude says.

'That's a familiar situation for you, I think,' John Nganga says. 'What do you advise?'

'First, we need to take out the shooter.'

Nganga nods. 'That's my plan. Once we've dealt with your casualties, I'll send up a flare as a signal for the rest of the team to put down suppressing fire. I'm going to try and get around the back of the convoy and into the field behind the cottages to flank the shooter. If we can take control of those cottages, we can set up a command centre and a medical point and go from there. Will you help me?'

'I'm with you.'

The four of them slosh back along the ditch to the back of the convoy where the Range Rover is boxed between two crumpled Trojans. They scramble up the bank and run across the road to crouch beside it. There hasn't been any shooting for a couple of minutes. Weir climbs in the front passenger seat. The rear passenger door opens and Rosanna jumps down beside Jude.

'How is Professor Sieff?' he asks.

'She's come around but she's pretty confused,' Rosanna says, looking around her. 'What now?'

'Counter-attack,' Jude says.

A couple of minutes later, the medic sticks his head back out of the door. 'I've given the driver painkillers and I'm going to splint his arms. The professor seems okay. No sign of concussion. I'll keep an eye on her.'

'Okay,' Nganga says and looks across at Jude. 'You ready?'

'I'm ready.'

Beside them, John Nganga pulls the cord on a pyrotechnic flare and it shoots out over the convoy towards the power station before exploding and drifting downward, casting stark white light across the road and the wreckage of abandoned vehicles. There is an immediate response. The distinctive pop of a rifle-grenade leaving a launch tube.

'Down!' Jude shouts.

They curl up flat against the side of the Range Rover.

The grenade detonates over one of the nearby vehicles and shoots out fragmentation in every direction. Jude hears the hiss and spatter of supersonic metal shards striking steel and tree bark. The police officer beside Jude grunts and swears, blood squirting out of his thigh.

While the contingent on the grass bank lay down covering fire, the paramedic applies a HemCon pad to the wounded police officer's artery and ties off his upper leg with a tourniquet, using the windlass rod to tighten it against his groin. Then he presses a field dressing against the pad and puts the officer's hand on it. 'Press down hard.'

Nganga unslings the man's rifle and gives it to Rosanna. 'Are you up for this?'

She nods.

'Let's go.'

Keeping low, Nganga runs to the back of the Trojan at the rear of the convoy and crabs along it, keeping below the lid of the boot with his bony knees higher than his head. Jude and Rosanna follow. Nganga takes a small shaving mirror from his breast pocket and holds it out so he can see around the corner.

The firing is continuing, both sides exchanging fire.

'Middle cottage,' Nganga says. 'Second floor. Let's go!'

They sprint out of cover and across the road to the beech hedge that surrounds the cottages without the shooter spotting them. Staying close to the hedge they run around the back. The middle cottage has a small wooden gate at the rear, leading through a garden to a back door framed in thick, sinewy wisteria.

At the gate, Jude freezes and crouches down. Nganga and Rosanna go down with him. Jude tears a length of couch grass out of the ground and strips it of its leaves. Reaching through the slats of the gate, he moves the stem carefully from left to right until it touches something. Lifting it ever so slightly, he catches a glint of light on a trip wire. Beside him, Nganga switches on a torch, its red-lensed light tracking the black wire from the door handle to a claymore on the lawn with its steel legs planted in the ground.

Nganga looks at the mine and at him, and Jude can see the shock in his eyes.

They move along the hedge to the gate leading to the adjacent cottage, Nganga running the red-lensed torch back and forth across the grass as they do so. When they reach the gate, Jude uses the couch grass to establish that there is no tripwire connected to the handle and they let themselves in. In the space between the two cottages there is a point where it is possible to step between two bushes.

Slowly, carefully, they ease themselves along the cottage wall towards the back door.

# 75

# Taking Hope Cottage

Pilar surveys the ambushed police convoy from the bedroom window of Mrs Emory's cottage. She is watching for signs of movement or tell-tale muzzle flash from between the trees on the far side of the road. In the distance she can see several burning buildings including Rose Cottage, her home since leaving Argentina. The accumulation of a carefully constructed identity now utterly destroyed. Strange, but she doesn't feel any sense of loss and she isn't afraid, even though the enemy fire is getting steadily more accurate. Rather she feels a sense of release at shedding her disguise. She is once again her true self and soon she will be reunited with her brother and her fiancé, in that special part of Catholic heaven reserved for those who have fought and died battling the British.

She pumps another grenade into the launcher and fires it in an arc that she hopes is high enough to carry it over the vehicles and into the sodden field beyond, where the enemy are sheltering.

She crouches back beneath the window sill and hears it detonate with a satisfying thump.

A few seconds later, as she is loading another grenade in the launcher, a prolonged burst of fire strikes the wall above and behind her. Ghillie whimpers. He's terrified but won't leave her side.

'Easy now,' she says, stroking his trembling back. She feels sorry for him.

More gunfire chews up the brickwork at the front of the cottage. They've pinpointed her location. It's time to move. Keeping low, she goes out onto the landing and is halfway down the stairs when she hears movement in the kitchen. She raises a hand to stop the dog.

Gripping the M4A1 tightly, she continues slowly down the stairs, trying not to make a sound. Above her Ghillie is watching anxiously from the landing. When she reaches the bottom, she turns and fires an entire fifteen-round magazine down the corridor at the door separating it from the kitchen. She is changing magazines when the splintered door is kicked open and a woman with wild red hair is standing there pointing a gun at her.

Rosanna pulls the trigger.

The dog howls.

John Nganga is lying spread-eagled on the kitchen floor, gasping for breath. Jude rips the Velcro fastening on his body armour, which has five bullets lodged in it, and lifts it over his head. He rips Nganga's shirt open and considers the mass of bruising on his chest.

'You'll live,' Jude tells him.

'I thought I was finished,' Nganga gasps.

Rosanna steps into the kitchen holding the G36 in one hand and the suppressed M4A1 in the other. 'Pilar Allan is dead.'

She hands the M4A1 to Jude, who checks the breach and sees that there is a grenade in the launcher. He holsters his pistol and slings the carbine across his back.

'Put up another flare,' Nganga says. 'That way they'll know we succeeded.'

She takes a flare out of the map pocket on his thigh and steps out into the back garden and shoots it over the roof. By the light of the descending flare, Jude approaches the claymore facing away from him on the grass, kneels and switches it to safe before removing the detonator from the fuse well.

'I better check the front garden,' he says, dropping the detonator in a water butt under the eaves. He collects Nganga's torch from the kitchen and goes out the front door, advancing slowly on the gate. Sweeping the torch across the grass, he spots another claymore planted on the lawn. Again, he makes it safe and removes the detonator.

As he stands up, he sees the first of the police officers approaching, carrying the wounded between them.

Thirty minutes later a control point has been set up in the cottage with a first aid post and the casualties are being stabilised in the beds, and on the sofa and the carpets.

Communications are still down and the helicopters have departed, presumably because they ran low on fuel. In the absence of reinforcements, Nganga and Jude have agreed that their only option is to continue on foot to the power station to seize the control room and determine the damage to the reactor. An Ordnance Survey map of the site and architectural drawings of the power station are taped to the kitchen wall. Nganga is standing in front of them with a medic wrapping a bandage around his entire upper body. Beside him on the table are a stack of linear-shaped charges alongside an assortment of battering rams and *hoolie* crow bars.

There are three other officers in the room methodically filling magazines with bullets. Two more on overwatch on the upper floor and an officer in the shadows at the front and back gates.

'We're about a kilometre from the power station,' Nganga says. 'There are eight of us. With you two that makes ten and eleven with Professor Sieff. We have no working vehicles so we have to walk. There's only one road, the Sizewell Gap, and it runs straight through the marsh on a raised embankment.'

Ruth Sieff is sitting watching them from a stool by the Aga, sipping from a mug of sweetened tea made for her by Jude.

'If the coolant pumps and all the emergency back-up systems have been disabled or sabotaged, how long before the core melts down?' Jude asks her, drinking from his own mug.

'Two hours, perhaps.'

'We have no way of knowing how much time we have left,' Rosanna says. 'It may already be too late.'

'It hasn't exploded yet,' Jude says.

'There may still be time to limit the damage if we can get there and manually open the coolant valves and reinsert the control rods,' Ruth Sieff says. 'Hopefully we can find some of the site engineers, if they're still alive. First, you need to get me to the control room.'

Simon Conway

'We have just enough breaching charges to blow our way into the control room,' Nganga says, loading them into a backpack which he puts on his back.

The back door opens and a soldier in uniform steps inside with a police officer at his shoulder. From the pips on the rank slide of his muddy smock, Jude assumes that it's the platoon commander from the defensive position on the Aldringham estate.

'I'm Lieutenant Parker,' he says. He looks incredibly young: in his early twenties with blood smeared across his face.

'How many men have you got?' Jude asks him.

'Ten able-bodied. The rest are dead or wounded. We walked into an ambush. We have no comms.'

'Neither do we,' says Nganga, 'bring them in. And the sentries.'

Soon the kitchen is crowded with muddy, sodden soldiers and police officers, all steaming in the heat. Nganga delivers a swift briefing including the objective, the proposed route and actions on contact with the enemy. In the absence of radio communications, he will exercise command and control by whistle blast. Weir is to carry the trauma kit. When Nganga is finished, he looks to Jude who scans the room, making eye contact with each of them in turn.

'You all know what we have to do,' Jude says. 'You understand the importance of it and the consequences if we fail. An entire city depends on us. Hundreds of thousands or even millions of lives are at risk.'

Nobody moves or says anything. Their faces are grim but determined.

'Let's go,' Jude says.

Nganga nods gravely and picks up a carbine.

'Follow me.'

They go out through the front gate and advance up Sizewell Gap, spread out in an extended line on either side of the road, heading towards the floodlit dome of the nuclear reactor.

# 76

# Fowle supreme

The Turbine Hall is the most impressive thing, the tips of its vast blades spinning at more than twice the speed of sound, creating a deafening vibration that shivers your limbs and thrums through the concrete floor. It's big and loud and hot. Guy is halfway across the hall beneath the blades when the pitch of the roar changes, and the turbines begin to decelerate. Soon it will be as quiet in the hall as it is under the white dome of the adjacent building, where the nuclear reactor vessel hangs serenely above a pool of glowing aquamarine water. The only incongruity is the blood billowing out of the body of one of the nuclear engineers, who is floating in the gently steaming pool.

The malware in the operating system has unlocked every door and Guy has been moving throughout the station complex on a shooting spree. Without the constabulary there to protect them, the engineers make easy pickings. Even so, some escape, fleeing across the car park in the direction of the marsh where a platoon of 3 PARA pulling back from Goose Hill crossed a canal and climbed a slippery bank rigged with trip-wire-activated claymores.

He stops on the red line outside the control room door and stares up at the black hemisphere of a camera. Only the shift supervisor is authorised to allow visitors in the control room. The Station Director is only admitted with the supervisor's agreement. Even the Prime Minister needs permission.

Impatiently, Guy presses the intercom button again.

The locks retract with a hefty thud and the door swings open. Inside, he finds Inspector Fletcher, not his real name, sitting in the reactor operator's chair with his unlaced boots up on the console eating pistachios from a bowl, splitting the shells with his thumb-nails and catching the nuts in his mouth.

The thirty-year-old cream-coloured computer consoles with their stubby keys look strangely dated under the spaceship strip lighting.

'Shouldn't you be outside?' Fletcher asks.

Guy knows Fletcher's real name is Baranov and he is a Russian born on the steppe in Kazakhstan where the first Soviet nuclear bomb, nicknamed Joe One by the Americans, was detonated.

'The helicopters won't be back for a while,' Guy replies, 'and I thought I'd check on how you are getting on.'

The Russian shrugs.

'As you see, it's all chaos and murder.' Baranov gestures casually towards the bodies of control room engineers and reactor operators strewn haphazardly across the room. There are deep gouge marks in the consoles caused by automatic fire and many of the screens, dials and switches are shattered. The far wall is covered in blood splatter dripping downwards like flung paint with the shift supervisor slumped at its base. 'A new dark age is coming.'

Guy takes the pack off his back and sets it down on one of the consoles. His back and shoulders are drenched in sweat. He rolls his head on his neck to relieve the cramp in his muscles.

'I suppose it's inevitable that I would feel a sense of anti-climax when the time came,' Baranov tells him, unscrewing the cap of the vodka bottle and flicking it across the room. 'They teach you to feel like them, think like them, speak and write like them. And you spend years doing so and then when the time comes and the secret is out, you discover you have become like them in some way. Smaller, diminished.'

Ignoring him, Guy removes the jammer and sets it beside the pack. Remaining in the pack, he has two surface-to-air missiles, the *Katana* sword, three rifle grenades and a few cardboard cartons of ammunition.

'How's the reactor?' he asks, as he replenishes his ammunition, thumbing the bullets into the magazines and then distributing them amongst his cargo pockets along with the rifle grenades.

'The turbines are shutting down, the pressure relief valve is locked open and the control rods are fully retracted,' the Russian tells him, looking at the screens in front of him. 'It's too late to flood the reactor with boric acid solution. Radioactive water is escaping the primary coolant system and soon the relief tank will overflow into the main containment building. You got out just in time. The core is beginning to boil.' He smiles, wryly. 'Neutrons are colliding in ever-increasing numbers. It's like sitting on a bomb. Watching it explode in slow motion.'

'You've seen the real thing,' Guy says. It's written in his Moleskine.

Baranov looks surprised. 'Yes, with my father in 1989.'

'What was it like?'

'It was the most colossal thing I ever saw. There were seven underground tests that year. I watched the last one from the roof of the laboratory on the river Irtysh. I remember the earth hurtling like a tidal wave across the steppe and the ground collapsing into the void created by the explosion. A surge of smoke and dust that rose into the sky.'

'Are you staying here?'

Baranov smiles. 'I wouldn't miss it for the world. You think you can get far enough away when this thing blows?'

That's exactly what Guy is planning: heading north at speed, perpendicular to the wind direction. 'Is it irreversible yet?'

Baranov sucks his teeth. 'Soon.'

'I better get back out there then.'

'I think so.' He taps one of the screens and Guy joins him at the console. The closed-circuit TV cameras on the perimeter and the approach road are still working. 'The police and the paras are coming.'

Guy is surprised that they have regrouped so quickly. He suspects that Jude Lyon is out there. He has come to understand that the intelligence officer fooled him. That his diffuse and difficult-to-read aura is a form of disguise. It masks substance: intelligence and determination. It fills him with anger at his own folly.

'I'll leave the jammer here,' he says. 'It'll keep the helicopters away.'

'Be my guest.'

'Lock all the doors behind me and switch off the lights.'

'Of course.'

Guy slings the pack over his shoulder and heads for the door. He pauses before exiting and looks back.

'Why?' he asks.

The Russian stares back at him. 'I could ask you the same question.'

'I don't need a reason.'

'And you will never know mine, Mr Fowle. Go. Let me finish my mission.'

Guy closes the door behind him. He pauses on the walkway at the top of the steel steps and smiles. It's true that there was nothing recorded in Grom to suggest Baranov's motivation. His aura is an embodiment of an elemental principle, Guy thinks, of storms, rain and war.

How can he have misread Jude so badly?

He goes down the stairs and sprints the length of a corridor, bursting through a series of steel doors, hearing them slam and lock behind him. Within less than two minutes he is outside in the rain and the wind again, sprinting towards a gap he cut in the fence earlier.

Beyond is a maze of ditches and mud banks, tidal flats, grassy hillocks and dark lagoons that are fringed by reeds. He shrugs off the pack and leaves it by the hole in the fence. He unlaces his boots and kicks them off. They'll only slow him down. Barefoot, armed with his rifle and the sword, he heads towards the churning, wind-lashed marsh.

With the rifle slung across his back and the sword in one hand, he wades across a ditch chest-high in water and into the wetland beyond, heading diagonally towards the raised embankment with the approach road on it that is known as the Sizewell Gap. Now that the power station's lights are off, the darkness is almost complete.

He'd prefer to be on higher ground with the sniper rifle but he abandoned it on the barge at Ragpicker's Wharf. If he hopes to defeat the enemy he will have to do so at close quarters and still leave himself enough time to get away before the reactor explodes.

He feels intensely aware and alive, the way he felt when the Serbs came for him in the courthouse. The way he has felt since his escape.

He slides the *Katana* out of its sheath.

# 77

# Staff-versus-sword

The rain makes it difficult to see the person in front of you, the road a barely visible vein between the flailing bushes on the narrow verges. Jude battles against the wind and the water streaming across the tarmac.

Shapes move and mutate. Grotesque fingers reach for him. Ahead on the left-hand verge, one of the paras yells and lets off an entire magazine into the darkness. The headless body of a fellow paratrooper is lying in the bushes beside him. They break right at the shrill sound of a whistle blast, and make for the embankment. The commanders form a tight group midway down the bank, just above the water's edge, and the rest are in the bushes on the verge, pointing their guns outward. They quickly establish that, in addition to the dead para on the road, two police officers from the back of the column are missing. It makes Jude feel angry and despairing. He puts his arm around Ruth Sieff's trembling shoulders and she leans into his chest.

'What now?' Rosanna asks and he can hear the fear in her voice.

'We keep a tight formation,' John Nganga says, his ivory-tinted eyes the only visible part of his face. 'We stay off the road and we follow this ditch.'

'And the claymore threat?' Parker, the young lieutenant, says with panic in his voice.

They hear the by-now familiar sound of a rocket-propelled grenade leaving its launch tube. It flies directly over their heads and lands beyond them, exploding in the ditch with a wet thump. Mud rains down on them.

Fowle is directly behind them.

'The other side. Now!' Jude yells.

Jude pulls Ruth Sieff up onto the road after him and lifts her over his right shoulder in a fireman's lift. He crosses as the second grenade lands in the ditch where they were seconds before.

The whistle of shrapnel and hard clods of mud hit the road behind them.

Jude plunges through the bushes and skids down the bank on his left side keeping Ruth Sieff away from the ground. He enters the water at the same time as the third grenade explodes on the road. He hears someone scream. Seconds later, Rosanna slides down beside him and sinks under the water. He lets go of Ruth and grabs at Rosanna's collar. Another body tumbles into him and he is knocked off his feet. He surfaces and reaches around him. A floating hand strokes his face. He lunges and pulls Rosanna up out of the water.

Her head hangs back. Her eyes are closed.

All around him there is gunfire aimed at the road.

He wades forward against the tide, carrying her with him towards the nearest solid ground. He pulls her up onto a bed of reeds. He slaps her face. No response. He scoops the mud out of her open mouth and rips open her jacket, pressing his hands against her chest to feel for the rise and fall of her breath. Nothing. He starts chest compressions, fingers-interlocked, the heel of one hand pressing down on her chest-bone.

Twenty-nine, twenty-eight, twenty-seven . . .

At some point, Weir the police medic climbs onto the reed bed beside him and starts running his hands over Rosanna's body. He finds the ragged hole in her inner thigh where a piece of shrapnel sliced through the femoral artery. He shakes Jude's shoulders.

'She's gone,' he shouts.

Jude howls with rage.

He pulls the M4A1 from his back on its sling and points it at the raised embankment. A burst of gunfire from the verge reveals Fowle's position. Rather than give in to the rage, Jude hones and channels it. Controlled three-round bursts: left and then right of the firing point to box Fowle in and then he pulls the trigger on the launcher and watches as the grenade arcs across the sky and detonates on the edge of the road.

*Die, you.*

Leaving Rosanna's body, Jude slips back into the water, where the remains of the team are huddled. Nganga has his arms around Ruth Sieff who is shivering uncontrollably.

'If we head north-east across the marsh, we'll reach the perimeter fence,' Parker says, pointing with a compass. 'It's just a couple of hundred metres.'

'Go quickly,' Jude tells them. 'Stay close together. I'll provide cover.'

He waits for them to get moving, the rain pummelling his face. After a few minutes, he begins to follow them, slowly and carefully, pausing often to check if they are being pursued. He crosses a ditch and pulls himself out of the mud onto a spongy island surrounded by rushing water.

*Come, Fowle. I'm waiting.*

The team can't be far from the perimeter by now.

Jude senses that there is someone behind him. He turns and sees a flicker of movement. He lets off a burst of gunfire that lights up the marsh and glimpses Fowle dropping flat.

He advances slowly at a crouch, scanning left and right.

Behind him there is an eruption of sound, an explosion that lights up the marsh and the raised blade in Fowle's grip. Jude is just in time to raise his rifle and block the sword's descent. It slices through the rifle's polymer magazine, scattering bullets, and strikes the trigger housing.

Sparks fly. A siren swells and ebbs.

Jude retaliates with a slant side-kick and feels his boot hit Fowle's knee. It's too weighed down with mud to carry much momentum. A grunt in return. Jude spins away and sees the flash of the blade as Fowle strikes again. He just manages to deflect the blow with the rifle stock. In staff-versus-sword training they teach you to keep the psychopath with the oversized razor blade as far away as possible. But the terrain won't allow it. It's too wet and spongy for deftness, reach or speed. His staff is half the length it should be. Instead he launches himself forward in an over-arm strike, the rifle's butt hitting the blade and pushing it down into the mud on the right. Before Fowle can pull it out, Jude strikes high and misses Fowle's head, and then low, the rifle sweeping across from the left into Fowle's shin, unbalancing him. Dropping the rifle, Jude lunges forward with his shoulder and hooks a leg behind Fowle's calf, knocking him to the ground.

They roll over and over on the sodden and slippery ground, grabbing and grappling, exchanging hand and elbow strikes.

There are more explosions from the power station.

Fowle comes out on top, his white teeth bared like fangs, and head-butts Jude who drops his chin, taking it on the bony ridge of his brow. He hears an angry roar but can't tell if it's him or Fowle or both of them. His eyes are full of blood and mud.

They roll.

Jude's on top when he feels the icy steel of Fowle's knife in his side and then he's on his back with the *Kerambit* claw in his hand.

He slashes Fowle in the side, between two ribs.

They are hooked like fish, steel barbs twisting.

They roll together down a mud bank and land in a fast-flowing stream. They lose their grip on each other. For a brief peaceful moment there is nothing but blackness and the temptation of giving up. Then Jude surfaces and scrambles up the opposite bank, pulling himself painfully upwards with fistfuls of reeds. When he reaches the top, he unclips his pistol and points it into the darkness, his whole arm shaking. The other hand pressed against the wound in his side.

The perimeter lights come on.

He glimpses Fowle disappearing down a mudbank.

He looks over his shoulder and is relieved to see that the dome of the reactor is still intact. It hasn't blown. Yet. He needs to get there.

He climbs to his feet and staggers across the marsh, slipping and sliding in the mud, but determined to reach the power station. He will have to draw deeply on his training in the containment of pain if he is to make it. He falls several times and is almost overwhelmed but each time he gets back up and continues.

Beside the hole in the fence he finds Fowle's backpack. Slowly and painfully, he picks it up and carries it through onto the tarmac.

'Stop!'

The doors to the operations building have been blown off their hinges and there are two policemen pointing their weapons at him.

He drops the pack.

The policemen are talking into their chest-mounted radios. The jammer must have been switched off. Two marine commandos approach at an angle from the helipad.

Jude advances with one hand raised and shouts above the noise of the siren: 'It's Jude Lyon.'

'Stop there,' a commando orders him, from just out of reach.

The other opens the flap of the pack with tip of his barrel.

'Control this is Three-Two,' he says, looking inside. 'A surface-to-air missile launcher and two warheads.'

Jude rocks on his feet, trying to keep the pain boxed in. 'Tell Gold that the helicopters can land.'

## 78

## Neutrons colliding

Jude follows the trail left by John Nganga and his team, the blown doors and scorch marks on the walls and floors; the smell of explosive residue in the windowless corridors. He has a first field dressing from one of the commandos tied against his wound, the bandaging wrapped around his torso.

He climbs a metal staircase one painful step at a time, pausing to catch his breath between each one. It seems to take an inordinately long period of time. At the top he sees two paratroopers carry a woman's body out of the control room onto the gangway. There are several bodies there already, including a man dressed in a police uniform that he does not recognise.

He follows the paras back in, through a door hanging on one hinge. Ruth Sieff is sitting wrapped in foil blankets at the reactor operator's console and John Nganga is talking to the head of the nuclear accident response team in the approaching helicopters.

Nganga looks across at him and Jude sees the alarm in his eyes.

'Medic!' he calls.

Jude sits heavily against one of the consoles.

'Where's Fowle?' Nganga asks.

'He's heading north-west towards Goose Hill.'

Nganga informs the paratroopers out beyond the canal on the Sizewell Belts to move to intercept him.

Soon the paramedic Weir is running a line into him. Someone else has put a foil blanket around his shoulders.

'What's the situation?' he asks.

'The SCRAM is unworkable and the main relief valve at the top of the pressure container is locked open,' Ruth Sieff tells him.

'We need to open the coolant pumps to allow fresh water in from the North Sea and close the relief valve to stop any further leakage of radioactive coolant. Then we need to reinsert the control rods, which will stop neutrons colliding in the reactor. All of that needs to be done manually and quickly before the melting core ruptures the reactor vessel. Luckily, we have regained control of the door-locking system in the containment building. However, the level of ionising radiation means that the response team can only be exposed for a short period.'

'When will they be here?'

'Just a few minutes,' John Nganga says. 'They've refuelled at RAF Lakenheath. We currently have a couple of American F15s as top cover.'

'If Fowle reaches it, take out Goose Hill,' Jude says.

'If he makes it past the paras, I'll authorise a strike,' John Nganga says.

'Good.'

'Have you spoken to Calthorp?'

'Yes. He told me that Yulia has spoken to the Russian president, who has offered technical assistance as a gesture of goodwill.'

Jude laughs, bitterly. 'That bastard.'

'It appears to be a genuine attempt at de-escalation.'

'Let's hope we live to see the result.'

'Stop talking,' Weir tells him. He sticks a fentanyl inhaler between Jude's lips and thumbs the plunger.

Jude feels the pain relief washing through him like an incoming tide.

On the screens, the Pumas land in an arrowhead on the helipad. Engineers in bright yellow HAZMAT suits with dome-like helmet visors are escorted across the apron towards the reactor building by SAS troopers.

'I'm opening the main entrance to the reactor building,' Ruth Sieff says, pressing a button. On the response team net, the team leader confirms that they have entered the security airlock at the entrance. Ruth Sieff closes the main door and unlocks all the internal doors.

After that, all they can hear are the crackling dosimeters on the team suits and the sound of them wading through knee-high water that is bubbling up out of the relief tank.

'The valves on the coolant pumps are now open,' Ruth Sieff says, after an agonising pause. 'We have water flowing into the primary and secondary systems.'

The team leader reports that he is climbing the gangway to the top of the reactor vessel. His breathing is laboured.

'They're running out of time,' Ruth Sieff says.

'How long before we can get a second team in there?' Jude asks.

'A second team is being prepped for flight in London but we're looking at another hour before they get here,' Nganga replies.

'Does the team inside know that?' Jude asks.

'They know what they have to do,' Ruth Sieff replies. 'Strength and blessing upon them.'

'Strength and blessing,' Jude echoes.

'The relief valve is turning,' the team leader says over the radio, with what sounds like a waterfall in the background. Gradually the sound of running water diminishes and then stops.

'The valve is closed,' Ruth Sieff confirms. 'The final task is to reinsert the control rods using the drive mechanism on the pressure vessel head.'

'They're not going to survive, are they?' Jude says.

From the expression on her face, the answer to that is clear.

'Manually deactivating the electromagnets holding the control rods now,' the team leader gasps. Freed of the electromagnets, the rods fall under gravity into the core. Within two seconds the neutron flux in the reactor has decreased by ninety per cent.

'It's done,' Ruth Sieff says. She speaks into the radio, 'All personnel in the containment building evacuate now!'

The sound of the dosimeters is deafening.

# 79

# The triumph of will

Guy watches as three Puma helicopters approach from the south and descend to land at the floodlit power station. The white dome of the reactor is defiantly intact and he has concluded that the series of explosions he heard earlier must have been the police blasting their way into the control room. The outcome of careful planning is now out of his hands. He should have more closely heeded the Prussian General von Moltke's warning: *No plan survives contact with the enemy*.

The remaining Apache sweeps low overhead, its searchlight piercing the darkness and lighting up the marsh ahead. He wishes he had his missiles. At first the light is blinding and then it begins to blur and rotate like a kaleidoscope.

He feels dizzy. He's losing too much blood and he's struggling to breathe. He has a punctured lung. He staggers forward into the driving rain, cursing Jude Lyon.

He reaches the steep bank, where fragmentation mines cut down the platoon from the north as they obeyed the order to fall back to the reactor from Goose Hill. He slides down beside the body of one of the dead paratroopers. Undoing a clip on the para's webbing, he takes out the Immediate First Aid Kit and unpacks it. Ripping the tear in his shirt to widen it, he presses the chest seal against the ragged gash in his ribs. He unpacks two dressings and presses them either side of the nozzle to fix the seal in place, wrapping the bandaging tightly around his chest. He then rips the morphine auto-injector pens that are hanging from the man's neck and stabs one in his thigh.

He lies back for a moment with his head in the cold mud, waiting for the euphoria to come.

Ahead of him the Apache's searchlight continues to roam the flooding wetlands and churning watercourses, at one point silhouetting a line of soldiers. The remnants of the platoon whose dead colleagues lie scattered around him. They are heading back towards their positions in the low hills to the north. He assumes that they are doing so in an effort to block his escape. Digging around in the mud, he finds the dead para's bullpup SA80 assault rifle. He picks it up. Ejecting the magazine, he clears the breach and reinserts the magazine. He pulls back the cocking handle and makes it ready.

He takes filled magazines from the man's pouches and buttons them in his cargo pockets. Then, he reaches across and slides the bayonet from its scabbard on the man's belt and fits its hollow handle onto the muzzle of the rifle.

There is a village a couple of kilometres to the north-west where he can find a car and head north. He just needs to get through the line of paras and cross the hills.

He has essence enough for that.

Who knows, the reactor may still blow. He imagines London as an irradiated wasteland that is off limits for hundreds of years. The beginning of a new Dark Age for a country that he has hated with all his being since the time that he first became aware of his destiny.

He slides down the bank and slips into the rushing water of the canal. He kicks with his feet, travelling diagonally with the incoming tide, and it carries him across to the other side. He drags himself up the far bank and pauses for a few breaths on all fours before climbing to his feet like a wraith rising from the grave.

Buoyed with morphine, he steps lightly across the spongy grass, gathering in speed as he feels his body filled with the triumph of will.

*I am Death! The destroyer of worlds!!*

He spears the first soldier with the bayonet and dances away before the body falls. The second, he trips and spears on the ground like a bug on its back. The third struggles and Guy is obliged to pull the trigger with the bayonet still inside him, the bullet tearing through the para's body at point-blank range. He drops and rolls away from the answering fire into a torrent of water. He can hear people shouting. The searchlight is turning towards him. He sinks further into the water and dives down into the darkness, grabbing at reeds on the bottom and pulling himself forward, fist over fist, as the searchlight sweeps over him.

He resurfaces and climbs out of the water, continuing north towards Goose Hill. Glancing back, he sees the searchlight roving behind him and beyond it the dome of the reactor. Abruptly, the siren stops and he realises that there is unlikely to be an explosion after all.

Grom has failed. His hope for a new era is dashed.

Anger slashes through the morphine and his head spins and his vision dims. He stumbles and falls to his knees, dropping the rifle. His head lolling on his neck. At first his breaths are little more than tortured gasps but slowly he gets it under control, inhaling and exhaling. Feeling his chest expand and contract.

Steadying.

He stabs himself with the second morphine auto-injector and waits for the joy to begin.

It doesn't take long for him to realise that he will live. Now is not the time to give up. There will be other opportunities. New vulnerabilities. He has options.

He looks back towards the hill.

He just has to cross it and then his escape route is clear. He picks up the fallen rifle and climbs to his feet again. One step at a time. He could walk the length of the British Isles if he chose to.

He has just reached the stand of tortured salt-lashed pines at the base of the hill when he hears the whistle of airborne rockets.

*Fuck!*

He is hurled backwards as the hillside explodes in flames before him.

# 80

# The day after

As the sun rises over the North Sea, Jude walks out through the ruined entrance to the operations building. The storm has passed but water sparkles everywhere: on the overhead pylon lines and the helicopter rotor blades, on the perimeter fence and beyond it on the thousands of acres of reeds and grasses. He navigates the rows of emergency response vehicles, heading for the outer perimeter, and steps through the gap in the fence.

Out on the marsh, floodwater is bubbling back into the sea.

There are already police teams out with dogs, searching for bodies. So far, there is no sign of Guy Fowle. Jude's been warned that if he was on Goose Hill when it was incinerated by multiple thermobaric warheads, the body may never be found. There is still smoke rising from the tree stumps and the blasted earth.

John Nganga joins him. They stand beside each other in reverential silence.

'You saved a city,' Nganga says, eventually.

'We did,' Jude replies, without any satisfaction. It cost too many lives.

He turns back and walks towards the white tent that has been put up to house the uncontaminated bodies. He's been told that the bodies of the fallen in the reactor building may never be recovered. Inside the tent, there are long lines of identical black body bags on wooden trestle tables. A solemn police officer with a clipboard leads him down one of the aisles and stops beside one. He carefully opens the zip partway and stands back for Jude to approach.

Rosanna's damp skin is pale as marble, her mouth slightly open and her face framed by her hair like Millais's Ophelia. He bows his head and says the only words he remembers of the mourner's *Kaddish*, 'Shelter her soul in the shadow of thy wings.'

He looks up and feels the tears coursing down his cheeks.

'Sir?' He turns to find a green-suited paramedic standing beside him. 'I've been asked to take a look at your wound.'

Disconsolate, Jude allows himself to be led away to the first aid post.

Inspecting the wound, the paramedic tells him that he is lucky that the blade did not pierce the abdominal cavity, instead lodging and twisting in the subcutaneous fat and the hard layer of muscle beneath.

'You're lucky you've got muscle and the blade was short,' the paramedic says, as he stitches the wound. 'It's ugly but not life-threatening.'

Later that afternoon, a police car drives Jude, tightly bandaged and freshly anaesthetised, out along the Sizewell Gap. By daylight, it seems like a much shorter distance than the night before. The only signs of the battle are the scorch marks on the tarmac. At Hope Cottage, the vehicles of the convoy have been pushed off the road and down into the ditch to open the road. All the bodies have been removed.

They slow for the cordon at Leiston Village. Staring out through the windows at the satellite trucks and the scrum of journalists, he wonders if Kirsty McIntyre is amongst them. He owes her a call but he's too tired. Instead he lets his head fall forward on his chest and gives in to sleep.

He wakes as the car comes to a halt a couple of hours later at the entrance to the cul-de-sac in Shoreditch. Just in time to see the same teenage lookout as the last time he was home cycle away at speed. Soon Kirsty will be on her way. The welfare officer sent with him from Sizewell offers to come in but he turns down her offer. He climbs the stairs to the top, gripping the handrail. It seems to take forever to open the three locks.

Inside, he takes off the borrowed police jacket and throws it against a wall. He puts the kettle on and walks over to the window.

The lights are back on in the city, courtesy of an electricity transfer from France. Of the towers, only the Gherkin is in darkness. A charred hulk.

Below him a black cab pulls up at the entrance to the cul-de-sac and Kirsty gets out.

He lets her in.

Entering the flat, she takes one look at him and tells him to sit down on the sofa.

'I told you to stay out of London,' he says.

'I've never been very good at doing what I'm told. You know that. Besides, you didn't tell me that Sizewell B might blow up and the city was at risk of being irradiated.' She takes off her coat, and puts it over the back of a chair. 'Anyway I figured you'd sort it out. And it seems you did. According to my sources in the police you're quite the hero.'

He stares at the rug. 'A lot of people died.'

'I'm sorry about that,' she tells him. 'But you're alive and the city is intact, and I'm very pleased about that.'

She brings him tea, which she insists on sugaring, and a bowl of warm water and a clean dishcloth from one of Sanjay's well-stocked but rarely used kitchen drawers.

'I'm going to run you a hot bath,' she tells him, as she dabs at the dried mud and blood on his face, 'and then I'm going to sit with you to watch you don't drown.'

He's too exhausted to protest. She kneels before him and starts unlacing his boots while he leans back on the sofa. He is beyond exhaustion.

'Don't worry.' She winks. 'I've seen a grown man naked before.'

*Crack!*

He looks up at the window and sees the flattened bullet lodged there and the compression wave of tiny fissures that radiate out from it like a paint splash.

He begins to laugh. It's painful at first and deeply inappropriate but soon he's beyond caring.

*Crack! Crack! Crack!*

Three more bullets strike the glass. They look like raisins in the Garibaldi biscuits that Jude remembers from old-style army ration packs.

*Thank fuck for Sanjay and the barter economy.*

'What is it?' Kirsty says, wide-eyed, dishcloth in hand.

'Armoured glass,' he tells her, clutching his side.

His yellow-taped phone pulses: a message from an unknown number.

I will kill you

# THRILLINGLY GOOD BOOKS
## FROM CRIMINALLY
### GOOD WRITERS

CRIME FILES BRINGS YOU THE LATEST RELEASES FROM
TOP CRIME AND THRILLER AUTHORS.

SIGN UP ONLINE FOR OUR MONTHLY NEWSLETTER AND BE THE FIRST
TO KNOW ABOUT OUR COMPETITIONS, NEW BOOKS AND MORE.

VISIT OUR WEBSITE: WWW.CRIMEFILES.CO.UK
LIKE US ON FACEBOOK: FACEBOOK.COM/CRIMEFILES
FOLLOW US ON TWITTER: @CRIMEFILESBOOKS